P9-DII-105

# Grantville Gazette IV

# Grantville Gazette IV

Sequels to 1632
Edited and Created by
## ERIC FLINT

GRANTVILLE GAZETTE IV

A Baen Books Original

Baen Publishing Enterprises
P.O. Box 1403
Riverdale, NY 10471
www.baen.com

ISBN 10: 1-4165-5554-4
ISBN 13: 978-1-4165-5554-4

Cover art by Tom Kidd

First printing, June 2008

Distributed by Simon & Schuster
1230 Avenue of the Americas
New York, NY 10020

Library of Congress Cataloging-in-Publication Data

Grantville gazette IV : sequels to 1632 / edited and created by Eric Flint.
    p. cm.
 ISBN-13: 978-1-4165-5554-4 (hc)
 ISBN-10: 1-4165-5554-4 (hc)
 1. Fantasy fiction, American. 2. Seventeenth century—Fiction. 3. Alternative histories (Fiction), American. I. Flint, Eric. II. Title: Grantville gazette 4.

 PS648.F3G75 2008
 813'.54—dc22

                                        2008005953


10  9  8  7  6  5  4  3  2  1

Pages by Joy Freeman (www.pagesbyjoy.com)
Printed in the United States of America

# Contents

# Preface

## Eric Flint

Some remarks on the contents of this fourth volume of the *Grantville Gazette*:

Once again, I had to go through my usual dance, trying to decide which stories should go under "Continuing Serials" and which should be published as stand-alone stories. This is a dance which, as the *Gazette* unfolds, is getting . . .

Really, really complicated.

In the end, I parsed the contents of this volume in such a way that only David Carrico's "Heavy Metal Music" fell into the category of "Continuing Serials." I am even willing to defend that choice under pressure, although—fair warning—my defense will lean heavily on subtle points covered by Hegel in his *Science of Logic*. (The big one, not the abridgment he did later for his Encyclopedia. So brace yourselves.)

That said . . .

Well, to give just one example . . .

"Poor Little Rich Girls," by Paula Goodlett and Gorg Huff, continues the adventures of the teenage tycoons-in-the-making that Gorg began in "The Sewing Circle" in Volume 1 of the *Gazette* and continued in the story "Other People's Money" in Volume 3. Eventually, many of these characters will probably appear in a novel that I'm planning to write with the two of them. (As will the characters in David Carrico's story, in a novel he and I are working on.)

1

The same will probably prove to be true, sooner or later, with many of the other stories in this volume. The truth? The distinction I make for the *Gazette* between "continuing serials" and "stand-alone stories" is pretty much analogous to the distinction the law makes between first and second degree murder. The one is premeditated in cold blood; the other more-or-less happens in the heat of the fray.

There are times I think of just throwing up my hands and publishing *all* of the stories in the *Gazette* as "continuing serials." And, in my darker moments, contemplate changing the title of the magazine to *The 1632 Soap Opera.* That's because, like a soap opera, the characters just seem to go on forever and ever in one episode after another. Unless one of them is actually Killed Off—and then, sometimes, you don't really know For Sure—they'll keep re-appearing. Often enough, in somebody *else*'s episode.

On the other hand, I'm not a snob about soap operas. I used to be, until many years ago my wife's work schedule required me to tape her favorite soap opera so she could watch it when she got home. Initially, I did so holding my nose—and bound and determined to watch only the first few minutes to make sure it was taping properly. This was back in the early days of VHS when I didn't trust the technology involved. (And still don't, but I admit I'm something of a technophobe.)

Before a week had passed, I found myself watching the entire damn episode! Day after day! It was then that I first discovered just how addictive soap operas could be.

In defense of the *Gazette,* I will say that the characters in *this* soap opera are wrestling with a far broader range of concerns than the usual fare of love pining from afar, emotional misunderstandings that somehow last for years when a simple five-minute conversation could settle it, and, of course, the inevitable jealousies and adulteries. Not that the magazine avoids those, either, of course. But the characters also wrestle with political issues, religious issues, worry about their livelihoods and scheme to make a fortune or at least a decent income.

In short, the *Gazette* is an ongoing chronicle of the way an alternate history would *actually* evolve, if you looked anywhere beyond the narrow circle of Ye Anointed Heroes and Heroines. The distinction between this and a soap opera—or The World's Great Literature, for that matter—is mainly in the eye of the beholder.

Yes, sorry, it is. It is widely known, of course, that only women watch soap operas, just as only women gossip. In my innocent youth, I believed these nostrums, until a quarter of a century working in transportation and factories proved to me how ridiculous they were. You can find no better example in the world of gossip than what machinists are doing standing around the tool crib or truck drivers are doing at lunch tables in a truck stop. Of course, if you ask them, they will insist they are engaged in the manly art of shooting the breeze. Just as, if you ask the electricians and millwrights in the maintenance shop who are watching daytime television while waiting for something to break down that requires their expertise, they will insist they are not actually *watching* the soap operas showing on the set. No, no. They are merely interested in ogling Whazzername's figure.

If this state of affairs irritates you, I can only shrug my shoulders. Don't blame me, blame Homer. To this day, the *Iliad* stands as one of the world's all-time great soap operas. The much-hallowed "epic" as it exists today is simply a cleaned-up pile of gossip. What it *really* was, in its inception, were the stories with which bards entertained the courts of Mycenaean kinglets by chattering about which gods and goddesses lusted for which mortals, their mutual jealousies, and what they did to advance their . . . ah . . . "causes."

For that matter, blame the Old Testament. Sure, sure, a lot of it deals with Sublime Stuff like the creation of the universe, etc., etc. But there are whole swaths of the books in the Bible that look suspiciously like soap opera plots to me.

It's not even peculiar to western culture. If you want to read the Greatest Soap Opera of all time, you can do no better than start the massive Hindu epic, the *Mahabharata*. I say "start," because you may or may not finish the multi-volume work. (I did finish it, myself. But that was after I'd learned to enjoy a good long-running soap opera.) I believe it is still, to this day, the longest epic ever written.

The word "epic," of course, is what scholars call a soap opera that was written a long time ago, which gives it the patina of respectability. They will defend their use of terms by pointing to such episodes in the *Mahabharata* as the philosophical discourse between Krishna and Arjuna which is separately known as the famous *Bhagavad Gita*.

Very sublime, the *Bhagavad Gita*; yes, yes, no doubt about it. It's also just one episode out of a multitude which follow (by and large) the adventures of the five Pandava brothers and the wife they share in common, Draupati. (Don't blame me! I didn't come up with the kinky stuff, although it's sure fun to read about.) One of the central adventures of which involves the sublime subject of how the foolish oldest Pandava brother lost their wife in a game of dice.

So, I figure the *Gazette* is in good company.

This will be the last paper edition of the *Gazette* that duplicates in toto the electronic edition (with the inclusion of a new story written by me for the paper edition). Beginning with *Grantville Gazette V,* which will probably be published some time next year, paper editions of the *Gazette* will henceforth be selections from several issues of the magazine.

The reason for the shift is simply because the publisher for the paper edition, Baen Books, can't possibly maintain a one-to-one ratio of paper-to-electronic editions. That was more-or-less feasible when the *Gazette* first got started, because it was originally a magazine that was only published occasionally, not one with a regular schedule.

Beginning with the eleventh issue of the electronic edition of the *Gazette*, the magazine's success enabled us to establish it as a regularly published magazine, paying professional rates, and with a bi-monthly publication schedule. That eleventh issue came out in May of 2007. As of the time this paper edition of *Gazette IV* starts showing up in bookstores, six more volumes of the magazine will have been produced—which is to say, more volumes than have been published in paper over a four year period.

Baen is a book publisher, not a magazine publisher. Even before the magazine shifted to a bimonthly schedule, the electronic edition had already gotten far ahead of any possible paper publication schedule. At the rate we were going, the tenth issue of the magazine—which was published a year ago—wouldn't have come out in paper until sometime in the year 2014. And, as I said, six more volumes have been added since then.

Being a low-minded author, this naturally leads to a sales pitch. I urge anyone interested in the ongoing 1632 series to consider buying a subscription to the electronic magazine. (See details at the back of the book.) You won't be able to assume, any longer, that whatever gets published will eventually appear in a paper edition.

Eric Flint
January 2008

# FICTION

# The Anatomy Lesson

## Eric Flint

**Amsterdam**

"I've got a headache," Anne Jefferson announced.

Her fiancé, Adam Olearius, cleared his throat. "It might be better to say, you have at least two of them."

Anne removed the hands rubbing her temples long enough to glare at him. "Oh, very funny. Very, very funny." Then went back to the rubbing.

"I wasn't actually trying to be witty," he said. "It's just my diplomat's reflexes."

"You call piling another headache onto the one I've already got being *diplomatic*?" she grumbled.

"Not you, dearest. I was speaking of Europe." Olearius leaned back in the chair in Anne's salon, turned his head, and peered out the window.

"How shall I count the ways?" he mused. "It's a headache for the king in the Netherlands; for the prince of Orange; for Duke Ernst Wettin, the USE's regent in the Oberpfalz; and . . ." After a pause, he waggled his hand back and forth. "Probably even a headache for Gustav Adolf himself. Or his prime minister, at least."

"And me," Anne said forcefully. "Especially me."

Her tone was quite surly.

"And you, of course."

7

## Brussels

"Yes, yes, gentlemen, I know it would be easiest if I simply forbade the girl and her brother to undertake their proposed change of residence to Amsterdam." Not quite glowering at them—almost, but not quite—Fernando I, King in the Netherlands, stared at the five advisers sitting around the large table in his council chamber. "Unfortunately, the situation is delicate."

"The emperor is not likely to go to war over the issue, Your Majesty," pointed out Pieter Paul Rubens.

"No, he isn't. If for no other reason than that it's convenient for Gustav Adolf to have the heirs to the Palatinate officially held captive by the Span—by the Netherlanders. It keeps them out of his hair."

The near slip did cause the king to glower at his advisers. He still hadn't gotten used to referring to himself as "Netherlander" rather than Spanish. Being, as he was, the younger brother of the king of Spain and having considered himself Spanish all his life until very recently.

That was hardly the fault of the advisers, of course. But Fernando figured that being glowered at from time to time was a reasonable part of their duties.

"*At the same time,*" he continued, "the emperor of the USE—who is also, I will remind you, the king of Sweden and the high king of the Kalmar Union—is officially the protector of the dynastic interests of that family. Being, as they are, Protestant and not Catholic. And being, as they are, the family whose claim to the Bohemian throne was made null and void by the Holy Roman Emperor of the time, my now-deceased uncle Ferdinand II of Austria. And while it could be argued that their claim to the Bohemian throne was . . . what's that American expression?"

"Dicey," provided Alessandro Scaglia. "Your Majesty."

Fernando gave him a thin smile. "You needn't toss in the honorific every two minutes, Alessandro. Thin-skinned, I am not."

Scaglia nodded. "Sorry, Your—ah, my apologies. I'm afraid I'm still engrained with Savoyard court custom."

Fernando's smile expanded. The two Savoyard dukes whom Scaglia had served as an adviser, Charles Emmanuel and his son and successor Victor Amadeus, had both been notoriously fussy about protocol. Fernando's private opinion was that their prickly attitude stemmed less from personality than from the objective situation of the Savoy. An independent duchy located between France, Italy and Spain—and which controlled several strategic passes through the Alps—had damn well better be prickly about protocol. Fernando's own relaxed attitude was due in no small part to the security of his situation. Given the size of his army, his demonstrated military skill, and the difficulties which the terrain of the Low Countries posed to any invader, he didn't care that much how anyone addressed him, as long as they were polite.

All the more so given the influence of his new wife. Whatever Maria Anna's upbringing might have been, in the Viennese court, the former archduchess of Austria was almost shockingly informal. Perhaps that was a residue from her adventures during the Bavarian war, when she'd smuggled herself through war-torn regions with the help of commoners.

She exhibited the informality that very moment. Leaning forward over the table and giving Alessandro a rather arch look, she put into words what Fernando himself had left unspoken.

"Well, of course. If I'd had to do the dance the Savoyard dukes had to do to keep from getting swallowed up over the past few years, I'd be insisting you had to throw in every single title I might have a claim to in every other sentence. And pity the poor chambermaids! 'I shall empty the chamber pot now, Your Majesty and formerly Your Highness.'"

She gave her husband a sly smile. "Fine. It's an exaggeration. In the ever-so-modern Netherlands—in the palace, at least—we have actual plumbing."

Fernando chuckled. "And very good plumbing it is, too, since I took on the service of the Van Meter woman. Which, oddly, brings us back to the subject at hand. Because we can now toss that item onto the pile, out of which we seek to extract a coherent position. I'm thinking that it would ill behoove a monarch who chose to hire a woman to design and build the plumbing in his palace—"

"An *American* woman," Rubens interjected.

Fernando gave him an astringent glance. "—to object if another woman chooses to study medicine."

He now swiveled to face Rubens squarely. "And I'm afraid your point about the Van Meter woman being an American speaks against your advice, Pieter, not for it. The Americans are the first to insist that they are not entitled to any special privileges." He raised his hand. "And spare me a recitation of the many ways in which, in the real world, they do get special treatment. That simply makes them all the more intransigent on the subject."

He leaned back in his chair. "The point being, that if I refuse to let the girl do as she wishes, I will incur the displeasure of the Americans as well as the emperor whom they advise. And, between us, I think I would rather risk Gustav Adolf's ire than theirs. I don't need a Swedish king's advice and assistance. I do need that of many of the Americans."

"That leaves the prince of Orange," said Scaglia.

The king made a face. "Yes, it does. And who knows what schemes Frederik Hendrik has in mind, concerning this?"

It was a rhetorical question, not a real one. Fernando provided the answer himself. "But you can be assured it will be devious."

## Breda

Had Frederik Hendrik heard that last remark, the Prince of Orange would have laughed sarcastically. He'd have appreciated the general sentiment, but would have filled the king's ear with a detailed explanation—nay, lament—concerning the impossibility of coming up with a devious scheme to take advantage of the blasted girl's stubbornness.

Not that he hadn't tried. Alas, the situation was too hemmed in by other factors to give him any maneuvering room.

You could start with the fact that he was glumly contemplating his options from the vantage point of his library in the House of Orange-Nassau's ancestral estate in Breda, overlooking the gardens. Which, appropriately enough, were rather bleak-looking at this time of year. Instead of being able to contemplate his options from the vantage point of the library in the small palace he maintained in Amsterdam, overlooking the harbor.

True, the harbor was an even bleaker sight, this time of year. But it was—even in mid-winter—a much busier and bustling sort of bleakiness. Vibrant with the energy of the Netherlands' largest and most dynamic city. A city which was now, for all practical purposes, *terra non grata* for the man who was supposed to be its prince, a figure second only to the king in his stature in the Low Countries.

"Well . . . not *that*, exactly," Frederik Hendrik muttered to himself, staring at the flat landscape beyond the window. He was exaggerating out of irritation, and knew it. Whenever he visited Amsterdam, which he did quite regularly, the benighted Committee of Correspondence who actually ruled the city were always punctiliously polite. Gretchen Richter, for a marvel, was even cordial and friendly. But velvety as its cover might be, it was still her fist and not his that held the power in Amsterdam. And the woman was not hesitant to remove the glove when she felt it necessary

As had been very forcefully demonstrated to the burgomasters and patricians of the city less than two months earlier, when they tried to resume their previous positions of authority in Amsterdam after returning from their exile during the cardinal-infante's siege. Their self-selected exile, as Richter had bluntly pointed out. She and Amsterdam's commoners had remained in the city throughout the siege, after all. It was thanks to *them*—not the patricians and burgomasters residing comfortably elsewhere—that Don Fernando had never been able to take the city and had eventually agreed to the current settlement of the war.

"So you can go fuck yourselves," had been her final words, according to the many indignant accounts which Frederik Hendrik had heard from the patricians afterward. "You can have your property, and that's it. Your posts and positions are either gone—and good riddance, since half of them were useless—or someone reliable and worthy now sits in your place."

He'd had little sympathy with the complaints. He'd *told* them they were fools to think they could march into Amsterdam this soon after the siege and get anything but a boot in the ass. And the fact that the boot was a woman's boot didn't matter in the least. She was a big woman and a strong one, and had the devil's fury to tap when she chose to do so.

"Well, not *that*, exactly," the prince muttered to himself. As tempting as it was, at times, he didn't really think Richter was Satan's minion. Just someone who had concluded that the near destruction of her family and her own rape and forced concubinage were outrages perpetrated not simply by the immediate parties involved, but by all of Europe's high and mighty. Who would now pay the price, whenever and wherever she could charge it. If nothing else, she owed that much to the young brother who'd been killed in the battle of Wismar.

And . . .

There really wasn't much anyone could do about it. The one time he'd raised the problem with the king, Fernando hadn't been much less blunt than Richter.

"It's your headache, I'm afraid, not mine. The displeasure and discomfiture of patricians and burgomasters is not much of a burden for me. Certainly not compared to the alternative. You know perfectly well that the Committee of Correspondence in Amsterdam can choose to secede from the Netherlands, if they feel pressed enough."

"They wouldn't dare!" one of Frederik Hendrik's courtiers had exclaimed. One of his soon-to-be-discharged courtiers. The idiot.

"Oh, wouldn't they?" the king had demanded frostily, giving the courtier in question a look that was downright icy. "As I recall, you were nowhere near the siege of Amsterdam at the time. While I, on the other hand, commanded the army besieging the city. For *months,* with everything I had—and I still couldn't take it. So don't tell me what Gretchen Richter and her people are and are not capable of daring. And, more to the point, doing."

He'd turned away then, and looked out over his own gardens in Brussels. "It wouldn't even be that hard for them. They have enough military strength in Amsterdam to close the city and keep it closed for months. More than they had, in fact, since I caught them off guard and today they are most certainly not. They've made an agreement with me—with us—and they're keeping to it. But Richter, whatever else she is, is very far from a trusting soul. Given her history, it's hard to blame her. So while she's kept the agreement—meticulously, in fact—she's also kept the city militia large and well-trained and has rebuilt and even strengthened the city's fortifications."

He shrugged. "Not forever, of course, if I brought the full weight of my army to bear. But they could certainly withstand a siege for as many months as they've already demonstrated they can—and long before then, they would have reached an accommodation with Gustav Adolf. There is no reason, after all, that Amsterdam couldn't become another province in his empire instead of a city in my kingdom. Not if the matter was pressed to the hilt."

The same courtier seemed to have no limit to his idiocy. "That's not possible! We've signed a treaty with him."

Again, came the icy royal gaze. "So we did. And so what? Treaties can be torn up. And while you may have forgotten that

Gustav Adolf has an eye for acquiring new territory, I have not. And while you seem to have missed the sight of Admiral Simpson's ironclads patrolling the Zuider Zee—how did you manage that, by the way? the things are huge—have you even *been* to Amsterdam since the siege?—I have most certainly not. There is no way, unless you have overwhelming forces—which I do not—that a large port city can be taken by siege if the defenders control the adjoining waters. Only a lunatic would even try."

The courtier finally wilted away and the king turned back to the prince of Orange. "Anyway, you have my sympathies, Frederik Hendrik. But my position as king—by the same terms you not only agreed to, but even insisted upon—give me only limited powers within the provinces, and even more limited authority with regard to the affairs of the towns and cities. And what internal powers I do have in the cities are what you might call negative. I can, by law, prevent a church from being suppressed. I cannot, by law, establish a church."

That was a major fudge, of course. Nothing, by law, prevented the king in the Netherlands from subsidizing and supporting a church—so long as he did it in his private capacity and using his own resources, rather than those of the state of the Netherlands. Given that the king was far and away the richest man in the Low Countries, the distinction was to a considerable degree a formal one.

"The burgomasters are therefore your cross to bear, not mine," the king continued. "And I'm not about to run the risk of another war over an issue like this one. Quite frankly, from everything I can see the Committee of Correspondence does a better job of running Amsterdam than the patricians did. The disease problem is certainly much better."

So, there it was. And while most of Frederik Hendrik's advisers were well-nigh ecstatic at the recent news that Gretchen Richter would soon be leaving Amsterdam to return to her family in the Germanies, the prince himself did not share their sanguine expectations. Richter was, alas, a superb organizer, not simply a firebrand and agitatrix. By now, the Committee she'd forged was very solid and durable. She'd be gone, but it would remain—commanded by lieutenants whom she'd chosen and trained personally. In a generation, things might change. But they wouldn't change any time soon—and then, for all he knew, the changes would be for the worse.

On that, for sure, the king had spoken truly. The committee *did* run the city better than the patricians had. Even most of the merchants and burghers were now becoming reconciled to its rule, if they weren't highly placed in the patricianate. Business was booming again, and Richter had been very careful not to play favorites.

And if that left the Prince of Orange with the awkwardness of having a country whose provinces were dominated by wealthy and conservative patrician families, and whose principal city was the most radical in Europe except for possibly Magdeburg and Grantville itself, then so be it. He'd just have to scheme and maneuver around the situation, as deviously as he could.

Which brought him back to the problem at hand. He turned away from the window and picked up the letter from the girl's mother.

Written in a very fine hand, on the best paper you could ask for. The hand wouldn't be her own, of course, although the signature was and she'd have dictated the contents. But she'd have employed a secretary who, among other things, had splendid handwriting. In exile or not, officially in the captivity of the Netherlands or not, she was still Elisabeth Stuart. Sister of the king of England, the widow of the Elector of the Palatine and—very briefly—the queen of Bohemia. Among her ancestors she could name another king of England, a king and queen of Scotland, several kings of Denmark and Norway, and the Lord only knew how many dukes and duchesses. Among the latter of whom could be counted the redoubtable Marie de Guise, another woman who'd plagued the counsels of Europe's rulers in her day.

He sighed and dropped the letter back onto the table. Given that she'd written it, there was no longer any point in trying to persuade the mother to dissuade the daughter. She wouldn't have written the letter at all if her daughter hadn't talked her into it. And, that done, the matter would no longer be of concern to Elisabeth. By all accounts, to use one of those picturesque American expressions, Elisabeth Stuart had the maternal instincts of a brick. Children were a burden and, what was worse, they piled still more burdens atop their mothers. This particular burden having been shifted to someone else, she was no more likely to reconsider the decision than a mule.

King Fernando could have forbidden the girl and her brother from making the trip to Amsterdam, of course. He and he alone could even have enforced it easily, since they resided in exile in Brussels, right under his nose and the nose of the many guards he'd placed over the family.

From the opposite end, Frederik Hendrik could—in theory—bar them from entering any of those provinces assigned to the House of Orange to supervise. And—in theory—that would apply to Amsterdam as well, since—in theory—Amsterdam was simply one of many cities in the province of Holland.

Theory, theory, theory. In practice, the moment he did so the Committee of Correspondence would immediately issue an invitation to the pestiferous girl and her brother. Given Richter, they'd do more than just issue an invitation. They'd personally see to smuggling the two youngsters into the city and keeping them guarded against any attempt to get them out.

No, that alternative was just nonsense. Frederik Hendrik disliked the prospect of having two such potentially important figures in European politics rattling around essentially unsupervised in a city like Amsterdam, especially given their ages. The girl was sixteen; the boy fifteen. Both ages at which even the dullest villager could get themselves into trouble.

But . . . all the alternatives were worse. Much worse.

He turned from the window and summoned his secretary, who'd been standing politely by the door some distance away.

"We'll need to write the girl a formal letter of invitation. Her brother also. I leave the wording to you. Just make sure to be polite, if not effusive. I'll sign it when you're done."

## Magdeburg

Hands clasped over his stomach, Mike Stearns leaned back in his chair and gave Fernando Nasi that placid look that made anyone who knew him rather nervous, unless they knew him very well.

Since Francisco did know the prime minister of the United States of Europe very well, he remained unfazed.

"Explain to me again," Stearns said, drawling the words a bit, "why time needs to be taken from my busy schedule to discuss what we think of the impending visit of two teenage noblefolk to Amsterdam. To put it as bluntly as I can, who gives a damn?"

"Well, first, some corrections needed to be made to your summation. Imprimus, they are not 'visiting' the city, they propose to relocate indefinitely from Brussels to Amsterdam. Secundus, to call them 'noblefolk' is to understate the reality. 'Royalfolk' would be a lot more accurate."

"The girl's not a princess and the boy's not a prince. In fact, I'm not even sure if they have any titles at all."

Francisco shrugged. "Like most Americans, unaccustomed as you are to the fine points of aristocratic etiquette, you're missing the key element. Titles don't really matter, in the end. What matters is blood line. Should they find it to their advantage—not likely at the moment, of course—there is not a royal house in Europe that would hesitate to marry off one of their princes or princesses to either one of those children. They have at least half a dozen kings and queens in their ancestry. It would take overheating my laptop to figure out how many dukes and duchesses."

Mike grimaced. "You're right. I keep forgetting that people in the here and now take that 'blood' nonsense dead seriously. Me, in my crude West Virginia coal miner's way, I figure the title makes the big shot, not the other way around."

Nasi grinned. Whatever his origins, Stearns was about as far removed these days from a rural bumpkin as the Ottoman emperor. He'd driven Europe's very sophisticated political elite half-mad, over the past few years. But he did enjoy putting on the act, from time to time.

He dropped the grin and leaned forward. "Mike, seriously, this is not trivial. Duke Ernst in the Oberpfalz has already written at least one vigorous letter of protest to the emperor concerning the matter."

"Why?" said Mike—who then proceeded to make nonsense of his own pretense at bumpkin ignorance. "The heir to the Oberpfalz is the oldest brother, Karl Ludwig. *He's* still in Brussels. *He's* not proposing to budge an inch from under the noses of his Spanish captors-although-we'll-pretend-they're-not. Neither does the mother, who's the official regent. If you look at it her way."

"Nevertheless. Ernst is worried about a precedent being set. He figures the last thing the Oberpfalz needs is to have any of the official heirs show up before he's had time to . . . ah . . ."

"Whip the province into good enough shape that the heir can't meddle with it. How's that? Of which dastardly scheme I approve, by the way. I'd far rather have one of those very capable Wettin brothers running the Oberpfalz than some royal flake. And from what you've told me in the past, Karl Ludwig is flaky even if he probably doesn't qualify as a flake-capital-F. I still don't see why it's any concern of ours what his younger brother and sister do."

Francisco squinted at him. Mike was normally more astute than this. "In other words, you do not think it's something to give any thought to. The fact that two youngsters in line of succession to the throne of England as well as the Palatine—you could even make a case for Bohemia—will be spending the next year or so in close proximity to an American nurse. And probably just as close proximity to the Amsterdam Committee of Correspondence, if I know Gretchen."

"She's leaving Amsterdam soon."

"Her spirit will remain—as you've said to me by now perhaps a hundred times."

Mike scowled. Francisco was heartened and pressed on.

"Not to mention close proximity to Thomas Wentworth, if the former—and very capable—duke of Strafford and chief minister of England can finally pull himself out of the dumps."

Mike glared at him. Then, unclasped his hands and sat up straight. "Well, thank y'all very much, Francisco," he drawled. "I was sorta hoping I might have a light day today."

## Amsterdam

"At least agree to *see* the boy, Thomas," said William Laud. The archbishop of Canterbury—or former archbishop, if you listened to his enemies—shook his head at his friend Thomas Wentworth. "And you *must* cease and desist from this pointless melancholy."

Wentworth looked at him in silence, for a moment, through lowered lids. "He supported my execution, you know."

Laud threw up his hands with exasperation. "And people accuse *me* of being stubborn! That happened almost seven years from now—"

"Six years and six months." Wentworth smiled sadly. "I don't keep count of the exact number of days. But I never forget the date. It comes to me when I wake up, each and every morning. May 12, 1641. The day I was beheaded."

Laud glared at him. "*And* in a completely different universe."

"Different, yes. Completely different? That's laughable, William, and you know it."

Before Laud could continue, Wentworth raised a hand. "Just to keep from having you natter at me endlessly, I'll invite the boy for supper. I'll even be polite to the murderous little bastard. But he may very well decline the invitation, you realize. And I'm hoping he does."

## Brussels

"Good Lord!" exclaimed Rupert.

"You shouldn't blaspheme," reproved his older sister Elisabeth.

"But look at this!" The fifteen-year-old boy held up the letter he'd just opened. "Another invitation. And this one's from *Wentworth*, of all people."

"For someone who insists as mightily as you do that under no circumstances will you allow your former-or-somewhere-else historical fame as a soldier to determine your life in this existence—'nay, nay, I'll be an artist instead'—I can't help but notice that it's the invitations from political figures who excite your interest. *Not* the invitations from artists. Of which we've received any number, including from Rubens and Rembrandt."

The boy scowled. "Rembrandt's claim to fame comes entirely from that other universe. In *this* one, he hasn't done anything worth talking about yet. Well, not much."

Elisabeth waited.

"Okay, Rubens is different. I admit."

"And stop using that hideous Americanism."

"Okey-doke." And then he burst into inane teenage laughter.

"I don't for the life of me remember why I asked you to come along."

"Because I'm your closest relative. Your best friend, too."

Elisabeth considered the matter. "True, on both counts. I still can't imagine what possessed me."

Rupert gave her a sly look. "You'll need me, sister. You watch. When you puke your guts after seeing your first operation. I'll be there to console you and point out how ridiculous it was anyway, the idea of a girl like you becoming a doctor."

## Amsterdam

"You get no special privileges," Anne Jefferson said firmly. "Not a one. You scrub like everybody else."

"Certainly, Madame Jefferson."

And that was *another* thing! The girl was invariably polite. Even gracious. For all that Anne wanted to work up a quiet and pleasant mad at being placed in this awkward situation, the damn girl wouldn't let her.

Even Elisabeth's appearance drove Anne nuts. Half-consciously, she'd been expecting someone . . .

Royal-looking. Anne wasn't sure what that meant, exactly—a long nose being looked down was the central image, of course—but whatever it was, it certainly wasn't what had presented itself to her that morning.

Herself, not itself. Very definitely, herself.

For starters, the girl was *pretty*. Not stunning, not gorgeous, nothing mythical or legendary in the least. Just pretty enough to have gotten elected prom queen any time she ran for it, in any West Virginia high school Anne could think of. The kind of sweet-looking prettiness that attracted boys but didn't make other girls resentful.

But Elisabeth wouldn't have run for prom queen, because she was *shy*. She didn't look down at people, she looked up at them from a slightly lowered gaze.

What kind of damn princess is shy?

"Don't call me 'Madame.' I think that's only for married women and I'm not married yet."

"Certainly, Mad—. Oh, dear. What appellation would you prefer?"

Anne didn't have it in her. She just didn't.

"How about you call me 'Anne.' And I'll call you 'Elisabeth.'"

Slowly, a shy and gentle smile spread across the girl's face. "Oh, I think that would be splendid."

All the way there, the next day, Rupert was practically bouncing off the walls of the coach.

"Oh, how marvelous! I can't believe the luck! You're to be cutting up *Joe Buckley*!"

Elisabeth sniffed. "First of all, *I* shan't be cutting up anyone. Madame Jeff—ah, Anne—will be doing the anatomy lesson, not me. I'll just be one of the people observing. And, secondly, who in the world is Joe Buckley?"

Rupert clasped a hand to his forehead, in the overly histrionic way that a teenage lad will demonstrate shocked disbelief.

"I can't believe you've never heard of *Joe Buckley*. The rascal's exploits were *legendary*. In his prime, the most notorious cutpurse in London."

Elisabeth sniffed again. "I can't imagine why I'd be acquainted with the names and doings of a foreign city's criminal element. Or you would be, now that I think about it."

Rupert gave her his *girls-don't-understand* look. And a splendid one it was, too.

"Just accept it as good coin. The man's a *legend*."

"The man's dead, now. And how would a London cutpurse wind up the subject of an anatomy lesson in Amsterdam?"

Her brother looked a bit discomfited. "Well. He had to flee London a few years back, since he'd gotten too well known. Then had to flee Paris, after he gained too much notoriety there also. Apparently, he turned up in Amsterdam just a few weeks ago."

"Indeed. And they caught him and hung him, as he so richly deserved." Elisabeth frowned. "Or perhaps they behead them, here in Holland. Although I can't imagine that Anne would choose a corpse without a head for an anatomy lesson.

Rupert looked more discomfited still. "Well. Well. He wasn't either hanged or chopped, it seems. The story is that he got drunk a night or two back and fell into the harbor in a stupor. Drowned, before anyone could fish him out."

Elisabeth burst into laughter. "Some legend!"

Her brother got a sullen look on his face. "So what? He's still *Joe Buckley*. You watch, sister. He'll be remembered long after you're forgotten by the world."

She turned her head and gave him a serene sort of look. "And you are forgotten also, no doubt. Given your firm resolve to devote your life to the higher pursuits instead of seeking fame and glory on the fields of war."

"Well."

Before he could come up with a lame remark, Elisabeth peered out the window. "Oh, look! We've arrived."

Rupert got another sly look on his face. He rummaged around in the sack he'd insisted on bringing with him, and came out holding a small bucket. "I brought this for you. To barf in, like you will."

There being no suitable rejoinder that wouldn't be undignified—worse still, might tempt her with blasphemy—Elisabeth just sniffed and prepared to disembark. As short as she was, that was always something of a chore, if modesty was to be preserved.


## Brussels

Fernando chuckled, after reading the letter which had just arrived. "Well, that should relieve our good prince of Orange of a small burden, Pieter."

Rubens cocked an inquisitive head.

"That nurse of yours. Anne Jefferson. The one you used as a model so many times. Apparently, a shrewd woman, and devious in her own way. It seems the prospect of having a royal student didn't appeal to her any more than it did to any of us. So—devious, as I said—she arranged the poor girl's very first introduction to the medical arts to be an anatomy lesson. Imagine it, if you all. Delicate little Elisabeth, having to watch at close hand while a human body is cut up into pieces."

Rubens' eyes widened. "That must be the same anatomy lesson that my young friend Rembrandt will be attending."

"Rembrandt? Why would he . . . ?"

"Oh, not as a doctor—although, like any good painter, he has a keen eye for anatomy." Rubens grinned. "No, this is his way of handling a problem I've had to handle myself."

It was the king's turn to cock an inquisitive head. Rubens elaborated. "He did that painting, in another universe. A very famous one, apparently. *The Anatomy Lesson.* As you know, I find that having to maintain my art under the suffocating weight of a body of work I'd done elsewhere and elsewhen is difficult."

The king nodded.

"Rembrandt faces the same problem, only for him it's even worse. He's a young man still, which I'm certainly not." The artist shrugged. "So, perhaps for that reason, his solution is different from mine. Where I avoid work I did, he seeks it out. He'll do, in this universe, the same painting that he did, in another—but without trying to copy it. And he'll let posterity decide which of the two is the better."

Fernando chuckled again. "Let's hope he leaves out of it the inevitable climax. When the girl starts vomiting."


## Breda

Frederik Hendrik's spies and informants in Amsterdam were even more numerous than the king's, and the city was closer. So he'd gotten the news the day before.

"Yes, it'll be happening . . ." He looked at the clock. "Right about now, I estimate," he said to one of his courtiers, sounding cheerful. "Remind me—at a suitable time, perhaps two weeks from now—to send that marvelous Anne Jefferson a short letter of thanks."

The courtier winced. "I hope someone thought to bring a bucket."


## Amsterdam

"—lobes to the liver, as you can see. This liver is abnormal, however, because of the man's quite obvious alcoholism. If you look closer, you'll be able to detect—"

Elisabeth peered more closely, as instructed. It was absolutely fascinating!

Her brother, known as Rupert of the Rhine in another universe, the royalist hero of the first English civil war, had left the chamber some time back. Looking very pale, and taking the bucket with him.


## Brussels

Three days later, looking philosophical, the king in the Netherlands laid down the letter from Amsterdam which had just arrived, after reading it to Rubens.

"What's that American expression, Pieter?"

"It's Scots, actually. In their own way, the Americans are worse cutpurses than the man on the table. Penned by a poet named Robert Burns who won't be born—wherever that birth happens— until sometime in the next century. 'The best laid schemes o' mice and men, gang aft a-gley.' "

He said the rhyme in English, a language in which he was fluent and the king was now adept.

"Yes. That one."

## Breda

Frederik Hendrik, of course, had gotten the news much sooner. And was considerably less philosophical about it all.

"Well, there it is, I'm afraid. We'll need to develop a policy, after all. Whether we like it or not."

The courtier he favored least was the first to speak up—which explained a good deal of why he favored him the least. Would the man ever learn to think before he opined?

"The first thing, of course, is to see to it that the girl—and the boy, even more so—is closely supervised."

"In *Amsterdam*?" The prince of Orange glared at him. "Do I need to remind you again that, in Amsterdam, 'close supervision' is something that Gretchen Richter can do better than anyone. Much, much, much better."

There was silence, for a time. Then the courtier he favored the most said the inevitable. "Best to ask Richter for a meeting, then. We can at least see to it that no harm comes to the two children."

"No physical harm, yes. Richter and her people can certainly see to that."

God only knew what they would do to their minds, of course. But he left that unspoken. Even his dullest courtier understood that much.

## Magdeburg

"This is shaping up very nicely indeed," said Mike Stearns, almost chortling.

"Yes, not badly at all—for a matter I had to twist your arm originally to get you to pay attention to."

Alas, the needle was pointless, as such needles always were. Stearns simply grinned.

On some petty level, Francisco found that mildly frustrating.

But only mildly so. Had he been in the service of the Ottoman emperor, as he'd once planned, he'd have been a lot more frustrated after needling his employer.

As frustrated as the term could possibly mean, in fact. Lying at the bottom of the Sea of Marmara, with a garrote around his neck.

So, all things considered, he did not regret the unexpected course his life had taken.


## Amsterdam

By the end of the meal, as the servants were clearing away the plates and dining ware, Thomas Wentworth finally realized what an insufferable dolt he'd become. Odd, perhaps, that it took a conversation with a teenage boy to do what none of his closest friends or his wife or his children had been able to do.

But, so it was. And he thought he understood the reason. Those of his friends and associates who'd been famous enough to survive in Grantville's often spotty historical record, were all his age or even older. Here was a boy who'd been more famous than any of them—and he was fifteen, with his life fresh and still uncut.

Wentworth rose and went to the window, clasping his hands behind his back. The day had been clear and frosty, as was often true in Amsterdam this time of year. The moon was new, so the stars were quite clear, even through the window.

"We've not discussed political matters at all," he said brusquely. Without turning his head to look at the boy, he raised a hand. "Nor do I propose to do so, unless you'd care to. I didn't invite you here for that reason."

"Why did you, then?"

"To be honest? Because my friend William Laud insisted. But I'm glad he did, now."

He studied Orion for a moment. It had always been his favorite constellation. "It's difficult, isn't it? Having a life already recorded somewhere. Even more difficult, I imagine, for someone your age than mine."

There was a short pause. Then the boy said: "It's very difficult."

Wentworth nodded. "I imagine, at some point—no, six or seven points—you made yourself the same solemn vow I made to myself.

'No! I shall not read another blasted word of it.' And then, a short time later, found yourself digging through yet another record."

"Another scrap, it'd be better to say. The American records are ghastly poor."

Wentworth shrugged. "You can hardly fault them. It's not as if that town ever expected it would be plunged into this situation either. Their records of their own history are quite good, actually. But what they have concerning Europe—even England—is what you'd expect."

He went back to the table and resumed his seat. "It's like an addiction, isn't it? You swear you won't, and yet you do."

"I've made one vow that I intend to keep, though," said the boy, in that firm and certain way that only teenagers can manage. "I shall not—*shall not*—allow what I did in that other life to determine what I do in this one."

"An excellent vow. But be aware of the pitfall."

The boy frowned. "Which is . . . ?"

"Don't allow your determination *not* to follow that same course become what determines the life you have now. Who knows, lad? You may well find a day comes when your duties *here* require you to be a soldier. Should you shirk that duty, simply because you once followed it in another time and place, you are simply letting that other life guide you still."

"I . . . understand, yes." The boy cleared his throat. "I should say this aloud, I think. In that other universe, I was among those who called for your execution."

Wentworth shook his head. "That's putting it a bit too strongly, I think. I found no record that you *called* for it. It's true that when others did, you supported them."

The man and the boy studied each other, for a time. Then Wentworth rose from the table and went back to the window.

"You need to understand this. I have decided—just this evening, finally—that I have no choice—in this world—but to seek the overthrow of your uncle, the king of England. I will do my best, assuming I succeed, to avoid having your uncle suffer the same fate he did in that other world. But I can make no promises. Charles . . . is a very difficult man."

The boy's chuckle was far harsher than any chuckle coming from a fifteen year old throat should ever be. "Yes, I know. He parted company with me—or I, with him, the records aren't quite clear—when he refused to do the reasonable thing after our defeat at Naseby and make a settlement with Parliament."

Wentworth grinned, at that point. Like an addiction, for a certainty! He knew, as if he'd been there watching, that—time after time—the boy hadn't been able to keep his promise. Time after time, just as Wentworth had done himself, he'd been drawn back irresistibly to those scraps and pieces of a history that had not happened except in a world that God had sundered from this one. By now, he'd have his other life almost memorized. What was known of it, at least.

But there was still serious business at hand, so the grin was brief. He turned around to face the boy squarely. What had to be said next, could only be said looking him in the eye.

"I can make no promises, except one. Nor can you, except that same one. You may find a day comes, in this universe, when you are supporting my execution. Just as I may find a day comes when I walk to that scaffold. Or stand and watch, while another man of the time—perhaps Charles, perhaps even you—makes the same final walk. But let us never be able to say, either one of us, that we do it 'again.' Because, whatever we do, we will be doing it for the first time, and for those reasons that seem good to us in the universe that God chose to place us in. Not a universe that, for us, no longer exists. For you, at your age, one could almost say never existed."

He waited, to let the boy think. When enough time had passed, he said: "I can make that promise. Today, if not any day until now. Can you make it, Prince Rupert of the Rhine?"

The boy's smile was shy, almost gentle. He looked much like his sister, in that moment.

"I don't know if Prince Rupert of the Rhine could make it. But I'm just Rupert Stuart. And I can."

Thomas sighed. "I stand corrected. Very well, then, Rupert. Will you come to visit again, now that you'll be in Amsterdam for a time? We needn't discuss political matters, if you don't want to. I simply ask because I could use a good friend young enough to keep my own eyes on this world instead of another."

"Oh, I'd like that myself. As long as you don't ask me to attend another anatomy lesson."

# Poor Little Rich Girls

## Paula Goodlett and Gorg Huff

"Will you two just give it up?" Heather asked, exasperated. "What good is that valley girl impersonation going to do you? No one here in Badenburg has ever heard of a valley girl."

"For sure, Heather, for sure," Vicky Emerson answered. "We're just getting into character. Gotta play dumb for the marks, you know."

"Like, haven't you ever seen *The Sting*?" Judy Wendell asked, with a sort of stupid look on her face. Then she dropped the pose and cracked up.

Heather shook her head. "This is just silly. We know what we want to buy, and we know that people, not marks, are starting to sell. The market is down since Guffy Pomeroy died, and people are nervous. All we have to do is show up at the wedding. They'll come to us. Mrs. G said so."

"Yep," Judy confirmed. "They'll come to us and pat us on the head, and treat us like a bunch of idiots, like we're too young to know what we're doing just because we're only fourteen. Then they'll try and dump their stock on us, because they'll think we're too stupid to know better. I'm getting a little tired of that part, but we can use it. Make them think there's a problem and they'll start dropping the prices."

Judy looked like she was ready to rub her hands together in anticipation, while Vicky looked energized. Susan Logsden just rolled her eyes, while the others grinned.

"Seriously, all of you," Susan remarked, "We ought to be able to double our net worth at this wedding. Mrs. G arranged a loan on our HSMC stock, so we've got a lot of cash to work with. Make the best deals you can, then get Mrs. G involved. She can look like she's trying to save us from being dumb, and people will drop their prices. It should work. I want to walk away from this with enough . . ."

Susan's voice trailed off, but Heather knew what she meant. Susan wanted to be rich enough and secure enough that she wouldn't ever have to be afraid of anything, ever again. She was still worried that something might go wrong, that she might have to go back to her mother. She didn't want that and all the girls knew it. For Susan, the building panic in the stock market was an opportunity for security. For Judy, it was a game, a game she enjoyed and played somewhat ruthlessly. Vicky seemed to be treating it like a contest between the girls, a contest she wanted to win.

Heather shook her head again. Money was nice to have, sure, but she just wanted to have a good time and enjoy herself. Hayley, Gabrielle and Millicent felt the same way. "If I can make a deal, I will. But I'm not going to spend every minute looking for them. It's supposed to be a party, you know."

"Well," Vicky explained, "all those resistors and transistors, the integrated circuits and stuff are pretty complicated. They used to have special rooms to build them in, back up-time."

At first, the older gentlemen in the group treated her with amused condescension. Gradually, though, they started to look a little concerned. The girl's comments stuck a chord matching some of the things they had read lately. Sensing the change in attitude, Vicky threw out a few more comments, this time about how difficult it was to compress natural gas and store it, and then wandered away.

Arend Nebel had never been convinced that gas-powered stoves were a good idea. After listening on the fringes of the girl's discussion, he was even less impressed with that investment. Master Drugen became interested in soldering irons first, because he thought they would be useful when making jewelry. Then he discovered that soldering irons were useful for producing a good seal on gas pipe connections in stoves. Arend didn't see the relationship.

"Henning, are you sure your father was right? That girl said the gas was hard to store, that it could leak and cause a disaster. Maybe we should sell our interest in that company before that happens."

"Arend, you know my father was careful. He believed the oven works was a good investment, or he wouldn't have put so much of his money into it. You are giving in to this atmosphere of panic. If Father was still alive, he would say the same thing. We have only to wait, and we will be rich."

"I wanted to be a goldsmith. I still want to be a goldsmith. All three of us, even Justine, must now work like peons while all we do is wait, and wait some more. I'm tired of waiting, and I do not want my future wife to work, like one of these . . . these . . . common women of Grantville."

"Research at the library is hardly common, Arend. Justine enjoys the work. She is becoming quite modern, you know. She even spoke of continuing the work, after you are married." Henning knew he shouldn't have teased Arend that way. Justine did enjoy the work, though, and Arend's attitudes were making her unhappy. Perhaps the marriage wasn't as good an idea as Father thought. Time would tell.

"Very well, we will speak to this girl. Perhaps she knows something we do not."

Vicky wondered what the two young men wanted as they approached. *So help me, if someone else tries to hit on me, today . . .*

But no, that wasn't what they wanted. They just wanted to talk about the gas ovens. Vicky figured that the oven works would be a success, over time. Once the problems of transporting the compressed natural gas were solved, the business would expand rapidly. Until then, business would be a little slow, but the investors' estimate of being able to sell ten thousand ovens in the next two or three years was pretty solid.

Vicky knew that the oven works had about half a dozen investors, all down-timers. The one up-timer involved led a team of down-timers trying to come up with designs for cooking stoves, camp stoves, space heaters and so on. They had a couple of working prototypes and a plan for mass production. It was a good investment, one she would be happy to have. Still, she let the young men explain all this, while she waited for them to make up their minds.

Vicki tapped her finger on her lips thoughtfully. "Well, even though it's risky, this does sound interesting. I do want to reinvest the many thousands of dollars I was fortunate enough to make in the sewing machine company."

Arend said, "I'll sell you my thousand shares at nine dollars each."

"That seems awfully high," said Vicky. "One explosion of a home and there goes my investment. What if someone died of a gas leak in their home? Of course, Heinrich, on the design team, is awfully cute!" Vicky batted her eyelashes.

Arend pulled Henning off to the side and whispered in his ear for a minute. Both nodded to one another, then walked back to Vicky.

Finally, the young men made a real offer. A good offer, the one she was waiting for. She signaled Mrs. Gundelfinger, who came rushing over, clearly intent on protecting Vicky from someone who was trying to take advantage of her youth. Her attitude increased one man's determination to sell, and he lowered the price again. Curiously, the other man seemed to believe Mrs. G's protective act. He backed out of the deal, which was a bit surprising. But Vicky was still able to buy one thousand shares of the oven works for the discount price of three dollars per share.

After finalizing the deal, Vicky asked how Judy was doing. When she heard the answer, she decided to look for another sucker.

"You are an idiot, Henning. And don't think I'm going to accept that worthless company stock as Justine's dowry. You should have sold it."

Henning studied Arend with irritation. The stock wasn't worthless, but Arend refused to see that. Even if it had been worthless, selling it to a child was more than Henning was willing to do. Arend actually seemed pleased to have foisted the stock he considered worthless onto a child. In a way, that attitude bothered Henning even more than the money he believed Arend had thrown away. It was money that, at least in part, was to have provided support for his sister.

A beautiful, warm autumn Saturday in seventeenth-century Germany was too good to be ignored. It seemed like every family in Grantville was out and about and had some business in town.

"Oh, Bill," Blake said, "will you just look at her. She's gorgeous. She's a dream. She's, she's . . ."

"A pretty girl. But has red hair." Wilhelm Magen was looking elsewhere. "That one, the one with the blond hair, is who I like. What is name?"

"That one over there? I think she's Vicky Emerson," Blake responded after following Bill's look. "C'mon, she's too tall and too thin. That redhead, Judy Wendell, now, she's the really pretty one of the bunch."

Bill Magen and Blake Haggerty were taking advantage of the crowd and using part of their lunch break to indulge in a bit of girl watching. The boys watched with interest as the group of girls known as the Barbie Consortium arrived at Tyler's Restaurant.

"Not a single one of those girls would look at you, even if you saved her from a fire or something. Stuck up, snooty rich girls aren't going to be interested in you police types."

Startled, Blake turned to see Brandy Bates standing behind him. He had known Brandy since they were kids and she had even been his baby sitter for a while. She'd been nice to him back then, when he was a little kid and wondered about his real mother and why she had left. Brandy lived just down the street and had kept him company sometimes, even when she wasn't babysitting. He had really needed someone back then and Brandy had always been ready to listen. In spite of the four-year age difference, they had been close.

The change in Brandy had happened suddenly and Blake didn't care for the results at all. One day, right after the winter break, Brandy had quit going to high school, just a few months before her graduation. She had started hanging out with her cousin, Marlene, and with the crowd at the Club 250. Hanging out with Marlene was bad enough, Blake thought, but he really didn't understand why Brandy continued to work at the Club 250. That crowd of crooks and lowlifes hadn't improved since the Ring of Fire.

"Jeez, Brandy, don't sneak up on me that way. None of those girls are stuck up or snooty. Susan Logsden is living with her grandfather, right on the same street we live on. She's always nice. Besides, there's nothing wrong with being police officers after we get out of the army. So, why wouldn't one of those girls get interested in one of us?"

A bit late, Blake remembered the lessons in manners his step-mother had tried to drum into him. "Brandy, this is my friend, Bill Magen. Bill, this is Brandy Bates."

Brandy ignored Bill's extended hand and stared past him as though he didn't exist. Bill blushed, dropped his hand, and turned his attention elsewhere.

"Yeah, right. You're short and you're scrawny and you probably don't even shave yet." To Blake's increasing irritation, Brandy continued to ignore Bill. "Judy Wendell is way out of your league, and always was. Besides, she's jail bait."

"I wasn't even thinking about anything like that, Brandy. They're just pretty girls, and I'm not too blind to see it," Blake answered sharply. "Y'know, Brandy, I used to like you a lot, but lately, you don't act like you care about anything. Ever since you went to work at the Club 250 and started hanging around with Marlene, you've just gotten mean."

"Why should I care about anyone? Being nice doesn't get you anywhere."

"It doesn't look to me like being mean is getting you anywhere either, Brandy," Blake retorted. "I liked you a lot better back before you started acting like this. Maybe you ought to find something else to do with your life. Hanging out with those losers at the Club 250 is just going to get you into a mess of trouble someday. Besides, it's pretty stupid to hate Germans, especially when you're stuck in the middle of Germany. I thought you were smarter than that."

"Blake, look at this," Bill interrupted. "Is maybe trouble coming."

Blake followed Bill's gaze and saw two men standing on the other side of the street. One of them seemed to be staring daggers at a well-dressed German woman who was about to enter Tyler's restaurant. The animosity in his eyes was obvious, even from across the street.

"He looks really pissed off. I wonder why. What do you suppose she did to him? We need to get back on duty anyway, Bill. How about we wander across the street and look official? It might stop trouble before it starts."

"Right," Brandy snorted. "Official! That's a laugh. You don't have a gun and you look like you're dressed up in your father's uniform. Real impressive."

Blake's feelings were stung again. It was true that the uniforms were new and didn't fit very well. Even so, Blake was still proud of his uniforms, and proud to have been selected for MP training after Basic.

"What's next for you, Brandy, have a bunch of kids and nowhere to go but down?" he snapped.

Turning away from Brandy, Blake said softly, "Sorry, Bill. She used to be such a nice person. I don't know what happened, but she's just not the girl she used to be. I wish . . ."

Henning Drugen stiffened as he saw the two young men head across the street. They didn't appear to be moving with any purpose, but Henning was nervous. Arend just wasn't making any sense lately.

"Arend, let's go. They look like children, but they are wearing 'MP' armbands," he muttered. "I told you this wasn't a good idea."

"They are puppies. And we are doing nothing wrong," Arend answered. "We cannot be arrested if we are doing nothing wrong. I am just watching that woman. I have done nothing."

Henning was still amazed by the Americans. They just didn't bother people who appeared to be obeying the law. There were no suspicious looks and no indistinct mutterings directed toward new people in town. Grantville's residents let you make a life on your own merits, in your own way. It was very unlike his family's experience, when they tried to start over in Jena after the destruction of Magdeburg. Henning much preferred Grantville. The town was a fine place to start a new life.

"That woman destroyed me. She and those girls, they are all demons. They gave me only a pittance. She owes me and I will make her pay. Why do you defend her?"

"They paid you, and paid in good money. They also paid exactly what you asked," Henning answered. "It is your own fault that you fell into the trap they set. I told you to wait."

"Helene Gundelfinger and that girl made a fool of me. I lost everything. We all, even Justine, must work like slaves. This is not what I intended."

"Arend, they did not make a fool of you, you did it to yourself," Henning responded. "It was my father and his gold that allowed you to join us when we left Magdeburg. I believe in my father's choice. We have only to wait, just a while longer, and the oven works will begin to pay. And you didn't lose everything, anyway. I will pay the dowry in time. The Americans have a saying . . . something about getting out of the heat if you can't work in the kitchen. You panicked. I came here only to tell you that I will have nothing to do with this plan of yours. I am leaving."

"I must have my money. I will marry Justine only if I have it."

"Justine and I wish to stay in Grantville. Now that our father has died and our property is gone, we have only the investments that he left. Justine and I must make our own way, for now. My sister does not want to marry you if you are going to cause trouble. We have jobs and we are willing to work. This idea you have, that Helene Gundelfinger owes you something, it is not right. We will not help you."

As he watched Henning's back recede, Arend Nebel's thoughts grew more and more hate-filled and angry. First, the Gundelfinger woman and that girl had impoverished him. Now, Henning had deserted him and Justine had proven she was a faithless woman. He would be avenged against them all.

"I'm not going to listen to this," Vicky yelled, while grabbing her jacket and purse. "I'll do what I want and it's none of your business. You can just count me out of this whole thing." Helene suspected that even Vicky didn't know if "whole thing" meant the consortium itself, her long-term friendship with the other girls, or just the intervention her friends had attempted.

After Vicky had slammed out of the room, the rest of the girls stared glumly at Judy. "Well, that didn't work very well," Gabrielle Ugolini muttered. Gabrielle clearly considered her overstuffed book bag the most important part of her wardrobe. She still wore her up-time clothing and probably would until it wore out or she outgrew it.

The girls had been trying to explain to Vicky the consequences of spending too much of your investment capital. It was supposed to be an intervention, like people did up-time for alcoholics or drug users. The idea was to try to save Vicky before she blew her share of the fortune they had made. They had picked the private room at Tyler's, hoping that Vicky wouldn't want to make a scene in a public place. The idea hadn't worked very well.

"It might have gone better if you hadn't called her an overdressed scarecrow, Millicent," Judy responded. "You know she's sensitive about being so tall." Judy was dressed well, but it wasn't a new outfit. She bought what she needed, but was selective about it. Helene was convinced that if Judy began wearing old grain sacks to school, every teenager in town would start wearing the same thing.

"Well, she is. Overdressed, I mean." It was easy to see that there was a certain amount of jealousy in Millicent's comment, true as it was.

Millicent's mother, Anita Barnes, didn't seem to have realized that Millicent was growing up. Compared to the departed Vicky, Millicent looked like a child, tiny and delicate, with a mane of dark curly hair that overpowered her face. Helene knew that Millicent's tiny size was a source of great frustration to her. She often complained that "looking like a ten-year-old" was the reason she wasn't allowed to spend any of her own money, and also why, to her extreme irritation, her mother still picked out her clothes. Vicky might hate being tall, but Millicent envied her height and her mature appearance.

Susan Logsden spoke up. "There's no reason for her to buy a new outfit practically every week. She's spending money like it was water. I hoped she would see sense, and listen to us. Not Vicky, though. She's going to go right on doing the same thing until she's broke." Susan didn't seem to mind that her clothing was more worn than that of the other girls. Susan was so focused on getting rich that Helene sometimes found her intensity a bit worrying.

"Life was a lot simpler before we had any money, wasn't it?" Judy asked. "I didn't realize how complicated this was going to be. There's so much to learn. I have nightmares about being smothered in balance sheets. Sometimes I dream the market really crashes and we all wind up back where we started."

"You dream that, too? That's my mother's nightmare. Every day she tells me I need to sell everything and put the money in a savings account," Millicent said. "When I try to tell her that I'm earning a lot more than three percent this way, she just looks at me like I'm crazy. She's still trying to make me do things her way."

"It is a little scary sometimes. Even my dad thinks so," Judy responded. "Savings accounts may be safe, but you have to put money to work if you want to make more of it. Maybe we can find a way to reassure your mom. Does anyone else have anything we need to talk about?"

Gabrielle, Susan and Heather all shook their heads. "Let's get this show on the road, Judy," Heather Mason remarked in her practical, down-to-earth way. "If Vicky won't listen, then she won't listen. If Hayley can't be on time, she'll just have to learn on her own. Frau Gundelfinger, what's today's subject?"

Helene Gundelfinger smiled at her serious young protégés. She hadn't intended to become their tutor, but most of the girls wanted to understand what they were doing. They listened to her advice, took the time to absorb everything they could and based a lot of their decisions on her experience and knowledge of the area. With a bit of carefully impartial input from Judy's parents and sister, the girls were well on their way to becoming extremely intelligent business investors. They were also very good at gathering information on what was happening in the business community. Helene couldn't resist the opportunity to teach such curious and inquiring minds.

"Today, we continue the discussion on diversifying our investments," she began. "Millicent, your mother might be happier if we do this. It is not a new concept. If you buy one ship and it sinks, you have lost your whole investment. If you buy a share of a dozen ships and one sinks, the others pay for the loss. The same thing is true about investing in the businesses that are starting up. If we diversify we can invest in more risky ventures because we're risking only a small part of our money in any one venture. It is very simple, yes?"

Helene expected the girls to nod and smiled when they did. Basic theory like this was nothing new to them. Specifics were more complicated and that's where Helene came in. She had agreed to become their business manager and "adult face" after the girls had invested in the Higgins Sewing Machine Company on their own. She was impressed by their intentions and by the information they had found on a new business startup.

Helene wasn't sure where they got all their information, but between them, the seven girls knew nearly every up-timer in Grantville. At the very least, they knew someone who knew someone else in the small town. Helene had come up with some cash and joined the "consortium" when they invested in that first start-up. Helene provided experience and contacts, the girls provided information on what was going on with the up-timers. So far it was working remarkably well.

"So, we continue . . ."

Judy grinned at Frau Gundelfinger's daughter as she left the meeting. It was kind of unusual for a woman of Mrs. G's status to keep a child with her as much as she did, especially when the child was just a toddler. Judy thought that Mrs. G just wanted the kid exposed to Grantville's attitudes from a very young age.

From some of the comments Mrs. G had made, Judy was pretty sure that she'd had a rough time after being widowed. Some brother-in-law was giving her trouble, using her involvement in business as an excuse to try to take over her property. Women were allowed to do business here, something that had come as a shock to most of the up-timers. Still, there was some prejudice against them. The "glass ceiling" in seventeenth-century Germany was a lot harder and set a lot lower than it had been in the twenty-first century. Consequently, Mrs. G embraced Grantville and its attitudes.

Having the kid around didn't bother Judy or the other girls. She was a cute little thing, and was really polite and quiet most of the time. The Barbie Consortium did, now and then, worry about what would happen if Mrs. G got involved with some guy, though. Especially if he were some older dude, who might object to the amount of time and effort she put into teaching them.

"NNNNNNNNOOOOOOOOOOOO!!!!!!!!"
The anguished scream coming from her daughter's bedroom made Vickie Mason jump nearly out of her skin. "What on earth?" she asked her husband, "Arnold, what in the world?"

"I don't know, dear," he responded, "but whatever it is, it isn't going to be good. Heather hardly ever makes any kind of noise. I think she's got to be the only quiet teenager in the world."

The slamming of a door and the thumping on the stairs told Arnold and Vickie that they would soon hear about the problem. It was a bit of a worry. Heather just didn't make scenes. She was just about the most practical person in the family, and even seemed a bit coldhearted sometimes. Even the news that her favorite aunt, Gayle Mason, would be going to London and facing unknown hazards during the journey hadn't caused this kind of uproar.

"It's broken," Heather wailed as she ran into the room. "It's broken and there aren't any more! What am I going to do now?"

"Honey, it can't be all that bad. What are you talking about, anyway? What's broken?" Arnold asked, worried.

"My CD player, Dad. It just quit, right in the middle of "Walking to New Orleans." I'll never get to listen to my music again. I'll be stuck listening to VOA!"

Arnold hid a grin. It was odd for a young girl who was as practical as Heather to be obsessed. It was especially odd for a girl born in the late 1980s to have this particular obsession. Doo-wop music, early rock and roll, even early 1960s folk music were what Heather enjoyed, as well as some blues and jazz. She didn't care much for any other type of music, like country, classical, or opera. Her CD collection was pretty impressive for a young girl, but it only included the types of music she preferred.

"Maybe someone can fix it, honey. Try Larry Dotson at the hardware store," Arnold suggested.

"I could lend you my cassette player, and some tapes, if you like," Vickie offered, hiding her own grin. Arnold anticipated Heather's next reaction.

"Eeeeyyyyeeewww, Mom," Heather muttered, right on cue. "like I really want to listen to 'Blue Eyes Crying in the Rain' a million times."

"It beats nothing, doesn't it?"

"Not by very much," Heather answered, aware now that she was being teased. "Do you want anything from downtown? I need to go to the hardware store and talk to Mr. Dotson. Maybe someone will sell me a player, but it will probably cost a fortune."

"You can pick up a loaf of bread, please, and be careful in town. I swear, getting around Grantville lately must be as hard as getting around New York City used to be. So many people!"

"Yeah," Heather commented, as she grabbed her bag and turned to leave, "sometimes I wish we were back in the old days. Or up in the new days. Or . . . whatever . . . you know what I mean."

Arnold and Vickie exchanged a look. Yes, they knew what Heather meant. They felt the same way sometimes.

"Velma's either getting really drunk or really brave," Brandy remarked. "Why do you suppose she started hanging around here, anyway? She used to do her drinking out of town."

"Nowhere to go and no way to get there, I guess. She's been drinking here a lot lately, and she never stops spouting off. She's decided it's the Germans' fault that she lost her kids. It sounds crazy to me, but her money is as good as anyone's," Fenton answered. "You know, if she keeps trying to flirt with old Ape, Wilda is going to snatch her bald. That ought to be a sight to see."

Brandy started to laugh, but stopped suddenly as she felt someone press against her and reach around to grab her breast. Without thinking, she drove her elbow into the body behind her. The muffled "Oooof" sound made her smile. As the offender stepped back, Brandy turned and dumped a full mug of beer over Freddie's head. Freddie wasn't especially big or strong and stood wheezing and dripping beer all over the floor. The rest of the customers started laughing and making remarks, poking fun at Freddie.

"I told you to keep your hands to yourself, you little weasel. Touch me again and I'll break the beer mug over your head instead of just dumping the beer."

Being pawed by the clientele of the Club 250 had never been something Brandy enjoyed. The club itself had long ago lost its rather meager attractions for her. The place was a pit, and she was starting to hate it.

Blake Haggerty's question "What's next, a bunch of kids and nowhere to go but down" as well as his remarks about her "meanness," had been on Brandy's mind all day. She had to admit that Blake was telling the truth. She wasn't getting anywhere, and probably wouldn't ever get anywhere, if she kept on this way. She had watched her cousin Marlene trying to cope with all those kids after Donnie and Melodie had snuck away from home. That had been instructive, too. Why Marlene was willing to live with a man who had two girlfriends in the same house was something that no one understood, especially Brandy.

Brandy was convinced that she just didn't want to wind up like Marlene, Melodie, or Velma. She needed to do something, make some kind of change, even if she hated to think about another wrenching adjustment. Brandy wasn't sure what kind of life she did want, but almost anything would be better than winding up like those three.

"What's going on in here?" Ken shouted, obviously drawn from the office by the noise. "Can't a person get anything done around this place?"

Brandy said, "This jerk tried grabbing my boobs again. I'm sick of it and I'm not taking it, anymore. I told him last week to keep his stinking hands to himself. If you won't stop him, I will."

"And I told you last week to stop pouring beer on the paying customers, Brandy. They PAY me money, you COST me money, and you're NOT even a good waitress," Ken yelled. "You know he's harmless. Can't you even take a joke? I ought to fire you."

"Go ahead, Ken," Brandy yelled back, glad for an excuse to do it. "I'm tired of this crummy dive anyway. Better yet, I quit. I know I can do better than this. Take your rinky-dink job and shove it!"

"Tell me that when you come crawling back, you useless bitch. What are you going to do now, huh? Make a living with your so-called brain? You can't keep more than two drink orders straight and you don't know how to do anything else, either," Ken kept on. "You're useless and you're stupid on top of it! Waitresses are about a dime a dozen, so it's not like I'll miss you. Maybe I can find a waitress who can actually work this time. You damn sure don't."

Velma Hardesty, who was listening avidly, decided it was time to throw her two cents in the pot and stir up some more trouble. "I'll work for you, Ken. That pizza joint isn't any fun, anyway. There are too many precious little rug-rats, and their darling moms and pops. I'm tired of not seeing any interesting people." Leaning forward over the table, Velma flashed her cleavage at Ken. "I'm a lot more fun than that little tootsie is, I guarantee."

Ken stopped his tirade and stared at Velma with his eyes alight. "You're hired. You can start right now. Even with a few beers in you, you've got to be better than she is."

Brandy started laughing. The by-play between Velma and Ken, along with his hateful comments, had convinced her that she was right to leave. She couldn't stay here and listen to Ken's crap anymore. She had to do something, anything, else.

Brandy kept laughing as she gathered her things and began the walk home alone. As she walked, things she didn't like to think about, emotions she usually tried to ignore crept into her mind and got the better of her. By the time she got home she was nearly hysterical. She was so glad to be home, finally, that she dissolved into her worried mother's arms, and started to cry.

"So, do you want to tell me what happened?" Donna asked the next morning, as she poured Brandy a cup of coffee. The coffee was a rare treat these days. The scant teaspoon of sugar she used to sweeten Brandy's cup was just as rare. Sugar was hideously expensive and Donna couldn't afford much of it. Still, she had been waiting for what she hoped was happening for several years and felt like a small celebration was in order.

"Exactly what you told me would happen, Mom. I got sick of the job, sick of the people, and I just couldn't take it anymore,"

Brandy admitted. "You were right. It's no kind of life for anyone. Satisfied?"

"I wouldn't say satisfied, Brandy. I'm sorry you've been hurt, and I'm sorry you've wasted four years finding out that I was right," Donna answered. "I never wanted you to hang out with that crowd, and I'm very, very glad you've come to your senses about them. What I meant was do you want to tell me why you started hanging out with those people in the first place?"

Brandy's face froze. Donna realized that she had pushed this subject too soon, and Brandy still wasn't going to talk about it.

"What did happen last night?" she asked.

"I got tired of being pawed is what happened. I dumped a beer over someone's head and got fired. I'm sure I'll get a real good reference from Ken, won't I?" Brandy sneered. "Not that I'd get a good reference from anyone. What am I going to do now? I've never done anything but wait tables. And I've never worked anywhere but the club."

"You could take a week or so off and spend some time thinking, if you want to. We can afford that. Marvin Tipton stopped by to see me a while back. He said that he's talked to Peggy Craig and arranged a job for you, if you ever want it. You can start at the elementary school lunchroom Monday if you want to. Marvin promised that the job would be there when you wanted it."

"Great, Mom. I can go sling hash for a bunch of brats, what fun."

"Brandy," Donna snapped, "you said yourself that you've never done anything else. If you really mean this, you're going to have to get your GED and you're going to have to prove that you can work at a real job. You can't spend four years at the bottom of the barrel and expect to start at the top somewhere else. Be realistic. It takes years to get ahead."

Donna could tell that Brandy hadn't thought that far. Sitting there, surprised at her mother's vehemence, Brandy took a sip of her coffee and thought for a while. "This isn't going to be easy, is it, Mom? A GED? Go back to school after all this time?"

"Heather, have you seen Vicky lately?" Judy asked. "I tried to call her, but she wouldn't come to the phone."

"Every time she sees me, she turns around and heads in a different direction," Heather answered. "Gabrielle even went over to her house, but the housekeeper said she wasn't home. Gabrielle said she knew it wasn't true, because she had just seen Vicky go in."

"This is stupid. We were just trying to help."

"You know, Judy, the spending might not be the whole problem. It seems like Vicky's been a little weird since before the Ring of Fire," Heather mused. "Do you remember when she told us her Mom was pregnant? It seems like it started back then. She got kind of moody, and now she's competing against everyone. It seems like she's out to get people."

"Yeah, come to think of it, she hasn't been acting very happy about anything, has she?"

"I don't know what her problem is, Judy. She's still calling people 'marks,' too. It's kind of mean."

Judy fell into thought for a few moments. Vicky was competing with everyone, dressing to attract attention, trying to stay in the spotlight. Maybe jealousy was at the heart of her problem. Judy said, "Maybe she was competing with her friends, because she couldn't compete with her little brother. Maybe that's part of the problem. It's not something we can fix, but it might help if she talked to us about it. We've all been friends forever and I just hate it when we fight."

"Yeah, me, too. You don't have an extra CD player, do you?"

Heather's abrupt change of subject didn't really surprise Judy. Heather probably didn't realize how uncaring she sounded, but that was just Heather. She always tried to avoid emotional conversations.

"Afraid not, and I'm being very careful with the one I do have, too. I'm not sure they can even be fixed if they break, can they?" Judy asked.

Heather's face was glum. "Mr. Dotson is going to try to fix it. But he said not to hope too hard."

"Officer?"

Bill Magen looked towards the whisper. One of the men he had noticed a few days ago was standing in shadow, motioning at him. Blake started forward, but Bill stopped him with a hand on his shoulder. "Let me," he whispered, "He's German and may not have much English."

Moving toward the man, Bill began speaking in his own language. After a hurried conference, during which the man darted looks all around, Bill nodded and the man hurried off.

As Bill rejoined Blake, he noticed Blake's querying look. "Is a worried man, this Henning is. Do you remember the men we saw, the ones at Tyler's? And that man who looked so angry?"

"I remember. That one guy looked really mean," Blake remarked. "I wondered why he was staring at that woman."

"That man is Arend Nebel. The woman is Helene Gundelfinger. He was part of the stock panic a few months ago, you remember hearing about it?"

"Oh, yeah. All that stuff. I remember. A bunch of people got silly about rumors, wasn't it? So, what's his problem?"

"Is not silly, Blake," Bill answered. "Is very serious to this man, Arend. He lost a lot of money and is very angry. Henning, he says that Arend is dangerous and is planning something. Henning does not know what, but wanted we should watch Arend."

"There's not a lot we can do, Bill, except spread the word around. If he hasn't done anything, we can't just go arrest him on someone's suspicions."

"I will ask Sergeant Grooms when we report in," Bill remarked. "We can watch for this Arend Nebel, at least. He might try something."


"Well, Brandy, do you want the good news or the bad news first?" Jessica Whitney asked as she walked into the office.

Brandy's hopes sank. The tests hadn't seemed that difficult, except for the math test. Wincing, she answered, "You may as well just dump it all out, Mrs. Whitney. How bad was it?"

"Not nearly as bad as I think you think it was, Brandy. You passed the language arts portions with flying colors, as a matter of fact. Do you do a lot of reading?"

"Not especially. I used to read some magazines, sometimes. I've tried reading a few books, but I never really found anything I liked very much. Some of them were just silly. And some of them were a real bore. Who could believe," Brandy asked with a grin, "that humans could colonize the entire galaxy? And why would some woman run away to sea and become a pirate? And, if she was any good at it, why would she give it up for love? Sure. That makes a lot of sense. Come on!"

Jessica smiled in response. "Well, I suppose everyone has their own preference in entertainment. You know, you also passed the social studies portion of the test. The only problem areas are science and math. It's going to take some study and a fair bit of work, but you could have your GED in a couple or three months. Are you willing to work on it?"

"I need to pass those tests. I'll work on it and I'll study, if you tell me what I need to do. It will have to be part time, though. I'm not going to let my mother support me, so I'll have to find another job real soon," Brandy answered with renewed hope.

"Do you have one lined up, yet?"

"I guess I could go to the elementary school lunchroom. Peggy Craig says I can start there, anytime I want. I'm not real crazy about the idea. I don't really like kids very much, but a job's a job," Brandy answered.

"People say that there's nothing wrong with any kind of honest work, Brandy. And there isn't. But, have you ever thought of aiming a little higher? Anyone can serve food in a cafeteria, but not everyone can read and understand English as well as you could, if you worked at it. Have you heard about the Grantville Research Center? They could use some younger people, and it looks like you could be a help to them," Jessica responded. "Their budget isn't that large, so I'm not sure what they'll pay. And I warn you, you'd have to do a lot of reading. It won't always be interesting reading, either. Research is so much harder without the internet to rely on that you might think that the job is pretty hard to do, at first."

"You think I could get a desk job? Would they hire me, Mrs. Whitney? I haven't done anything like that, ever."

"Give me a day or so to talk to Laura Jo or Meg. I'll let you know, okay?" Jessica smiled warmly at Brandy. "You scored really well on reading comprehension. They need that. If you can pay enough attention to all the little details, you can do it."

"And how was your day?" Donna asked as Brandy slumped into a chair.

"My brain hurts. My eyes are going to cross if I have to read another word." Brandy groaned. "I never knew that so many people could have so many questions. Where do rubber trees grow? What is the melting point of . . . whatever it was, I can't remember. "What's the chemical composition of . . . something? It might be easier to wash pots and pans all day. Why am I doing this, again?"

Donna grinned at her tired daughter as she rubbed her own aching legs. In spite of her complaints about the research, Brandy seemed to be enjoying herself. Donna was glad to see that Brandy was beginning to look like her old self. She looked happier and somehow softer, less like the hard-edged barmaid. "We go through this every evening, Brandy. You're doing it to make a better life for yourself. How are the studies coming along?"

"Pretty well, I think. Mrs. Whitney says I can probably pass the test in a couple of months. I got to sit down and have lunch with Justine, today, too. She's just about my age and her English is pretty good. I like her."

"Why don't you plan to invite her over in a few weeks, then?" Donna asked. "You and I are going to have a little celebration, pretty soon."

"What do we have to celebrate, Mom?"

"Oh, lots of things. Your new job, new friends, old friends, and most of all," Donna paused as she placed a packet of papers on the table, "I made the last payment on the mortgage today. The house is all ours, finally. Now, with the extra money, maybe we can remodel that garage."

Brandy smiled at her mother. Donna had wanted to pay off the mortgage for years. Converting the garage to a room to rent would add even more money to their budget. Donna's excitement and happiness at her success was infectious. "I'd like to invite Blake, if you don't mind, Mom. And I really ought to include that pal of his. Bill Something . . . Magen, I think. I sort of owe both of them an apology."

"There is girl, again," Bill muttered with a sigh.

Blake followed Bill's gaze and saw Vicky Emerson walking toward them. Even to Blake's untutored eyes, Vicky looked like a wealthy young woman. He had recently paid the bill for having his uniforms altered to fit and was still surprised at the cost of the clothing he had seen in the shop. The simple alterations hadn't cost that much, but the price of fabric for new clothing was incredible. With fabric that expensive, Blake couldn't imagine what Vicky's outfit had cost.

Bill sighed again. "Her parents must be very wealthy for her to dress so well. They must be arranging a very good marriage for her."

Blake stared at Bill in surprise. Bill had some of the strangest ideas sometimes. How could anyone think that an American parent would arrange a marriage?

"She's only fourteen or fifteen, Bill. Her parents won't have marriage in mind for years, and even then they won't arrange it. She'll pick her own husband. Besides, she's the one who's rich. Her mom is a teacher and her dad works at the power plant. You can't get rich that way."

Bill looked at Blake in surprise. Blake had the strangest ideas sometimes. How could any responsible parent not arrange a proper marriage? And, how could any young girl be rich if her parents weren't? And, there was just no way that this girl could be only fourteen years old. She certainly didn't look that young to Bill.

"Justine, what happened?" Brandy asked. Justine had run past her, crying and in a panic.

Justine stood at the washbasin, holding a wet cloth over her left eye. Her normally neat appearance wasn't in evidence today. One of her sleeves was torn, her hair loose from its usually neat braid and her face was flushed. Her right eye leaked tears and she appeared to be shivering with fright.

"What is going on around here?" Barbara Monroe boomed, causing both young women to jump. "What on earth? Justine, what happened to you?"

"That's what I'm trying to find out, Mrs. Monroe," Brandy answered, "but Justine hasn't had a chance to answer me."

Barbara approached the shivering Justine and coaxed her to lower the cloth. The flesh around Justine's left eye was beginning to show some spectacular color. It was going to be a remarkable shiner.

"Who did this, Justine? Tell me. I'm going to call the police right now." Barbara was outraged. "Who ever it was is going to spend a few days in jail."

"No, please," Justine cried. "Please do not, Frau Monroe. Do not, I beg you."

"Young lady, no one is going to attack you and get away with it. Who was it?"

Justine stubbornly refused to answer, until Barbara gave up her questioning. "Brandy, I don't know what's going on, but if she won't let me call the police, why don't you take her to your house? She's in no state to work. Besides, I don't want anyone to see her this way. You'll both still get paid for today, I'll see to that. Keep her with you for the weekend, even. Maybe by Monday she'll come to her senses and turn this person in. Wait here, while I go get Reardon Miller to walk you two home."

Brandy could tell that Justine had been a little afraid to leave the building, but the presence of Mr. Miller reassured her. The walk to Brandy's house was fairly short and no one bothered the girls. The streets weren't exactly deserted, but almost everyone in the neighborhood worked, so the area was nearly empty. Once they had entered the house and locked the doors, Mr. Miller headed back to the research center.

Brandy got Justine settled on the couch in the living room and made a couple of cups of mint tea. After serving Justine, she sat down and tried to organize her thoughts.

Brandy looked over at Justine, who sat quietly and seemed to be beginning to relax. "Who did this?"

Justine began crying quietly. Brandy was dismayed at how quickly the tears began. "Justine, just tell me. I'm not going to call the cops. I just want to know so we can stay away from whoever did it."

Justine seemed to calm down and finally began to speak. "It was Arend. He was the man I would marry, if Magdeburg had not been destroyed, if we had stayed at home. My father, he brought him with us, when we fled. He has gone mad, Brandy. He did this when I told him I must come to work. He screamed that I have helped to destroy him, and that I am becoming too much like the Americans. He screamed that he would kill me, if I did not stop."

Brandy could tell that this wasn't the whole story. Her own experience left her feeling that Justine was leaving out a lot of details.

"What else did he do? This isn't all of it, Justine."

Justine couldn't answer at first, she was crying so hard. "Henning, he does not know. Arend, when we ran from the city, he . . . he . . ."

"He got you alone, when your brother and your father were doing something else, and he raped you, didn't he?"

Justine wept hysterically and it seemed a long while before she was able to speak.

"I have been so afraid. Arend swore to me that he would kill me if I told of this. He was to be my husband, he said, and I must obey. *Mein brudder*, Henning, Arend, he would kill him, too. Arend, he is mad. I fear to tell Henning. Arend will kill him and I will have no one. I do not want to be alone in the world. We have no home, no money, and now I am . . ."

When Justine shuddered to a halt, Brandy knew what words she had been unable to speak. "No, Justine. You are not spoiled. You are not ruined. It wasn't your fault, and you didn't deserve it," Brandy asserted. "No matter what you think, no matter what he said, that much just isn't true."

"You do not understand . . . You do not. I feel so . . ."

Brandy's own tears started rolling down her face. "Dirty. You feel dirty and ashamed and you don't think you'll ever be clean again. You feel so dirty that you can't imagine ever being worth anything to anyone. Not even to yourself."

Justine's eyes widened in shock as she looked into Brandy's eyes, and understood what she saw there. "You! It happened also to you?"

"Oh, yes, Justine," Brandy said. "It happened to me, and I don't even have the excuse that I was running from soldiers. I deliberately went somewhere I wasn't supposed to go and was doing something I wasn't supposed to be doing . . ."

"Like at a certain frat party, with a certain young man I told you to stay away from, maybe?" Donna knew she should have kept quiet. She hadn't been able to stop the words. Both young women stopped talking, exactly what Donna didn't want.

"How long have you been standing there, Mom?"

"Long enough, Brandy, long enough," Donna admitted as she walked into the room. "You two were so intent that I guess you didn't hear me come in. I've thought for years now that something must have happened to you and that whatever it was, it had to be pretty ugly. You just wouldn't tell me and I wasn't sure what to do except wait. Go on, finish your story," she continued, as she sat down and put her arms around her daughter. "Get it out."

"I don't know all of it, Mom. I think he slipped me some kind of drug, maybe. I have flashes of memory, sort of pictures in my head." Donna held her daughter tightly as Brandy started shaking. "They're awful. He did things, things that make me sick to think of. I couldn't talk about it. What would you have thought of me, if I told you? What would anybody think?"

All three women were crying, and talking at once. In Brandy's case, years of poisonous thoughts, self-recriminations, fears of betrayal and discovery poured out. For Justine, it was months, but the feelings of degradation weren't limited by the time. Eventually, the emotional storm began to wear down. Gradually, over a space of time, the weeping diminished. Finally, Donna stood and shook herself into some kind of order.

"Okay, you two. It's out. You can go on with life and we can make it better. There's not a thing we can do to the man who hurt Brandy, Justine, but there is something that can be done about this Arend person. You need to tell your brother."

"*Mein Gott*, Henning! It is so late, he will be worried. I must go. He does not know where I am. He was to meet me after the work, and I am not there."

The knock on the door startled everyone. Donna was relieved to find Blake Haggerty standing on the porch, along with another young man in an MP uniform. Behind them stood another man who, judging from his looks, could only be Henning Drugen, Justine's brother.

"Mrs. Bates, do you know where Brandy is? We were passing the research center and found Henning here going a little crazy trying to find his sister. Mr. Reardon said that Miss Drugen might still be with Brandy."

"They're both here, Blake. Gentlemen, come in," Donna answered. "There's a bit of a problem, and you're just the people we need to see."

Mary Emerson smiled as Gannon sat down at the dinner table. For a change, all four of her family would have a chance to talk over dinner. The last two years had been incredibly hectic. Between Gannon working the "B" shift, her own work at the library, young David's birth, and the Ring of Fire, Mary sometimes felt like she had lost touch with her family.

"There's nothing like a dinner with two beautiful women to make a guy happy," Gannon joked. "A couple of gorgeous blondes, a bouncing boy, and a quiet dinner at home seems like heaven to me."

Mary and Vicky both grinned at Gannon, pleased to be together. Even the two-year-old David gurgled happily in his highchair, chanting "Da, Da" sounds and making the usual mess with his food.

*So much has been going on in our lives*, Mary thought. The

addition of the housekeeper and her daughter to the household, while relieving her child-care concerns and domestic responsibilities, had also added an element of reserve between Mary, Vicky and Gannon. Tonight, with Margrethe and Eva away, Mary had both the time and the privacy to pay attention to her husband and daughter.

"Vicky, I swear it seems like you've grown-up all of a sudden. I never noticed that outfit before tonight. It looks really good on you."

Vicky blushed, a bit, and breezily answered, "Well, I haven't had it very long. All my old stuff was getting kind of short. I wonder if I'm ever going to stop growing up and start growing out."

Gannon looked a little embarrassed suddenly. He hastily changed the subject, "All your investments must be going pretty well then. I was kind of surprised when I had to buy a new shirt. Just couldn't believe the cost."

"Oh, I'm in pretty good shape, Dad. I can afford a few things."

"You know, Gannon," Mary said, "that reminds me about our own savings. That money is just sitting in the bank, not doing much. Don't you think that we should probably take advantage of having a financial genius in the house? Vicky, I used to think that you might be a little young for this, but now, with you so grown up and all, maybe you could recommend some investments for me and Dad."

Vicky sat at her desk and thought hard. "You've been stupid," she told herself, "You've been stupid, silly, jealous, and acting like a brat." The other girls might have a point. She had been a little extravagant lately. Maybe she hadn't really needed quite so many new things.

Still, Vicky knew she was good at this investing game. Not quite as good or as focused as Susan, but certainly as good as Judy. She could be even better if she wanted to. And, suddenly, she did want to. If Mom and Dad trusted her, she wasn't going to let them down.

Vicky reached for the phone and glared at the offending instrument. Making this call wasn't going to be easy. She had to stay in the consortium. She needed their input. She was going to have to talk to Judy.

☆     ☆     ☆

"I'm sorry, Millie," Anita said. "I didn't realize you were in here."

Millicent blushed furiously as she wrapped the towel around herself. "I hate being called Millie, Mom. It sounds like a name from 'Little House on the Prairie.' It seems like I'm old enough that you could call me by the name you gave me."

Mom looked a little strange, kind of shaken up or something. She didn't even complain that Millicent had been rude, just stood aside and let her leave the bathroom.

Anita stared at her own reflection while she washed her hands. When she realized that she was looking for wrinkles or gray hair, she shook her head at her own vanity. Of course she was getting older; everyone did, unless they died young. She just hadn't thought about Millicent being a part of "everyone." She was going to have to rethink some things. Millie, *No, Millicent* she corrected, might be small, but she definitely wasn't a little girl any more.

The young trainees, Blake and Bill, knew the correct procedures and called in the person Donna needed to see. After Marvin Tipton finished taking Justine's statement and left, the boys stayed for a few minutes, talking to Brandy.

Noting that Justine and her brother were having an intense, emotional conversation, Donna drifted a bit closer. If Henning was blaming Justine for what had happened, he was going to get an old-fashioned chewing out.

In fact, Henning was blaming himself. "No, Henning, is not your fault," Justine was insisting. "There was no other thing to do. He did not touch me, after that time. He never touched me at our rooms, not until today, when I would not listen to him."

"What!" said Donna. "You've been forced to live with this wretch! It's going to be a little crowded, Justine, but you and Brandy can share her room. Henning, you can sleep on the couch. Neither one of you is going back to anyplace this guy might be able to get into. You'll just have to stay here until he's caught."

Donna overrode any protests, and directed Blake to go with Henning to collect any belongings, right now, and hurry up about it. Henning and Justine gave in with good grace and a show of relief. Bill Magen would stay at the house and wait for Blake and Henning to get back, just in case.

☆        ☆        ☆

Arend Nebel stood silently in the deepest shadow he could find, seething to himself. So far, he had managed to avoid the police. He had returned to his rooms only to see Henning and the young MP leaving the premises. That they were burdened with bundles and bags as they left only made Arend angrier. They were going to pay for this. They were all going to pay.

His jumbled thoughts settled on one object of his anger. The blonde girl, the one who had stolen his stock that day, she was the responsible one. Yes, that one, the girl who had acted as though the stock was worthless until he dropped the price, she would be the first to die. Arend fingered the knife he carried. When he finished with the blonde, he would take care of the other witches, the faithless Justine who had gotten away, and then the Gundelfinger woman.

"Oh, yes, I am too going to work," Brandy said. "And so is Justine, so is Henning and so are you, Mom. We're not going to live in fear of that creep. We're still going to have our celebration this weekend, too. I just got my normal life back, and I'm going to keep it. No cowardly little weasel is going to stop me."

Donna smiled inwardly as she looked at her daughter. Brandy might not be completely healed, but she was improving, just a little bit, every day. So was Justine. Living life the way you wanted to was the best revenge against a bully. *Never let the bastards get you down,* Donna thought.

"Fine, Brandy," she answered. "You will be careful, though? You won't go running off alone, or into dark alleys, stuff like that?"

"Yes, Mom, we'll all be careful. We'll either be on the bus or in some other public place all the time. Just don't worry."

"Frau Bates," Henning began, "I must talk to you. It is not right, that you should open your home to us this way and not accept some payment. You must let me . . ."

Donna interrupted, brusquely, "Henning, I'm not going to charge someone for a bed on the couch. It wouldn't be right. But, I have been thinking about something, and maybe you could help. This isn't a very big house, and it's been around a few years, so it isn't very fancy. Now that we're here and cars are pretty useless, so is the garage, at least as a garage. I think we could make that space into a bedroom, or maybe even an apartment to rent to you and Justine. Do you know anything about that sort of thing?"

Henning grinned. "I learn. I learn the electric, for the 'Kelly Construction.' I learn it so I may teach, someday, that all may have the lights. I will ask my friends. Maybe I can get, what is it, a discount."

Vicky was preoccupied as she walked toward another meeting with her friends and Helene. The last few days had been really busy and very informative. She had learned that her parents just didn't understand business, and that they knew it. They were even a little intimidated by the thought of investing. There wasn't that much in the family savings account, although there should have been more. Her parents had good jobs that paid pretty well, but they tended to spend most of their salaries.

Most of the family's wealth was tied up in equity on the house and in a boatload of up-time equipment stored in the garage. Back when she had realized that she had sold her Barbie dolls too soon, and for too little money, she had made a comment about selling stuff too quickly. So, Mom and Dad hadn't sold anything, just stored it. Vicky hadn't realized that they were waiting for her to tell them what they should do.

The realization that her parents weren't uninterested in her, that they were just not sure what to do, was a shock. Mom and Dad didn't want to mess up her chances by trying to second-guess her decisions. They were proud of her but didn't want to put any pressure on her.

Vicky was so busy thinking and planning that the arm that snaked out and grabbed her was a complete surprise. The rage on the man's face scared her and being thrown hard against the building made her see stars for a couple of seconds. She felt the front of her blouse being grabbed and then she was being dragged into the space between two buildings.

"Bitch, harlot, thieving Daughter of Eve," he hissed. "You thought you could cheat me, destroy me, all to buy pretty clothes. You will not do this, not to me. I am a man, not one of you whimpering, soft up-timers. You hide behind evil magic. You cheat me. You use your looks to trap me. Maybe I fix the looks."

Vicky felt a sting on her cheek and saw a knife in front of her eye. The man giggled, with a high-pitched insane sound. The face was familiar, but she couldn't place him. Her head hurt and she couldn't remember.

"Who are you? Why are you doing this? Let me go," she screamed, trying to pull away.

He threw her against the wall again, hissing "You do not remember Badenburg, little whore? You stole my life in Badenburg. I steal your life now. I will use your beauty, yes, and then I will destroy you."

Vicky felt him grab her blouse again and saw the knife begin to come up. "No!" she screamed and pushed him as hard as she could.

He fell back a little and she felt the blouse tear. Suddenly, out of nowhere, a nightstick came down. It hit the wrist of his knife hand and she heard the sound of cracking wood as the knife flew away. Then there was a blur as someone else pushed the madman away.

Tears still blurred her vision and she blinked rapidly to clear them. Blake Haggerty and another young man were handcuffing the madman, even while he struggled and kept screaming that she was a demon and had destroyed his life.

Another policeman, this one in civilian clothes, had arrived and was helping Blake control the lunatic. The other uniformed young man approached Vicky and pressed a clean cloth to the cut on her cheek. She realized that her blouse was torn to a rag when the young man handed her his jacket. The madman was screaming, "She destroyed me. She stole my life to buy clothes. Women, they are all whores." Vicky looked down at the expensive rag she wore and began to wonder if some of what he screamed was true.

Susan and Judy were the first of the Barbie Consortium to arrive at the mob scene that the street had become. By the time they learned that Vicky had been attacked the rest of the girls had shown up, as well as half a dozen police officers. The police officers were trying to weed out the real witnesses from the crowd and telling people to move along, trying to clear the area. The officers told the girls that they could take Vicky to the doctor's office and then home. They also reminded Vicky that they would need to take her statement.

Doc Adams cleaned and bandaged the cut on Vicky's cheek, but insisted on calling her mother. "She'll want to know, Vicky," he responded in answer to her protests, "and she needs to know. You are a minor, after all."

The cut wasn't especially deep, so only cleaning and bandaging was needed. "She just needs to be careful and keep the cut clean and dry. Yes, she'll have a very faint scar for a while, but it should fade in time," Doc Adams said, in answer to Judy's worried questions.

Mary Emerson, frantic with worry, met the girls as they were leaving the doctor's office. "My God, Vicky, what's going on? The nurse said you were attacked! Who did this?"

"I'm fine, Mom, just fine," Vicky said, as the rest of her friends clustered around her. "Mom, let's just go home, please. We'll talk about it there, okay?"

Once at home, Mary heard the whole story. After the explanations, Vicky said, "We drove him to it, Mom. It's our fault. If we hadn't taken advantage of him, and of other people like him, it wouldn't have happened."

"What are you talking about, Vicky?" Heather asked. "You know as well as I do that a whole bunch of people laughed themselves silly when we bought their stock. They thought we were a bunch of stupid kids. They were glad to sell, and didn't care if we took a big loss. I heard some of them laugh about it, when they thought we couldn't hear them."

"Not everyone, Heather. Some of them were just regular people who were scared, and afraid of losing everything. We encouraged it and we took advantage of it. Some people asked for a lot less than they should have. You know they did," Vicky said.

"We paid them what they asked for, Vicky. It's not our fault if they didn't know what they were doing," Heather insisted stubbornly. "All they had to do was hold on, and everything would have been okay. I'm not taking blame when someone acts like an idiot."

"Don't you think we should have told them?" Vicky asked, earnestly. "Maybe we should have tried to teach them, not just take advantage."

"Everyone we bought stock from was selling that stock for more than they thought it was worth," Judy said. "It didn't matter if they were rich or not. It didn't matter if they were in a panic or not. The one thing we know about every person that sold us stock that day is that they were willing to dump what they thought was worthless paper on anyone who would buy it. If they were willing to dump it on people they thought were a bunch of dumb girls who didn't know any better, they don't get any sympathy from me.

"I did tell a couple of people, you know. I tried to tell one guy, some cousin of the mayor of Eisenach. He was scared to death about his investment, but he wouldn't dump it on someone he thought didn't know what it was worth. He wouldn't listen to me so I got Mr. Kunze to explain it to him. Besides, I agreed to pay what they asked. It's just like a run on the stock market back up-time. Some people panic and some people . . ."

Bang! Bang! Bang! The knock on the door sounded like gun shots and startled everyone. Mary, not at all amused, went to answer the door.

"Do we really have to do this, Bill?"

Bill got a really stubborn look on his face. "We will. I wish to know about this Vicky, und how she is. We have only to knock on the door and ask that she is all right. Then we will leave."

Blake wasn't convinced that things were going to be that easy. Girls still made him a little nervous. They just didn't think the way he did. Still, he followed Bill up the walk to the Emerson house, determined to see this through.

It wasn't Vicky who opened the door. It was her mother. Bill stumbled a bit, introducing himself, and Blake stepped in to explain that Bill wanted to check on the welfare of her daughter. Mary Emerson's eyes seemed to see right through Blake's lame explanation.

"Come on in, officers," Mrs. Emerson said, with an odd emphasis on the word "officers." "I'm sure the girls will be glad to see you."

"Girls?" Blake asked.

"Oh, yes, didn't you know? All of Vicky's little friends are here. They brought her home and stayed to make sure she's okay." Again, there was a funny emphasis, this time on the word "little." Blake had the feeling that that Mrs. Emerson might be trying to send him some sort of message.

The young men followed her into the living room, and found a cluster of girls, all talking at once. The girls fell quiet for a moment, until Vicky recognized Bill as the man who had saved her from harm. She even stood up and thanked him sincerely for saving her life. Blake was just a little miffed by this. After all, he was the one who hit Arend Nebel with his baton. Bill hadn't been the only one there.

Blake came out of his momentary rush of memory only to hear Bill inviting everyone to Mrs. Bates' celebration, tomorrow afternoon. Somehow, Bill had phrased his invitation to include everyone in the room, as well as anyone else who wanted to come. Mrs. Emerson, faced with the joint acceptance of all seven girls, didn't say anything right away, but she did drag Blake into the hall for a quick talk. His ears still burning, Blake left with Bill a few moments later.

"Uh, Bill, there's something we need to talk about," Blake muttered. "Something that Mrs. Emerson told me."

"The mother, she worries, as all mothers worry about young girls," Bill acknowledged. "I know girl is too young, now. But, I will marry her one day. I know this. I wish only that she will remember me while we are in army. I will be ready in six, seven years. She will marry me then."

Bill's absolute certainty confounded Blake. Blake couldn't imagine what would be happening to him in the next six days, much less in six or seven years. How could Bill, who was only a couple of months past eighteen, just like Blake, be so sure of the future?

"If you say so," Blake remarked. "That's if you live through the next few hours."

Surprised, Bill looked at Blake, the question written all over his face.

Grinning, Blake answered the unspoken question. "Buddy or not, I'm not going to be the person who tells Mrs. Bates that a bunch more people have been invited to her party. You get to do that all by yourself, my friend."

"Bill and Vicky, sitting in a tree, K-I-S-S-I-N-G," Hayley chanted, much to Vicky's chagrin.

"Good grief, Hayley," Millicent muttered. "Grow up, why don't you?"

Hayley grinned as she answered, "Well, maybe they aren't now, but they will someday."

"I don't think so," Mary said, glad to see that the girls were recovering their normal natures. "At least, I better not catch them at it anytime soon."

The girls all giggled and blushed and continued to poke good-humored fun at Vicky for a while, until Vicky asked, "Millicent, what did you do to yourself? You look different."

"Oh, just a little haircut." Millicent preened, pleased that someone had finally noticed. "The stylist said that my hair was overwhelming my face, so she got rid of a bunch of it. She said it detracted from my looks."

"Ohhhh, a stylist, was it?" Susan grinned. "You couldn't just go to the beauty shop, like the rest of us?"

"Beauty shops are for peons," Millicent pretended to sniff haughtily, "Us real rich folk go to see a stylist."

Even Mary had to laugh. Millicent did look much different. Without the mass of hair, she no longer looked like a moppet, but more like the young woman she was. She still looked like a little pixie, but she didn't look like a child anymore.

Vicky was the first to arrive at the Bates home, along with Judy. Arend Nebel's screamed imprecations had had a profound affect on her. She felt she had to make amends, somehow. She knew that most of the group didn't really share her view. Still, some people had been hurt, and Vicky felt responsible.

When Brandy answered the door, Vicky handed over the covered dish that she had brought for the party. "I know we're early, Brandy, and I'm sorry. I just really need to speak to your guests."

Brandy looked at Vicky in surprise. "How do you know Justine and Henning?" she blurted out.

"I don't know them, exactly. But, I've done them some harm and I have to fix it. Could we see them, please?"

Brandy escorted Vicky and Judy into the kitchen, where Justine and Henning were sitting at the table, enjoying a quiet moment before the party began. After introducing everyone, Brandy sat down with the rest of them and stared at Vicky and Judy, curiosity in her face.

Vicky touched the bandage on her cheek, and tried to speak, but wasn't able to. Judy, watching with concern, decided to step in.

"The reason we're here is that Vicky kind of thinks we may have done something bad. We didn't mean to, exactly, but looking back on it, maybe we did. We took advantage of people and we didn't realize that they were people just like us. People trying their best to get ahead and do well. We feel kind of bad about doing it, and we want to make it up to you, somehow."

Henning looked at the girls with interest. He could tell that they meant their words. The shame on Vicky's face was clear to see. He recognized her, just as Arend had. She was the girl who had driven down the price of the stock Arend had sold. She had convinced Arend that a lower price was better than no price at all. Arend had sold all the stock he owned and come close to ruining himself.

Henning; however, was a sharper player of the game. In spite of Arend's urging, Henning had continued to hold on to his father's investments. Those investments would begin paying, and soon, he felt. Not everyone had sold their stock at bargain prices. Quite a few people besides the girls had continued to buy instead of sell.

"You should not worry. Arend, he was always a bit impatient," Henning explained. "Always, he was in a hurry, never able to wait. You did not cause his madness. I discovered, recently, that he was always not the man I thought I knew."

Vicky started crying. "I feel so bad. I never meant to hurt anyone. I keep wondering how many people are in the same boat, just because of me. I'll never do that again. Never. I'll be honest and give honest value, I swear."

"Is not so bad, to be, how do you say . . . sharp trader," Henning answered. "What is American saying, Ah, yes, I have it . . . 'never give a sucker the break even.'"

Judy burst into laughter. It took a while for her to calm down and explain.

"How did this happen?" Donna wondered. From a small celebration with a few friends, her "mortgage-burning" get-together had somehow become a full-blown party, complete with covered dishes, music, and dancing in the street. It wasn't exactly what she had counted on. It was nice, even enjoyable, but not what she had planned.

She wandered around, talking to people she knew and meeting the people she didn't know. Some of Henning's friends from work had stopped by, ostensibly to check out the garage she wanted to remodel, and wound up staying. Susan Logsden and all her friends were here, along with a German woman and her little girl. Susan had introduced Mrs. Gundelfinger as her teacher although Donna wasn't too clear on what the woman taught. Young Blake Haggerty had even set himself up as a DJ, with one of those silly microphone things.

Donna headed toward Blake, intending to ask him for some

slightly quieter music. Heather Mason apparently had the same idea, since Donna heard her pleading with Blake to play her favorite Fats Domino CD. Blake good-humoredly gave in, and the loud music got toned down a bit.

"Thanks, Heather," Donna said. "I was beginning to wonder if my hearing would survive that last number."

"Me, too, Mrs. Bates. I just hate that stuff," Heather said. "It's a really nice party, you know. I'm having a lot of fun."

"I'm glad to hear it, dear. It isn't exactly what I had planned, but what the heck. I'll have a big audience when my time in the spotlight comes."

Heather looked at Donna curiously. "Spotlight?"

"Oh, yes, Heather. This whole thing started out as a little celebration for me. I made the last payment on my mortgage a couple of weeks ago. The house is paid for, finally."

"But that's just nuts, Mrs. Bates." Heather blushed from the top of her head to the tips of her toes when that exclamation rang out. During a lull in the music, Blake's microphone had picked up her words and sent them flying through the crowd. Everyone around them turned to look at Heather, who now seemed to be a complete loss for words.

Donna stared at the girl and said, "Perhaps you'd like to explain that remark, young lady."

As the flustered Heather looked for a way out of the limelight, Vicky Emerson started to apologize for her. "She didn't mean it the way it sounded, Mrs. Bates. Heather just isn't very diplomatic."

"I should say not. I've worked and slaved for years to get where I am. Some teenager doesn't need to be telling me I'm nuts."

"I'll be glad to explain it, Mrs. Bates, really, I will. Vicky's right, I didn't mean it the way it sounded. I was just surprised that you'd be willing to keep your money locked up that way," Heather said.

"Money? What are you talking about? I said I paid off my house, nothing about money." Donna was becoming interested in spite of her annoyance. The whole town knew these girls were getting rich, and knew they'd gotten their start by selling their toys.

"Money, Mrs. Bates. This house represents money, and quite a bit of it, at that. Every house in this neighborhood is worth a fortune, at least a half-million dollars. Some of them are worth even more than that. What you've got is a great big chunk of money that's just sitting here, not growing and not doing you any good. I'm sorry, but it isn't the smartest thing you could do," Vicky explained. "I'm recommending that my parents pull their equity out of their house, with a second mortgage. Then, we'll invest that equity. Some of it will go into OPM, and some of it will go into new companies, to spread the risk. It's called diversifying."

People from all around the neighborhood were listening with interest. Everyone knew about savings accounts, but hearing business theory from teenagers who were getting rich was, well, weird. The attention had grown beyond Vicky and Heather's ability to cope with. They desperately wanted out of this. Judy, always the showman, stepped up and took Blake's microphone.

"Okay, everyone. Give us a few minutes. Listen to some music and relax. Since everyone seems so interested in this subject, we'll get something organized and be back in a few. Just enjoy the party."

The audience watched as seven teenaged girls and one adult went into a huddle. They huddled so long that some people, who were just watching them, started to get bored. It was almost thirty minutes before Judy returned to the microphone and started speaking.

"The first thing that we really need to mention is the difference between what's happening now and what was going on back up-time. Economically, I mean.

"Up-time, we had what's called a saturated economy. That means that there was business and production from all over the world. There wasn't room for a lot of expansion, unless you had some fancy new technology or something. If you wanted to open a business, you had to compete with all the businesses what were already there, so it was really hard to make money.

"Down-time, things were different. Most of Germany, most of the world we landed in, was in the middle of a big depression, as well as in the middle of a big war. It's not like that, now, here in Thuringia. We have all sorts of things that people know how to make, and all sorts of things we are making. And, we have millions of people to sell these things to. My sister says it's like the beginning of the Golden Age, back in America, near the end of the nineteenth century. Right now, right here, we have the beginning of what's probably going to be about fifty years of rapid expansion, a 'bull' market.

"That means that what you should do with your property is different. We already have tourists coming to see the Ring of Fire. The roads and the waterways are going to get better, so more and more people will come. That means that your property is worth a lot more than it was up-time."

Nothing that Judy was saying was really new to anyone. Everyone had heard the same words, or read them in the paper, or seen people talk about it on TV. It was the same old thing, but now the information changed a bit. Judy took a note card from Susan and started talking about a subject near and dear to the hearts of average Americans, taxes.

"Even up-time, having your home paid off wasn't really the most profitable thing to do. It was safe and it was simple, but not profitable. Now, in a new Golden Age, it isn't even very safe. As the property values go up, so will the taxes. It will take a few years for the taxes to catch up, because the government has put a twenty percent per year limit on those taxes. The government had to limit the growth of the taxes or half the people inside the Ring of Fire would get evicted when the taxes come due in a few months. Think about that.

"The taxes you pay will go up twenty percent per year for at least the next ten years. That's just to catch up to the value of your property today. It's like it was back in the Silicon Valley, in California, when houses that people bought for fifty thousand dollars in 1960 were worth three million dollars in 1999. The government is protecting you from being forced out of your property, because no matter how much the assessed value of your home goes up, the taxes aren't going to go up more than twenty percent. That's still a lot of money, though. Taxes that were a thousand dollars last year are going to be twelve hundred this year. In ten years, they'll be about sixty-three hundred. How hard is it going to be to save that kind of money?

"If you leave your equity in your home, you're probably going to have to sell it in a few years, just to pay the taxes that are going to come due. You'll have to do that unless you have something else to make you rich. Bad news, isn't it?"

The crowd began to murmur. Hearing this on TV didn't have quite the same impact that an earnest young woman talking from the heart had. She made it so clear.

"Now for the good news. Investing in stocks and bonds is

probably safer now than it was up-time, as long as you're even a little bit careful. Don't go financing a trip for someone to raid King Tut's tomb, okay?"

Laughter echoed through the crowd. There had been a lot of silly talk about gold rushes and treasure hunting, nearly ever since the Ring of Fire had happened.

"A lot of new companies are starting up. For the first time in history, an awful lot of them are going to make it, too. But, there's a little more bad news. If you don't invest, you're going to get left behind. With the property values going up, the taxes are going up, and without some kind of investments, you're actually more likely to lose your house if you pay it off.

"What you need to do is refinance your home and get about half or three-quarters of its market value. Then, you invest the money, either in new businesses starting up, or in mutual funds that will probably pay you something like ten percent a year interest. A good new business could pay you more like fifty percent a year on your investment.

"So, even after you make your mortgage payment, the investments will pay you more money than you pay out. Probably a lot more, but it depends on what you invest in. You just have to be careful, like I said. That's why Heather said what she said."

Judy then stepped away from the microphone and found herself answering question after question. She and the rest of the Barbie Consortium, as well as Helene, after people got more used to her, spent the rest of the evening answering questions for their half-disbelieving audience.

"The thing is, money gets really complicated," Vicky explained. "Everything is all tied together, like the value of your property, and the value of the dollar. The value of the dollar is so high right now that wages probably aren't going to go up very much for a few years, but the taxes will. It will get harder and harder to save money, so you need to invest while you have the chance.

"And, we've all got to stop thinking like we did back up-time. Almost every up-timer is an irreplaceable resource and knows more about how to do things than the down-timers do. We all need to start good businesses, or invest our money, and even get every bit of training we can. Just being able to read English puts you ahead of the game, so don't waste your time in a job anyone can do. If you have things that people want, sell them and then invest the money. Just ask Heather what she'd be willing to pay for a new CD player."

Donna was trying to both listen and maintain her grip on Helene's daughter. The little girl was determined to get to her mother and squirmed loose just as Helene was trying to bring one of her discussions to an end. While she was running as swiftly as she could, the little girl naturally tripped and fell with a thump. She began crying at the top of her lungs.

The man at whose feet she fell gently helped her stand and brushed her off a bit. Donna had met him earlier and even asked him about matching the brick on her house. He was very tall, with broad shoulders and a thick mane of black hair that he wore in a single braid. *If I were only a few years younger,* Donna remembered thinking during the introduction.

The little girl stared trustingly into his face and held up her arms, wanting to be picked up. He hesitated a moment, looking around for the child's parents. Helene caught his eye and nodded. He then picked her up with great care and set her on his shoulder so she could look all around. Her excitement and glee were really something to see.

Donna and Helene moved toward him, arriving at about the same time. Helene stood, mute, and stared up at him, obviously intrigued. Donna grinned to herself. This might be another budding romance, like the ones she had noticed this day. Bill and Vicky, while much too young, were obviously interested in one another. And, to Donna's extreme relief, Brandy seemed to be developing an interest in Henning. She had been afraid that Brandy might have lost all interest in getting married after her experience. Donna wanted grandchildren, someday, and was glad to see that it might happen.

Well, there's no point in just standing here, Donna decided. I guess I can go introduce them.

Judy didn't like what she was seeing. Mrs. G looked kind of funny. Like she was really interested in the man she was talking to. She got Susan's attention and motioned toward Mrs. G. "Look at that, Susan. What do you think? Is it what I'm afraid it is?"

Susan took a long look. "Probably." She sighed. "Probably."

☆        ☆        ☆

*So many changes,* Vicky thought as she looked at the people gathered in Tyler's Restaurant. She had been changed by the events of the last few weeks, she knew. In a way, though, she had found her place. She had a mission, now. She wanted to teach the up-timers and the down-timers, too. Not everyone understood the opportunities and dangers of their new world. She didn't want another Arend, but there were reasons, good reasons, to work the stock market.

Susan still wanted to be rich enough to be safe. Gabrielle wanted money to pay for medical school and become a doctor. Millicent still wanted to be treated like a grownup with something to contribute. Hayley and Judy had things they wanted to do, too, although they didn't really talk about it much. Heather, even after buying another CD player, spent a lot of her time researching ways to transfer her music to some other media, just in case this one broke, too.

Mrs. G stood at the front of the room, giving a lecture, as she did every month. This meeting; however, was a little different. Instead of teaching half a dozen young girls, Mrs. G now spoke to a growing, enthusiastic audience. Blake Haggerty was here, learning how to invest the money Heather had paid for his CD player. His friend, Bill Magen was here, too. Mrs. Bates and Brandy were taking notes, learning everything they could about investing the money they received for the new mortgage. So were about ten more people, all determined to learn everything she had to teach.

"Maybe," Vicky thought, "the biggest changes are still to come."

# 'Til We Meet Again

## Virginia DeMarce

The worst thing about working for Mechanical Support was that the facilities were scattered out all over Grantville, even now, two and a half years after the Ring of Fire. They'd never been able to take the time to centralize them; they didn't really have any central place to put them if they had the time, and definitely not the extra resources to re-pour the pits and such. So there were men here and men there—never enough in one place for the really heavy jobs, so you had to stop and call one of the other sections in to help. Three service stations. The shops at the car dealerships. The repair and body shop that had belonged to Bernie and Cy Fodor.

Billy Nelson whistled. "Here a lift, there a lift, everywhere a lift, lift."

No, not everywhere. If there had been lifts everywhere, the crew's life would have been a lot simpler.

Billy looked up at the circular metal saw with exasperation. These days, when a heavy truck had body damage beyond what you could fix, there wasn't much to cannibalize. They took thin sheets of steel rolled down by Saalfeld, cut pieces, bolted them together, dropped the result down over the motor and frame, and bolted it on. The results weren't sleek. They looked like rolling boxes. But they still rolled and they still transported material that the military needed. At least, it was easier to fix windows and windshields onto the straight steel pieces—just fit in a straight piece of glass cut to fit. Forget about wipers; forget about windows that went up and down. Forget about safety glass, for that matter. Just keep the truck rolling and box in the cab so the driver won't freeze in winter. Even if you were only moving at twenty-five miles per hour, the wind chill generated by a truck was a lot worse than what the driver of a horse and wagon was exposed to. So build a new body for that truck parked next to the shop.

If the metal saw didn't quit on you, that is. The metal saw had just quit. He could hear a hum in the engine, over all the rest of the noise in the shop, but the blade wasn't turning.

"Cut the power to the saw, but leave it on to the winch, so we can bring it down and take a look to see what is wrong." His regular partner, Foster Caldwell, flipped the switches, brought the saw down, then came over to help, flipping the power to the saw back on before he came.

"The motor, actually, sounds okay." Foster and Billy looked at it. The power just wasn't turning the saw. "Problem has to be in the connection."

They knew the routine. This wasn't the first time it had happened. Turn off the power to the saw. Unscrew the bolts, take off the blade, lay it aside. Turn the power to the saw on again. Work back, step by step, through the wiring, power on, power off, until they found out where the problem was. A lot of this wiring was nearly burned out, they way they'd been overloading it. They found bad spots in the insulation all the time.

"Unscrew the bolts" was easier said than done. Somebody had screwed them on with a power driver the last time. And somebody, not necessarily the same somebody, taken the head that fit these nuts to use at one of the other shops, probably, because it sure wasn't in the tray here. Muscle power time. Billy stuck his head out of the bay and yelled, "Merton." Merton Smith was their muscle. He'd worked for the mobile home moving company before the Ring of Fire. He'd been wrestling double-wides ever since he dropped out of high school.

It took all three of them, and a jerry-rigged extension to the wrench, to get the fourth bolt loose. Still, that took less time than sending someone to visit every other Mech Support shop location looking for the right head. Which somebody might have put in his pocket and taken along on a run to Jena, for all they knew.

"What are the odds that Bobby took the head?" Foster asked.

"No bets," Merton answered.

The others saw to it that Bobby Jones made most of the delivery runs. He'd complained about it, once, that the others were shirking the unloading and reloading at the other end. Foster had said, "Well, it's this way. If I go out, then Billy and Merton have to put up with you. If Merton goes out, then Billy and me have to put up with you. If Billy goes out, then Merton and me have to put up with you. If you go out, then none of us have to put up with you."

It took Bobby three days to work though the logic of that one, figure out that he'd been insulted, and decide to be offended. But Bobby was that kind of guy. If one of the other shops called and asked for that size head, he'd just put it in his pocket, intending to drop it off, not bothering to check it out, and forgetting to take it to the guy who wanted it. It would stay in his pocket until someone asked for it, or until he found it when he washed his overalls and brought it back.

It got dark early in January in Thuringia. The only bulb that they had in the overhead fixture wasn't giving them enough light to see by. Merton turned it off and strung a light from an extension cord, throwing the cord over a line just above the saw, so they could see what they were doing better. Nearly four hours they had lost over the damned wiring for the saw. None of them were electricians, but it would have taken even longer to get an electrician to come look at it than to do it themselves. At least they had the manual for the thing. Finally, the rotor was turning as it should. Just get the blade back on and they could start fresh in the morning.

All three of them were focused on it. Merton and Foster were holding the blade in place. Well, Foster was bracing it and Merton was holding it in place, one foot on the ground, the other leg bent with his foot on a rail, leaning forward to give himself a bit more leverage. Billy was standing next to Merton, starting to set the bolts. One on; five to go. Out of one ear, Billy heard the delivery truck. Good thing Bobby was back; the headlights were on the fritz and had been for two weeks. One more thing to fix. It seemed like they never had time to fix their own stuff; there were always more urgent projects.

Bobby came in, said, "Hey, what are you doing with the lights off?" Foster started to turn. Bobby hadn't pulled off his leather, fur-lined driving gloves with the outside seams yet. As he reached to flip the light switch, the tip of his next finger flipped another switch. The wrong switch. The single bolt sheared. The huge saw blade jerked and flew off the rotor, spinning to an angle.

"Billy died instantly." Jeff Adams was glad to be able to tell Iona that. He didn't think that he needed to tell her that Billy had been cut in half. He'd have a word with the mortuary, too. If they arranged the suit right and only opened the top half of the casket, Iona could have a viewing for Billy, the way she wanted it.

It had been harder to tell Mary Ruth Caldwell. They had saved Foster. He had been hit at the first thoracic vertebra. He would have diaphramatic control of his breathing but little or no rib breathing; shoulder movement and some arm and hand movement. Foster would be an incomplete quadraplegic. She would have to be prepared to keep him in assisted living for the rest of his life. The only ameliorating circumstance was that, at least, Mary Ruth could afford it. She'd been office manager for her father Thurman Jennings at Town and Country Properties before the Ring of Fire—had turned herself into an agent, since it. The way the real estate market was in Grantville, these days, Mary Ruth would be doing fine. For a woman with a quadraplegic husband, that is. Financially, she would be doing fine, even paying the cost of care for Foster.

Billy's body had slowed the blade, some, deflecting the angle. They had to amputate both of Merton's legs above the knees. The blade had sliced the bent one right through the kneecap, all the way off; the other three inches above the knee, through the bone. James Nichols and his team had to complete the amputation and take a few more inches of bone so they could fashion a muscle and skin stump. Merton had been too unstable for anything else. Reattaching legs was beyond their capabilities, these days. Controlling infection was pretty much within them. The EMTs had gotten Farrell and Merton to the hospital in ten minutes after Bobby Jones had come running out of the shop into the middle of the highway, yelling.

Jeff Adams sighed. Farrell and Mary Alta, Merton's parents, were sitting with him, now. If Farrell could just manage to control his impatience, Merton could be salvaged. Not just for being alive, but for having a life worth living, double amputee or not. Farrell had a M.Ed. and a B.S. in industrial arts; he'd been terribly embarrassed when Merton dropped out of school, since he was always lecturing kids on the importance of finishing and getting a start on a decent career. If Farrell would just control himself, after a few months they could get Merton out of rehab and into a GED and tech school program. If Farrell didn't yell at him too often in the meantime.

That would be another day's trouble. Jeff looked back at Iona.

The pipes wailed through Grantville's streets. "Abide With Me." Iona had chosen it. It was Billy's favorite hymn. The up-timers, almost all of them, had associated bagpipes with Scotland. While there were Scots in Grantville, now, the Germans also had a remarkable variety of bagpipes or instruments that it was hard to tell from bagpipes. Both the way they looked and the way they sounded.

This procession had a fairly long way to go, all the way from the funeral home downtown to the new cemetery behind St. Martin's in the Fields, the Lutheran church just outside the Ring of Fire, off the main road leading to Rudolstadt.

Pipes followed by a wagon and a procession of mourners had become part of Grantville's regular sounds and sights.

Archie Clinter hadn't been willing to accept Iona's resignation. First he appealed to her sense of responsibility. "Where are we going to find a replacement?" When that didn't work, he went into paternalistic/counseling mode. "You know, Iona, everyone recommends that recent widows shouldn't make impulsive decisions. You should continue where you are for at least a year after Billy's death, before making any decision so drastic as resigning your job and moving to a town where you will be the only American. I just don't feel right about letting you do this."

Iona looked at him, cocked her head a little to the side, and remarked, "You know, slavery really has gone out of fashion, these days. You can't refuse to accept it."

Archie looked shocked. He meant it all for her own good, of course. She was right, though. Legally, he couldn't refuse to accept her resignation. So he bucked it up the chain to the superintendent of schools.

Which meant that Iona was sitting in Ned Paxton's office, going over it all again. *Men!* She didn't dislike men, as a group. She did dislike their general tendency to think that they knew what was best for you.

"Ned, Quedlinburg asked me to do this before Billy— well, before he died. I didn't turn them down because I didn't want the challenge. I turned them down because I didn't want to leave Billy, and there wasn't any job for him up there. Now— I'm not going to be any farther away from Billy in Quedlinburg than I am in Grantville. Graves don't count."

Ned looked at her. "The one thing that Germany doesn't have a shortage of is musicians. Surely they can find a down-timer to teach music at the new women's college they're starting up north."

Iona looked at him with exasperation. *Men!* she thought again.

"Well, of course they could. Mary Simpson and the abbess aren't looking for just a music teacher to be a music teacher. They're looking for an American woman to be a music teacher. Because it's a college for young women. Because it's a college for the young, mostly down-timer, women who are going to marry some of the most influential men of the next generation of the USE."

She reached across the desk, picked up his substantial bronze letter-opener, and pointed it at him. He automatically scooted his swivel chair back a few inches, but she brought the point down onto his blotter rather than toward his face.

"A lot more influential than those men that the girls we're turning out from the high school here in Grantville will be marrying, Ned. Than most of them, anyway. The positions in that abbey, the way it was set up before the Ring of Fire, the slots for the canonesses—that's what they're called, not nuns—was for daughters of the high nobility. The most upper of the upper crust. That part isn't going to change right away. It's bound to, eventually, but not right away. From the start, though, they're throwing open the college section that's starting up next fall to the daughters of anyone who can pay the tuition. And stretching that down into the school they already run, which is a sort of quasi-secondary school for daughters of the high nobility, the little sisters and nieces and cousins of the canonesses. The next generation of canonesses, some of them. Do you really think that half the rich merchants and upper bureaucrats in the USE aren't going to want to send their little girls to a school where they can be taught by ladies from the high nobility and mix with their daughters? That the lower nobility, if they can afford it, won't want their daughters in a place where they can associate with girls from the high nobility, even if they have to swallow associating with commoners and scholarship students as part of the deal?"

The point of the letter opener came down on the blotter again.

"So do you want those girls educated without any up-timer input? Or do you see what Mary Simpson is getting at? Put in some American women as teachers. Let those girls—they'll be what we think of as high school as well as college age, figure from about fourteen to twenty or twenty-one—see what we're really all about. Every girl in Grantville has contact with dozens of up-timer women. Just because they live here. For the time being, in Quedlinburg, it's going to be me or nobody."

The point of the letter opener came down again.

"I don't have all that many ties in Grantville, Ned. No parents, no children or grandchildren. I'm from Pennsylvania, you know that. Billy was from Fairmont. We just lived here because I had the job and didn't like to drive that far every day on those curving roads in winter. It didn't matter to Billy where we lived. We bought the house; it was just a place for him to park his rig when he was off the road. No sentimental ties. No old family traditions. Just a house that we bought through a real estate agent. The kids didn't even grow up in it, really; I took the job at Fluharty after Kyra started high school. I'm free to go."

Ned cleared his throat. "Do me a favor, Iona. Don't sell your house. Rent it out. Let Mary Ruth Caldwell handle it. She'll be needing the money. Don't burn your boats. Take a leave of absence. One year, two years, I'll leave that up to you."

*Men!*

Iona had quite a bit of luggage. Four suitcases and a trunk. No matter that she had gone along with Ned Paxton about renting out her house, she knew in her heart that she wasn't coming back to Grantville except maybe for an occasional visit. The college would provide her with a room, and she was taking what she would want to have in that room. Music. Photos. Clothes. Her favorite foam rubber pillow that supported her neck just right when she slept. Two old-fashioned rubber hot water bottles. She didn't mind saying goodbye to the rest. Archie Clinter thought that she should have rented a storage place, but she didn't want to bother. She was renting the house out furnished.

She'd hired a wagon to take her down to the train. As far as Halle by train; by boat on the Elbe to Magdeburg. Then over to Quedlinburg. Thank goodness she wouldn't be slogging overland in a wagon, the way it had been raining the last week.

The driver was headed the wrong way. She had said her good-byes at the school the day the spring semester ended. She leaned forward, "We're supposed to be going to the depot."

He turned his head. "I haff my orders."

She looked up at the steps of the turreted old red brick building. A couple of hundred people, at least. She blinked. Every one of them under twenty-five; every one had been in middle school music classes at some time in the past ten years. Down at the bottom of the steps, Vicki Saluzzo.

Now, that had been a lively fight, as the school system had bearded the NUS army, demanding that it not tie up in that original, romantic, "for the duration" enlistment statement people who were needed a lot worse to do other things in Grantville's civilian world. They'd pried out the Saluzzo twins, Jim and Vicki, to teach physics and music; that had been followed by a "reevaluation" and a fairly large release of up-timers who had already been soldiers for two or three years into the reserves. Which was turning out to be very beneficial to Grantville's economy.

Vicki raised her baton.

Smile, the while I bid you sad adieu.
When the clouds roll back, I'll come to you.

The young voices went on. "'Til we meet again."

Iona blinked once more, smiled, and waved at them. The driver turned the wagon and took her down to the depot, with no more fuss.

As soon as she found her seat, she opened her notebook. There was a whole curriculum to plan between now and September. She thought she had better have several different options to present to her new colleagues. It was never a good idea to start a new job by giving the impression that you were overbearing.

As the modified pickup truck cab section that was pulling the little train moved out of the built-up part of the Ring of Fire, paralleling the highway to Rudolstadt, it started to gain speed. Iona looked out the window as it passed St. Martin's in the fields.

*Goodbye, Billy. 'Til We Meet Again.*

# One Man's Junk

Karen Bergstrahl

Martin Schmidt paused, his spoon barely touching the stew. His stomach would have him attack the stew bowl like a starving wolf but his mind held him back. Carefully, he took one spoonful and then put his spoon down. A sip of beer helped but his hand shook slightly. Reminding himself he was a man, not a wolf, he looked at his host before taking a second spoonful.

"Eat up, boy. When you've finished there will be time enough to talk." Herr Glauber beamed across the table. "Here, Adolf, fetch another pitcher of beer and get me another ham sandwich." The older of the two boys beside Herr Glauber shoved his chair back and got up with a grin and a glance at the crowded bar of the Thuringen Gardens.

"Yes, Papa. Heinrich, more stew or a sandwich?" Adolf asked his younger brother.

"Sandwich, please," Heinrich replied. The boy drained his mug with a gulp and belched loudly. "And hurry back with the beer."

"Manners, son, manners!" Herr Glauber clouted the youngster on the shoulder. "Your mother didn't raise you without manners."

"No, Papa." Heinrich sat up straight, tucked his folded hands in his lap and assumed a pious expression, or what would have been one save for the crossed eyes.

"Brat. I'm surprised I don't beat you daily." Herr Glauber's stern expression slipped and he reached over to ruffle his son's hair. "You must excuse the boy. Since his mother's death . . . Go ahead and eat, Young Schmidt. It does no good to talk business on an empty stomach."

Martin, chewing a bit of tough meat from the last of the stew, contemplated his host. Herr Glauber did not have the look of a man who missed many meals. A closer look showed the lines and loose flesh common to those who have lost a great deal of weight quickly. No, his host, while not starving now, had seen hunger recently. Martin carefully fished a bit of gristle out of his teeth and took a mouthful of beer to wash down the stew. Just as he opened his mouth to speak Adolf reappeared with two large pitchers clutched to his chest and a plate of sandwiches balanced precariously atop the pitchers.

"Here, Young Schmidt, take a couple of sandwiches for later. Young men are always hungry." Herr Glauber shoved the plate toward Martin and out of the grasping hands of Heinrich.

"Thank you, sir. Thank you very much for the meal," Martin said. He hurriedly selected a pair of sandwiches and carefully wrapped them in his handkerchief.

"See, Heinrich? Our guest is polite, as you should be. He is full of questions but instead of spewing them at me like bees circling a hive he waits. I've the right of it, don't I, Schmidt? You're as full of questions as my boy is of mischief." Herman Glauber grinned across the table.

"Yes, sir. I am," was all Martin could manage. His thoughts tangled and knotted and he couldn't fashion them into a coherent question.

"First, we have never met before yet I invite you to share a meal with my family. Why should I do so? Secondly, I am a Master Carpenter, you are a blacksmith. In fact, you claim you are a journeyman blacksmith and the masters of your craft deny you the title."

A sick feeling welled up from Martin's stomach. He was a journeyman—but one without papers to prove his claim. Or tools, or friends, or anyone who could say, "Yes, I know Martin Schmidt is a journeyman blacksmith." Slumping down in the chair, he ducked his head to hide the shameful flush.

"Ah, boy, don't hang your head." Glauber's voice was gentle. "I didn't invite you here to shame you. You are hardly the only journeyman to arrive in Grantville without his papers. Old Hubner denied your claim so he could charge the Americans a journeyman's wages for your work while giving you an apprentice's wages. Some of the others are doing the same."

"I . . . I thought that might be so. He was within his rights to deny me my rank. I have no proof." Martin's voice trailed off as his thoughts twisted again to the beginning of the week when he had accused Master Blacksmith Hans Hubner of just such an action. In the space of ten minutes he had listened to a lecture on the sin of claiming rank he did not hold, been fired from his job without pay, and informed that no other blacksmith in or around Grantville would employ him even as a sweep. So it had proved. Named as a malcontent and troublemaker, Martin had found no one was willing to hire him. "I thought my work would show . . ." With a helpless shrug Martin sat, waiting for the lecture he was certain would come from this Master.

"Adolf, our guest's stein is empty. Refill it. Journeyman Schmidt, those last sets of hinges you made were for one of my jobs. I've seen poorer work from the hand of a master. You, my boy, arrived in Grantville too late or too early. Too late because Hubner and his cronies gobbled up the smithing jobs and control who is hired. This they can do because so few of the Americans speak German. Had you been hiding in the hills when first this town appeared, you might be one of them. Six months, or maybe a year from now, there will be too many jobs for the masters to control. Too many jobs and too many of the Americans will speak German for Hubner's tricks to work. Adolf, my stein is now empty and so is this pitcher." Fishing a handful of coins and some paper money out of a pocket, the older man shoved them at his son and waved him off. Pulling the remaining pitcher over, Glauber filled his stein. Beside him Heinrich was giggling. Every time Herr Glauber had mentioned Master Blacksmith Hubner, Heinrich had puffed out his cheeks and sucked in his lips, in a nearly perfect parody of Herr Hubner.

Heinrich Glauber grinned widely and winked at Martin. Finding himself smiling back, Martin also felt his stomach settling. Perhaps there was some truth to Herr Glauber's words. "Sir, it may be so. However, my intemperate words have put me out of work."

Herr Glauber nodded in agreement. "Yes, son, they have. But your words caused your American bosses to look into the way wages are paid out. If they did not completely understand your words they did understand their point. Master Blacksmith Hans Hubner no longer distributes the pay to his underlings. That alone has gained you friends among many of the journeymen—not that they dare show their regard openly."

"Oh!" this information startled Martin. It did explain why he had found his pocketknife tucked into his boots the morning before. He'd been whittling kindling and had left it beside the forge when Master Hubner had called him from the shop.

"Adolf tells me you are in his English class and that you are doing very well. That is good, very good. Heinrich, go tell your brother he was to fetch more beer, not chat with the barmaids." Glauber remained silent until the boy had left the table. Then he reached over to his tool belt which rested on the extra chair and with a thud threw a hammer in front of Martin. "Journeyman Schmidt, can you make one of these?" Glauber asked in a challenging manner, his face serious.

Picking up the hammer, Martin found his hands caressing it. Made as a single piece, the shaft and head gleamed with a soft silvery glow. The grip was blue, fitted tightly over much of the shaft and it was dotted with a pattern of oval holes. At the bottom, in yellow lettering was "Estwing" on one side and "Safe-T-Shape" on the other. Both sets of lettering had a shape suggesting a wing around them. Two months ago he would have found the blue material a puzzle. Now he recognized it as what the Americans called "plastic." Hefting the hammer, Martin found it fit well in his hand, the balance inviting him to swing it. With a sigh he set the hammer on the table and admired its form. From the side the shaft was roughly as wide as his thumb but from the back . . . As the shaft arose from the blue plastic grip it narrowed, gracefully but rapidly, until it was only an eighth of an inch thick. This narrow edge continued for a handbreadth until it again swelled to form the head. With his finger Martin stroked the hammer, admiring the daring form. After a final caress he looked up and into his host's face.

"No, Herr Glauber. I cannot make such a hammer. I don't think even the Americans could make such a hammer now. Not for lack of craft but for lack of material. Give me the steel this is made from and time to learn its tricks and . . . maybe. It would be a Masterwork indeed." Pushing the hammer back across the table Martin found his hand reluctant to let go of it. What had the Americans' world been like that hammers were made of such steel?

"Ah, an honest answer, Journeyman. What about these?" Glauber now opened his fist and scattered several sizes of nuts and bolts on the tabletop.

Puzzled and wondering if this was some joke or worse, a trap, Martin gathered the metal bits up and set them in order. A glance showed that Herr Glauber was leaning toward him, his face a studied calm. Gathering three of the hardware pieces up and setting them aside Martin pushed the rest back toward Herr Glauber. "These, sir, these I could make. Had I tools and a shop, I could make these."

"Ah, good. Good. And those three little ones?"

"I've never made such small screws before. Given practice I could probably make something like them." Shrugging, Martin picked up the tiny screws and handed them back to Glauber.

"Only something like them?"

"Yes, sir. The same size and thread but I don't know what metal they are made from. It is too light for steel."

"Ah, I see. According to the person I got them from, they are made of aluminum." Glauber seemed pleased. He took a long drink from his stein and pulled out his pipe. "But, Journeyman Schmidt, you can make the others."

"Yes, sir. I could, if I had the tools. If you have need of more bolts and nuts, then you had best talk to the Americans."

"Did you know, young man, that the Americans have been searching out such hardware? That they are careful—very careful—to save any such pieces when they disassemble any of their machines?"

"No, sir, but it doesn't surprise me. Bolts and nuts are fiddly things to make. I've heard that the Americans had machines to make them by the thousands back in the place they came from." Now that was a thought for an apprentice or overworked journeyman to contemplate. A machine to do the dull, repetitive, boring, but oh so precise job of making threaded fasteners.

"Ah, yes, young man, so they did. And will again—sometime. Until then someone will have to make them."

"Well, sir. Any good blacksmith can make bolts. Given examples he could duplicate those. He wouldn't turn out thousands but he should be able to make several hundred. If I had a shop and tools even I could make them." Martin looked across the table.

Glauber was back to beaming at him, as though he had said something especially bright.

"Yes, yes, young man. Indeed. Your lack of tools is a problem." Herr Glauber tapped his teeth with his pipe stem. "Have you any engagements for the next few days?"

"No, sir, none." Disconcerted, Martin stared; wondering just what Glauber had in mind.

"Good. Now Master Blacksmith Hubner has declared that you are not to be employed by anyone, at least not as an apprentice or journeyman blacksmith. As a master myself, I'm custom bound to honor his decree." Herr Glauber's face was serious as he intoned Hubner's decree. Looking directly into Martin's eyes, Glauber's face slipped into a sly grin. "However, I've got work to be done that requires only strong muscles. A journeyman blacksmith might think such a job beneath him. A bright young man could find benefit in it. For the duration of the job I'll match your journeyman's pay and provide for two meals. It starts tomorrow morning. Might you be interested?"

"Yes, sir," was all Martin could manage without his voice breaking. "Yes, sir." A job. An hour ago any job had been beyond Martin's hope.

"Good. Adolf will collect you from the Refugee Center. The work is hot and dirty but it is honest and I pay honest wages."

"Thank you, sir, thank you."

Adolf showed up at six. From the sack he was carrying he offered Martin several fresh rolls, still warm from the ovens. "Papa likes these rolls so he sends me out every morning to get them. I got an extra dozen. If you don't eat them Heinrich will," Adolf cheerfully said.

Munching companionably the two young men set off down the road. They caught a ride with a produce wagon in exchange for a pair of the fresh rolls and Martin listened as Adolf traded gossip with the farmer and his wife. Before the young men alighted the farmer's wife swapped several apples for the remainder of the extra rolls. She waved and wished them well, commenting to her husband that they reminded her of her sons.

"We're just up this street behind us, Journeyman Schmidt. Papa and Heinrich should be there already," Adolf commented, still waving to the farmer's wife.

"It will be easier if you just call me Martin. My status as a journeyman is suspect." With a rueful grimace, Martin began walking in the direction Adolf had indicated.

"Sure, Martin. Put the long face aside, your status is not in question with my father. Papa has been talking about how fine your work is. Come on, this is it. We best be quiet, lest we disturb the house owner." Adolf opened a wooden gate and led Martin along the side of the house. When they came to the back of the house Martin could see that the yard dropped down abruptly and then leveled off before meeting the neighbor's fence. Down on the lower level was a small shack covered in some kind of vine. From under the back porch an old dog ambled out to walk beside them.

"Martin, this is Killer. He likes to have his ears and tummy scratched."

"Not much of a watchdog, is he?"

"No, he's not. I think he was her husband's dog. She doesn't seem to like him."

"Whose husband?" queried Martin.

"The old woman who owns this house. She's . . . well, Papa will tell you about her. There's Papa now." Pointing to the overgrown shack Adolf grabbed Martin's arm. "Come on, there are steps over this way."

"Ah, Adolf. There you are at last. Journeyman Schmidt, I hope my son has not talked your ears off on the way." Herr Glauber met them at the bottom of the stairs. "This is Bauer Mohler. He's renting us the use of his wagon and team. And here is our problem." Glauber waved a hand at the shack. "The owner of this property has determined to have this ruin fixed up so that she can rent it out. Already the top floor of her house holds two families and she hopes to see more income."

"It looks as if one good wind will tumble it down. It'll be leaky and with all those vines, full of spiders and such. Who'd rent such as this?" Mohler asked.

"She'll find someone, houses being that short in town. She'll get a goodly rent for it, too. A grasping and mean-spirited woman, she is," Herr Glauber explained. Patting the pocket of his coat he added, "I did some repairs for her before. This time, when I agreed to clear out this shack and fix it up, I made certain to get a contract, one drawn up by a good American lawyer and checked over by a good German lawyer. I made sure that everything we clean out of it belongs to me. First, we need to cut down these vines and see what is left of her shed."

Bauer Mohler reached into his wagon and brought out three sickles, a long rake, and a scythe. Standing at the edge of the growth of vines, he began the long, graceful, and backbreaking sweep with his scythe. Herr Glauber removed his jacket and carefully laid it on the wagon seat before taking one of the sickles.

"Gather the cuttings to the side, just over there," Mohler directed. "I'll be taking them back with me."

"Sir, if I might ask, why?" Heinrich, swinging a bit wildly in his attempts to cut the vines, piped up.

"Nasty stuff, isn't it? The sheep love it and it puts the weight on them. No, son, not like that, here." The big farmer chuckled. He rescued Heinrich from his entanglement and set the boy to raking cut vines on the canvas.

"What is this vine?" Martin, no stranger to hard labor, was finding the vine cutting difficult. For each stem cut three more seemed to spring up, grasping for his hands, legs, and the sickle.

"The Americans call it Kudzu and swear that it grows as you watch it. My boys and I cleared the doorway just last week—just look at it now!" Herr Glauber stopped and mopped his face. "One of the Americans told me you can hear it growing on a still night."

"The strange thing is that it hasn't overgrown the entire town," Adolf added, puffing as he pulled several long vines off the roof.

"Yes, yes, my boy. The Americans know of ways to stop it, although it is a long and hard fight. Fire kills it and their alchemists brewed up substances that would slow it down. Fire," Herr Glauber declared with a grin, "is often impractical."

"Yes, Papa, but what about the goats? Why couldn't we have turned goats loose in here?" Heinrich asked as he struggled to gather a tangle of vines that trailed from the shed to the growing pile in the corner of the yard.

"Ah, well, first the goats would have taken days to eat all this. Second, my son, all the goats were busy in other yards." Pausing to sharpen his sickle Herr Glauber turned to Martin. "Goats and sheep will eat this cursed vine down to the ground. It grows back, but not as strongly. Then winter's cold stops its growth. If the goats come back to eat it again through the next year and the ones following eventually it dies."

"Given several years of goat nibbles, anything will die," announced Heinrich.

"Careful, Henny, or Papa will buy a herd of goats and make you the goatherd," Adolf teased his younger brother.

"Not a bad idea, not a bad idea. I think I may suggest it to our council. We could rent out the goats and sheep in small flocks to clear these yards," Bauer Mohler mused as he ran the whetstone over his scythe blade. "The older children could manage it."

"I did consider such a business," admitted Herr Glauber, "but I know little about goats or sheep. Besides, some of the American children are already doing so. Still, for someone who knows goats . . ."

Bauer Mohler nodded in agreement and returned to cutting kudzu. The men worked steadily as the day warmed. Finally the shed emerged from its green shroud. Martin considered it while he straightened the kinks from his aching back. It was larger than he'd thought. Big enough for a small family—if Herr Glauber could make it sound. The roof had an ominous sway to it and the siding looked rotten in spots. A call came from the yard above and proved to be lunch. Two boys, looking to be about ten or eleven, towed a small red wagon filled with wrapped sandwiches and a small keg of beer. Herr Glauber paid the boys and Adolf unloaded the food onto a blanket in the shade. Martin took the opportunity to examine the wagon.

Shaking his head and muttering, "Steel, fine steel for a child's wagon." Martin joined the rest of the men.

"Yes and there must be a hundred such wagons in this town. The town is full of entrepreneurs. The blond boy is American. His mother sells lunches and dinners to workingmen. The wagon belongs to him and it was his idea to deliver the food. His friend is German and translates for both mother and son. The German's family rents rooms from the American's and they have several such little enterprises going. I'd not be surprised to see them wealthy come this time next year," Herr Glauber cheerfully explained. "Hard work and new ideas make for wealth. Is it not so, my boys?"

A chorus of "Yes, Papa" echoed from Adolf and Heinrich.

When the last crumb of the food had gone Herr Glauber announced it was time to open the shed and begin clearing it out. It was not as a dignified Master Carpenter that he led them back to the door of the shed, but as a mischievous boy, his glee hardly held in check. "Treasures await within!"

Puzzled by Herr Glauber's comment, Martin assisted Adolf in prying open the door. In the gloom within all he could see was brown—rust brown. The shed appeared to be completely filled with rusty metal objects. What wasn't rusty was so covered with dust as to appear rusted. At the front he could make out a gasoline lawnmower, its green and yellow paint barely visible under the layer of dust. A few Americans still used them despite the ban on using gasoline for anything but official vehicles.

"Heinrich, up on the wagon with you. We'll pass things up to you and you must stow them carefully. Adolf, Martin, stand there at the door and start passing items out to Bauer Mohler and myself." Herr Glauber was almost cackling with glee. "Ah, treasures indeed!"

As he and Adolf got into the rhythm of grab and pass and the first tightly packed objects went to the wagon Martin began to understand Herr Glauber's meaning. Here was a shed packed with steel. Most of it, like the lawnmower, probably would be beyond repair. But the items could be taken apart to repair other such and if not, still they would yield nuts, bolts, screws, and washers by the dozen. And gears, oh, yes, beautiful gears such as those on this push mower with the broken handle. The steel blades, nicked and rusty could be cleaned, straightened, and turned into fine tools.

"Here, Martin, can you reach that thing?" Adolf was pointing to something that looked vaguely like a metal chair frame. "It's tangled up and I can't get these rakes loose."

Reaching over, Martin lifted the chair frame so easily he nearly fell over. Coughing in the dust stirred up; both young men retreated outside. In sunlight Martin examined the chair. It con-sisted of a continuous tubular frame with flat metal arms riveted on. Across the back and seat sagged the remains of woven plastic strips. Hefting the chair, Martin wondered at its light weight. He rubbed the dust off a portion of the frame and felt it. Eagerly he pulled out his knife to test the metal and stopped, suddenly aware Herr Glauber was standing beside him. Apologetically, he made to hand the chair to Glauber.

"No, son. Go ahead and test the metal. Just do so where it won't show. That should clean up and with a nice new leather seat it will fetch a fancy price in Jena or perhaps Amsterdam," Glauber beamed.

"It isn't rusty, and so light . . . Is it more aluminum, sir?" queried Martin. He picked a spot sure to be covered and scratched the metal frame with the knifepoint. "Soft . . . very soft. How do they work it?"

"Yes, I've seen such chairs around. That is aluminum. It doesn't rust. Unfortunately," Glauber sounded regretful, "it will be years before they can make more of it. Still, that lack makes what remains all the more valuable. Come, son, we've scarcely begun to empty our treasure house."

Adolf and Bauer Mohler had continued to pull objects out of the shed while the aluminum chair held Martin's attention. Now, stepping back in and letting his eyes adjust he caught a glimpse of something. The chair had intrigued him, now his heart pounded. If . . . if it was what he thought . . . and if he could persuade Herr Glauber . . .

"Hey, Martin, there's an anvil for you. Papa said he thought he'd seen one in here. Come on, help me with this bed frame." Adolf tapped Martin on the shoulder and pointed. "Take that end and I'll just remove these shovels and up she goes."

By late afternoon they had cleared back to the anvil. In a corner stood a forge, and a bench covered the other wall. Hanging on the walls and in front of the forge were a blacksmith's tools. Tongs, swages, punches, chisels, anvil dies, and clamps in a multitude of sizes and shapes sat draped in cobwebs, dust, and rust. On the bench was a grinding wheel with an electric motor. A leg vise stood anchored on a massive wood post. Dazed, Martin opened a drawer in the bench. Fullers and hardys filled it. Another drawer held anvil dies. Still another drawer was filled with rasps and files. A dozen hammers, each different in size and shape hung neatly on the wall. Tucked down under the bench was a bickern and a second, smaller anvil. The quench tub held not water but more tools.

"Well, Journeyman Schmidt, do you think these tools would be a start to a blacksmith shop?" Herr Glauber asked.

"More than a start. With this, what few things might not be here can be made. All the masters will bid for this."

"Yes, if I were so foolish as to look for a quick profit. I've a mind for a longer, higher profit. There is a building I've rented space in with thought to storing these treasures. It could make a good blacksmith's shop I think. I just need a blacksmith."

"Oh, sir, you should have masters fighting each other. None like working for another, all would be pleased to have such a shop." With a pang of regret Martin mentally cataloged the shed's contents.

"Young man, I've no wish to start a war amongst the blacksmiths in town. Besides, the shop I've got in mind would not suit most of our masters." Herr Glauber blew out his breath and eyed Martin.

"Sir?" A cautious hope grew in Martin's heart.

"A Master Blacksmith would argue with me constantly. Besides, masters don't want to do 'fiddly' little things. Now, a good solid journeyman, that's what I want for my shop."

"What 'fiddly' things, sir?" Martin clamped down tightly on his hope, striving to keep his voice level.

"Why, bolts, nuts, washers, screws and such." Grinning, Herr Glauber clapped Martin on the shoulder. "Interested, Journeyman Schmidt?"

"But, sir! The masters have banned me," Martin pointed out.

"Oh them. For a bit I thought to give you the title of 'Shop Manager' and argue that you were not employed principally as a blacksmith. Set my lawyer on working it out. Then I got a letter back from Masters Ritterhof and Eisenbach. Those two confirm you as a journeyman—one they consider worthy of being considered for master. The letter will serve to stop Hubner and his bunch." Glauber rocked back and forth on his feet, a wide grin splitting his face. "Have I found my shop manager?"

"Yes, sir." Standing straight and fighting tears, Martin took the hand Glauber extended and shook it. "Yes, sir. I'll make all the fiddly little bolts and nuts you want."

# Chip's Christmas Gift

## Russ Rittgers

Chip and Joachim had just finished working out with quarterstaffs, six-foot-long hardwood sticks, at the von Thierbach estate manor, absorbing a new collection of bruises to join those of the previous two days. Chip wanted to practice techniques he'd previously learned in the army and Joachim simply wanted to gain another weapon in the event they were attacked while on the road. Chip hadn't exactly had quarterstaff training but his close combat training sergeant had taught his company something about using his rifle to block sword strokes. At the same time he'd also said, if they're that close to you, run like hell if you're alone, otherwise block, use your rifle butt, or punch him with your bayonet if you've got it fitted.

Chip didn't have a rifle at Joachim's home in Thierbach where he'd come for the Christmas holiday or in Jena for that matter, but he did have six feet of salvaged galvanized pipe his dad had kept when he replaced their home's plumbing ten years ago. Wrapped in sticky black electrical tape with a dirt covering, it didn't look like metal, didn't resonate like metal. No sword would ever slash through it like Alex Mackay's had destroyed Chip's pool cue on that fateful night at the Thuringen Gardens.

He and Joachim had padded their arms and legs and wore old helmets pulled out of storage from the days his von Thierbach ancestors had worn them into battle. Fortunately or not, with the advent of the crossbow and firearms, armor was on the way out and it wasn't going to be coming back.

"I'm exhausted, sweaty and need a bath," Chip said, pulling off the tight padded metal helmet which showed a number of fresh dents. Sweat was pouring down his face as he stripped off his arm padding and upper clothing to cool down. The horse barn they had been using was dim and cool but out of the wind and snow. "I haven't had a series of workouts like this since I was in the army," Chip said, wiping his upper body with a linen towel.

"What's it like, being in the American Army?" Joachim asked, sitting down next to him, placing his helmet on the bench and stripping off his own padding.

"I don't know," Chip mumbled, as he loosened the padding covering his legs. "A lot of exercise, getting your body into shape, practicing maneuvering into formations so they can be used during battle, close combat training, a lot like this but with and without our rifles. Actually, after we achieve a certain proficiency, we hardly ever shoot our rifles. Then there are all the lectures. Medical, technical, history, battle tactics, what's probably happening now in the world, and of course, patrol duty."

"So that's how you fought Josef with a knife and lived?" Joachim asked.

"*Ja*, and got the scar to prove it," Chip answered, tapping his scabbed-over healing cheek. "It was good that I was almost sober when we met that night. You were enjoying yourself with Inga at the time."

"Speaking of Inga, don't mention her to Papa, at least in connection with me."

"He doesn't want you to use a prostitute? That's a more up-time position than I would have expected of him."

"Oh, it's not that. He doesn't mind that at all. In fact, he thinks of it as a part of my education. But having a long-term relationship with her, especially with her having someone else's child, never. That should be for wives only."

"Ah," Chip smiled, nodding sagely. "The double standard is alive and well out here in the countryside, I see," he said, redressing himself in his cooled linen shirt. He tucked it into his pants and but left the collar string untied. "Boys get to play house but not the girls," he explained.

☆　　　☆　　　☆

"The maid Karla began heating water an hour ago and a bath is waiting for both of you in the usual place with your usual clothing," Frau Thierbach told them as they reentered the manor house. "Four days you've been here and three baths. How can you be so dirty?" she dramatically asked, throwing up her hands.

"Mama, you are so forgiving when it comes to the smell of soured sweat," Chip said affectionately, winking and then kissing her cheek next to her ear. She giggled and gave him a playful swat in return. On the second day after they'd arrived, she'd told him to call her "Mama" and used the familiar "*du*" with him.

"I don't know how you do it," Joachim sighed as they entered the room where their bath had been set up.

"Do what?"

"How you charmed Mama that way. I've never seen Papa do what you just did."

Chip shrugged and grinned. "Mostly it's confidence, then spotting her mood and having the knowledge on how to use it. She knew I wasn't serious, just having fun. I'll bet your father knows every mood your mother has, so it's just a matter of if he's in the mood. Now if it was just the two of them in the room . . ."

Both young men rinsed their once-sweaty shirts in the tub's clean warm water and hung them to dry on a piece of string stretched across the small ground floor room otherwise used as a summer kitchen. They decided their first day to alternate who should bathe first while the other waited and this time it was Chip's turn to go first.

"I want to soak a bit," Joachim remarked lazily, resting in the large wooden tub, used in the fall for wine fermentation. "Would you tell Karla to bring in some more hot water? This has gotten just a little cool."

It wasn't that cool, Chip thought sarcastically. More likely he wanted the von Thierbach's housemaid Karla to help scrub his back. Or something. Well, it wasn't like she objected or it was a secret from his parents.

He was walking towards Karla at the end of the hallway and just as he was about to talk to her, he heard the sound of music. A violin? "What is that I'm hearing?" he asked Karla.

"Fraulein von Ruppersdorf brought her violin with her, Herr Jenkins," Karla answered politely.

"Ah. Thank you. By the way, the young Herr says the bath

water is getting a little cool and specifically asked that you bring him some more hot water."

Karla wasn't fat nor was she thin; she was what Grandpa Hudson called "healthy." She was plain-faced but when she bowed her head and blushed with a smile, she became almost attractive.

Chip followed the music to the library. Its door was closed but Chip knocked. "Come in," he heard Katerina respond.

The young brunette with striking features was sitting on a straight-backed chair with the sheet music spread on the table before her, the base of the violin tucked against her collar bone. "Oh, Herr Jenkins!" said Joachim's second cousin, with a surprised look, her fair face flushed, a strand of black hair escaping from her bun. "I'm sorry if the errors in my playing bothered you. I try to practice only when the men are out."

Chip smiled delightedly. "I didn't have the opportunity to be bothered, Fraulein von Ruppersdorf," he replied, delighted by her lack of composure at his appearance. "In fact, I'm a poor player myself. At least you can play the music as you read it. Everything I play, I have to struggle to read to get the notes right first and then play by ear. I've made far too many errors to ever complain about someone else. Please continue."

He'd never heard the work she was raggedly playing and both the violin and bow looked strange to him. The first major difference he noticed was that her violin was narrower than the one he had in his room in Jena. The bow was also significantly shorter than the one he used and it curved out, not in. The third was that her violin didn't have a chin rest and definitely no shoulder rest. And finally, the sound of the music was also softer. Gut strings, he supposed, made from young sheep gut rather than cat gut, a common misconception up-time. Hey, let's hear it for another use of lamb intestines, he mentally cheered.

Katerina stopped playing abruptly. "I am so sorry, Herr Jenkins, I simply cannot concentrate on the music this afternoon. Perhaps . . . you would care to play something that you know," she offered, lifting her violin and bow to him.

"I'm not certain," he said, taking the violin reluctantly. "There are many changes between your time and mine to the instrument and besides, I haven't practiced since I left Grantville two months ago."

"Please," Katerina requested, her dark eyes meeting his and

her lips imploring. "For me. I should like to hear a tune from your time."

Fortunately, he thought, the tuning of the strings hadn't changed in four hundred years, still in fifths, whatever that was. He tucked the violin under his chin and drew the strange bow across the strings. It sounded right but what should he play?

"This is a tune from almost a hundred fifty years before my time and was popular with both armies in our only civil war," Chip said finally. "The lyrics are of a man describing his loving relationship with a girl when he was a boy. They then parted and have gone different ways but he hopes to join with her after death. A soldier's song, of a man well aware that he may die before they meet again. It is called 'Lorena.'"

A couple of false starts and he launched into the tune he'd first heard as background music in a documentary about the Civil War. His timing was off but he was able to repeat the last part of the song without a flaw and the double stop at the end came out smoothly.

"That was marvelous!" Katerina beamed, clapping her hands to Chip's slight embarrassment.

It wasn't that good, Chip thought, but wasn't going to argue if she thought it was. Besides, humility would take you only so far and he wanted his relationship with her to last for a long time. He didn't know if he was in love but there was certainly a fair amount of lust involved in his thoughts about her.

"What else can you play?" she asked.

"Several things, Fraulein, but one thing that has changed between your time and mine is that we have a chin rest on this part of the violin," he said, tapping the base side of the bottom. "Most violinists also use a shoulder rest which clamps onto the other side of the violin to hold it even higher. I'm afraid my neck would ache if I played many tunes but I will play one more.

"This one is from the same era and I play it two different ways. The first and more popular is the tune 'When Johnny Comes Marching Home,' a happy welcome for the returning soldier. The second, not so well known is, 'Johnny, I Hardly Knew Ya,' the lament of a wife when she sees her husband return missing an arm, leg and eye." Actually, the description of the returning soldier was far worse but as far as Chip knew, he had the only copy of the words and music in Grantville, something he'd picked up at a Morgantown folk music shop. He'd have to copy it someday and put it into the Grantville musical archives.

Chip launched into the merry tune and played it twice before transitioning into the second melancholy version. He played that twice and then hopped back up to the first to finish.

"Why did you go back to the first tune?" Katerina asked when he finished.

Chip smiled ruefully. "I hate to end on a sad note and besides it reminds me of how people quickly forget the damage a war can bring to the men involved. Oh, I'm sorry if what I just said brought unhappy memories back to you," he said quickly as he saw her face cloud. "Here, let me play one more tune. This one was originally played by the English to mock Americans during our war for independence but we took it and made it our own."

Chip played "Yankee Doodle" and then sang a translation of its words to her, pantomiming the movements described in the song. Katerina laughed delightedly.

"Please, call me Katerina or . . . no, just Katerina and I will call you Chip as everyone else does," she said, taking her violin back from Chip and put it away with her music. "You must also say '*du*' to me as well. Come, let us see what trouble Joachim is getting himself into," she said, taking his arm.

"Better yet," Chip said, his heart thumping wildly at her touch but still not forgetting about Karla, "why don't we talk with his mother? I haven't heard half the stories I should have heard about how Joachim got into trouble when he was young."

"You don't have to give anyone a gift, at least not here at home," Joachim protested when Chip asked what kind of presents he should give his family.

"But they've been so nice to me, especially your mama and papa."

"Of course they have but I suspect you're thinking of my cousin." Joachim grinned. "Let those who have eyes, see," he quoted.

Chip flushed. "Perhaps a little."

"Chip, just one thing, probably unnecessary to say but she is my cousin and a noble lady, not to be trifled with like some of the girls we know in Jena. Use her unkindly and well, our friendship will be at an end," Joachim told him in all seriousness.

"Not to worry," Chip responded calmly. "I have nothing but the most honorable intentions towards her. Well, almost," he slyly smiled to his friend. "You wouldn't blame me for trying to kiss her, would you?" he teased. "Or if she returned it? Not that I have. Yet, anyway."

"That . . . would be different. Just remember, she's a lady, not a trollop."

"In my time, sometimes the two were hard to distinguish just looking at their class," Chip answered. "But Julie was . . . never mind," he abruptly ended his thought. Didn't matter now anyway.

"I have an idea, Chip. Katerina was talking about you playing the violin. Perhaps a concert before we attend the Christmas Eve service in Thierbach would be best. We'll be staying at our house in town beginning the day before Christmas Eve. Play some tunes from your time."

"A good idea." Chip grinned. "They certainly won't hear any of them this far from Grantville for years."

Chip had rigged an impromptu chin rest and shoulder rest for Katerina's violin, making it possible for him to play several songs for his host family this evening. *Viedel* in German meant violin, no doubt where the word "fiddle" came from, he reflected, tuning it once again. Gut strings took a lot more tuning than steel wire wrapped over nylon. He'd tried the collar bone position a few times so he could sing and play at the same time, but his playing in that position was still awful.

They'd arrived in Thierbach yesterday afternoon and after dinner today he'd played a number of tunes, mostly slower ones and a few religious ones. Somehow, Santa, Rudolf and Frosty hadn't seemed appropriate. As with Katerina, he spoke the lyrics and then played the tune except for one song Joachim had helped translate into German.

As they walked to church for the Christmas Eve service, Katerina's arm on his, she asked, "Why are you bringing my violin? Is there a problem with the organ?" she lightly questioned.

"No, no, nothing like that," Chip replied, avoiding her question. "Just something I want to do."

". . . And now, a guest of the von Thierbach's, Herr Chip Jenkins, has something for us," the church's pastor said from his pulpit.

Chip walked steadily forward from the von Thierbach pew, carrying Katerina's now-unwrapped violin with him, and stepped up to the platform level below the altar.

"Thank you, Herr Reverend," Chip began. "Some of you may have heard of a town of Americans from the future who suddenly appeared as if by magic not far from Rudolstadt south of Jena several months ago. I am one of them. If there was magic involved, it was not of our making. We have no explanation for it.

"This is my first Christmas in Germany, far from the land I grew up in. I met Joachim von Thierbach at the University of Jena a short while ago and he was kind enough to invite me to stay with him and his family for the Holy Season. So, why am I standing up here with this violin? Not because I am a particularly good musician, I assure you. But I did beg Herr Reverend Taller this morning for this opportunity. I am here because of another story and a song which will probably never be written as it was then.

"The story is that there once lived a Father Mohr, the priest of a church this size in Oberndorf in Austria. It was already Christmas Eve and Father Mohr wanted a new hymn for that evening's mass. He persuaded his organist, a man named Franz Gruber, to set to music a poem he had written two years earlier at a pilgrim church. For whatever reason, Franz Gruber did not write it for organ. I think because he felt the words were better suited to be sung softly, not over the sound of an organ. So in a matter of hours, this song was first sung to the accompaniment of a guitar at the Christmas Eve mass.

"Two years later, Franz Gruber published the hymn. It was then spread by at least two families of singers to several countries. Since that time, the words have been translated into almost as many languages as there are countries. I would like you to hear it as that first church did, on Christmas Eve, accompanied by soft music. I have written out several copies of the hymn and I see they are being distributed among you. Listen as I play it the first time and then begin to sing."

Chip tucked the violin under his chin and eyes closed, began to play his Christmas gift to Katerina, the von Thierbachs and the people of Thierbach. Undoubtedly the translation wouldn't be the same as the original German, but they'd never know it. He definitely knew he had the first four words right. As he began the second time, he heard Dieter von Thierbach's light baritone voice above the others, *"Stille Nacht, Heilige Nacht..."*

# Dice's Drawings

## Dan Robinson

To hell with them all. Dice had lost his Karen, forty-five years of hard work, twenty years as a damned Linotype operator and twenty-five as a damned pressman after the damned computers had taken his damned job away. God how he hated that pressman's job! A quarter century hauling paper and permanently stained fingers, but he'd stuck with it.

Then, to top it all off, right before he was ready to retire and tell the whole world to take a flying leap, the local chunk of world had taken a flying leap and Dysart Clifford along with it!

Dice grumbled out loud as he walked the ten blocks to his two-bedroom house with a single bag of groceries. Sixty-four years old, over $523,000 in a Fidelity Retirement account, and a paid-off boat and house on Sutton Lake—all shot to hell. Now, here he was stuck in the 1600s with no retirement. All because he got a bargain on the house in Grantville when the mine shut down. Why hadn't he gone to Sutton that Sunday? Why did the Ring of Fire happen to him?

Dice grumbled louder and noticed that people were stepping off the sidewalk to avoid him. For good measure he snarled at the next pedestrian and delighted when the shocked down-timer almost fell over himself getting out of his way.

It's damned hard to snarl when you're laughing inside.

With his mood much improved, his step lightened and the final blocks home passed quickly.

☆   ☆   ☆

Elfriede Schützin made her choice. Her husband had died a year ago and her year of mourning was over. As a shoemaker in Coburg, he had made a passable living. As a widow, she had not. When news of the Ring of Fire and the Americans had reached her town, it was not a difficult choice at all to leave Kurt and Anna with neighbors while she went to check out the Americans from the future.

Perhaps she could find work there. The Americans she had seen were all lords, of course, in their marvelous vehicles from the future and their fine clothes. Such as they would surely need a good cook. So, with letters of recommendation from her neighbors and priest, she set out for Grantville.

Four months later, she was still in the refugee center. Kurt and Anna were in the Grantville school and she was taking English lessons, but there were no American lords, and no grand castles. There were also lots of people like her looking to the rich Americans for a better life.

And although she had not found work with one of the Americans, she had found a niche at the refugee center. With girlhood lessons at her mother's knee well learned, she combed the dense woods around the center for the ingredients that made her, if not the head cook, at least the head recipe maker. With the help of the old folks around town and books from more than one home, she quickly identified the edible plants, herbs, berries and other kitchen essential that grew wild in the steep West Virginia hills. More and more Americans were finding reason to be around the refugee center at dinnertime.

"Trudy, haff ve got eggs today?" she had asked her friend and head cook at the center.

"*Ja,* Effi. Lots of zem." Gertrude was her best friend at the center. They bunked near each other, laughed together, and watched each other's children. The crowded refugee center was like a community where neighbors looked out for each other.

But Gertrude Zeiss had Hermann. And Hermann was a popular workman among the down-timers. They would not be staying long at the refugee center.

"If you vill keep an eye on Anna, Kurt und I vill go chopping."

"Shopping, Mama. It's pronounced mit a 'shah,' not a 'chah.'"

Effi slung her big net bag over one shoulder and pulled her

machete from its leather scabbard and wielded it like a sword. "Ven I say chopping, I mean chopping!"

"*Javol, mein Kapitan!*" Her nine-year-old saluted, laughing, and slung his own net bag to march out behind his mother.

Dice's good mood lasted until he opened the door to the dark house and the dark TV. He could turn on all the lights and play a tape, but that would just make them wear out faster. There weren't going to be any more light bulbs, TVs, or VCRs for quite some time and he was determined to make them last. He looked longingly at the TV and heaved a sigh for the Pittsburgh Pirates. Just on the other side of the dark TV screen was the twentieth century and Three Rivers Stadium where the Pirates would be playing Cincinnati tonight. He plopped in his chair and looked out the window, almost in tears.

Outside on the sidewalk was the German bag lady with her tote full of dandelions. Several weeks before, she had knocked politely on his door with her prepared speech, "Mai I pliz haff yoo dandy lions?" She seemed so sincere and with his consent immediately fell to harvesting the weeds. She was young, clean, thirty-something, with blonde braids tightly coiled on each side of her head, a brown down-timer blouse, and sturdy green skirt that hung to her ankles. He was so taken at her industriousness that he had pointed out a patch of mint growing by the back door. "*Ach! Minze!*" She happily placed a few starters in a carry-cloth.

What she was doing out so late was none of his business.

Dice walked through the dark house to the kitchen. He never kept the refrigerator too full in the best of times and nowadays it was getting downright bare. The freezer held a lonesome Swanson turkey pot pie and a partially consumed half gallon of Neapolitan ice cream with freezer-frost thick on the lid. Lots of ice, though. Since he'd run out of Scotch, the need for ice cubes had diminished considerably. He put the few groceries away and left out the brown bread and sausage for his supper. At least the beer had improved. He drew a frothy mug from the recycled one gallon Heineken keg.

In the back yard, a thump and an "oof" indicated a trespasser or a critter down from the hillside behind his house. Neither was welcome, but if it was a two-legged critter, it gave him an opportunity to vent a little of his anger and liven up the night a bit.

Two steps took Dice to the shotgun in the broom closet and two more brought him to the back door. He unlocked the door, slapped the porch light, threw the door wide, and racked a shell into the chamber.

Spread-eagled and unmoving on the ground beneath the thick limb of the maple tree, was the German bag lady. Blood oozed from her right eyebrow to make a bloody trail across her temple into her still neatly arranged hair.

Elfriede woke up with a ringing headache. Above her an old man stood with his feet apart like an avenging angel. His white hair, lit from behind by the electric light, framed his head like a halo. He held one of the American "shotguns."

With a snap, Effi realized what had happened. She had run into something in the dark. She also recognized the man as the one who had permitted her to take some of his mint. Sitting upright slowly, she threw her skirts modestly back around her ankles.

"Mein Sohn. Ich kann nicht meinen Sohn finden! "

"Try it in English," Dice grumbled.

"Iss same in English." she said as though to a child. "I can not my son find. He come back here." And then louder. "Kurt! *Wo sind du? Verstecken sie nicht sich von mir!*"

A small voice came from the bushes by the corner of the house. "I'm not your son."

"Well come on out so we can see who else you're not."

"Don't shoot. I'll come out!"

Dice felt a proper fool waving his shotgun around under these less than threatening circumstances and placed the gun on the porch.

"What's your name, boy?"

"I'm Cody Brown. I stay with the Lawsons."

Dice looked at the tow-headed youngster in the light from the porch. He was probably one of the foster kids that Bill and Corda took in for extra income. Dice took momentary pleasure from the fact that the checks from the county wouldn't be coming any more. But that was probably why the kid was out after dark. Bill didn't do much for free. No point in Dice picking on the kid; the boy would have enough troubles.

The German bag lady was unsteadily trying to stand. Dice and Cody each took an arm and helped her upright and into the kitchen. In the better lighting inside, he could see a spectacular bruise forming.

Dice liberated some ice from the solid lump of cubes in the icemaker, wrapped them in a clean towel and whacked them a couple times on the tile countertop to break them up. A wet paper towel swabbed the little trail of blood and a Band Aid covered the small cut.

As he worked, Dice noticed the boy's nervousness. He was also curious why and from whom the kid was hiding.

"Cody, do you know where her son is?"

"Uh . . ."

"Is he outside?"

"Uh . . ."

He turned to the German woman. "Is your son in trouble?"

She shook her head, wincing at the pain. "Chust him I vant to find."

Cody thought about it for a second, then went to the screen door. "Kurt, It's okay."

The German boy appeared at the door and looked sheepishly inside. Cody opened the screen door and led the second youngster into the kitchen. "I'm sorry, Frau Schützin. We went into the woods to hunt for some herbs for you, and it got dark before we could get back."

Dice stifled a smile. No one could fabricate a believable excuse out of thin air like a nine-year-old. The two boys stood together like condemned prisoners, clearly expecting not to be believed.

Effi looked relieved, "Then all ist goot. Kurt, get your bag und we will take the herbs you have gathered back to the shelter."

The boys' faces fell. They were truly caught in a lie and they knew it.

"There are no herbs, are there?"

"No, ma'am."

Dice put his two cents in. "You were playing, weren't you?"

"Yes, sir."

"And because of your actions, Kurt's mother has been seriously hurt." Dice tried to look stern; and mostly succeeded.

"Pliz, Trudy may I alzo borrow ein vun qvart baggie?" Effi asked politely. The dark haired Kitchen Policeman In Charge took a Ziploc off the drying line and carefully put it right side out. Effi filled the baggie with her signature Dandelion Salad and placed it in her tote bag atop the precious Rubbermaid containers that were filled with venison stew and cheese grits. Containers weren't needed for the fresh loaf of crusty brown bread and the loop of dark sausage.

Around dark, Dice arrived home to see the German bag—correction—Elfriede seated primly on his front steps. He briefly considered running, but decided he could endure a weepy female for a while. He hadn't seen the neighbor kids warn their mothers that he was coming or their diaspora from his front porch and retreat behind window blinds to watch the show.

"I haff come to t'ank you, Herr Cliffort. You vas very kind to Kurt und me." She was so sincere and so calm that Dice had trouble keeping his smile under control. In her unhurried speech, she showed the food she had prepared for him and could she pliz use his kitchen to make him a hot meal?

Now Dice was an old coot. But Mama Clifford didn't raise no dumb puppies and he was well aware of the barren nature of his cupboard. Turn down a hot meal? Not bloody likely!

She firmly ejected him from the kitchen and set him down at the end of the table with a salad of green leafy strips, pieces of boiled egg, grated yellow cheese and the last of his Thousand Island dressing from the refrigerator. It was very good! But the edge of one leaf piqued his curiosity. Unfolding one of the larger pieces—it was a dandelion! Damn! No wonder she was harvesting the stuff! Clatter of dishes, clank of saucepan and skillet, even a beep beep beep of the microwave. Now he *was* impressed. He was tempted to peek, but restrained himself by pretending to read a magazine but his ears were tuned to the noises from the kitchen.

"Oakee Doakee. Iss ready!"

Elfriede placed bowls of hot food on the table and stood with her hands folded primly before a spotless white apron. Flowers from who knows where made a yellow and purple centerpiece.

This wouldn't do. From the cabinet, he retrieved a second setting and placed it at the opposite end of the table.

"Now iss ready," he deliberately mispronounced, and held her seat expectantly. Flustered, she paused uncertainly before taking the offered seat.

The food she had provided was rich and tasty. The tender

chunks of venison, carrots, potatoes, onions, and celery in a thick clear broth was unlike the canned stew he used to nuke in the microwave. Also there was a casserole of yellow something that he had at first mistaken for mashed potatoes. But it was topped with baked yellow cheese and delicious.

To Effi's delight, he praised her stew, made from scratch from available provender. But she wanted to have something American, too and had made some thrice cooked cheese grits from Sarah Jane Mason's recipe. She had a moment of panic when he stopped for a second at the first bite. But then appreciation showed on his face and he took another big bite.

"What is this?"

Now she was confused. Sara Jane had pronounced her grits to be very good. "Iss gritz. Iss not goot?"

"Grits?" These were better than the horrible stuff they served instead of hash browns at the restaurants. "No. Yes. They're very good! Excellent!"

"Eggs of Lent? No. Cheese—*Käse*—*Fromage!* You like?"

"God! I need a dictionary!"

"Ach! I haff a dikzhunary!" She bounced up and retrieved a precious paperback English-German dictionary from her bag, borrowed especially for this event.

In minutes, they had pulled their chairs and placemats around to the long side of the table and were looking up words between bites.

Dice leaned back in his La-Z-Boy with a bulging belly, a book and a beer. It reminded him what it was like to be married. But since Karen, women had always been too much trouble. He never dated much and when he did, his dates usually bored him by talking too much about people he didn't know or didn't like. After a while he stopped asking them out. He would come home, nuke a dinner, watch some TV and go to bed.

Until the Ring of Fire.

Now he was an old fart that people thought was a bit "tetched." That was okay before, but now, after two evenings of company and activity, he discovered that he had become a lonely old man.

Clattering from the kitchen stopped and Elfriede came with her much emptier bag to the living room. Her smile lit the room better than electricity ever could, but Dice was a realist. The pretty, thirtyish blonde would have no reason to find an old man like him attractive. He was satisfied that she had been grateful enough to bring him a dinner. But he could still stall for time. The thought of her leaving sent his brain scurrying for a reason to delay the return of solitude.

During the meal they had looked up "printing" and "press" in the *Wörterbuch*, so she knew he was a *Drucker*, but he had an ace in the hole. Actually it was a press in the basement.

His plan. His project. His salvation.

"Would you like to see *mein Druckerpresse*?"

Effi had seen printing presses before. They were big wooden machines with iron frames of lead type. But her eyes lit up when he asked her to see his press. And he had remembered the German word, too. She now had a reason to stay longer in this fine house. And instead of treating her like a servant, he had insisted she dine with him at his own table! It wasn't a castle, but it was beautiful and clean and quiet. To find quiet, she went to the forest. But to live in a quiet, peaceful place like this with a man who treated her so kindly would be heaven.

And though he was old, these Americans stayed vigorous way beyond the age when most normal people shriveled up and died. He was strong. She had felt his forearm the night before and he had good breadth of chest. That would be from pulling the big wooden handle on his press. He was hearty. She had seen him striding down the sidewalk like a much younger man. But what would a rich American want with a poor German widow and two children, and whose English was so poor and whose skills were hundreds of years behind his? Ah well . . . she could dream.

Dice flipped on the stairway and basement lights and led the way down the stairs. The full basement was divided without walls into Dice's areas of interest. The laundry corner held the water heater, washer and dryer and the double tub. The furnace sat squat in the middle of the floor and boxes were stacked three deep along one wall. The entire west half of the basement was given to his new workshop. This was where he was going to stop being a pressman and start being a captain of industry.

There, on a sturdy table, was the Clifford Mark I Hand-Powered Rotary Press. It was little more than a foot square, two feet tall, and had a big handle and a flywheel. Dice spread ink on the fountain roller and started cranking. When the ink covered the plate, he handed the job over to Elfriede. Dice stood on a box at the end of the table and put on a rubber finger cap. He flipped the engagement lever and fed a dozen sheets of bond paper into the top of the machine one sheet at a time. As the press engaged, the speed slowed momentarily, but Effi picked up the pace without instruction. One sheet per second slid smoothly onto the catcher!

Dice showed her how ink was spread by the rollers onto the plate cylinder and how the impression cylinder grabbed the sheet of paper, transferred the image from the plate, and then dropped the paper into the receiving tray.

"No electricity!" he said proudly, "and it will take any kind of paper at all!"

Her eyes grew big. This was marvelous! It was simple! She could see and understand every step of the process. The ink goes onto the raised letters and is pressed against the paper. But it was tiny compared to the presses she had seen. With every turn of the handle little metal fingers grabbed the waiting sheet of paper from the wooden board on top, carried it to press against the inky letters and immediately dropped the printed piece into the tray. And it was fast! Sixty sheets a minute instead of two!

It was at that moment that she really understood both the gulf between the Americans and people of her time, and how truly alike they were.

Here was a man who had put uncounted hundreds of hours into a dream, taking the progress of centuries and using that knowledge to build a machine for her time. She walked slowly around the table, trailing her hand over his invention. There was a combination of old and new, shiny rollers and metal pieces in roughly cut sides. Screws and springs and wedges of wood. But it worked. Because he dreamed of making things better. Just as she had dreamed of finding a better life at the end of the yellow lined roadway to Grantville.

She looked at the walls. They were covered with paper and drawings of machines. Not just his press, either. On one wall, in the center, was a black and white photograph of a smiling young man sitting at a machine that towered over him. His hands were poised over buttons lined up in rows beneath his fingers. His drawings, dozens and dozens of drawings, surrounded the picture. She recognized some of them as pieces from the machine. She touched the photo.

"Dieses ist Sie, ja?" she said softly.

There were tears welling in the man's eyes.

"Yeah. That's me." He snuffled and blinked back the tears before she could notice. Stupid computers! His first Ring of Fire had been in 1977 when he'd been told he no longer had a job. A damned minimum wage teeny bopper on a computer had replaced him.

His spread hands encompassed the wall full of drawings. "And that's my Linotype." How soon before he could build one? Probably never. But with his drawings, someone, years from now, would be able to figure it out.

Upstairs, they paused at the front door. Dice looked down at Effi. So young and beautiful. How could he ask her to stay? What could he possibly offer this wonderful German girl half his age?

Upstairs, they paused at the front door. Effi looked up at Dice. This rich American . . . so intelligent, kind, and sensitive, so strong and self-sufficient . . . what did he need her for?

He looked ready to say something and she held her breath.

"Uh . . . would you . . . maybe like to go out to dinner with me?" he stammered out, feeling like a teenager. "There is a new restaurant downtown. You could bring Kurt and Anna."

Effi smiled. "I vould like that very much."

# The Class of '34

## Kerryn Offord

### The High School Stables

"Isn't that JoAnn's horse you have there?" asked Matt Tisdel, walking towards Liz Manning who was saddling her horse.

Liz ignored the interruption and continued slipping the headstall and bosal over Speedy's head.

"I mean, you do know that's 'Speedy'? Does your sister know you have him out?"

With a heavy sigh Liz ran a hand gently down the side of Speedy's neck. She muttered a set-upon "Yes."

"You aren't thinking of riding him home are you? I mean. JoAnn wouldn't call him Speedy for nothing."

Liz turned from Speedy to stare at her tormentor. "Yes, Matt. Yes, I know this is Speedy. Yes, I know he is fast. I have been riding Speedy for a while. I am perfectly capable of riding a horse. I am perfectly capable of riding Speedy. Okay? Now if you will excuse me, I have to finish saddling up if I want to get home before it gets dark." With that she made her way over to the saddle and blankets straddling a rail beside the saddling area.

With Liz moving Matt had a clear view of the bridle she had been fitting. The sight shocked him. "Isn't that a hackamore? Don't tell me you are thinking of riding that animal with a hackamore?" he asked in horror.

"Okay, I won't tell you. Though what business it is of yours I don't know."

"I'm not totally ignorant when it comes to horses you know. It takes a really good rider to control an animal like Speedy with a hackamore."

"What are you trying to suggest, Matt?" Liz asked, fire growing in her eyes.

Matt was taken aback at how the conversation was deteriorating. "Nothing. Nothing. Here, let me help with that," Matt offered, trying to regain lost ground by reaching to pick up the saddle sitting ready on the rail.

"Thanks, but I'm perfectly capable of saddling a horse." Liz grabbed the saddle blanket and pad before Matt could lay a hand on them and set them over Speedy's withers. Turning back to the saddle she found Matt had carried it over. Reaching out she grabbed the heavy western saddle and pulled it from his hands. "Thank you for your help. I could have managed quite well without it." Quickly she threw the saddle over Speedy's back, letting it down gently. First checking that there were no wrinkles in the saddle pad and blanket, she then bent down and reached under Speedy's belly for the girth. She had just grabbed the cinch when she heard the heavy tread of someone else coming. Loosely buckling the cinch she looked up to see who had come in.

"Hi, Liz," Kevin greeted her, running his eyes up and down Liz, pausing to stare at her breasts. He waved a couple of pieces of paper in her direction. "I've got tickets for the senior prom. What time do you want me to pick you up?"

Liz managed to stifle her immediate reaction, a loud negation. She had heard stories about Kevin Simmons, and there was no way she wanted anything to do with him. Standing straight, her right hand gripping Speedy's mane for support, she shook her head. "I'm sorry, Kevin. I've already got a date for the prom."

The look on Kevin's face wasn't pretty. "Who?"

Breaking eye contact with Kevin, Liz cast about for a name Kevin would believe. She caught sight of Matt leaning against a stall, the raised eyebrow the only indication that he had been listening. She pointed. "Matt. He asked me earlier."

Kevin followed Liz's pointing arm. He obviously hadn't noticed Matt in the shadows. Anger flashed over his face.

"That's right, Simmons. Liz is going to the prom with me."

Kevin's hands tightened into fists for a moment. Then relaxed. He blasted Liz with an angry look before turning on his heels and stalking out of the stables.

"What color dress are you wearing?"

Liz had been following Kevin's departure with her eyes. The tension only left her body as he moved out of sight. Matt's question barely penetrated. Swinging to face him she asked, "What?"

"What color is your prom dress. For the corsage. You don't want them to clash."

"White." Liz responded automatically to the question as her heart fluttered for a moment. There had been a flash of something in Matt's eyes, quickly lost in his normal surly expression. "But you don't have to be my partner. I was going to go with a group of girls."

Shaking his head, Matt walked up the off-side of Speedy, stopping to rest a hand on the horse's neck. "Simmons is a real piece of work. If you don't go as my partner he'll get really nasty. He won't forgive you for refusing him."

Liz sighed. Then looked at Matt. He looked so solid and comfortable as he stood quite relaxed, idly rubbing at the base of Speedy's ears. She ran her tongue over her suddenly dry lips and passed her gaze over Matt before returning to doing up the cinch. All those miles Matt swam every day did wonders for his shoulders. Slightly distracted Liz turned her attention back to Speedy, giving him a nudge in the stomach to get him to exhale. She tightened the cinch another couple of notches, then turned back to Matt. "Are you still swimming every day?"

"Every day," he replied smiling at the nonsequitur.

"Even in winter? What about the ice?"

"Oh, I break that first. It can be real difficult trying to swim in unbroken ice."

"Maaatttt." Liz shook her head as she smiled at Matt. "You know what I mean. Isn't the water cold?"

"Well, of course it's cold. It's got ice forming on it. Okay, okay." Matt fended off Liz's mock slaps. "Nah, if you swim every day you don't notice the cold so much. Besides, when it gets colder I wear a triathlon wetsuit. You should come out and watch sometime. Well, I'm off."

As he reached the stable door Liz called out, "Dutch?"

Matt paused and looked over his shoulder. "Well, of course

Dutch. I'm not made of money." He made a hasty exit as Liz reached for something to throw.

Her hands empty, Liz stood staring at Matt's retreating back, a smile on her face. The sight of his broad shoulders receding into the distance did funny things to her breathing. She was brought back to earth when Speedy bumped his head into her back. Hastily she turned her attention back to saddling her mount.

## The Senior Prom, The Calvert High School Gym

Liz scanned the room as she and Matt glided around the gym. She was enjoying herself considerably. There had been many a wide-eyed stare when she turned up with Matt. Even now there were eyes following them around the dance floor. A few of the stares were less than friendly. "Did you notice David Bartley came with Brent and not Sarah?" Matt nodded. "And the guy Sarah came with. Did you see him?" Matt was starting to grin. "Did you notice Trent came with a girl? I'm surprised Brent came with David. You don't suppose he's stopped playing the field?"

"No, I think it's still a case of so many girls, so little time. If he brought a date there would be some kind of expectations."

"Well, if he's not careful, he's going to find himself propped up at an altar by a couple of shotguns," said Liz, a little disgusted at Brent's behavior.

"Whereas, if Trent is involved in a shotgun wedding, it'll be his girlfriend with the shotgun props," Matt said with a smile.

Liz looked wide-eyed at Matt. "Do you know her?"

"Not really, but I've noticed how Trent behaves whenever she's around. If you want all the dirt you should talk to Glenna Sue Haggerty; she seems to know her."

When the music stopped they started to walk towards the refreshments. In the shadows by the drinks table Liz spotted something. "Matt, over by the curtains. What do you think Kevin is doing?"

Matt looked over towards Kevin, then back to Liz. "If Simmons is acting true to form he's probably spiking his date's drink. Come on, I can see your friend the stable manager and his girlfriend. We should pass on a warning to them. If anybody can handle Simmons it'll be that pair."

"You mean because Erika is a police officer?"

"There is that, but I was thinking your Mr. Muller can be very physical when he needs to be."

"Rudi? But he's as gentle as a lamb."

"Next time you see Sims, ask him to describe the bit of dental reconstruction his father did when your Rudi hit a guy who was giving Officer Fleischer a hard time. I'm not saying your Rudi is violent, but when he hits someone, they stay hit."

"Oh."


"That wasn't so bad now, was it?" Matt asked as they left Rudi and Erika searching out Kevin and his date.

"No, and I'm glad we passed on a warning."

With the band now playing music more suited to the down-time dancers Matt and Liz abandoned the floor. As they walked back to the buffet tables Liz saw some of her friends and steered Matt towards them. "Hi, guys. You look all danced out. Joe Calagna, isn't it?" she asked as she looked at Glenna Sue Haggerty's date.

"Yes, and you must be her friend Liz." Joe did a graceful bow and kissed the back of her right hand.

"Very nicely done, Joe," observed Richelle Kubiak's date. "Hi, Liz. Has Matt been treating you well?"

"Thanks, Jonathan. Matt's been treating me fine. I didn't know you could dance."

"Mom's an Astaire and Rogers fan," Jonathan Fortney responded. "I think she married Dad because he could dance, and she's made sure both her kids could dance. She seemed to think it offered social benefits." With that he gave Richelle a quick cuddle. "I think she might be right. How about you, Matt? I wouldn't have thought you had time for dancing."

Matt shrugged his shoulders. "Miz Maddox struck a deal in exchange for additional coaching," he said, as if it explained everything.

"You get roped in as an extra male for her ballroom dance classes at school as well?" asked Joe.

Matt nodded. "You, too? I thought your aunt might have taught you."

"Oh Aunt Bitty did. That just made Miz Maddox more anxious to get her claws into me. Males as partners are rare enough; one who can actually move on a dance floor without tripping over his or his partner's feet, now those are like hen's teeth."

Liz examined the crowd, her gaze locking on one specific person. "Poor Julia. Prom queen, and her date unable to dance. Matt. Do you think you could . . . ?"

Matt looked at Liz, his eyes dancing, "Wander over and ask her to dance? Sure. If that's what you want. Are you all danced out?"

"A bit. And I'd like to chat with Tina."

"Have fun," Matt said. He dropped a kiss on her cheek before setting off towards Julia.

"Hey. Where's Matt going?" asked Tina Logsden.

"He's just going over to ask Julia to dance."

Tina looked at Liz wide-eyed. "Oh boy, DEAD. Girl, you are so DEAD."

Confused, Liz stared at Tina before turning her gaze onto Matt, who had just joined her cousin Julia. "What do you mean?"

"Lady Bountiful has just sent her faithful cavalier to dance with the poor wallflower. What do you think I mean?" Tina giggled as she watched the emotions passing over Julia O'Reilly's face as she debated whether or not to accept her cousin's largesse. "I think, right now, Julia would have been happier if you had been voted prom queen, rather than have her friends see you lending her your boyfriend."

"Matt's not my boyfriend. I told you what happened. He was in the stable when Kevin asked me to the prom. I'm really grateful that he didn't deny it when I claimed he had already asked me to the prom."

"Yeah, Right." Tina gave Liz a very superior smile and let her eyes drift from her friend to Matt and Julia who were now gliding around on the dance floor. Her eyes back on Liz she asked, "Have you ever asked yourself what a guy with no time for horses was doing in the stable just when you needed him?"

"Oh," responded Liz a little taken aback.

"Right. 'Oh.' I think the guy's got the hots for you," she said with a smile.

"Well, nothing can come of it." Liz shook her head gently, a blush growing. "Matt's said he wants to join the Marines. He reckons that they'll have more use for his swimming than the army."

"If he wants to use his swimming, surely the navy," Tina said.

Liz stifled a giggle. "That's what I said. Matt said that the navy has boats precisely so they don't have to swim."

As Liz, Tina, and a few of the unpartnered girls started talking amongst themselves the couples slipped back onto the dance floor.

It was the change in the beat of the music that drew them out of their huddle. "I think it's absolutely disgusting and shouldn't be allowed," muttered Tina, her eyes brimming with humor as she joined most of the guests in watching the couples dancing with the floor to themselves.

"What are they dancing?" asked Liz.

"Well, I'm no expert, but I think it's supposed to be a Tango," said Paola Villareal. "It sure looks like they are enjoying themselves, doesn't it."

"Yeah. They're really dancing up a storm. Who is the guy with Miz Stevenson?" asked Liz.

Tina looked at Liz. "Didn't you see the Christmas ballet? He was the Sugar Plum Fairy's cavalier." At Liz's shaking head, Paola and Tina exchanged horrified looks before turning back to the cultural desert that was their friend. "What about 'Bad Bad Brillo' and the continuing adventures of Brillo? Surely you have seen some of those, even if just on TV?"

"The Brillo saga. Yes, I've seen some of that. So, what part did he dance?"

"Lizzzzz. How could you fail to recognize Brillo?" Tina asked in a pained voice.

"Because Brillo's not a horse, obviously. You know Liz and her horses. If its not a horse, she's not interested. It's a wonder she didn't try to bring Speedy as her partner tonight, " Paola said. She turned her attention back to the dance floor. "It's a conspiracy," she muttered to her friends, pointing at the dancers. "Look at who has joined Miz Stevenson and her partner. There's Glenna Sue's sister Miz Haggerty, Miz Salerno, Miz Matowski, Glenna Sue and Joe, and Richelle and Jon. You realize they're all from the ballet. I bet those down-timers are guys that partnered the en pointe dancers in Nutcracker. It's a recruiting drive I tell you."

Liz, Tina and Paola, like most of the rest of the guests, stood watching the dancers dance the Tango, leaving the floor to the experts. It was a pleasure to watch, but too soon it came to an end.

Matt came to collect Liz for the next set and escorted her to the floor for yet another slow number. Tina turned to Paola. "Well, there is a lineup of guys holding up the opposite wall watching the dancing. It doesn't look like any of them are going to come over here to ask us to dance."

Paola looked at the males, then back at Tina, "You're right. If we want to dance, there is only one thing for it. We'll have to do the asking." Paola turned and offered Tina her left hand, "Miss Logsden, may I have the pleasure of this dance?"

"Why Miss Villareal, I'd be delighted." Tina smiled and she put her right hand in Paola's left and started onto the dance floor.

"Hey, just a minute. I asked. That means I get to lead," protested Paola.

"But next dance it's my turn to lead."

## The Graduation Picnic at the old quarry.

"Richelle. Are you all right?" Liz Manning asked. Richelle was bent over in the bushes, vomit pooling in front of her.

Richelle Kubiak looked up at the voice, Her wide unfocused eyes dominated a porcelain white face. "I do not feel so well."

"That's an understatement. Have you had anything to drink?" Liz asked.

Richelle tried to focus on her friend, "Drink? A little small beer."

"I mean alcohol. Have you had anything stronger than the small beer?"

Richelle tried to shake her head in negation, but the effort told on her and she collapsed back onto her hands and knees, dry retching.

"If it's not that, then is it something you ate?" Liz asked, wrapping her arms around Richelle's trembling body. She looked around for help. "Diana, can you come here? Richelle's unwell."

Diana Cheng made her way quickly over to Liz and Richelle. After a hasty physical assessment, she used a stick to stir the pool of vomit and sniffed it. "Come on. Liz, you take the other side. We need to get Richelle warm."

"Is Richelle all right?" someone slurred.

Liz turned to the voice. The pale face of Maria Pflaum struggled to hold eye contact.

"Hell. Maria, are you all right?"

"I don't feel so good."

Liz and Diana exchanged looks. It seemed that something was going around. Leaving Richelle in Liz's care, Diana knelt down beside Maria and checked her over. "What have you been eating, Maria?"

"Nothing. I haven't eaten anyth . . ."

Diana waited until the dry heaving stopped. "Are you sure?"

"Nothing, I've only had a drink of small beer since I arrived."

Diana looked over at the barrel of small beer sitting innocently on the back of a wagon. "Liz." As Liz turned to face her, Diana continued, "would you check out the drinks barrel and bring back a cupful?"

Leaving Richelle wrapped in a picnic blanket, Liz moved over to the beer barrel and tapped it for a cup. Sniffing it first, Liz then took a small sip. Looking back at Diana, she shrugged her shoulders before taking the cup to Diana. "What do you think?"

"Well it doesn't smell bad." Taking a small sip and then spitting it out Diana looked at the cup of offending liquid. "I don't know. The only thing I can think of is someone has spiked the barrel with booze. But what kind of dumb idiot would do a thing like that?"

"I can think of one name," said Liz, "but I wouldn't think it would be him. He should have learned his lesson at the senior prom."

Diana looked around the picnic site. There were a couple of girls suffering some kind of mystery illness. "If it is alcohol I suppose it's too much to hope its not home made 'shine.'"

Liz looked questioningly at Diana, "What?"

"People who know what they are doing throw out the first couple of ounces of flow to get rid of the methanol." Seeing Liz's confusion, Diana elaborated. "Methanol fractions off at a lower temperature than ethanol, so the first bit of flow contains some methanol. It's a toxin. If you don't dump it, anybody drinking your alcohol risks blindness, or," she passed her eye over Richelle and the other girls huddled in blankets around the fire, "you get illness. Mind you, they could just be reacting to too much alcohol."

Diana and Liz's contemplation of the huddled shapes by the fire was disturbed by a scream and splashing. Both looked towards the sound, to the beer barrel, then, with dawning horror, at each other.

☆        ☆        ☆

Matt Tisdel was used to the walk to the swimming hole at the old quarry. It was one of his favorite swimming holes. The short municipal pool made training for distance swimming difficult; all that constant turning every few seconds or so interfered with the rhythm of his stroke. He was deep in his daydreams of what might have been but for the Ring of Fire when the high pitched scream penetrated. Looking up he could see splashing near the pontoon anchored fifty yards from the beach. Dropping into a jog Matt made his way towards the water. As he neared the bank he saw a girl strip down to her swimsuit and dive into the water. Sprinting now, he ran to the bank. Looking down the ten feet into the water he searched for the would-be rescuer. Spotting a body floating in the water Matt quickly stripped down to his swimsuit, then after scanning the water for any floating or submerged branches, jumped feet first into the water.

The frigid water almost robbed him of breath as he went under. Shooting to the surface in the shallow water he searched for the floater. Spotting the body he struck out with a powerful freestyle stroke that quickly closed the distance. Arriving at the floating body he quickly rolled the girl over. Kicking to stay afloat he felt for a pulse. He couldn't feel anything. Looking towards shore he could see people gathering on the short pier that jutted into the quarry. Rolling onto his back he took hold of the girl and kicked out for the shore. "She's not breathing," he called as helping hands dragged the bleeding girl out of the water. With a hand holding onto the pier Matt looked back towards the pontoon. There were a couple of people on it trying to drag someone out of the water. Their movements appeared uncoordinated.

"Are you all right, Matt?"

Matt looked up to see John Sullivan looking down at him, "Yeah, I'm okay. What about the girl?"

"Henry Sims and one of the girls are giving her CPR. Look. They seem to be having trouble out on the pontoon. Could you swim over and help? I'm worried about those guys still in the water. It's not so bad if they keep moving, but staying still in the water like that. Well, I've got a bad feeling about them."

"Okay, I'll start hauling them back if they can't manage on their own. Just make sure you have people ready to receive them."

Matt launched into a fast crawl and swam for the pontoon. Thirty seconds later he was helping get the last couple of swimmers out of the water. "Huddle together for warmth you guys." Pulling himself onto the pontoon Matt looked down on the shivering young men and women. A couple were going blue around the lips. Looking around the quarry Matt searched for a boat. Anything that floated. There was nothing. "Everybody. You have to stay huddled together for warmth. You understand?" The shivering swimmers nodded. "Right, I'm going to swim back to shore to get a rope or something. You just stay out of the water. You understand?" Seeing their nods Matt dived back into the water and struck out for the shore.

Helping hands dragged Matt onto the pier and quickly toweled him down before throwing a blanket around his shoulders. Shivering Matt turned to John. "I wouldn't risk swimming them back if we can avoid it. Is there a boat out here?"

"No," said John.

"Hell. Anybody know how the pontoon is secured?" Matt asked, looking around the faces congregated on the pier.

"I think it's a concrete anchor on a chain," suggested Mark Higgins. "The chain is attached to the pontoon by a shackle. If you can undo the shackle the pontoon should float free. I'll run back to the wagons and see if I can find any rope."

"Dieter and I'll get a couple of horses to help pull the pontoon," said Julia O'Reilly as she grabbed her boyfriend, Dieter Klaus Schmidt, by the hand and dragged him off towards the horses.

Still shivering, Matt turned to John. "The guys on the pontoon seem a bit punch drunk. Does that make any difference to anything?"

John Sullivan was thoughtful for a moment before nodding. "Yes. It means we better get them on dry land and warmed up quickly. They're ripe for hypothermia, and if they are drunk, that's even worse. Look, Matt. If you're planning what I think you are, you're going to need some equipment. Stay here while I get a few things together."

Matt watched John run off, to return a few minutes later with a backpack in his hands. Mark Higgins and a couple of down-timers arrived at the same time, carrying some lengths of hemp rope.

"None of these will do on its own, but if we join them together, it should be enough," Mark said. He started unraveling the bundles of rope.

"Here, let me do that." John grabbed two lengths of rope and expertly joined them. "Matt," he called, "there's a large screwdriver, some knit caps, a thermos of hot water, and a couple of survival blankets in the backpack. Get them to wear the knit caps. Remember, we lose up to thirty percent of our body heat through the head. Try to get them to drink some of the hot water, and wrap them in the blankets. Here, use this as a leader. We'll attach the ropes when you get to the pontoon and you can haul the rope over. Much easier than swimming pulling a rope." John passed Matt a stick with heavy line wound round it.

Matt nodded in understanding. He put the roll of string into the top of the backpack and pulled the end free. He made a loop and tied it to a pile on the pier, then put the pack on and adjusted the straps. Then he lowered himself back into the water. It felt colder this time.

Matt barely felt the increased drag of the pack as he swam back out to the pontoon. He shivered when he pulled himself out of the water. The first thing he did was loop the string around a cleat. Then he emptied the backpack. He had to physically put the hats on the shivering men and women. One by one, he forced them to drink some of the hot water. After that, he wrapped them in the survival blankets and left them huddled together. He'd done the best he could.

He looked back to shore. Julia and Doug had almost arrived back with a pair of horses. It was time to see about undoing the anchor.

The shackle was old and rust had built up. Pushing the end of the screwdriver through the hole of the shackle, Matt applied all his strength. His body was starting to shake when the shackle squealed and turned a bit. Switching the screwdriver around Matt made another half turn. Half a dozen turns later a thought struck Matt. Going back to the pack he removed the ball of string, and unraveling it as he went, moved back to the shackle. Quickly he tied a loop of line to the chain. Now, when the chain was released they would be able to recover the anchor relatively easily.

There was a cry from the shore. Matt hurried to the front of the pontoon and started hauling on the line as he pulled the heavier rope toward him. With the rope in hand he secured it to the pontoon and hurried back to the shackle. With a few more turns the chain dropped free to be caught by the line Matt had tied to it. Letting line out, Matt waved to the people on shore.

Slowly the pontoon started to move as the horses, aided by help-ing hands, hauled on the rope.

Helping hands carefully lifted their shivering friends from the pontoon and rushed them up to where fires had been lit. John stayed with Matt as he dried off and dressed in the clothes some-one had recovered from where he had dropped them less than twenty minutes earlier.

"Help. Help. We need help. We have someone in the early stages of hypothermia," called Janie Abodeely as she ran up to the camp. "We need someone to ride to the nearest phone to call the emergency services. We might have another three or four cases." As she arrived at the campfire Janie looked at the girls huddled around the fire with Diana and Liz caring for them. "Oh hell. Is everything all right here? Liz? You came on a horse didn't you?" Not waiting for a reply she hurried on. "Look, I'll give you a note. You have to ride to the nearest phone as quickly as you can."

After hurriedly writing on a page from a notebook Janie grabbed Liz and dragged her towards the line of horses feeding from baskets set at their feet. "Which is your horse?" she asked still pulling on Liz's arm.

"Speedy. That one over there," Liz pointed.

"Oh good. Do you know the shortcut?" At Liz's nod Janie con-tinued, "Quick, where's his tack." Liz looked around. The space where she had left Speedy's tack was bare.

"Someone must have taken it," Liz called. She ran to Speedy's head, stuffing Janie's note into her pocket. Untying the halter rope Liz quickly looped it over Speedy's neck and tied the end to the front clip. She then threw herself up onto Speedy. Bareback and with only a halter for control Liz led Speedy off towards the shortcut.

Fifteen minutes later Liz burst out of the valley and surprised the workmen gathered around the hut. Speedy staggered to a halt and helping hands caught Liz as she slipped from his back. Strug-gling to stand, Liz pulled at her pocket, her whole body shaking, as she tried to get Janie's note. "Help, we need help," she said.

As someone took the note, Liz collapsed from a combination of emotional exhaustion, coming down from the adrenaline rush, and her rubbery legs refusing to support her.

Reading the hastily scrawled note, Michel Kuhn detailed one of the boys to throw something over the horse and walk it around to cool it down. He then hurried over to the phone and made a call to the emergency services. After a few moments of conversation he gathered most of his crew, leaving a couple of men to look after the up-timer and her horse. Grabbing what equipment they could they started towards the site of the picnic.

## The Hospital

"What have you got for us, Doctor?" Police Chief Preston Richards asked Dr. Adams.

"Well, three of the five who went into the water are in a stable condition. They should recover, but they will be in the hospital for a couple of weeks. For the other two, the prognosis isn't so good. Tina Logsden suffered severe head injuries when she dived into the quarry. She appears to have forgotten that the quarry shelves on that side. She is also suffering from hypothermia with complications, including cardiac arrest, probably due to the shock of the cold water. Young Glenna Sue Haggerty is critical. She has suffered a number of cardiac arrests in addition to hypothermia. We are still trying to stabilize her heartbeat."

"Do you have any idea why things happened like that? It seems everybody was okay, then suddenly everything went wrong."

"That's for the coroner to say, but there are indications alcohol was involved. In addition to our five hypothermia cases there were a couple cases of what appears to be alcohol poisoning." Dr. Adams held up his hand to stop Chief Richards interrupting. "They should be all right. But I want to keep them in for forty-eight hours for observation."

"Are you saying that the kids drank too much and then went swimming?" asked Chief Richards.

"I wish I could say that, but it appears that someone spiked one of their beverage barrels with spirits. Pretty cheap spirits at that. Diana Cheng, one of our new medical students, saved a sample and ran it through the lab. There were traces of methanol in it."

Seeing the shocked look of his audience he continued, "Oh, don't worry, the amount was too small to cause any permanent harm. The worst affected, Richelle Kubiak and Maria Pflaum, should make a full recovery." Dr. Adams gave Chief Richards and his officers a rueful look. "Given the girl's families, I wouldn't want to be whoever it was that spiked the drinks. Do you have any ideas as to who might be responsible?"

"Officer Fleischer followed up a hunch. She located a couple of bottles of cheap alcohol and a few doses of those horse steroids that went missing just after the Ring of Fire in the bedroom of one of the students," said Officer Bernadette Adducci, the juvenile officer.

"Who?" asked Dr. Adams.

"Normally we wouldn't say until our investigations are complete. But under the circumstances," Officer Adducci took a deep breath, releasing it, with the name. "Kevin Simmons."

"Oh." Dr. Adams nodded his head in understanding. There had been one fatality so far from the picnic. Kevin Simmons had taken a horse and, having poor horsemanship skills, failed to properly secure the saddle. At some stage, as he galloped away from the picnic site, the saddle had slipped, spilling Kevin. Unfortunately, he had caught a foot in the stirrup. Kevin's battered and bloodied body had been found, missing a boot, caught in undergrowth. "That's going to hit his parents Lorraine and Peter pretty hard. Does it all have to be made public knowledge?"

"Under the circumstances there isn't much point in revealing more than necessary. It won't bring those girls back, and Kevin Simmons can't be punished.

What about the Manning girl? I understood she was in a pretty bad condition," said Chief Richards.

"Liz Manning should be okay. She's a little stressed out." Dr. Adams grinned for the first time. "Based on the time Janie Abodeely wrote on her note and the time the emergency call came through, Liz Manning had just set an all time record for racing a horse through that shortcut. She wiped a good three minutes off her sister's record. I would think the less Liz remembers of that ride the better. Her sister JoAnn was always the risk taker of those two."

"Right. Dr. Adams, is there anything we can do before we go?" asked Chief Richards.

"There is one thing. If it hadn't been for the bravery of Matt Tisdel things could have been a lot worse. He seems to have behaved completely differently from what people would expect if they listened to his uncle Melvin Sutter. Is there anything we can do for him?"

Chief Richards looked to Officer Adducci. As the juvenile officer Bernadette knew more about Matt Tisdel than he did. "I'll have Officer Adducci look into it, Dr. Adams. Matt does seem to have covered himself with glory, just like some of your new intake of medical students, and he shouldn't go unrewarded."

## Public Notices: *Grantville Gazette*. Deaths.

Glenna Sue Haggerty—On May 28, 1634, at Grantville Hospital. In her 18th year. Dearly loved daughter of Gary and Laurie, and beloved sister of Cameron, Duane, Marcie, and Blake. Dearly loved member of the Grantville Ballet Company. Glenna Sue will be sadly missed.

Tina Logsden—On May 25, 1634, at Grantville Hospital. In only her 18th year. Tina will be badly missed by her sister Susan and her grandfather. We will miss you xxx.

Kevin Simmons—Loving son of Mickey and Lorraine, loving brother of Andrea. Died in his 18th year in a riding accident.

# Magdeburg Marines:
# The Few and the Proud

## Jose J. Clavell

**The Hudson Residence**
**City of Grantville**
**Thuringia Region, Germany**
**Monday, 6 December 1632 AD**
**1600 hours local**

"Well, can you repair it?"

Charles "Duke" Hudson asked the question to the pair of legs sticking out from under his sink. He was a tall, no-nonsense middle-aged man whose brown buzz cut hair had gone mostly to gray, especially in the last two years. The response was garbled, so he bent over and repeated his question. The response come back garbled again. This time, recognizing the futility of answering while under the sink, the owner of the legs slid out from under it and stood. The blonde woman was almost as tall as Duke was. She was also muscular and in her thirties. For some reason, the term Valkyrie came to mind every time Duke looked at her.

"Yes, Duke. I can repair it. But it's going to cost you," Margaret "Lulu" O'Keefe replied. In addition to being the General Manager of O'Keefe Plumbing and Heating, she was also a close friend of both Duke and his wife, Claire.

"How much, Lu?"

Lulu grimaced before replying, not a good sign in a plumber, "But let's wait for Claire. That way I only have to be subjected to verbal abuse one time."

"That much?" Duke exclaimed, surprised.

"Duke, it's not like I can get in my truck and drive to Fairmont for parts anymore," Lulu said as she cleaned her hands with a kitchen rag.

Duke didn't need the reminder. Over a year ago the life of everyone in the West Virginia town of Grantville—and history itself—had changed forever. In a brief instant, on a Sunday afternoon. When, under unexplained circumstances, in what everyone now called the Ring of Fire, the whole town and its inhabitants were transported back in time to 1631 Germany. They'd wound up in the middle of the period that historians knew as The Thirty Years' War. Since that day, daily life had become a struggle for survival. Bits and pieces of the past—or future, depending on how you looked at it—ground to a halt, just like Duke's broken trash compactor.

Lulu sat at the kitchen table and pushed her toolbox next to her chair with her foot. "Maybe you need to retire the beast and accept the inevitable. Who knows, maybe one of these days someone will reinvent it. Anyway, it's just a labor saving device. And I know you're as well aware as I am that we have plenty of cheap manual labor available. In fact, I don't understand why Claire hasn't hired a maid. Think of all her responsibilities, working for the government yet. Where is she, by the way?"

"She's helping a German family that just moved down the block, the Hoffmans," Duke answered. "The man used to be a mercenary officer of sorts, I'm told. But now he wants to join our Military Police unit. He seems like a dependable sort and his wife, Ilse, is pregnant with their fourth child. So, Claire went to lend a hand with the kids and the house. You know how she likes to keep busy."

"Yes, I know. We all like to keep busy." Lulu sighed as she found a more comfortable position in her chair.

Unsaid between the two friends was that in Grantville everyone kept busy to forget. There wasn't a family in town that had not been affected by the event. In the case of the Duke and Claire, their two grown kids and grandkids were left behind. Lulu had lost her fiancé and older brother the same way.

"Well, while we wait, would you care for a beer?" Duke asked.

"Don't mind if I do. This is my last call before heading for home and another exciting night of educational TV and movies repeated for the umpteenth time."

Duke opened his refrigerator, took out two beer bottles and passed one to Lulu. The bottles were recycled but the labels announcing the latest product line from the Thuringen Gardens were new. He pulled a chair and sat across from Lulu.

She took a long sip before smacking her lips. "Wow, I think this batch is the best one yet."

"I think you're right," Duke replied, after doing his own tasting. "So, Lu, how's business?"

"I can't complain," she answered. "The business is booming, thanks to all the new construction. I've hired six more employees and we may need to hire more. The family is also discussing the possibility of starting our own plumbing fixtures manufacturing. We think there's an untapped market out there for the wonders of indoor plumbing, especially with this weather. And you, how are things with the MPs?"

"The usual," Duke said, relaxing into his chair. "Brawls after payday, fights just for the sake of fighting. Dan Frost still wants to form a Military Police unit like the Italian carabineers. But he's having problems finding someone to fill in for Elizabeth Pitre now that she's with the toy trains. And I don't want the job. She originally asked me to be her top kick."

"She made a good choice," Lulu said. "It's a damn shame that it didn't work out for you two." Lulu paused a moment and looked thoughtful. "You helped her become the kind of officer she is now. I remember when she was just a wet behind the ears shave-tail, wearing her cowboy boots in utilities."

Duke smiled fondly at the memory. When they were first introduced, Pitre had gone pale as a ghost when someone let her know that her new platoon sergeant was a former Marine DI. "Don't be so harsh, Lu. No one packed for the Ring, remember. She was only supposed to be in town for Mike's sister's wedding. I really didn't have to work too hard with her. There was a lot of good material already there. Besides, she had her colonel father's example to provide her a good starting point. She is definitely one of the best young officers I ever had the pleasure to train. Heck, I considered her good enough to be in the Marines. If anyone has the wherewithal to get that harebrained transportation scheme off the drawing board, it's going to be her. But, she needed a first sergeant with more transportation experience than I have, so I'm out."

"That's high praise coming from you, Duke." Lulu continued to stare intently at her beer bottle until she suddenly asked. "Do you miss it?"

"Miss what? The Corps?"

"Yes. The green machine, Uncle Sam's misguided children, our Corps."

"Yes," Duke admitted. "Sometimes. But I put in my twenty years and left others to carry on the mission. No one is irreplaceable, Lu. Besides, I wanted to keep my promise to Claire to return to our hometown."

"Come on, Duke," Lulu said. "You weren't like every other Marine. I did twelve years, you know. After Dad died and I had to request a compassionate discharge, I only got a pat on the back and a farewell bash at the NCO Club. I hear that you, on the other hand, got a phone call straight from Headquarters, Marine Corps, to try to get you to reconsider your decision. I've never heard of the Sergeant Major of the Marine Corps doing that for any other gunnery sergeant."

"So what." Duke shrugged. "Like I said, Lu, I promised Claire and I don't like to break my word. And just how did you hear about that, anyway?"

"Willie Ray told me one day. It was a while back, one day when we were shooting the breeze at the Gardens. And just in case you want to know, he was happy that you didn't decide to stay in. Otherwise, after the Ring of Fire, he wouldn't have had any family left in town."

"I think," Duke muttered, "that my brother talks too much."

"Maybe so," Lula said, grinning a bit. "But he told me that it wasn't until you accepted the job with Dan and the MPs that you started overcoming your doldrums. Then you took young Pitre under your wing and that helped to finally return you to your usual cheery self. Well, almost." Lulu leaned back in the chair and took another sip of beer before she went on. "That led me to suspect that you miss the Corps as much as I do."

"So what if I do? The Corps, like the rest of the twenty-first century and my kids are, and pardon the pun, past history." His bitter reply warned Lulu that she was getting closer to overstepping the line.

"Sorry, I know how much you miss Kathy and James. It was thoughtless of me."

Duke relaxed visibly before replying. "And I know how much you miss Billy and your brother. So why we don't drop the subject and talk about something else?"

"Fine with me," Lulu agreed, glad that they had managed to avoid a tender subject. "Have you heard the latest scuttlebutt about John Simpson?"

Duke shook his head and made a shivering motion. "No, I haven't. That's way above my pay grade and that's the way I like it."

Lulu snorted and plowed on in. She leaned forward with a conspirator's smile. "He's been put in charge of a special project. By Mike Stearns, no less."

Duke snorted and took another sip of beer. He was clearly amused. "Are those two talking again? I'm kind of surprised. I'd have thought that even after the elections, those two would still have some irreconcilable differences on most issues."

John Simpson's first attempt to push himself into a leadership position after the Ring of Fire and, later, his party platform during the elections that saw Mike Stearns elected as the new nation's president were generally reviled. That had strained his relationships with most of the town's residents. Most of the up-timers saw him as a representative of the managerial class. Considering that the closure of the local mines had condemned Grantville to a slow death, he wasn't a particularly popular man.

"They're talking. Just barely. But . . ." Lulu's reply was preempted by a familiar voice calling from the living room. "Duke, I'm home. Where are you?"

"In the kitchen, Claire," Duke called out. He heard his wife talking to someone and wondered who had dropped in.

"Ah, there you are," Claire said. "Hi, Lulu. I see you're loafing around my kitchen and drinking my beer instead of working hard. Let me guess, my compactor is dead, right?" Claire, a short and plump, but attractive, middle-aged brunette took off her woolen watch cap and mittens before kissing Duke.

"Well, girlfriend," Lulu answered with a grin, "unless you want to pay me a lot for handcrafted parts, I think you'd better call for a burial detail and the Wilson kid can play taps on his bugle. How's Mrs. Hoffman?"

"I guess Duke told you about our new neighbors," Claire

answered. "She's about ready to pop, I think. But after three live births and two miscarriages, Ilse is pretty much matter-of-fact about the whole thing. Let's hear it for Teutonic phlegmatic practicality." Claire rolled her eyes a bit when she made that last comment and moved toward the sink and the coffee pot. She took the pot off the heating element and rinsed it out, saying, "And Duke, you have a visitor. John Simpson is waiting for you in the living room."

Lulu almost gagged on her beer. Duke's face was a study and he appeared to be speechless for a moment. She and Duke exchanged puzzled glances and then looked at Claire, who continued making coffee. Claire was apparently totally without a clue as to the bombshell that she just dropped on her kitchen. Duke finally managed to clear his throat. "Come again?"

"I said that John Simpson is waiting for you in the living room. I found him at our doorstep, ready to push the bell, when I got home. I told him I was going to make some coffee and that I'd find you. Will you tell him that it will be ready in a couple of minutes?"

"Sure, love," Duke replied. He stifled a laugh when he saw Lulu making signs to ward off evil in the direction of the living room. He made a severe face in her direction and rose to go see what John Chandler Simpson wanted.

Duke entered his living room to find Simpson carefully looking at his "love me" wall. This was the first time Duke had seen Simpson up close. The older man was tall and distinguished looking, regardless of his secondhand coat and clothes. Simpson looked to be at least in his late fifties or early sixties. Surrendering to the inevitable, Duke cleared his throat, catching Simpson's attention.

Startled, Simpson turned around. "Oh, sorry, Mr. Hudson," he said. "You caught me unaware. This is quite an impressive collection of awards and recognitions, sir. We haven't actually met, I'm afraid. I'm pleased to meet you. I'm John Simpson." Simpson advanced with his right hand extended to shake hands.

Duke was put a little off guard by John Simpson's unexpected friendly demeanor. He shook Simpson's hand automatically, noticing the firm, confident grip, and stammered a response. "Thanks, Mr. Simpson. My wife asked me to tell you that coffee will be ready shortly. Would you like to have a seat?"

"Don't mind if I do, Mr. Hudson," Simpson said. "And I'll gladly accept a cup of coffee. It's a little chilly out there at this time of year." As Simpson sat down, Duke noticed an unnatural stiffness in his left lower leg. A stiffness that was familiar to anyone who had been around military hospitals. Two purple hearts had gained Duke a somewhat regretted experience with those institutions.

Simpson noticed his gaze and replied to his unspoken question. "I lost my lower leg to an RPG in Vietnam. I was with the Navy's riverine forces. The boat section under my command was ambushed by the NVA as we tried to relieve a South Vietnamese battalion. I lost a lot of good men that day."

A shadow of sadness swept over Simpson's face. A veteran combat leader himself, Duke didn't need to be told what was going through this man's mind and he didn't have to wonder which loss was more important to him. That spoke volumes about Simpson, the man. Embarrassed and oddly intrigued by this revelation, Duke could only offer his apologies. "I am sorry, Mr. Simpson. It was rude of me to stare."

"I don't mind it too much," Simpson said. "I saw by your wall that you're in a good position to understand. In fact, that's the reason I'm here. Mike Stearns has asked me to head a new project. When I started to look for people who could help me with it, your brother was kind enough to tell me about your qualifications."

"My brother may be exaggerating a bit there, sir. And frankly, I don't know if I can be of any help to you." Duke immediately got the impression that his low-key answer provided the right tone. Simpson smiled at him.

"I doubt it, Gunnery Sergeant Hudson. I think you're the right man for the job. And, I have a proposal for you."

**The Hudson Residence
City of Grantville
Thuringia Region, Germany
Tuesday, 7 December 1632 AD
0230 hours local**

Claire Hudson woke up suddenly and realized that her husband was not beside her in bed. She raised her head and looked around the darkened room until she saw him sitting in one of the recliners by the window. He was staring out into the night, deep in thought. She then looked at her nightstand clock and almost cursed at the early hour, before continuing to stare at him. Even after more than twenty-five years of marriage, he was still occasionally an enigma to her. Tonight, though, she had a pretty good idea what was on his mind. Damn John Simpson, she thought.

Claire still felt as much in love with Duke today as she had when she was seventeen. Through all those years Duke had been a gentle, caring husband and truly her best friend. Now, as she watched his not-quite ominous presence in the darkened room, she couldn't fail to think of that other aspect of his persona, the warrior. It was an aspect that he had struggled to keep hidden from her and their kids through his time in the Corps. Unlike other Marines she knew, he seldom raised his voice or tried to run his family like an extension of his unit. Watching other women struggling with husbands who, unlike Duke, couldn't keep their lives in the Corps separate from their lives at home had made her feel truly blessed.

Still, she was very much aware of his potential for, and expertise in, applied violence. Not from him, of course. She had tried early in their marriage to get him to open up and confide in her. But that was before she learned from older and more experienced Marine spouses to let sleeping dogs lie. In an organization of close-mouthed professional warriors, her husband set unbeatable standards for that trait. However, other Marines and occasion- ally their wives had slipped up and told her of his exploits. The stories were usually told with a strange measure of admiration, awe and wonderment at his courage. Sometimes they seemed to describe a legend in the making. Even when the Corps deigned to recognize those exploits, like his Silver Star after the Gulf War, it had come as a total surprise to her. That day, darn the man, he just told her that they were giving him some kind of award and it would be nice if she and the kids could dress up and attend. The presentation and the divisional parade that followed managed at the same time to annoy her with his discretion and make her feel truly proud as she stood with the wives of the other men receiving awards.

Now, once more, the warrior aspect of his persona was being summoned. After Simpson and Lulu left, Duke had told her about

Simpson's proposal for a new Marine Corps. And then he had refused to discuss it any further. She knew that he was conflicted and had an inkling of the source of that conflict. She had hoped he could resolve it on his own. But, Claire chided herself, she knew full well that, in a roundabout way, it all depended on her. She was no longer the innocent girl who was unaware of what the love of her life did for a living.

Claire thought hard for a few moments. Was she strong enough to demonstrate that she was a warrior's wife? Claire had never been either horrified or frightened of Duke's feats. She knew, all the way to her core, that as long as he and his brothers stood guard against all enemies, she, their children and their nation would be safe. So, maybe she was a warrior's wife after all, she thought. There was only one way to find out.

Clearing her throat, Claire said, "Duke, it's too early. Come back to bed."

Her husband, startled, broke from his introspection and looked at her for a long time before replying. "Sorry, sweetheart, I couldn't sleep and I didn't want to wake you up."

"I know, Duke. Come back to bed, please. It's too cold to sit up like that." She watched as he reluctantly got up from the chair, shed his robe and slid in beside her. Claire immediately spooned against his back, ignoring the chill from his skin and clothing. "Why you don't tell me what the problem is, Duke?"

"I don't know if I want to discuss it, Claire."

"Well, why I don't start then?" She felt his surprise as his body stiffened. *Don't chicken out now, Claire Louise*, she admonished herself. "You're concerned about me and my feelings, right? Don't be. Do you remember why I originally got you to promise to put in your twenty and move back to this town? Did you forget?"

Duke turned around under the covers to face her. "Claire, I think that you lost me there."

"The kids, Duke. I wanted them to know what it's like to grow roots somewhere. And we did that, in the few years that we had together before they grew up and left home. And, after the Ring, I am so glad that we did it that way. They grew up to be such wonderful people and friends. And, I hope, they have a great future ahead of them. Kathy, our wise little girl, found this marvelous young man and . . ." Claire stopped as she read his expression. With an accusatory tone, she snarled, "Stop rolling your eyes, Duke. I can see them."

Duke smiled and propped his head with his hand as he looked down at her. "But we are talking about the long-haired freak, Tim?"

"Yes, the no longer long-haired freak. When are you going to admit that you love him as much as I do? He says the same thing of you, by the way. Men, you have a funny way to show you care. I swear I'll never understand you at all," she said, with feigned disgust.

"We like to be mysterious. Yes, I like the freak. He actually grew up to be a solid man and a good husband for Kathy."

"Yes, he did. And I'm sure that the fact that he got a degree, a good job and even joined the Guard, helped. I'll remind you that without any prodding in your part, he went through their OCS and got commissioned as an infantry officer. Our Kathy is a warrior's daughter. She would never have settled for a lesser man. They had given us two beautiful grandchildren, well . . . three by now." Claire stopped and started sobbing as Duke hugged her tightly. They shared the pain for the grandkids that they could no longer watch grow up. It was a pain that time might ease, but never erase.

After a seemingly long time, Claire cleared her throat and looked up. "Thanks, sweetie. I'm better now. Anyway, Jamie, excuse me, James. He's a grown man now and hated that nickname with a passion. You told me that he was well on his way to following in your footsteps, right?"

"My last report from Patrick at Parris Island was that he was a shoe-in for honor graduate. By this time, I expect him to be well into his first tour." Duke smiled with pride at the memory and then chuckled. "And yes, he hated to hear that nickname from everyone else but you, Kathy or Kim Chaffin . . . "Okay, sweetheart. I see your point. But what about you? I was also doing this for you."

Claire propped her head with her hand as she unconsciously imitated his stance. "What about me? Don't worry. We're more alike than you ever guessed. Tell me why you decided to join the Corps. And please don't tell me that you liked the uniform. I haven't been a teeny bopper for a long time."

Amused, Duke studied her face for a while. "I don't know, patriotism; perhaps? We lost a lot of guys in the bombing of the Marine barracks in Beirut and I felt like I needed to do something."

"Well, I share those feelings, too. Or do you think I followed you around the world, bore your children and lived in accommodations that would shame any third world nation, only because of your ruggedly handsome looks?" Claire asked.

"No. I stood by you and made a home for you because it was my contribution to the common defense. And now, once more your country is calling you. And I'm ready to do my part, just like you are. And, by the way, I know you got a call from Sergeant Major Overstreet when you announced that you were retiring instead of accepting your first sergeant stripes."

"Damn, I'm going to kill my brother," Duke muttered.

"No you aren't," Claire said. "I didn't hear it from him. You see, I entertained a wives' delegation shortly after you put in your papers. It was headed by Mrs. Division Sergeant Major. All the wives in your chain of command came to see me. All the way down to Mrs. O'Rourke, your first sergeant's wife, even. Mrs. Overstreet had called them from D.C. to give them a heads up on our situation."

"The dragon squad?" Duke grinned. "They sent the dragon squad? I'm sorry if they give you a hard time, sweetie."

Claire giggled before laying her head back on the pillow. "Don't be silly. They were my friends and they were doing the same thing that I had done with the wives of the men in your platoon. I'm sure some of the wives of your lance corporals thought I was part of the dragon squad, too. Part of the unofficial job description for a senior NCO wife is making sure that a subordinate's wife is receiving the proper support as she attempts to accomplish all the difficult tasks expected of a Marine wife."

Duke knew this. He just hadn't realized, consciously, that Claire knew it as well. After a moment's thought Duke realized that at all those wives' soirées she had attended, more than diapers and husbands had been discussed.

Claire went on, "In fact, I wasn't totally sure we were doing the right thing, back when you retired. But after they heard my reasoning, they backed me up a hundred percent. It's kind of funny, but I occasionally miss the joy of helping a new Marine wife to get on her feet. Maybe I can get that joy back again."

Duke smiled into the dark. Yes, helping a young Marine to

get on his or her own two feet was one of the more intangible pleasures of the job. Funny, he had never realized that his wife could sympathize with that. Maybe she was right and they were more alike than he thought they were.

"Okay, sweetie," Duke said. "You've sold me on it. Tomorrow I'm going to call the admiral and . . ." He stopped when he saw the surprise in her face. "Yes, Mike is making Simpson an admiral. But, don't be too impressed. Last I heard, his navy consists of four people, counting himself, and no ships. Well, five, now, I guess. Counting me. Hey, would you like to make love to the whole one man Marine Corps? I've been told in good faith that I have ruggedly handsome looks." Duke leered and wiggled his eyebrows in a suggestive manner.

Claire suppressed her amusement and kept him at arms' length. "Hold your horses, lover boy. We need our sleep if we're going to start this Marine Corps off on the right foot."

"We?" Duke repeated, totally flabbergasted at the thought.

"Of course. You are going to ask Lulu, right?"

"Well, yes. After Simpson, she's my next call. But you said we."

"Ah, my ruggedly handsome boy toy." Claire grinned, reaching for him. "For over two hundred years, Marines' wives have known that if someone had bothered to ask us in the first place, a large portion of the problems Marines have experienced would have been resolved. But what can you expect from an organization that got its start in a tavern? And, if you think I'm going to miss this opportunity to make my mark in the name of marine wives, past, present and future, you're out of your ever-loving mind."


**Main Office**
**O'Keefe Plumbing & Heating Company**
**Main Street, City of Grantville**
**Thuringia Region, Germany**
**Tuesday, 7 December 1632 AD**
**1130 hours local**

"Here we are," Lulu said, pushing the door of the small room by the main office entrance open. "What do you think?"

"It's small, but I think it will do, Lu," Duke said. He entered the office, more a cubicle than a full fledged office, but it had real walls and a door. "Are you sure we're not going to have any problems with your family?"

"Duke, remember I'm the general manager," Lulu said, smirking a bit. "Anyway, this was my brother's office. We've only used it for storage since the Ring. Just consider it the O'Keefe Company's contribution to the support of the new Marine Corps. Claire is okay with all this, right?

"Lu," Duke said, shaking his head in bemusement, "she was the one who pushed me to agree. Not that she had to push too hard. By the way, Claire is taking charge of clearing our way through the government. She also had some ideas about how to equip ourselves that she wants to explore. Do you know a Tracy Kubiak?"

"Darnn, Duke, she really wants you out of the house." Lulu chuckled as she cleaned some spider webs with her hand. "Tracy? I think she runs a canvas tent manufacturing business from her home. She used to be a parachute rigger sergeant with the Eighty Second Airborne Division. Is she joining us?"

"No." Duke shook his head regretfully. "I think Claire wants to find out if she can be our supplier. Besides she just had a baby." As he talked, he curiously scanned the office contents for possible use.

"Oh," Lulu said. "Well, that would kind of cramp a woman's style. Okay then, what's first on the agenda?"

"We need to find some more Marines. Just the two of us, and Claire, is not going to cut it."

"Even if we have the strength of ten because our hearts are pure?" Lulu asked as she tilted her head to one side and opened her blue eyes in a wide innocent stare.

Duke snorted, amused. "Even then. We can only be in one place at a time. Do you know anyone who fits the bill?"

"Not that many," Lulu answered. "People here tend to join the army or the guard. We Marines stick out like sore thumbs. I know some WWII, Korea and Nam gyrenes but I think you mean relatively young folks."

"Yes. And I also need them with NCO experience. I think I already got one, though. Do you know Calvin Hobbs? He used to be a sergeant armorer with the Twenty Second MEU."

"I know his wife, Nancy," Lulu said. "She once told me he was into living history and weapons. Good idea, that. He may be a big help."

"I'm going to give him a call later today, Lu." Duke stopped for a second as he scratched his head. "You know, we need a corpsman, too."

"Way ahead of you, buddy. Do you remember Aunt Beulah's right hand woman, Mary Pat, Elizabeth's good buddy? Didn't she have a NCOIC working for her at military medical training? Dorrman, David Dorrman is his name."

"Yes, I remember," Duke said. "I was introduced to him when I was still working with Beth Pitre. You're right. He mentioned once that he had been an independent duty corpsman."

"He was also with the Fleet Marine Force and saw action. He's the one we definitely need to recruit." Lulu paused a moment, then straightened her shoulders as she faced him. "I've also got another one for you. But I'm not sure how you're going to feel. Just hear me out, before you say anything, okay?"

"If you insist. But so far, I like everyone that you've mentioned," Duke said as he crossed his arms and waited for her tale.

Lulu leaned against the doorframe. When she found a comfortable position, she started telling her story. "His name is William Musgrove, goes by Wild Bill. He used to work as a mechanic at Fairmont Jiffy Lube. Since the Ring, he's been working for the government in the repair shop. He was a corporal with amtracks. However, he left the Corps as a private with a BCD."

Duke eyebrows went up. "A bad conduct discharge, Lu? Just tell me there's more to his story than that."

Lulu, expecting this reaction, continued calmly after taking a deep breath. "There is. Just hear me out. I got this from a mutual friend, because Wild Bill is as closemouthed as you are. It seems that his track was redlined even after repairs and he told that to his platoon commander, a world-class asshole. The lieutenant, a rather fresh butter bar, courtesy of Canoe U and the Basic School, decided to take it for a test swim anyway, regardless of Bill's warning. His gunny was at the company, so there weren't any older and wiser heads around to reason with the idiot. Of course, to no enlisted person's surprise, the track sank. Bill had to rescue the trapped driver, who was not only his best friend but also his sister's fiancé. After they swam to shore, the lieutenant tried to put the blame on the driver. Bill lost his cool and hit the butter bar. He broke the idiot's jaw."

Duke had to shake his head. In twenty years in the Corps, he had seen variations of the same story repeated many times. "Wow, I can't say that I can blame him. But why the BCD?"

"The asshole's father was another Canoe U grad and an admiral. Bill had to take the BCD or face serious brig time."

Duke snorted in disgust as the picture become clearer. "Damn. I see. But are you sure he might still be interested in giving the Corps a chance? If I were him, I might still harbor some resentment."

"I can see him this afternoon and invite him to come over tomorrow to discuss it, Duke."

"Works for me, Lu. Next thing, recruits. We need to set high standards for the first class. I want down-timers mostly, with military experience, preferably as NCOs or officers."

Lulu nodded, as she followed his reasoning. "Let me guess—train the trainers, right?"

"Absolutely right, Lu," Duke replied, as he tested the chair behind the desk. "This chair is in severe need of oil for its wheels. Our main base is going to be in Magdeburg where King Gustavus Adolphus has set up his capital. It's a river town, so we're talking brown water operations. But if I understood the admiral's intentions, we're going to end up as a blue water navy soon enough. He's going to need Marines for both force protection and to provide his ground-fighting elements."

After making sure that the chair could support him, Duke sat down in a gingerly fashion. Lulu watched, amused. "This means that we're only going to have time to train one boot camp class here before we move the whole shebang over there," Duke said. "We need to concentrate on boots who can be trained to form the NCO cadre first. We need to have a rifle company in place in Magdeburg by the end of next year. If we do the job right, they can keep running the recruit training, so we can grow exponentially. I told the admiral we can have a battalion by the end of 1634."

Lulu raised her eyebrows as she digested the news. "Wow. That's quite a timetable, Duke. Now, I believe that Simpson went to Annapolis. They're brainwashed with the Mahan crap from day one. Still, I think it's doable. It's going to be hard on us, but doable. At least we have two advantages the guys at Turn tavern didn't have."

"Don't be so harsh, Lu. Without Captain Mahan's theories of sea power we would never have had the kind of navy or, by the same token, Marine Corps that was preeminent in the twentieth century. I just wonder how the admiral is going to apply those theories in this century. Anyway, you said that we had two other advantages. What are they? Don't keep me in suspense, Lu," Duke said, as he started clearing some of the supplies from the desk.

"Unlike them, we've got over two hundred years of accumulated Marine experience. And, of course, female logic isn't something they had either. It's a good thing you have me and Claire on your side."

Duke stopped emptying the desk and tried to repress his laughter. "I suspect I'm going to be reminded of that for a long time." He then went back to opening the desk drawers and looking at their contents.

"Say, Duke, I've got a question." Lulu cleaned a corner of the desk and perched on it. "What is going to be our policy for women in combat?"

Duke opened the last drawer and stared at its contents for a second. Then, with raised eyebrows, he slammed it shut. A perplexed Lulu could only ask. "What?"

Duke gave her an uncomfortable smile. "I think I just found your brother's stash of girlie magazines."

Lulu snorted. Then she continued speaking in a very matter-of-fact way. "Don't throw them away, Duke. I hear there are folks who pay good money for them."

Duke looked like he was expecting a joke. But when he saw her looking back without any hesitation, he decided to drop the subject and answer her question.

"When I originally talked to the admiral his plans were no females at all. I told him that if he wanted me, he'd better want you, too. I told him that because I'm not going to do everything by myself. He had to agree to that if he wanted me, so he did. And, of course, if we let you join, we can't refuse any other women who want to try."

Lulu smiled. "I'm the camel nose under the tent, I see."

"Sort of," Duke said as he leaned back in the chair. "The truth is that I'm not going to handicap myself by being forced to choose poor candidates just because they're men. I don't plan to waste my time like Jackson did at the beginning."

Lulu smirked in disgust at the mention of Jackson's name. There was bad blood between her and Jackson. After the Ring of Fire, she had offered her services to the new army. After Jackson told her he didn't needed either women or fat jarheads, Lulu was furious. In front of his staff, she had invited him to step outside so she could sweep the street with his bony doughboy ass. Luckily for Jackson's ego and health, someone had the presence of mind to get Dan Frost and Duke, who put a stop to the confrontation. Later, when Jackson had been forced to let women into his Army, Lulu had felt vindicated. But she had never tried to join up again.

Duke didn't need to be mind reader to know what his friend was thinking, so he continued talking. "Like the up-time Corps, women are going to be excluded from direct combat roles, like infantry, artillery and cavalry. I know that this is very restrictive compared with what the army allows. But they don't have to think about operating in cramped shipboard conditions or opposed beach landings. However, I don't plan to send them to the rear, either. If there is anything that the Croat raid demonstrated to everyone, it was that we don't have a rear. So, I expect every Marine, regardless of gender or duty, to remember that we are all riflemen first. I plan to train everyone under that standard. Can you live with that, Lu?"

Lulu thought for a second before nodding her approval. "Yes, I can live with that. I suppose I'd better brush off my combat skills then, eh?"

Duke smiled. "Yes. But you aren't the only one. I have to get in shape again, too. And we need to do it before we start boot camp. So, we can work up together." He started rummaging through the desk again. "Say, Lu, can you find us some pens and paper? I want to write down what we discussed so far and start working in the basic plan."

Lulu stood up and brushed her pants. "Sure, Duke. Meanwhile, can you clean the desk and the chairs? I'm going to get some of my boys to clean the place, later. You know, I remember seeing two manual typewriters in my dad's junk. I bet we can use them in Magdeburg."

"You bet we can," Duke grinned. "But I'm not sure if future generations of Marines are going to be happy with us. You know we're going to have to reinvent paperwork."

Lulu, a former administration and supply specialist, laughed hard as she exited the small office.

☆　　　☆　　　☆

## GRANTVILLE FREE PRESS
### May 11, 1633

### First Marines Complete Training
### by Jason Waters

*The early sun was not completely over the horizon when this reporter observed the last Marine "boot" passing the marker that completed the final force march of their training at the Hudson farm. Recruit Kimberly Ann Chaffin, 19, of Grantville, crossed the final line five seconds after the last man on her platoon at 0715 today, completing . . .*

## Outskirts, City of Grantville
## Road to Magdeburg
## Saturday, 21 May 1633 AD
## 0900 hours local

Claire Hudson wiped the tears out of her eyes as the last troops disappeared around the bend of the road. With a flourish, the high school band ended their rendition of "The Girl I Left Behind Me." As a sudden silence settled over the crowd, most started walking back into the direction of town. Claire felt rooted to the spot, a feeling shared by many of the women around her. All of them, with the exception of naval spouse Susan Dorrman, were Marine wives or sweethearts. She also felt a sense of déjà vu, as the memory of her participation in many departure ceremonies like this in the twentieth century mixed with the reality of 1633 Grantville.

After a deep breath, Claire took stock of the situation. She was now the de facto senior spouse, or the senior dragon lady in her husband's words. One of the last things that he had asked her to do while they were saying their goodbye was to watch out for all of them. As she looked at the mostly young women, she knew that she had a great task ahead. Gathering her flock around her, she stood by her neighbor and now duty translator, Ilse Hoffman and addressed the women.

"Ladies, tomorrow we will meet at my house for coffee at 1400 hours. That's two in the afternoon. Don't look so surprised; you married Marines and that's how they talk. Learn it. Bring your problems and we can discuss them and find solutions. The wives of Captain Lennox's unit are going to provide us with child care support like they did today at Ilse's house. You all have my phone number. If you need help or want to talk; I'm here for you. Thank you and I'll see you all tomorrow."

As the group broke up, Claire found herself walking with Susan and Ilse. Nancy Hobbs and Bill Musgrove's fiancée, Connie Miller, joined them. Nancy had her arm around Connie as she sobbed quietly. Her on and off relationship with Wild Bill seemed to be on at the moment. To the whole detachment's amusement, her overnight goodbye almost made her warrior late for the initial formation.

Looking at Claire, Susan told her, "Well this went well. At least we were not left at the pier watching the ships as they became smaller and smaller towards the horizon."

"Yes but watching a horse's rear end doing the same thing lacks some of the romance," a saddened Nancy shot back.

For several steps the group walked in silence until Claire started giggling. Then the whole group, including Ilse who had only understood part of the observation, part in hysteria and part in relief, broke into loud laughs.

Wiping her eyes, Claire spoke to her friends. "Well, it's obvious that except for Connie, we all have gone through similar experiences. At least Magdeburg is not at the other end of the world and hopefully we will be able to see the guys soon."

"They might be at the other end of the world as far as we are concerned, Claire," Nancy Hobbs replied as she kept walking with Connie. "I was hoping that after Calvin left the Corps, I would be able to keep him around but look at us now; back to square one. And this time, we have no phone or e-mail and we're back to the old-fashioned snail mail if we are lucky."

"She's right, Claire. Becoming a geographical widow again sucks. There's got to be a way to remain together," Susan added.

Claire kept walking as she thought about it. The other women waited for her insights. Finally, her mind made up, she addressed her friends. "Ladies, I have an idea but up to this moment it needed to be fleshed out. However, as I see that you all share my concerns, I feel that I can talk briefly about it. Obviously, we are going to have to refine it before we present it to the group at large. Let me talk to you about something that I'm calling Operation Exodus."

## Three Miles outside the City of Magdeburg
## Main road from Thuringia
## Monday, 6 June 1633 AD
## 1333 hours local

Gunnery Sergeant Hudson halted the Marine horse and wagon column with a sharp raised right arm sign. His "Detachment, Halt" command was relayed down the line by his junior leaders with loud shouts. He twisted on his saddle and gave the hand signal for leaders forward. As was usual whenever he did this, he couldn't stop feeling like an extra in a John Wayne movie. Loud commands once again relayed the order down the column. After weeks of training with Lennox and his cavalrymen (it was going to take Duke a long time before he felt comfortable calling them Marines) together with the practice gained during the journey, he knew mounted commands were now second nature for everyone.

Duke easily controlled his spirited mount, Henderson, with his knees. The horse tended to be easily spooked. Of course, Duke couldn't fail to appreciate the irony that a Marine infantryman who trained for most of his adult life to ride into combat in amtracks, helos and LCACs was now going into the breach on horseback.

Duke felt more than saw when the first of his gathering subordinates, Staff Sergeant O'Keefe approached him. The spires of Magdeburg Cathedral beyond the tree line beckoned him. Those spires marked the end of their two-week trip and the long months of preparation and training. The cathedral was the tallest structure on the horizon but there were other buildings, possibly new construction, that were starting to give it a run for its money.

"So, that's Magdeburg Cathedral," Lulu commented after stopping her mare, Lejeune, beside his horse.

"Yes, it is, Lu," Duke responded, looking at her intently. She looked tired, but as usual remained stoic about her discomfort. Lulu wasn't one to let her fatigue keep her from getting the job done. Once again, Duke gave thanks to the Lord for her and the remarkable group of men and women who had chosen to follow him to help in the formation of the new Marine Corps.

"Don't look like much from here," Lulu said, leaning forward on her saddle to rest her backside. Duke smiled, Lu was not a born horsewoman and he felt sympathy for her soreness.

"Wait until we get into town. The place is a goddamn phoenix. The admiral told me that for a city that was practically razed to the ground, its rebuilding is way ahead and starting to look a lot better that you could expect." Duke's eagerness for their new home and the tasks ahead started to color his voice.

Lulu smiled at her friend's enthusiasm but her reply was pre-empted by the arrival of the rest of their up-time cadre of former veterans. The first squad leader, Sergeant Hobbs, and the second squad leader, Corporal Musgrove were followed by their chief medic, Petty Officer Dorrman. Dorrman, or as he was now known, the "Chief", walked from his combination horse-drawn ambulance and first-aid wagon at the rear of the wagon formation.

"Magdeburg, I presume?" Dorrman asked as he wiped his brow with his soft "bonnie style" hat.

"Oh yes. We finally made it," Lulu replied, looking down at him. "After two weeks of invigorating horseback travel. Forget trucks, Humvees or helos, only horses for me from now on." There was more than a heavy hint of sarcasm in her tired voice. "Ouch, I can't feel my butt any longer."

"Gee, Staff Sergeant O'Keefe, did you forget already? The Corps never promised you a rose garden," Wild Bill, the youngest of the senior NCOs, joked to the chuckles of the tired group. Musgrove had definitely enjoyed the trip, occasionally commenting that he would have paid money for an adventure outing like this back up in the twenty-first century. The consensus of the older NCOs was that Wild Bill had been in the sun without a cover for way too long.

"Yeah, right, Musgrove. Tell that to my butt," Lulu shot back. Her humorous comeback was typical of the rapport that the cadre shared. Humor was a good way to ease the stress of daily life under wartime conditions. Her horsemanship had improved during the trip but everyone knew the relationship between her and her mare was, at best, an armed truce.

Duke, knowing that the conversation was only going to go downhill from there, stopped their usual mock insult humor fest cold with his instructions. "Can the chit-chat, guys. This place looks as good as any to stop for lunch. Get your people dismounted and let them take a break under the trees while we wait for the scouts' return," he ordered. "Also tell them to try to clean up a bit and secure all the loose ends. I want them to look

like Marines and not like a band of unemployed carnival people
when we arrive in town. Got it?"

"Or worse, like the army. No problem, boss." Hobbs, a quiet,
middle-sized man with unexpected depths, replied. The NCOs
quietly returned to the column and a series of barked commands
got the troops dismounted, under the trees and away from the
main road. The men went with an eagerness that indicated that
they, too, welcomed the rest stop.

Duke, after seeing to his mount and his own small needs,
watched contentedly as the others quickly got the temporary rest
stop organized. Captain Lennox had been a tough but skilled
taskmaster and instructor. *Take care of the horses first* was something Lennox believed down to his bones. And that belief was
now deeply ingrained in everyone. And, it had to be admitted,
riding certainly beat the hell out of marching. The horse herd,
which the Scotsman Lennox had personally selected, was destined
to become the Navy and Marine Corps' four-legged "motor pool"
in Magdeburg. That last thought brought Duke's attention back
to the cavalryman's special status.

When Simpson first approached him last December, seeking
help in the formation of a new Corps to support his planned navy,
Duke only expected to contend with one flavor of Marine. He was
honest enough with himself to recognize that the Scotsman was
an innocent bystander and not responsible for the "Horse Marine"
gaffe foisted on everyone by the secretary of state, Ed Piazza. He
even understood the rationale behind the decision. It just simply
caught him, Simpson and most especially, Lennox, by surprise when
President Stearns and General Jackson designated his new escort
cavalrymen as Marines, too. It made a sort of sense as in the here
and now—legations and embassies required protection by mounted
troops and on the other hand American tradition and custom was
that Marines guarded the embassies—but no one was happy with
the decision. Although Claire had found the whole situation side-
splitting hilarious, just like the rest of the wives.

At least, Duke consoled himself, unlike Lennox, he didn't have
to contend with the operalike dress uniforms that came with the
Marine guard's duty. That had been another of Ed's great ideas.

Throughout the preceding months, Duke and Lennox had had
long conversations about what being in the Corps meant, usually

over a cold beer at the Thuringen Gardens. In the process they had established a friendly working relationship. It had helped that Lennox had been favorably impressed with the Corps' basic philosophy that every Marine was first a rifleman.

Duke and Lennox had reached a compromise, of sorts. That compromise gave proof to the notion that two veteran NCOs could find acceptable solutions to any military problem—as long as there was the proper alcoholic lubrication. After the base and training organization was firmly established at Magdeburg, all of Lennox's new troops' initial training would be in Duke's hands. The plan was to start with the junior officers and then continue with the rest. That would provide every new Marine in both organizations with the same set of core competencies and values. Of course, Lennox would continue to run the specialized cavalry and diplomatic security escort training.

Overall, Duke was satisfied with the progress so far. The troops were shaping up well and had cemented the practical teamwork learned in their temporary boot camp at Grantville early in the year. Most of them would make excellent NCOs for the rifle company he needed to have in place by the end of the year. Duke watched as the group of men, following orders, sorted themselves into work details. Of course, security was quickly set up. Some things had not changed from the time of the Roman legions. Other troops saw to the horses and wagons after a detail brought water from a nearby creek for the mounts. The men were soon preparing their rations, doing general cleaning, and the all-important coffee brewing over the newly lit campfire. The last two weeks on the road had sharpened their field craft, and most had former mercenary experience, so their actions were quick and precise.

Only after the immediate tasks were completed did some of the Marines, accompanied by their new entrenching tools, seek some privacy to answer the call of nature. On their return, they were received with humorous catcalls and an occasional joker making the twenty-first century hand signal for gas attack. Duke found it mildly surprising, but amusing.

"Looks like Wild Bill's handiwork," Dorrman commented as he approached Duke.

"Must be," Duke agreed. "Chemical warfare was not in their training curriculum. And, I can't tell you, Dave, just how very happy I am with that." Another of the surprises that the past months had brought was Duke's growing friendship with the younger man. Dorrman, as he was outside of the chain of command and as senior as Duke, had assumed the role of confidant and sounding board for both Duke and Lulu.

"You were on Mike Stearns's side during that brouhaha in Congress, I gather."

"You bet," Duke said. "And I wasn't alone. As well, although he hated to admit it, the admiral supported the President's stance and would have quit in support of it."

"You really like the old man?" Dorrman asked.

Duke, after thinking for a moment, replied. "Yes, I do. And I was as surprised as you are, Dave. Simpson is not a man who is easily liked. Part of the problem is his own damn fault, I think. But, I can sympathize with his position. When we ended up here after the Ring of Fire, his domestic situation with his son, which was barely under control, went completely off into the abyss."

Dorrman nodded. "Yeah. Poor guy. I agree with you, Duke, the admiral occasionally has control issues. The sad part is that I can also see it from his point of view. Seventeenth-century Germany would not be the place I would have chosen for my forced retirement. Especially not in the company of a bunch of hicks."

Duke smirked before replying. "Then, of course, the hicks went ahead and formed an army. And, as a Navy man through and through . . . suffice it to say, and pardon the pun, he was totally out of his depth."

After a hearty guffaw, Dorrman continued. "He wasn't the only one. Remember the strange look Mary Pat gave me the first time I called "attention on deck" at the Sanitary Commission?"

"Yeah," Duke grinned. "But she got over that really quick. And later she found great amusement in the irony that an air force brat, who is now an army officer, has a navy petty officer as her NCOIC. The same way that her best friend has a Marine NCO as her platoon sergeant. Lucky for us, there's only one Coastie in the whole town."

"Damn leatherneck humor."

"Dumb squid."

Their friendly banter was interrupted when Lulu arrived from her rounds. "Everyone's doing well so far and . . . what you two are up to now?" she asked, curious at their caught-in-the-act guilty expressions.

Duke finally replied, somewhat sheepishly, "Nothing much, Lulu. Just thinking about our current situation."

Amused, Lulu snorted. "Right. Which part in particular? The lost in time part, the fact that we're supposed to start a new military service or that we are getting too old to play Lewis and Clark? And, let's not forget all the good folks who would like to see us dead or back in whichever hell we escaped from, hah?"

"Touché," Dorrman said. "I see that your new close relationship with Lejeune hasn't improved your humor."

"Respectfully, Chief," Lulu said, "bite me. I don't know how Lennox seems to enjoy all this riding, day in and day out."

Dave snorted before replying. "He was born in the saddle, Lu. The folks here are a lot hardier than we are and things are definitely different in these times. But speaking about Captain Lennox, Duke, have you changed your mind about accepting a commission like he did?"

"No," Duke shuddered. "Like I told Mike and Jackson, I feel that I'm doing the right thing. The admiral and I agreed that having up-timers as senior officers was a losing proposition in an organization that was going to be composed of almost a hundred percent down-timers. Besides, you know we don't have any trained Marine officers in our ranks to do the job. And it will be a cold day in hell before we tap the army for senior leaders."

The amused chuckles of his audience let him know that he was not alone on his low esteem for the army.

Duke smiled as he continued. "The training of good NCOs is going to provide the backbone for the new Corps and impact in their efficiency. Anyway, children, we get to recruit and train our own officers. I hope there are enough young whippersnappers in Magdeburg with the appropriate background to run through the Basic School. Still, it is going to require that we to find the right kind of leader to put it all together. We need someone who can be a disciplinarian but not a martinet, a people person, open to new ideas and concepts but still able to use his experiences and battle skills from this time effectively. In other words, we need an officer who is equally at ease on the battlefield or in the realm of academia. We need someone who can be a diplomat, move easily in the social circles and command a rifle platoon. An Archibald Henderson-type organizer, more than a Chesty Puller-style warrior, at least in the beginning."

Lulu, momentarily taken aback with Hudson's long list of requirements, was left speechless. It was a few moments before she was able to reply. "Shit, Duke. You don't ask for much, do you? I don't think Napoleon or Frederick the Great have been born yet, and Alexander and Caesar are long dead. Where do you think we're going to find this paragon of military virtue?"

Duke Hudson nodded as he considered the subject. Contrary to popular misconceptions, in the up-time American armed forces the Marines had been the true warrior intellectuals. The study of military history and other subjects was deeply encouraged and ingrained in their training. That was always surprising to those who considered leathernecks as simpletons who were always interested in the most destructive direct approach. One of Duke's personal deep-seated beliefs was that the origin of that curious inconsistency could be placed squarely at the feet of the constant bureaucratic inter-service warfare. The Marines had had to wage a hidden war for their survival every year since their formation. Actual war provided the occasional respite from the bureaucratic war that went on most of the time. The constant struggle for funds, material and missions with the much larger army, navy, and the air force had led to a relatively small organization whose leadership, both in the enlisted and officer ranks, was extremely flexible and adaptable. How to find the same flexibility and intellectual agility in down-timers was going to be interesting to say the least.

"Beats me, guys," he finally admitted. "I talked to the admiral about our requirements on his last visit to Grantville. He didn't have a good idea, either. However, he told me that he discussed the matter with King Gustav, in his role as our captain general."

A clearly puzzled Dorrman asked, "So, what did the king . . . excuse me, our captain general have to say?"

"Well, Chief, you have to remember that Gustavus Adolphus had a great reputation as a military thinker, according to our history. I expect that now, thanks to Julie, Baroness Sims, he's going to hang around to add to that image. One of his most remarkable qualities, according to the books, was his able selection of good subordinates. I'm sure he's got someone in mind."

"In other words, you don't know either, right?" Lulu asked.

"Not a clue, Lulu," Duke admitted. "And neither does the admiral. I asked him already. The king is keeping it close to his vest. He wants to wait to meet us first and do the introductions in person."

"Darn, I hate surprises." Lulu told him as she tried to dig a small rock with her boot.

"Take a number, Lulu. We are getting to the crunch now. I think we have a handle on the initial NCO manning, thanks to our recruiting in Grantville. The bottleneck, in my opinion, is going to be in our officer recruitment and training. As it stands now, our plan still calls for a fully manned company by year's end and a battalion by the end of next year. Of course, that's only here in Magdeburg. We also need to think about Lennox's requirements, which weren't in our original plans. By next year, he's going to have the equivalent of a short battalion with two companies. So, yes, you could say that I am anxious to meet the king's candidates and get the ball rolling."

Dorrman shook his head. "That's a very ambitious plan, Gunny. Do you think we're going to have the time to do it?"

"We don't have a choice in the matter, my friends," Duke said, grimly. "I don't have to read tea leaves to know that Richelieu and his friends are not going to give us the time we need for a leisurely build up. I wouldn't be too surprised that if by this time next year, we're right smack in the thick of it."

The nods of agreement and the silence that followed his statement proved that his two friends agreed with his assessment. Oh, well as Wild Bill said, no one promised us a rose garden, he thought.

Finally, Lulu cleared her throat. "And on that cheery note, I'm going to check how everyone is doing and see if Kim has taught the pup any new tricks."

Dorrman snorted. "I thought that sum of her repertoire was the ability to piddle on folks at the drop of a hat."

Lulu smiled as Duke tried to stifle a laugh.

"Well, my dear Chief, I'm hoping that Kimberly can teach Puddles to attack unsavory characters, like navy men." Lulu concluded with an innocent smile as she walked away.

"Hey, I resent that," Dorrman called after her before turning to Duke. "What are you planning to do now?"

"Do? Well Chief, it is my intention to sit down, wait and see if our company clerk can deliver lunch with the meager resources left. I left my NCOs to take care of business. I like to call that leadership. Don't you have a wagon to get ready?" Duke asked.

Dorrman smiled, amused by the seeming innocence of his

Marine friend. "Not as long as I have a corpsman striker; extra work builds his character. Anyway, Lucas is a lot better with the horses that I ever plan to be. So, let me join you and we can make sure that we don't get poisoned by our eager chef."

"That's a plan that I can live with," Duke told him as they walked towards the campfire.

Duke and Dorrman were sitting at the campfire conducting an impromptu tactical discussion with other Marines while they waited for lunch. When they heard a guard loudly announcing the scouts' return, they continued sipping their coffee. After dismounting and hobbling their mounts. the scouts left their horses in the hands of fellow leathernecks and joined Duke and the others at the campfire. Other Marines started to drift in closer to hear their report and silence quickly spread around the area. The scout leader, Lance Corporal Hans Hoffman, removed his sunglasses and began to come to attention before starting his report but was stopped by Duke's gesture. "Lance Corporal, relax. It's cold and it's been a long day for your guys. I want you all to sit down and drink your coffee first. The report can wait."

"*Danke, mein freund*," Hans murmured, as he sat down and sipped coffee from the cup someone put in his hand. Duke allowed him time to unwind.

Hans, a man in his early thirties and Duke's former neighbor, was the oldest and most experienced of the down-timer recruits. He was being groomed for a staff NCO position and, like Hudson, had rejected a Marine commission. The group that now surrounded the campfire waited patiently for his report while his fellow scouts, Gustav Franker, Noah Wilson and Dallas Chaffin also sat down to catch their breaths and warm up with coffee. They, too, had been wearing sunglasses. That suggestion from Dallas had quickly become the scouts' trademark. At last, Hans put his cup down, picked up a nearby stick and started drawing a rough map of Magdeburg.

"Admiral Simpson sends his compliments, Gunny. He's pleased that we finally made it. The navy yard is here, the embassy is here and the king's palace is there. In the yard, we can use a temporary barnlike building for quarters. However, I wouldn't move anyone inside until we have cleaned and disinfected it thoroughly. We'll need to use . . . what do you call it, Noah?"

"You mean the DDT, Hans?" Noah asked.

"DDT, *danke*. We should use it to kill all the fleas and other insects. I'm sorry, but it looks like tents again, tonight. We also need to dig new outhouses and a well to make the area livable. The admiral sent me and Mister Cantrell to check the site he's picked out for the permanent barracks. It's good and has a nice view of the river. There's space for all the planned buildings, ranges and the parade ground. As per your orders, I scouted two routes to get to the yard. One here, around the outskirts, is longer, but faster, as traffic is light. Noah scouted the other route through town. Noah?" Hans prompted Wilson to continue the report.

"Gunny, Dallas and I went through town. I got us a route but getting through is going to be a challenge. The place is like a zoo. There's traffic everywhere and no one to play traffic cop. It also stinks to high heaven, because the new sewer system is still under construction. On the other hand, it bustles with activity and energy just like Grantville, but multiplied by ten. Looks to me like a good place to live as long as you don't mind the stink or the noise. There's lots of new construction going on, so we may have problems hiring workers for the barracks. I talked to Swedish and German soldiers at the checkpoints and got the names of several of the local equivalents to a contractor. I also warned them to expect us, so we can go through the checkpoints without stopping. Hans?"

"*Danke*, Noah. Gunny, I discussed your request with the admiral. He told me that you could do whatever you think best. He also said that if you go with the main plan you really need to make sure that you show the colors. He also gave me a letter and a package for you. He said that he had wanted to wait and surprise you but thought that you could use something to start us on the right foot. Here it is." Hans passed Duke an envelope and a small package wrapped in oilskins.

"Thanks, Lance Corporal; you and your team performed admirably." Duke pitched his voice so everyone could overhear his compliment to Hans and his scouts. He then stood up to address the whole group. "Listen up, Marines. During the trip, I've talked to you about my ideas for our outfit. Right here, right now, is where we start making them a reality. We have a whole town full of civilians and allied soldiers who have never heard or seen Marines before. So, they don't have an idea of what to expect.

We have an excellent opportunity to make a good first impression and help jumpstart our recruitment efforts. We're going to ride through town and let everyone know that we've arrived. So, this is the plan. I want everyone to remain in formation, keep your horse under control and try to look sharp regardless of what we encounter. Tighten up your saddle and accoutrements. I don't want anyone falling off his or her horse in front of the crowd. Police your uniform and person and remember—today we create history. That is all. We will leave in two hours, but before we do, we will police this area. O'Keefe, Hobbs, Dorrman, Hoffman and you, too, Wild Bill. A moment of your time, please."

The other Marines moved away, some to start their preparations, others to continue their interrupted rest. Duke opened the admiral's letter as he walked away from the campfire. He quickly scanned the contents and a wide grin split his face. Lulu exchanged curious glances with the rest of her colleagues as they followed the gunnery sergeant, wondering what was going on. Duke stopped to open the package and started issuing his instructions. "Hans, I need you and your scouts to open the way for us into town and provide traffic control. Your people are going to be my road guards. Lulu, do we still have those orange construction vests we swiped from your great uncle?"

"Yes, in the first wagon. I was wondering what you wanted with them. So, Hans and his boys get to wear them, right?"

Duke stopped walking as soon as he was far enough from the main group not to be overheard. "Right, I want them to stand out like sore thumbs, Lulu. Get them those vests after lunch, please. Hans, I'm counting on you to prevent any civilians from getting in our way or getting hurt, but be polite about it. Discuss it with your scouts and maybe you can use some of the folks to help you practice your crowd control drill before we leave."

"Yes, Gunny." Hoffman replied, making a notation in his always-present notebook.

Duke turned towards the corpsman. "Dave, as soon as we arrive at the barn, I want you to collect a detail and start working on our new quarters' habitability and sanitation. The only living thing that I want sharing my bedding is my wife."

Dorrman laughed. "I share that feeling. It will be done, Gunny."

Duke then addressed his two platoon leaders. "Hobbs and Musgrove, after we arrive at the yard, we're going to conduct evening colors for the first time in Magdeburg. I want it to become a Marine responsibility from now on. Please, organize the troops and maybe get a little practice for the flag detail before we depart, okay?"

Puzzled, Sergeant Hobbs raised his hand. "Yes, Gunny, but isn't it going to be a tad too early for evening colors?"

Duke addressed the whole group with his answer. "Guys, have you seen how dark the night gets around here? Magdeburg doesn't have an electric grid yet. So, as much as I hate it, and until the night light situation improves, we're going to have to conduct evening colors while we still have daylight. Around 1700 would be my guess, just like the army."

Hobbs nodded his head as he followed the reasoning. "Makes sense. But it's going to feel funny. Well, we can adapt and improvise, Gunny."

Satisfied, Hudson smiled. "And overcome. That's the spirit, Hobbs. Now everyone, listen up. A month before we left Grantville, I wrote the admiral with some suggestions about our manning and organization. I am pleased to inform you that he not only approved my suggestions and the personnel actions I suggested, but to my surprise, has provided us the proper insignia. So, let me start with the junior man here. Hoffman, front and center." Hans, already standing in front of Duke, came to attention.

"Hans, I don't know what kind of officer you were before as a mercenary but you've impressed me in the short time you've been with us. As well as becoming my friend, you've shown me you have the makings of a good non-commissioned officer. Your wife Ilse has become an invaluable part of our ladies support efforts and a great assistance to Claire with the down-time Marine ladies. I'm sure she would love to know that we recognize your worth to the Corps with this promotion. Lu, Dave, can you do the honors and help Staff Sergeant Hoffman pin his new stripes."

Duke handed the metal devices to his surprised friends. Smiling, Dorrman and O'Keefe admired the well-made reproduction of a Marine staff sergeant collar insignia, a black painted metal device with three chevrons and a rocker with crossed rifles. Together, they approached Hoffman and carefully replaced his lance corporal devices with the new insignia before shaking his hand. Hoffman had stood ramrod straight during the proceedings, seemingly surprised and overwhelmed with emotion.

Hudson then singled out Corporal Musgrove. "Wild Bill . . . William, one of the most surprising things about you is that, unlike your nickname, you're one of the most evenhanded and well-controlled Marines that I have ever known. Of course, that's apart from your truly low sense of humor, which is better left unmentioned. We all know that you got a raw deal up-time, and had a promising career cut short. However, since you decided to join our quixotic enterprise, your enthusiasm and selflessness has shown us the kind of NCO that the up-time corps lost in the twentieth century. Is my pleasure to be able to remedy that situation in this century. On behalf of Admiral Simpson and myself, please accept the insignia of your new rank, Staff Sergeant Musgrove." Unlike Hoffman, Wild Bill had an ear-to-ear grin as his new stripes were pinned to his collars.

"Calvin," Duke said, "we all knew you reluctantly decided to leave the Corps to take care of your family when we were back in the old USA. It happened to many others, and we can't fault you for that. However, I am personally grateful that you decided to give our new Marines a chance, as your knowledge is going to come in handy in the months ahead. This promotion to staff sergeant is just a token of our appreciation and recognition of that experience." Hobbs snapped to attention and managed to keep a straight face through the informal ceremony but finally cracked up when Lulu hugged him.

"Funny, I don't remember being hugged during my last promotion," Hobbs commented as he struggled to glance at the stripes on his collar.

A mockingly serious Wild Bill replied, "Well, Staff Sergeant Hobbs, if I recall, you were then in an all male Marine unit. Of course, we certainly would not ask . . . or even tell."

"Wild Bill, I mean, Staff Sergeant Musgrove, shut up," Hobbs responded in the same vein.

"Aye, aye, Staff Sergeant," an unrepentant Wild Bill barked.

Shaking his head at their antics as he struggled to keep a straight face, Duke turned towards Dorrman. "Dave, everyone has been calling you chief since long before we started our planning. The admiral and I think it's time to make it official and make you the first official CPO of our new navy. He also told me to tell you to go ahead and advance Lucas to petty officer. Congratulations. I'm sorry you couldn't go through a formal CPO initiation. I know that you squids make a good deal out of it." As he talked, Duke handed one of the pair of chief anchors to Lulu and together they pinned the new insignia on the collar of a smiling Dorrman.

"Don't worry, Duke. I consider this two-week nature trip with you nuts a good substitute. Even so, I may have to institute a more formal program for the newer CPOs after we're established in Magdeburg. Lucas is also going to appreciate the promotion, although I may have to explain what a petty officer is. Thanks, guys."

As everyone shook Dorrman's hand, Hudson started removing his own collar stripes to everyone's surprise and then with a devilish smile, faced Lulu. As soon as she realized what he was doing, she went pale and a look of almost panic swept over her face as she tried to retreat. Her way was blocked by Dorrman and Wild Bill to everyone else's great amusement. "Lulu, you have been my friend for longer than I've known these reprobates. You were the second person to hear about Admiral Simpson's new Corps plans, but you were the first one to believe that we might have a chance. Since that moment, you've spent your every waking moment providing the logistics required. In the process you've reinvented the Marine military bureaucracy, while serving as a loyal second in command. Yet, you still found the time to become proficient in those fields that the up-time Corps female combat policies and your primary assignment in logistics left deficient. Of course, we all know that your pugilistic skills have earned the respect of down-timers far and wide." Duke stopped, letting the expected chuckles subside.

He then continued. "The admiral sent you the appropriate insignia but I would consider it an honor if you wore mine, Gunnery Sergeant O'Keefe. Sorry, they're a bit tarnished with my sweat, but I don't think you're going to mind too much." Hudson, assisted by Dorrman, pinned Lulu's new rank, ignoring the tears that ran down her cheeks as the other NCOs beamed their approval.

After a short round of hugs all around, he continued. "Our detachment is now Alpha company of the hoped for first battalion, Lennox's men are to become the first two companies of the second. Obviously, both he and we still need to recruit to our manning levels. If we work hard, I hope to see us fully deployed by the end of next year. I want you to start thinking about which people from our current ranks we're going to promote next. We have to fill all the open company enlisted leaders positions. It's my intention that we meet at the end of the week to discuss it. So, be prepared to defend your candidates. Yes, Lulu?"

"Err, Duke, pardon me but aren't you out of uniform?" she asked, looking at his now bare collar.

"Well, yes I am, Gunny. Thanks for noticing it. I just wanted to get the small and more important details out of the way. I would appreciate it if you and Hoffman do the honors," Duke answered, passing them a pair of rank devices.

"First Sergeant?" she exclaimed with a mixture of both surprise and pleasure as she looked down at the metal stripes with a diamond instead of crossed rifles. "I see you finally got the rank you ought to have had many years ago. Congratulations, my friend." Lulu hugged Duke first and then she and Hoffman pinned the new insignia.

After accepting everyone's congratulations, Duke continued. "Thank you, people. After we're all settled down in Magdeburg it's my intention to pay for the first round of drinks. We'll do that at a time and place to be announced later. New stripes need to be properly wet down."

"Darn, Top, is that the only way to get you to pay for booze? We may need to get you promoted more often," Wild Bill interjected, to the group's amusement.

"Hardee har har, Musgrove," Duke said. "Start counting your pennies. I expect everyone here to pay for at least a round. I'm not the only one being promoted. Now, lady and gentlemen, there is a lot of work to be done before we enter Magdeburg. I see that the so-called chicken stew seems to be ready and the rest of the troops have been served. Let's get our lunch and get this show in the road."

"Aye, aye, First Sergeant," the group chorused before returning to the campfire.

**Three Miles outside the City of Magdeburg**
**Main road from Thuringia**
**Monday, 6 June 1633 AD**
**1535 hours local**

Duke finished checking Henderson' tack and bridle, adjusting his leather straps as the horse contently munched on nearby grass.

After one final tug, he dropped the blanket and stirrups into place, then pulled his cover from his saddlebags. Like the rest of his small command, he had traded his road-weary bonnie-style floppy hat for a starched utility cover. His hands lingered on it for just a second as he thought of Claire starching and pressing it with her own hands. He missed her so badly that he could taste it. Putting aside his feelings of longing, he placed the cap squarely on his head, automatically checking the proper angle of the bill over his eyes with two fingers. Then, with his boot in the stirrup and his grasp on the saddle pommel, he hoisted himself into the saddle.

His Marines had policed the area well within the allotted time, providing ample opportunity to practice the drills required during their arrival in Magdeburg. Now ready, they stood by their mounts and wagons. The scouts took position at the head of the line, marked easily by their bright orange construction vests. As he watched the now silent ranks, Duke felt a momentary sense of pride in their achievements so far. Earlier, he had been especially touched, when each of the junior Marines had made the point of seeking him out to congratulate and shake his hand. Well, not everyone.

Kim Chaffin, his lone woman Marine, hugged and kissed him on the cheek instead as she whispered that she was doing it on behalf of his absent wife and daughter. That unexpected gesture had touched him deeply, making him glad that he had been able to walk away before his vision became completely misted. Later, looking into Noah and Dallas's beaming faces as they offered their own congratulations, he could not help but think that his son, James, had also been there in spirit.

In spite of all that, Duke could still have gotten depressed at the memories as he had many times before, but Wild Bill had unexpectedly come to his rescue with one of his practical jokes. Instead of being depressed, Duke found himself trying to keep a straight face as he watched Wild Bill and his whole squad of like-minded scoundrels fall on their knees, bow with their arms extended and touch the ground several times as newly promoted Gunnery Sergeant O'Keefe walked by. They loudly proclaimed that they were not worthy to be in her presence to a deeply mortified, but pleased, Lulu. Duke wondered what she would do to get even but rested assured that it would be entertaining.

Shaking himself out of his woolgathering, Duke looked down

at his watch and decided that it was time. He rode Henderson to join O'Keefe in front of the formation. As he rode bedside her, he asked her sotto voce. "How you are doing, Lu?"

Lulu answered back in the same way. "Petrified and exhilarated at the same time. I can't believe that we are here at all. Not after all the problems we had. I just wish that Claire were here with us."

Duke smiled fondly as he thought of his wife. "Yes, I would have loved that, too. But I'm sure she's with us in spirit."

Lulu smiled back before looking at the formed troops again. "Yes, she is. Lord, there are so few of us for what we need to do."

Duke looked at their Marines, too. "Few, but very proud. They'll do."

Lulu smiled in reply and Duke gave her a silent nod, which she returned before barking her first command in her much practiced parade ground voice. "Marines, prepare to mount. MOUNT." Then, together, Duke and she slowly trooped the line, looking for but not finding any discrepancies. Duke took heart in their confidence and smart bearing before returning to the front, where he addressed the formation.

"Ladies and gentlemen, in a short while we are going to enter the capital city of Magdeburg to join our naval brethren for the first time. There, waiting for us, is the beginning of a new chapter in Marine history. To those of us born in the twentieth century this is another episode in the over two-hundred-year-old continuous saga of glory and sacrifice. To those of you born in this century, is the first chapter of your own glorious tale. During your training, you learned of the likes of Manila John Basilone, Daly, Butler, Lejeune, Henderson, Chesty Puller and countless others. They were men and women like you, no more and no less. They helped write each page in those chapters with their selfless dedication, sacrifice, blood and courage. I hope that you, like me, have found their lives a source of inspiration. But at the end, they belong to a future that will never be. This means that in you now rests the requirement to write the first chapters in your own book. It will be a place where others, one day, will seek their inspiration. I know it sounds like a daunting task. But rest assured that, like those Marines who precede us, you now have the wherewithal to excel and shine on your own. Because, I'm telling you, you all have what it takes and my personal trust and confidence." Duke stopped, letting his words sink in before continuing.

"On a personal note, I am grateful for your heartfelt congratulations and I'm sure that I spoke for the rest of us in thanking you for your well wishes." Duke let a smile cross his face before continuing. "I am also sure that Gunnery Sergeant O'Keefe will find the time to acknowledge everyone's best wishes, especially those of second squad." A roar of laughter broke from the ranks at Lulu's toothsome smile aimed at the suddenly guilty looking party.

"Okay, listen up. folks. When we arrive in the city, we are not only going to be on display for the good citizens of Magdeburg, but more important, our comrades-in-arms in the army, navy and Swedish forces. Let's give them a show. What say you, MARINES?"

"OOO-RAH!" Their enthusiastic roar disturbed the horses and shook leaves from nearby trees. It was to Duke's complete satisfaction.

"Okay, let's shove off and get this show on the road. MUELLER!" Duke barked.

"Yes, Gunny, I mean, First Sergeant."

"Let's show our colors, son. Uncase the guidon!"

"Aye, aye, First Sergeant."

Duke watched as Joseph pulled the cover from the unit guidon that his wife, Claire, had sewn for them. The guidon was finished with a stitch from each of the wives, sweethearts, mothers and sisters of the company members in their heartfelt wish for their loved ones' safe return. It was a new tradition in the making for their new Corps. The bright scarlet color of the swallowtail pennant with the rich gold of the globe and anchor on its center added a festive touch to the formation as it fluttered in the early afternoon light.

Satisfied, Duke nodded again to O'Keefe to give the order to start them on their way to the city and an uncertain future. "Scouts, Post! Detachment . . . belay that. COMPANY, column of twos, by the left, Forward HOOO!"

First Sergeant Hudson then spurred his horse forward to take his place at the head of the column. Gunnery Sergeant O'Keefe and the guidon bearer followed, as they led A company of the 1st Marine battalion into the City of Magdeburg for the first time in the new Corps story.

## *Acknowledgements:*

A work of fiction has many helpers apart from the main author. In one where the author is trying to write in a second language, the helpers are crucial. So, to everyone who provided his or input at work or in the bar, a heartfelt thanks. Particular thanks go to Cindy Ridgley.

Last to my editor Paula Goodlett, who kept me on track with her corrections, suggestions and insights, this is a lot better work than the story that I originally started, many thanks.

# Elizabeth

## Ernest Lutz and John Zeek

Frank Jackson took a swallow of beer and settled back in to his chair. "Ah," he said. "Nothing better than beer on a summer day. Now, about the transportation problem we were discussing, Dan, we're going to have to support a larger army in the field. We've done pretty well with the vehicles around here so far, but they aren't going to be enough."

Dan Frost took a sip of his own beer and nodded. "I know it's a problem, Frank. Do you have any ideas on how to fix it?"

"Well, the obvious choice is to start building wagons," Frank said. "But if we do that we're going to need a lot of them. And that doesn't include all of the horses we'd need. Not to mention the equipment we'd need to outfit them, and the feed the horses will need when deployed."

"What about trains?" Dan asked.

Frank shook his head. "We're nowhere near ready with the rail lines we have right now. And with all the infighting going on with Quentin Underwood and company, I don't know when we'll ever finish the line to Halle. Torstensson is in town and one thing we discussed was the slow progress of the railroad."

Dan thought for a moment, letting his gaze travel around the room. His eyes lit on a Military Police lieutenant and an idea began to grow. "You know, Frank, there might be a way. Hang on a second, let me get someone." Dan waved and shouted, "Lieutenant Pitre, come here for a sec, will you?

"I think you need to talk to this Lieutenant Pitre," Dan said as the young woman made her way to the table. "She showed us some pictures the other day that may be a start on a solution to your transportation problem.

"Elizabeth, have you ever met Frank Jackson?" Dan asked.

"I think we talked a couple of minutes at Rita's wedding, sir. I know your wife, though," Elizabeth said, nodding at Frank.

"Frank, this is Elizabeth Pitre, New Orleans' gift to the Ring of Fire, MP lieutenant, and paratrooper," said Dan in introduction. "Elizabeth, General Jackson was talking about the problems we're going to have with keeping the armies supplied in the field. We don't have anywhere enough trucks to go around and we probably won't have enough for years. Would you tell him about the railroad your grandfather works on in England?"

"Well, sir, Granddad Spencer volunteers at the Imperial War Museum at Duxford, north of London. He works on a narrow-gauge railway that was standard in the British forces from WWI up into the 1960s. Besides a couple of paperbacks my granddad gave me, I've a bunch of pictures on my computer."

"Why don't you come over to headquarters tomorrow morning around ten? You've got me thinking and I want to bring a couple of other people to see your pictures," Frank said.

"Sir, I'll be there. I just need a few seconds to set up and plug in my laptop. I'll bring the books my grandfather gave me, too," Elizabeth said.

Elizabeth showed up at headquarters in a neatly pressed set of BDUs. She wore the black bar of a first lieutenant on her right collar, and the crossed pistols of the Military Police on her left. Instead of standard army boots, she was wearing black rubber riding boots.

General Jackson and two men were waiting in his office. One of the men was an older up-timer and the other was a down-time officer. She didn't know who either of them was.

"Elizabeth, this is General Lennart Torstensson and Charlie Schwartz. Charlie worked on the railroad link to the coal mine and helped to build the steam locomotive. He also worked on the B and O for more years than he likes to admit. General Torstensson is the captain general's chief of artillery," Frank said. "Gentlemen, this is Elizabeth Pitre, who, I'm told, might just have the makings of a solution to our transport problem. Why don't you set your computer up on this table and you can talk us through your pictures."

Setting up the laptop and getting to the right place took a few moments. Elizabeth began her presentation, "Sir, this picture is of a Simplex twenty-five horsepower gasoline powered locomotive pulling four cars at the Imperial War Museum at Duxford. It is on a six-hundred-millimeter gauge railway, which is very close to two feet. This was the standard size light railway used by all sides during the First World War."

Elizabeth continued showing pictures, "The beauty of this system is that you use prefabricated track you can lay virtually anywhere and very quickly. You can also move a great deal of material over one of these systems. Most of the freight cars were rated to carry a ten-ton load."

She showed pictures in a WWI diorama setting. "Another good thing about this gauge is that it is small enough to run through a trench close to the front lines."

Torstensson asked, "You said they could carry a lot of weight, can you carry big things like cannon on one of these little trains?"

"Yes, sir," Elizabeth said. She pulled out a small paperback book titled *Narrow Gauge at War* and showed them a picture of a railcar carrying a large fieldpiece and then another picture of a standard gauge railway gun being hauled over several cars.

"How hard would it be to build some of these trains?" asked Torstensson.

"Charlie, what do you think?" Frank asked.

"You know, I bet you could use a garden tractor for a locomotive on something like this," Charlie Schwartz answered. "I think we might just be able to come up with something that would work, but track is going to be the problem."

"Would you try to build something like this for us?" Frank asked.

"I'll be glad to help and advise, Frank. But you really need to have a unit to experiment with this and figure out what will and won't work," Charlie said.

"Would you command the unit, if I authorized the formation of it?"

"Frank, I said I'd be glad to help and advise, but I'm too old to command something like this. You need a bright young officer to take charge of this. I'll teach him everything I know," Charlie answered.

"Excuse me, sir," Elizabeth said, "Why don't you appoint Mr. Schwartz as a chief warrant officer? It would give him the rank and authority he needs to train everyone in this unit."

"Chief warrant officer? What is that?" Torstensson asked.

"Chief warrant officer is a rank used in the U.S. Army for technical experts. A lot of army pilots had that rank, back up-time. It's like what you do with master gunners in your artillery," Frank answered. "Elizabeth, that's a perfect solution. That is, if Chief Schwartz has no objection?"

"Hmm, Chief warrant officer, I think I could live with that," Charlie said as he looked at Elizabeth with a twinkle in his eyes. "But I need a really bright young officer to teach and to lead this unit. I originally said I'd teach him but it could very easily be a 'her.'"

Jackson and Torstensson looked at the young woman standing in front of them. They could see the obvious intelligence in her eyes and that she knew what was coming next. Torstensson had a question first, "Lieutenant, what is that device you have on your uniform above the words U.S. Army?"

"Sir, those are jump wings. That means I jumped five times out of a perfectly good airplane with a parachute and lived to tell about it," she said.

Glancing over at Frank, Torstensson said, "She's definitely tough enough to do this. And from this presentation, she has more knowledge about these little trains than anyone in this room."

"Lieutenant, you just got a new job," Frank said. "You're now commander of the First Railway Company (Provisional). Right now the company is you and Chief Schwartz. You two get together tomorrow and come up with a list of what you'll need to get started."

"Lieutenant, after you get things started, I'll send down a liaison officer to work with you to figure out how best to use these little trains of yours," Torstensson said.

"Sir, I was supposed to go on a duty swing with the Military Police starting ne—" Elizabeth began.

"You don't worry about any of that," Frank interrupted. "I'll deal with Dan Frost."

"Yes, sir." Elizabeth sighed. "If I'm going to be transferred, can I take a couple of people from the MPs with me? I'm going to need all the help I can get to make this work." Mentally she was kicking herself for not keeping her mouth shut.

"Let me know who you want from the MPs and report here tomorrow morning. I'll have a place for you and Charlie to start work," Frank said. "Go on now; you really did a good job with this and we need to pick your brains as much as Charlie's."

"Yes, sir." Elizabeth said. As she walked away she felt like she had just gone from the frying pan into the fire.

Before leaving headquarters Elizabeth and Chief Schwartz met up and had a cup of coffee together. The chief started out with some ideas he had. "I know someone we should get on board pretty quickly," he said. "Anse Hatfield. He ran a switch locomotive up in Detroit for a few years. Besides that, he has a couple of lawn tractors and other stuff that we might need."

"Hatfield. I think I've heard of him," Elizabeth said. "Isn't he also a bit of a gun nut, too?"

"Yep," Chief Schwartz answered. "and he can probably provide some weapons out of his stash. I bet we aren't going to have a very high priority for weapons."

"Works for me," Elizabeth said. "If he has any sort of railroad experience, that's a good thing. The tractors and weapons are gravy."

Chief Schwartz was walking by the power plant when he saw Anse Hatfield and three other men. They were sitting outside the little tavern up the road from the power plant. Two of Anse's companions were obviously German mercenaries. The other Charlie wasn't sure about. The fellow was wearing khaki work pants and a Blue Barn dog food baseball cap but also had a German farmer's shirt. His boots never came from a store, either. Charlie didn't know him and he knew most of the West Virginians.

"Hey, Hatfield. Got a minute? I need to talk to you," Charlie called.

"Sure, Charlie. We're just sitting here resting up from the afternoon shift," Anse replied. "By the way do you know the guys?"

"Can't say I've had the privilege, I'm Charlie Schwartz," he said, extending his hand.

"This is Wilfried Schultz, Bernhard Toeffel and Jochen Rau." Anse pointed to the Tavern and added, "Benno and Jochen run this place and Wili works with me at the power plant, pushing coal."

"Glad to meet you fellows," Charlie said, looking over the trio. Toeffel and Rau, both in their twenties, were obviously former mercenaries, but Schultz was harder to place. Schultz didn't look like a mercenary, but the gun on his hip didn't make him look like a farmer either.

"Okay, what do you need? Do you want a beer before we start talking?" Anse asked. "Benno makes a pretty good brew."

"No beer, Hatfield. I'm on duty," Charlie said, pointing to the bar on his collar. "I'm in the army now. You'll notice I'm a chief warrant officer. Since you're a friend you don't have to call me sir. You can call me Chief."

"Well, since I'm not in the army, how about I keep on calling you Charlie? The offer of a beer still stands. I'll even buy, just to show you I still like you even though you're an officer," Anse replied.

"Anse, that's what I want to talk to you about. Were you serious when you said you drove a switch engine?" Chief Schwartz asked, wondering if he could convince Anse to join his unit. "We could use a man with that kind of experience."

"Sure, I was serious. I ran a switcher for five years. And, what do you mean 'we'? You mean the army needs me? I don't mind the militia, but if you're talking full-time army . . . I need to think about it. Besides, what does the army need with some one who can run a switch engine? I don't see too many switchers around. That coal for the power plant would be a lot easier to move if we had one," Anse said.

"Anse, we're putting together a crew to build a narrow gauge railroad. It won't be like the one they're building to the oil field, though. It will be a tactical rail to follow and supply Gustav's army. Something quick and dirty, throw down the track, run a supply line faster than horses, pull it up and move on. You'd be perfect to train engineers, since you know how an engine is supposed to work," Chief Schwartz said.

"Well, it sounds like a good idea, but I repeat, what are you going to use for an engine? I still don't see any around," Anse replied.

"Don't you start laughing," Chief Schwartz said, shifting uncomfortably. "We're going to use a lawn tractor. I think eighteen to twenty horse power will be plenty for what we want. It will be small enough that we can load it on a barge or wagon to move it around. I don't notice anyone mowing their grass since the Ring of Fire, and those little motors are going to waste."

"What gauge are you going to use? And where are you going to get track? There's a lot more to a railroad than just an engine," Anse said, shaking his head.

"That's what this unit is for. We're going to solve all those problems and any others that crop up. For example you left out brakes and wheels. This is an experiment to find out if it can be done. It is important. You know how they supply armies in the here and now, don't you? We're trying to give them a better system. Gustav is going to be fighting a defensive war and you can't rob your own people and expect them to like it," replied the chief. That got the attention of all four men.

"Sounds like you at least have the questions figured out, Chief. But where are we going to get a lawn tractor?"

Schwartz noticed the change from 'you' to 'we' and began to think that he had just gotten an engineer. "Well, I was going to leave that to the engineer to figure out. If I remember correctly you had a nice Gravely ride-on tractor at one time. What ever happened to it? The government would pay for it, you know."

"Yeah, I still have it. Me and Hank are changing it over to run on ethanol right now. Don't know why, our lawn care business is pretty well dead. It's a twenty-seven horse power Professional Model, to be exact. Think it would work?"

"That's just what we need, nice heavy tractor with good power. Now all I need is someone to drive it since you're not interested," Charlie said.

"Wait a minute," Anse said. "I never said I wouldn't do it. If you're going to use my tractor I might as well go with it. I went through Nam as an enlisted man and what was good enough then is good enough now. With that condition, sign me up, Chief."

"Well, I just happen to have an opening for a sergeant in charge of a train crew," Charlie said. "Sew three stripes on your sleeve and meet me and Lieutenant Pitre at Frank Jackson's office at nine o'clock tomorrow morning. You better remember that he's General Jackson, and be on time."

"Lieutenant Pitre? You mean you're not in charge?" Anse asked noticing the looks on the faces of his three friends.

"No, Sergeant Hatfield, I'm not. We're working for a real U.S. Army officer who knows all about narrow gauge railroads. I'll see you tomorrow morning," Charlie said.

After the chief left, the three down-timers began to speak at once. "Lieutenant Pitre from the MPs? She threatened to arrest us after the business with Wili's cow came out," Rau finally said over the general noise level.

"*Ja*," Toeffle agreed, "und the police don't like our tavern."

"Guys, I get tired of sitting around just spinning my wheels. This is my chance to do something. Pushing coal at the power plant is not my idea of a long-term career," Anse stated.

"Und we will be helping protect farmers." Wili stated. "I will join."

"Are you sure, Wili? This isn't like being in a local militia."

"*Ja*, Ich go with my brother." Wili responded as he laid his hand on Anse's shoulder.

Toeffel looked at Rau. "Jochen, business is bad. We should sell the tavern und go with them." Then with a grin at Hatfield he added, "We are the real soldier here. Und we will protect the old men."


Later that evening, Elizabeth and her old college roommate, Caroline Platzer, were having dinner at the Thuringen Gardens. Elizabeth was not in the best of moods with this new assignment.

"What kind of miracle does this bunch of hillbillies expect me to pull out of my ass?" Elizabeth ranted. "At least with the MPs I'm doing something useful."

"Beth, like you've told me on more than one occasion, lead, follow, or get the hell out of the way," Caroline responded. "Who knows, you might actually get something going. I know you will do better than that bunch claiming to be laying a line to Madgeburg."

On that note, Elizabeth changed the subject. Caroline wisely followed her friend away from the subject of railroads for the rest of the evening.


Early the next morning, Elizabeth and Chief Schwartz met at Army headquarters. They were given a room with a table, a couple of chairs, and a telephone to use.

"Well Chief, I'm glad I got a couple of people from my old MP platoon. One of the first things we're going to need is a company clerk. Someone has to answer the telephone and track messages," Elizabeth said.

Chief Schwartz chuckled, "Ma'am, I think you're right. No military ever ran right without paper."

Elizabeth passed on some of her father's observations about armies and paperwork as she explained her background. She was an army brat of sorts. Her father was a reserve colonel who worked in the Pentagon as a civilian. Her mother had served as a nurse in the British Army. Her brother had served in the Coast Guard and was in his third year at Louisiana State University. Elizabeth told the chief about a videotape she found in the items she was planning to take home after Tom and Rita's wedding reception.

They found a TV/VCR and brought it into the office. Chief plugged it in and Elizabeth inserted the videotape. The tape started and Elizabeth forwarded it through scenes of a very young Elizabeth and her slightly older brother with their parents.

"This is what I think you'll be interested in," Elizabeth said. A very old man appeared in the screen with a man Chief now knew as Elizabeth's granddad. "This is my great-grandfather," she said. "He spent three years on the Western Front running these trains. I was probably about six when they filmed this; it wasn't long after that he died."

The old man began to speak, standing next to a locomotive like the one they had seen in the pictures. "Chief, you'll probably understand this a lot better than I did last night," Elizabeth said.

Chief Schwartz heard a man with an American accent asking questions of the old man and the old man's detailed answers. The interview continued for about ten minutes.

After finishing the interview, Elizabeth turned the TV off and turned to the chief. "What do you think?" she asked.

Rubbing his chin thoughtfully, the chief replied, "We might just be able to pull this off. The biggest problem we're going to have is track."

"Here's something else that might be of help," Elizabeth said as she pulled out her copy of *Narrow Gauge at War*. "We should probably get a couple of copies made of this book and get everyone to read it. Folks might have some ideas after seeing this."

"Good idea," the chief replied.

"I agree that we can probably pull this off," Elizabeth said. "Since I've been here, I've seen all sorts of stuff that people hang on to. We can probably come up with the stuff for the locomotives and cars pretty easily, but track is what is going to make or break us. I don't think it's as big a problem as some people might think, though."

"What do you mean?"

"Well, I've ridden over a lot of the territory in the Ring of Fire. Once I started thinking about it, I realized that there are a bunch of old railway rights of way. They didn't look as wide as normal rail lines," Elizabeth said. "We need to get out there soon and start looking around."

"Sounds like a good idea to me. At nine I've our first recruits coming to see General Jackson," the chief said. "He has a twenty-seven horsepower lawn tractor that he's willing to contribute as our first locomotive."

Elizabeth chuckled, "Chief, you and I are going to get along just fine. I need to go down to City Hall and find out where they found some space for us to set up a shop. I should be back in time to meet our recruits and I'll also start scrounging around for a clerk. What about tools?"

"Well, ma'am, I've got some things we can use and Anse Hatfield, he's our first recruit, has a bunch of stuff in his shed that will probably be of use to us."

Just then, there was a knock on the door and a young man stuck his head in. Sergeants Bicard and Born and Corporals Kerner and Schmidt from the MPs were reporting in for duty. Along with them was a young down-time man named Ludwig Bode. Bode didn't want to study classics any more, he said. When Elizabeth learned he could operate a computer and answer a telephone he was made the company clerk. Because he had had a year of ROTC, he didn't have to go to basic training, either.

"Sergeant Bicard, you're on your way to OCS," Elizabeth said. "After OCS, you come back here and take charge of the horse-drawn trams." Sergeant Bicard nodded his understanding with a smile on his face.

"Staff Sergeant Born, Sergeant Kerner, and Sergeant Schmidt, you three will have your hands full here," Elizabeth said. The three newly promoted NCOs nodded in understanding. "Sergeant Born will be the platoon sergeant of the horse-drawn tram platoon and Sergeant Kerner will be the Headquarters squad leader as soon as he trains our new recruit here to be a clerk," Elizabeth continued. "Sergeant Schmidt, you are now the mess sergeant. We will come up with a field kitchen where you won't have to cook over an open fire any more."

Later that morning, Anse and his friends reported to General

Jackson's office. When Elizabeth saw the three Germans with Anse, she and the chief had a quick discussion before going into General Jackson's office. After the meeting with General Jackson, Elizabeth asked them to follow her to the company office.

"Sergeant Hatfield, I don't know how you are able to attract some of the most dubious company in Grantville," Elizabeth said. Anse tried to respond, but Elizabeth cut him off. "At this point, beggars can't be choosers. I'll give the three of you a chance. But, I'll be watching and you better believe that I will run your rear ends clear out of Grantville if you get out of line, understood?"

Anse and the three Germans nodded their understanding.

"Ma'am, is there anything else?" Anse asked.

"Nope, just get with the chief to get directions on where to bring the tractor," Elizabeth said.

After directing Hatfield where to bring the tractor, Elizabeth and the chief then back to their office. They had a lengthy discussion about what else they would need besides people to operate and maintain equipment. The first thing was track-laying and maintenance crews. Second was communications, since they knew they wouldn't get radios. Chief Schwartz suggested old-fashioned telegraph.

Before going to lunch, Chief contacted Pearl Chaffin, a widow who had worked for years as a telegrapher on the B&O. She agreed to take an appointment as a warrant officer and to train the telegraph operators for the railway unit.

After lunch that day, Elizabeth and the chief met back at the office. They had a locomotive and a telegraphy trainer, but they weren't sure how they would get fuel. While discussing the matter, Chief remembered J.B. Torbert, who owned a still outside of town. J.B. Torbert was the town drunk before the ROF. However, finding himself in seventeenth-century Germany had been the motivitation for him to stay sober, one day at a time.

Chief Schwartz caught a ride with an army car out to Torbert's place after the discussion with Elizabeth. He called for J.B., but did not get a response. He saw some smoke coming out of the woods behind the trailer and walked out there, continuing to call for J.B. Torbert.

J.B. was out back tending his still. "Oh, hi, Charlie," Torbert said, "What are you doing out here?"

"Got something I'd like to talk to you about," the chief said. "You still brewing alcohol in that still of yours?"

"Yep, but only for fuel," Torbert replied. "And I've got a bunch of handyman jobs that are keeping me busy, too."

"Would you be interested in selling your still to the army?"

"The army," Torbert exclaimed. "What does the army need a still for? And what's an old man like you doing in the army?"

"You're now looking at Chief Warrant Officer Schwartz of the First Railway Company. We're going to build a unit that can lay track and operate a narrow gauge railroad," the Chief answered.

"Who's we and what's narrow gauge?"

"Well, we just got started yesterday. There's Lieutenant Pitre from the MPs, who will command. She's bringing four people from the MPs and we have a brand-new clerk. Anse Hatfield is bringing his tractor along. That's what we'll use for our test locomotive. He's got three down-time German friends of his who are joining, too," replied the Chief. "Oh yes, narrow gauge. That's when the track is smaller than normal. We're looking at something in the two-to-three foot range for a gauge. That's a lot lighter and easier to put down. Something like one of those little trains in amusement parks."

"What does she know about railroads?" asked Torbert.

"Actually, she's the one that General Jackson got the idea from. Her grandfather works on a military narrow gauge railroad in a museum up-time, so she's got some pictures. She showed me some real detail from an old videotape of her great-grandfather who actually worked on one during World War One," Chief Schwartz said. "And she's smart, really smart, someone who can look at something and come up with a solution where no one else can."

"Well, you're going to need someone to run this still. How about I come along with it?" Torbert asked.

"The lieutenant and I figured that's what you'd say. We'll take you, but she says if you fall off the wagon, you're gone."

"That sounds fair," Torbert said.

"One other thing; we'll probably make a lot of use out of your handyman skills. Do you have some tools to bring along?"

"Well, I've my hand tools, a power saw, a drill, and a couple of electric screwdrivers," Torbert said.

"That's real good. Can you have the still ready to move tomorrow morning? If you can, I'll send Anse Hatfield out here with some people to help you move it."

"I'll have it ready."

"Welcome to the First Railway Company, Sergeant Torbert." The chief held out his hand.

"Sergeant Torbert. I like the sound of that," Torbert said, shaking the chief's hand.

The next morning Private Ludwig Bode was playing solitaire on the office computer at his desk. The desk was in front of the TacRail office. Ludwig was congratulating himself on the easy job he had found. He was surprised when General Jackson and a younger man walked up the hall toward his desk.

"Gut Morning, General," Bode said. Coming to attention and trying to turn off the computer monitor at the same time wasn't working out too well.

"Is Lieutenant Pitre in, Private? Tell her I'm here to see her."

"Yes sir, General. The lieutenant and Chief Schwartz are going over the morning reports right now. You can go right in."

"Wait here, Bill," Frank said to the younger man as he entered the office. Inside he found Lieutenant Pitre and Chief Schwartz standing by the desk looking over some paper work.

"Good morning Lieutenant, Chief. I stopped by to see how things were going and to bring you a new man," the general said. "He will be perfect as your top sergeant, Lieutenant. He's a combat veteran up-time and in the here and now. With your two up-timer sergeants being the town drunk and a loafer whose only real job before the ring of fire was mowing grass, you need someone who knows what he's doing."

"Thank you, General," Elizabeth said. "We always need more people, but Torbert and Hatfield are doing a good job. And Torbert hasn't touched a drop since the Ring of Fire."

"Be that as it may, Plotz is yours." Frank opened the door and called, "Come in here, Bill. This is Bill Plotz, veteran of Desert Storm and Bosnia. He won a Bronze and Silver Star and has a Purple Heart with two clusters. He was a crew chief in the mine before it closed and acted as a sergeant in the Battle of the Crapper and at Jena. Besides that, he's one of the hardest men in town. He's just the man you need to get your people under control. The story about how Hatfield pulled one over on you about those coveralls is all over town."

"General, while Hatfield didn't show the best judgment with the coveralls," Elizabeth said, "I gave the okay on their issue. It was a good idea because many of my people were down to rags."

"Don't cover for him, Lieutenant. Maybe he's going to do a good job and maybe he should go back to shoveling coal at the power plant; time will tell. But for now you have First Sergeant Plotz as your top soldier and he's going to watch over Hatfield and his merry men." With that closing comment General Jackson strode out of the office.

Elizabeth turned to Chief Schwartz, "Chief, you were going to check with Sergeant Torbert about how much more of that rail from the lumber trail is serviceable. I think you should to do that now and then stop by the locomotive shop and pick up a coverall for yourself. I'll bring the first sergeant up to speed on the unit."

Elizabeth could tell by the worried look on his face that the chief thought she couldn't deal with Plotz by herself. It was also easy to see that Sergeant Plotz had little respect for her rank or skills. After a year in the MPs and her informal Officer Basic Course under Gunnery Sergeant Duke Hudson, Elizabeth knew she could hold her own.

"Well, First Sergeant, what do you know about railroads? You realize you're going to be serving over men more knowledgeable and experienced than you?" Elizabeth asked.

"Ma'am, I think the general made it clear my job is to keep the men in line and not to be creative. I'll leave that to the management types," First Sergeant Plotz replied.

"And you think I'm one of those management types, First Sergeant?" Elizabeth asked.

Plotz looked at Elizabeth's jump wings which she had transferred to her coveralls that morning. "No, ma'am. Two groups of people I never argue with are paratroopers and MPs and I understand that you have been both. So I guess you're not one of those management types."

"Actually First Sergeant, I'm one of the managers of our little enterprise and you're going to have to be one also if you stay with us. And as a management type your style had better fit with mine or we're going to be working at cross purposes, I hope you understand that. If you're going to be the first sergeant of the rail company you're going to have to learn to be creative. And First Sergeant, you mentioned the MPs. From what I remember from my reading of police records your command style is quite different from mine. And you're going to use my style. Is that understood, First Sergeant? Or do I tell General Jackson to find another home for you?"

"No, Lieutenant. I think I'll stay with the railroad for a while. You never know, I might become one of those management types."

"Fine, Top. Let's go down to the train shop and introduce you to the train crew, and then over to the mess to meet Sergeant Liesel Schmidt who runs our commissary squad or else you won't get fed. Then we'll go to the rail shop and meet the track crew. You know Hatfield and Torbert, but you don't know Born. All the soldiers need to know who you are."

Elizabeth and Chief Schwartz were at the unit mess having a cup of hot soup when PFC Rau came up to them out of breath like he'd been running.

"Fraulein Lieutenant, Herr Schwartz, I was out hunting and I came across something you really need to see."

"What is it, Private?" Elizabeth asked.

"Fraulein Lieutenant, it looks like some iron tracks going into a hole in the ground," Rau replied.

"Chief?" Elizabeth asked.

"Ma'am, it sounds like an abandoned dog hole mine to me," said Chief Schwartz. "We really need to look at this; there could be some stuff we could use there."

"I couldn't agree with you more. Let's grab some of the others and have a look," Elizabeth replied.

When they got to the old mine, they found about twenty yards of track going into a boarded-up entrance. It looked as if it had been abandoned for years.

Elizabeth and the chief looked at each other like they'd won the lottery. "Chief, am I seeing what I think I'm seeing?" she asked.

"Ma'am, I just wonder what else we're going to find once we get these boards off," said Chief Schwartz. "Anse, Bill, let's get everyone up here, get this place opened up and start getting this stuff out of here."

"Chief, why don't we move some of our prefab track out here? We could get some more equipment here and haul it back," Elizabeth said.

"Ma'am, I'll send word back to Torbert to get things moving this way. We'll also need some lights to go looking in this old mine. No telling what we'll find once we open things up. We should also get some lumber out here for trusses," Chief Schwartz replied.

The old mine was a beehive of activity. The track layers were starting to clear a route back toward the road while Elizabeth, the sergeants and Chief Schwartz were waiting for PFC Rau and some of the younger personnel to open the mine.

"Private Rau, you found this, you have the first look," Elizabeth said, handing him a flashlight. When the first board came off the entrance, Rau shined the flashlight in the hole.

"Fraulien Lieutenant, what is this?" asked Rau.

"Corporal Rau, you're looking at two narrow gauge coal mining cars," Elizabeth said.

"Fraulien Lieutenant, I'm not a corporal."

"You are now," Elizabeth said, glancing at Chief Schwartz with a smile on her face.

"Chief, how deep do you think this puppy goes?" Elizabeth asked.

"Ma'am, I don't know," Chief Schwartz replied. "But I'd be willing to bet that since we found one of these old mines there'll be some more around here."

"Ma'am, you should also talk to Henry Dreeson and some of the other old-timers," Anse Hatfield said. "There could be a few more of these abandoned operations around here."

"First Sergeant Plotz, take charge out here. Get Sergeant Torbert's crew to lay track right up to the end of this track. Then have Sergeant Hatfield's men continue clearing that entrance. When they finish, send them for their locomotive and don't let anyone into the mine until Chief Schwartz and I get back," Elizabeth said. "Chief, I think we need to go to town and talk to the mayor and some more of the old-timers."

About an hour and a half later, Elizabeth and Chief Schwartz arrived at City Hall and asked to speak to Mayor Dreeson. "Henry, we found something that could really help us out but first off, do you know Lieutenant Pitre," the chief said.

"Only by reputation. I understand you were a pretty good cop when you worked for Dan Frost," Mayor Dreeson said, smiling.

"Well, sir, sometimes I miss the police," Elizabeth said. "But right now I'm working on a military narrow gauge railroad. Mr. Mayor, we found an old mine with a couple of narrow gauge rail cars and a bunch of track. I don't know how much you know about what we're doing, but the track and rail cars are perfect for our project."

"I knew there was work on railroads, but this is the first I've heard about anyone doing something with narrow gauge," Mayor Dreeson replied.

"Mr. Mayor, we've been experimenting with narrow gauge for a couple of months now. We converted Anse Hatfield's garden tractor as our first locomotive, scrounged up a couple of others that we're converting, and we're now working on a larger locomotive based on a Subaru Justy," Elizabeth said. "At the same time we came up with a few cars on the old lumber trails that we're rebuilding. Our biggest problem is track. Strap rail is not worth a hoot and there isn't enough of the good rail we're finding on the old lumber trails. If we can find more of it, the First Railway Company can be truly operational."

"Why don't I call Ken Hobbs, and you can show us both what you've found. I think we might be able to help you out and in more ways than you think," said Mayor Dreeson.

"This was my uncle's old place," Ken Hobbs said as he looked at the mine entrance. "There are a couple more of these around here, too. You should be able to get a bunch of track out of them."

"What about the old Joanne mine?" asked Mayor Dreeson.

"You know, I didn't think about that," Ken replied. "Didn't they have a couple of locomotives, too? And what about the line that went through the middle of town? I seem to recall that the town didn't have enough money to pull up the tracks so they were just paved over."

"You know, I plumb forgot about that one," said Mayor Dreeson. "Bill, Lieutenant, you probably just got a couple of miles more track there alone. You also got me thinking about something. We need to go over to the Joanne mine. I think you'll want to see this. We also need to go back to City Hall and look at a couple of old maps."

*Why did I ever decide to go to Rita's wedding?* Elizabeth thought as she saw the latest effort of the 1st Rail Company (Narrow Gauge tactical) of the new U.S. Army. First Lieutenant Elizabeth Pitre was not a happy camper on this crisp September afternoon in 1633. She was a "volunteer" for this project by being in the right place at the wrong time. When she was stressed, the "Dis, dat, dese, dose, and dem" of a New Orleans' childhood came out.

"What da hell kind of goat rope organization do I have here," she muttered to Chief Schwartz. It wasn't that she didn't understand the importance of her job. She had been perfectly happy as an MP platoon leader and was in line for command of the next MP Company to be organized.

Elizabeth was looking at a derailed train consisting of a garden tractor locomotive and two narrow gauge flatcars. The flatcars were about twenty-feet long and looked like half-sized versions of standard gauge cars.

"First Sergeant!" Elizabeth called, "Get the train back on the rails, bring the track laying crews back, and let's get ready to go home. We'll do the after action review before we head back.

"Chief, is it what I think?" Elizabeth asked.

"Yes ma'am, another case of not leveling the roadbed enough," the chief said, "but the rails didn't break or spread this time and we laid a mile and a half of railway in six hours."

Elizabeth merely shook her head and walked off. Six hours of wasted work. Well, maybe not wasted . . . they were getting a better feel for what they could or couldn't do. They were learning what they needed to fix and what wouldn't work. She thought about the two months it took to figure out that they needed more than two drive wheels on a locomotive.

At the end of the tracks she arrived at the site of the derailment. Three men were righting the lawn tractor locomotive, with another sitting nearby holding his leg. "Y'all okay, Sergeant Hatfield?" she asked.

"Yes ma'am', he answered, "Just a little shook up. Toeffel twisted his ankle when he was thrown off the flatcar, though."

Elizabeth looked at the now dented tractor. "Hooah. Third time this week. What do you think caused it this time? Chief Schwartz thinks it's because the roadbed isn't level enough. Why do you think it happened?"

Sergeant Hatfield scratched his head and thought for a couple of seconds. "Mr. Schwartz is the railway expert, but I think if the tractor was heavier it would stay on these uneven rails. This locomotive should be heavier anyway, ma'am. Let me weld some seats over the front wheels and have two more men ride there to test it?"

"You might be onto something, Sergeant Hatfield. We'll try it tomorrow. At least we already have the track in place. Do you think the track can handle the additional weight?" Elizabeth remembered only too well the experiments to come up with strap rail before they found the dog hole mines.

"I think so, ma'am. These rails will hold a lot more weight than the strap rail they are playing with on the standard gauge lines so a couple of hundred extra pounds on a tractor should be all right."

"Well, by the time you get this turned around and back on the tracks, everyone else should be here." Elizabeth walked farther down the tracks to see what the laying crew was up to. Sergeant Torbert had a platoon of new German recruits working on clearing the route and laying prefabricated track sections. Sergeant Bach, who was also the bandleader, was there in his role as the platoon sergeant of the wire platoon. First Sergeant Plotz and the two were already discussing the events of the day.

"We were very lucky today. We didn't have a lot of clearing to do," Sergeant Torbert said. "If we're going to lay track in the woods, I'm either going to need a lot more people or equipment. I'd really like to have three or four chain saws. I'll talk to my brother tonight to see what he has hidden in his barn that we might be able to repair."

"Yeah, you got a lot of track laid, but you have to be more careful. It derailed again about half a mile down the track," First Sergeant Plotz replied.

"Afternoon, ma'am," Sergeant Torbert said as he saw Elizabeth approach.

"It'd be a lot better if we could keep the train on the tracks," Elizabeth said. She greeted her sergeants personally and then said, "You done good, Sergeant Torbert."

Once all the personnel were assembled, Elizabeth began, "Okay, we got a mile and a half of track laid in six hours, but the train derailed. Sergeant Hatfield thinks he can do something with more weight on the locomotive, but the chief thinks it is because of roadbeds not being level enough. We also need to be faster in laying the prefabricated track. We need to work out better procedures for using other troops when they are available."

"Ma'am," one of the privates said, "we can dig fast but we need some sort of tool to tell us when the ground we're digging is level."

Sergeant Torbert said, "That's right ma'am. In fact we need some sort of gadget we can use to find the most level place so we won't have to dig as much."

Elizabeth noted this as a project for the chief and Sergeant Hatfield.

Sergeant Bach said, "Perhaps my wire teams could be of some help, too. If we know where the track is going to be laid, we could go out and find the best places while we lay wire. That way you already have the telegraph line in before the track is laid."

"Good idea, Sergeant Bach. Anything else?"

Her soldiers were tired and hungry and just wanted to get back to their billets. It had been a long day. "Top, lets get our troops back to the train and get them home. It's been a long day and I still have to meet with the regimental commander to back-brief him," she told First Sergeant Plotz.

Elizabeth returned to the Hatfield farm after meeting with the staff of the 1st Grantville Volunteer Regiment (Hans Richter). The one bright spot of a disappointing day was that there were now more soldiers cross trained in track laying who could help her when the word came. She expected that word sooner rather than later.

She looked at the soldiers lined up at the mess railcar and felt a small twinge of satisfaction. *Well, that at least is something I did that turned out all right,* she thought. The kitchen car had three gas burners designed from a picture of her grandfather's crawfish boiler. It was also set up so a griddle could be used for breakfast cooking. Elizabeth loved food like only someone who was born in New Orleans could. That, combined with her father's continual carping about quality of military cooking, made her very interested in what she and her soldiers would eat. She detested the blandness of their diet and she normally carried a bottle of hot sauce everywhere. But supplies were running out and she kept what she had left for special occasions.

"Well, young Lieutenant, I've a treat for you tonight," Mess Sergeant Liesel Schmidt told her. "I was able to get hold of some fish for you today."

"Is there enough for the troops, too?" Elizabeth asked.

"Yes ma'am." Liesel knew that the only way Elizabeth would eat was after every soldier in the unit was fed first. "Corporal Rau was practicing with some of the new hand grenades and he accidentally threw one into the river. We have enough fish for a couple of days."

"I bet," Elizabeth said, restraining the urge to chuckle. She had too many relatives who thought game and fish limits were strictly advisory. Her father often said, with a big grin on his face, that he thought the reason her grandfather made sergeant was because of his skill in doing such things as fishing with hand grenades. "Sergeant Schmidt, what am I going to do with you?" Elizabeth asked.

"Well someday, you're going to teach me to cook this gumbo you're always talking about," Sergeant Schmidt replied.

"Tell you what, good Sergeant, I'll write out a copy of a sausage gumbo recipe off my computer and let's see what we can do next week. I've seen some good-looking venison sausage we should be able to use." Elizabeth was thankful that she had her laptop with her when she made the trip to Grantville. On it was most of her life in one form or another.

When she arrived at the company's orderly room, Elizabeth was surprised to see that the chief and her sergeants weren't wrapped up in their usual evening argument about what went wrong and how to fix it. Normally Chief Schwartz and Sergeant Hatfield would be locked in a tooth and nail fight about what should be done. Elizabeth was in no mood to referee tonight. She just wanted to eat and go back to her room.

To her surprise, there was no argument tonight. Elizabeth soon found out why. Her old college roommates, Mary Pat Flanagan and Caroline Platzer were waiting for her. With the support of the warrant officers and NCO's, they virtually dragged her to the Thuringen Gardens for junior officers' night.

Elizabeth went off with her friends and drank herself into oblivion. She ranted and raved the whole time about her frustrations over the last year, beginning with her belief that she was shanghaied into the railways.

Elizabeth got so drunk that she had to be carried home by First Sergeant Plotz and Sergeant Hatfield. Her friend Caroline put her to bed. As soon as she was carried out of the Thuringen Gardens, Frank Jackson's phone began to ring.

Thankfully, Diane Jackson was the voice of common sense and kept Frank from doing anything rash. Diane went over to Elizabeth's quarters and spoke to her first.

About an hour and a half after meeting Diane, Elizabeth appeared at the army headquarters in Grantville wearing the one set of U.S. Army battledress she saved for special occasions. She was thankful she left her dirty uniforms in her car before she went to Rita's wedding. But the rubber riding boots bore no comparison to the jump boots she had left behind.

As Elizabeth waited in General Jackson's outer office she was surprised to realize she really wanted to stay with the railroad project. When she was called into the inner office she found General Jackson, not behind his desk as she expected, but looking out the window.

"Come here, Lieutenant, look out there. What do you see?" Jackson asked.

As Elizabeth looked out all she saw was the typical scene of a Grantville street, people from the twentieth century and people from the seventeenth century, to judge by their clothing, going about their business, many of them riding the new streetcars. And she knew many would be speaking in the mixed German-English patois that was becoming the common street language of Grantville, and to a certain extent of the new U.S. Army.

"Just people, sir. It looks busy."

"Yes it is busy, about as busy as I've seen Grantville in the last few years, before or after the Ring of Fire. I wish Mike Sterns and Rebecca were here. They could put this much better, but I think that street is so busy because the people feel safe. And do you know why they feel safe, lieutenant?"

"Because of us, sir, that is, the army?"

"Bingo, Lieutenant, they feel safe because of us, and that means they trust us to protect them. Now how would you feel if the person who is supposed to protect you was dancing on the tables and falling down drunk?"

"Sir, for the drinking I've no excuse, but I wasn't dancing."

"But you did make a spectacle of yourself and passed out in front of half the town. By this morning the other half has heard about it. And you did have to be carried back to your quarters. Lieutenant, I got a number of calls about you last night, all of them wanting you relieved from command. This is a small town and everything you do is noticed and talked about. Your private life is normally none of my business, but when it becomes public it becomes my business. You have to be a model, someone people look up to and not a town joke. There are some people who are just waiting for you to screw up. And when you do, guess who gets the complaints?"

"General, I—"

"Stop, Lieutenant. I picked you for the job so I should get the complaints, but I don't want to hear any more about anything we can avoid. You have to realize you live in a fishbowl and there are a lot of hungry cats just waiting for a chance. Do you understand?"

"Yes, sir."

"You have to know how important this rail project is. We need a way to supply Gustav's armies that is better than horses and wagons, and this is the best shot we have. In fact it is one of the most important projects we have right now. And from what I hear, you're doing a good job. If you don't know that, it is partially my fault. I should have visited your unit and let you know. So we're going there right now. Besides, that tramway subsidiary of yours has made life a lot easier for people in Grantville."

"Now sir? We don't have anything prepared to show you. All we have is the track out to the farm and our training locomotive. It's not too impressive, sir."

"Call and have the engine and a flatcar meet us at this end of the track. We'll ride out on the train."

When they arrived at the railhead they saw Sergeant Hatfield, Corporals Toeffel and Rau with Private Schultz turning the lawn tractor locomotive around by picking it up off the tracks and rolling it around the flatcar. Corporal Lehrer and Private Schroder from the signal platoon were there, practicing hooking up a telegraph to an existing wire. As usual, the four men on the train crew were dressed in stained mechanics coveralls. All the NCOs' stripes were painted on, upside down. Private Schultz was wearing a set of coveralls that were too small. Hatfield and Schultz had their up-time pistols in holsters, but Toeffel had two wheel lock pistols stuck in his belt. Rau had a sheathed knife that must have had fourteen inches of blade strapped to his leg. As a finishing touch, all four were wearing ball caps with Blue Barn dog food logos on them. Lehrer and Schroder were wearing clean overalls and also wearing Blue Barn dog food caps.

With Hatfield and his crew riding on the engine driven by Toeffel, there was plenty of room on the flatcar for Elizabeth and the general.

"Tell me about this. What am I looking at?" General Jackson asked.

"Sir, all this line was laid by the original crew using the existing road as a roadbed; it's basically two-foot gauge tracks using prefab rail sections. This runs out to Hatfield's father-in-law's farm where we have a turning wye. Then the rail branches into two lines and they head off into the woods. Total we have right now is about fifteen miles of track, not counting the wye, our storage yard and three sidings. We tried using strap iron on the top of six-by-four-inch wooden rails to save material, but it kept breaking. Then we got lucky and found the twenty-pound rail that was used in the dog hole mines and on the lumber trails. The twenty pound is fine for narrow gauge, but if you want to make a higher capacity standard gauge line you'll need heavier track."

"And your people have put in this track since the project started?"

"Yes, sir. We're up to about one and a half miles a day on unprepared ground. This stretch on the road we averaged about two and a half miles a day. Right now we have about forty-five miles of track we have recovered, and we're building twenty miles of that into twenty-foot sections of prefab, with the rails and ties already together. That lets us lay track just like a big toy train. If the lines are replaced with new made heavier rail the old rails can be reused."

The general looked at the engine, "Lieutenant that really is just a big lawn tractor isn't it? And why isn't Hatfield driving? I thought he was your engineer?"

"Yes, sir. The engine has close to twenty-eight horsepower. We had to modify it to a 0-6-0 configuration to adequately transfer power to the tracks. Toeffel is driving because we're training rail crews as well as track crews. Corporals Toeffel and Rau are both trained drivers. Sergeant Hatfield likes to let both men get more experience, so I would bet that Rau was driving on the trip into town. Private Schultz is trained to be a brakeman, though with just one car he's along for his muscle more than his skill."

"Hatfield," the general called out, "how many cars can that thing pull?"

"Ten is all we have overhauled right now, General, and we have pulled them all at one time, loaded. Now that's on level ground. On a hill, it's about half that. But we're working on three more loco-motives. One is a bigger one using a Subaru with a four cylinder engine and four-wheel drive. It should be able to pull twice that load. You'll have to talk to Lieutenant Bicard and Sergeant Born about the horse-drawn cars. I don't know much about them," Anse answered.

"Lieutenant, how much can each car carry?"

"Sir, from what I can figure out, the coal cars are rated at two tons each, the lumber cars at five tons, and the flatcars at ten tons. However, we won't carry more than two tons a car because they start spreading the rails at about two and a half tons. We're also building some cars we can use for horse-drawn trams and they can carry about a ton and a half each."

"So on level ground with what is really a lawn tractor, you can move twenty tons at ten to fifteen miles an hour. Is that about right, Lieutenant?"

"Yes sir, though it is much closer to ten than fifteen miles per hour. And we're getting better. Give us better equipment and we can lay track faster. As we get more coal cars overhauled, we'll be able to haul a lot of ballast to level out the roadbed and smooth over rough spots."

General Jackson appeared lost in thought as they rode to the end of the track where Sergeant Torbert had a group of recruits clearing ground. A horse-drawn railcar was nearby, loaded with prefabricated track sections.

After watching for a while, the general asked, "Those all your men, Lieutenant?"

"No sir. Most of them are from the First Volunteer regiment we're cross training. Torbert works well with the recruits and we have cross trained about two hundred in track laying and clear-ing," Elizabeth answered.

"And what are they doing?" the general continued.

"They are laying what we call a training fork. They put in a switch on the branch and run a set of rails out in to the woods for about a mile and a half. They have to clear and level the ground first for the length of the fork. They have some prefab track sections ready to lay, and we're using the horse-drawn trams to transport the sections to them. Right now we have four forks, but they can be removed and the rail reused."

"Well, let's head back," said the general.

At the end of the rail they found that the crew had turned the engine around ready to head back.

"I want to stop at your headquarters and see your camp, Lieutenant," General Jackson said.

They arrived at the camp just as Sergeant Schmidt was feeding the first shift.

"What is that thing, Lieutenant, a stove on wheels?" the General asked.

"That's our field kitchen, General. I based the burners on my grandpa's crawfish boiler and the chief had it made in a metal shop in town. We laid a special siding for it as practice with switches," Elizabeth answered.

"I like it. And this is your design?"

"Well, yes. With the chief's help, sir. Want a closer look?"

General Jackson walked over to look at the kitchen. As he got closer he saw that the mess car was just one of the improvements; there were garbage cans and immersion heaters running off a bottled gas tank that was on a rail car parked behind the kitchen car. The soldiers were washing their tin plates and forks in heated water. In front of the mess car was a water tank mounted on rail wheels.

Just then Sergeant Schmidt saw him. "Want some fish, General? We have enough for everyone. I'll get you some. Grab a plate and wash it and your hands. No one gets fed unless they wash up. The lieutenant is a 'Teufel' for washing."

"I haven't heard that sort of lecture since I was in Basic Training," said Jackson.

"Sir, if there's anything I learned from my daddy it's the importance of field sanitation. He used to think it was a pain in the rear end. But he read an article in *The Field Artillery Journal* years ago about how the Afrika Korps had a large amount of soldiers who couldn't fight because they were sick. When he took my brother and me to France we walked through some of the British cemeteries from the First World War. He always got angry about how many men died needlessly from disease."

She continued, "I didn't know anything about the old way of doing things with mess kits, but between the chief and the up-time sergeants who were in the Army, we came up with the immersion heaters and the basic setup. The first sergeant told me that the old immersion heaters used dripping gasoline, which struck me as dangerous and a pain to deal with. So they came up with one that would use natural gas instead."

General Jackson was amazed by what he was seeing. "Lieutenant, I want to bring Ed Piazza and Greg Fererra out here to see this. We need a field kitchen and this plan would be perfect. We could mount it on a wagon instead of a rail car. What else do you have to show me?"

Elizabeth led him to her field office, where PFC Bode called up on the company computer the design for the field shower unit and a design for tent heaters that would run off the same bottled gas as the kitchen. Then they went to the shop tent to meet PFC Dressel, the company blacksmith and to see the natural gas/coal-fired forge that Sergeants Hatfield and Torbert had come up with for making small critical parts from scrap steel.

After that, Elizabeth took him to the signal shack, which was a purpose built car with a telegraph station on board as well as the company's one radio. "We started training telegraph operators before we got the radio and it wasn't too difficult to cross train the telegraphers to send Morse over the radio," Elizabeth explained to General Jackson.

"Eighteen miles of railroad, three hundred troops trained to lay track, trained engine crews, trained horse-drawn trams, you're making your own parts and your troops eat better than any in the field. You know, you have done a hell of a job, Major."

As Elizabeth turned to correct the General she saw the smile on his face.

"It's long overdue, Elizabeth," General Jackson said, as he held the insignia of a major out to her.

"Thank you, sir."

"Don't thank me, Major, you earned it. Now what do you need to make this unit ready to go? As of now this unit is no longer provisional and I think the army is going to want more than one battalion like this."

"Well, we need more blacksmiths to work on fabricating new equipment, one or two captains, a few more lieutenants, at least one more radio, and if possible a small sawmill. I already have a signal detachment that can lay wire and operate a telegraph system. I'd also like to transfer about two hundred and fifty men to fill out the track laying platoons and form a horse-drawn tram company. You talk about expanding to a battalion and more. If we do, I want to make Hatfield, Plotz, Born, and Bach warrant officers so they can command platoons. Promote Bicard to captain so he can command the tram company and Torbert to first sergeant as a start. Anything else we can build and we'll promote from within as I expand the TOE." Elizabeth paused, "And sir, this unit will be the One hundred forty-first Railway Battalion, otherwise known as the Louisiana Tigers."

"Well, before I ask why one hundred forty-first and why Louisiana, where's this band I keep hearing rumors about?" the general asked.

Elizabeth smiled and said, "Easy, sir, they're the wire platoon and some of the telegraph operators of the signal detachment."

Jackson smiled as he shook his head, thinking she's *got military bureaucrat in her blood and knows very well how to hide things in the open*. He then asked, "You know that Richelieu has changed the name of Virginia to Louisiana, don't you?"

"Sir, it's my home and I want to ram it up the rear end of the arrogant Frenchman that took the name of my home away from me. Besides, there are no alligators and bayous in Virginia. They sure don't grow rice there. And, I 'gaw-ron-tee' that there's no way they would ever come up with Tabasco Sauce there," Elizabeth said. "Besides that sir, I wanted my people to realize that there was more to the old United States than the great state of West Virginia."

"Does this have anything to do with the LSU football team being called Tigers?" the general asked.

"Well sir, the One-four-one is one of the Louisiana units that LSU got the tiger mascot from. My daddy served with the One-four-one until he had to leave for promotion," Elizabeth replied.

"Done," he said. "How were you ever able to get Plotz, Hatfield and Torbert to work together or work at all? That's really amazing," General Jackson told her.

"Well, General, it just took a half-English coonass to sort these hillbillies out." Elizabeth answered with a smile, "Really, they're all good men, sir."

On a cold spring morning in 1634 a new train was loading up in Grantville to move north. This was a different sort of unit from the normal volunteer regiments that completed training in the Grantville area.

First, a marching band was playing New Orleans style brass band music and alternating numbers with the fifes and drums. On the bass drum was written "U.S. Military Railway Band" around a brick-red colored shield-shaped crest with the head of a Bengal tiger on it; below the shield was a gold ribbon with the words "Try Us."

Another difference was the load on this train was made up of steel-wheeled railcars, not rubber tired vehicles. These trains were loaded on the standard gauge flatcars for transport to Halle, where they would be loaded on barges.

Large amounts and different types of equipment were moving out. Flatcars were loaded with prefabricated sections of rail, lumber cars were laden with rails, coal cars were filled with equipment, and there was one car loaded with spools of telegraph wire.

Another difference was that families were going with this unit. With the attached Volunteer Pioneer Regiment to provide security and track laying support, the total convoy numbered nearly two thousand personnel.

A young woman dressed in up-time U.S. Army battledress with a new gold oak leaf on her right collar walked the length of the train accompanied by an older man in overalls.

"Well Chief, I guess we're as ready as we'll ever be," Elizabeth said.

"Yes ma'am, I agree with you. Time to go," Chief Warrant Officer Charlie Schwartz replied.

"I'll meet you back at our train," Elizabeth told him. She then went over where two other young women were waiting for her.

"You take care of yourself and be careful," Mary Pat Flanagan said.

"And what am I supposed to do now that you're leaving?" Caroline Platzer asked.

Beth looked at her roommates of her last two years at WVU and said, "I'll miss both of you very much, but you know I'll be back." After hugging her friends, she went to the lead locomotive and pumped her arm up and down, the signal to move out. The 141st Railway Battalion was going to war.

"Well Chief, on to Halle. I hope the navy has the river open so we can travel on barges up to Scherwin Lake," Elizabeth said.

"Ma'am, it'll be a lot easier and quicker to get to where we need to go on barges," Chief Schwartz replied.

"I couldn't agree with you more. This is going to be a pain, but on the other hand, we're going to be needed," Elizabeth said.

"Well, we have the advance detachment with some equipment at the Schwerin Lake railhead, but we have to lot to work out on how we're going support the army," the chief said.

"Your idea of setting up an advanced base camp at Schwerin Lake is a good one," Elizabeth replied. "We'll just have to see what happens when we get there."

# CONTINUING SERIALS

# Heavy Metal Music
## or
# Revolution in Three Flats

~~~

## David Carrico

### Grantville, March, 1633

Franz hissed in pain as his crippled hand was flexed, twisted and pulled by Dr. Nichols' strong fingers. Sweat beaded his forehead as he endured the testing manipulation. He sighed in relief when the doctor finally released it.

"Sorry," Dr. Nichols said. "I know that hurt, but I had to see what the condition was." He made some notes in a folder, then looked up. "Well, as the old joke goes, I have bad news and good news. Which do you want first?"

Franz swallowed as Marla took his claw in both her hands. "The bad first, if you please," he replied.

Dr. Nichols looked at them both seriously. "I can't help you surgically. I'm sorry. The damage is severe, but I probably could have saved it if I could have seen it right after it happened. Maybe not, with the knuckles smashed in the last two fingers, but we would have had a good chance. Now . . . Frankly, it healed wrong. I'm not faulting those who tended you—fact is, they did as good a job as any down-timer could have done."

He glanced down at his notes, then back up, and continued, "I have—had, rather—a good friend back up-time who could have fixed it, even now, but he was a fully trained specialized orthopedic surgeon with all the appropriate tools and technology at his fingertips. All modesty aside, I'm a good surgeon, but orthopedics, especially with the small bones like in the hand, requires not only the training but the tools, and I don't have either one. Even if I did, I'm not sure I could justify expending them for what is, to be honest, a relatively minor injury. Our resources are so limited right now that they have to be reserved for truly major problems."

Franz looked down at where Marla's hands clasped tightly around the hand in question, sighed, and said, "I understand."

He raised his eyes back up to look into the doctor's, and a small quirky smile played around his mouth. "I truly did not believe you could do anything, but Marla insisted we come to you. Perhaps in my heart of hearts I wanted to believe that you Grantvillers could work just one more miracle"—he chuckled—"as if enough miracles have not been worked on my behalf already." He smiled at Marla, and his good hand rested on top of hers.

"Well, it is sorry I am that we have wasted your time, Herr Doctor." Franz started to stand up.

"Just a minute, young man. I said I had good news also. Don't you want to hear that?"

Marla pulled him back down, and spoke for the first time. "What do you mean, Dr. Nichols?"

"Well, we may not be able to restore the hand to its preinjury condition, but there are some things we can do to make it somewhat better than it is. Granted, the little finger and ring finger are total write-offs."

Marla saw his confusion, and said, "He means nothing can be done for them, Franz."

The doctor blinked at the interruption, then continued, "Er, yes, they can't be helped. Your wrist and thumb, on the other hand, seem to have totally escaped injury."

"A mark of the malice of Heydrich, " Franz said quietly. "To a violinist, the left hand thumb is just a resting place for the neck of the violin. The fingers are everything."

There was a pause, then Dr. Nichols said carefully, "You're saying he not only attacked you, he knew precisely what to do to cause you the most damage."

"Precisely."

The doctor's tone was glacial. "I think Herr Heydrich would be well advised to avoid our territory. I believe I would want to have words with him if I saw him."

"You'd have to stand in line, Doc," Marla snarled. "You're a surgeon, so with your hands you might understand better than most just what this cost a musician, but even you can't understand the grief and madness this caused. I do."

A swirl of appreciation for the woman at his side filled Franz, driving out the old cold ache. The doctor's expression eased to a warm smile.

"Far be it from me to get in the way of mama lion defending her cub. I would be proud to hold your coat, young lady, and see to sweeping up the leftovers if you ever get the chance."

They all laughed, and he continued, "Getting back to your hand, your index and middle fingers are not as hopeless as they appear to be. Granted, they're very stiff right now, but the knuckles escaped injury and the broken bones, although not perfectly straight, healed well enough. What you mainly have is stiffened and inflamed muscles and tendons, with some atrophy because you didn't exercise it while it was healing. The good news is there are some things you can do to help rehabilitate it. If you'll talk to Irene Musgrove, she will describe the procedures you should follow, but basically massages with oil, alternating hot and cold soaks and some exercises with a stiff rubber ball will help bring them back. It will take a while, and I'm not going to lie to you, they won't be as good as they were before the injuries, but you can have more use out of them than you do now."

"Any improvement is more than I have, Doctor. I will do as you say."

"Good. Let Irene know if you can't find a rubber ball, and we'll see if we can requisition one from some kid's toy box." They all laughed again, and the couple stood and left on that note.

Outside the office in the evening twilight, they snugged their coats up against the chill spring breeze and walked slowly down the sidewalk together. After a block or so, Franz sighed, and said, "Well, now we know." He looked over at Marla, walking head down and hands in pockets, and saw tears coursing down her cheeks. Stopping her with his hands on her shoulders, he turned her to face him and gently wiped them from her face. She threw her arms about him, and began to sob convulsively.

"It's . . . not . . . fair," she said brokenly.

"Sshh, sshh," Franz murmured as his cheek rested against her hair. "The good doctor did not take anything from me except false hope. I lost my hand, I gained you and the music of Grantville. I consider it a fair trade."

"But," she said, her voice muffled against his chest, "I wanted to hear you play. It's not fair," sniff, "that you love the music so," sniff, "and can't play it now." Snuffle. Her arms tightened around him again.

Franz took her by the shoulders again and moved her out to arm's length, then lifted her chin and stared at the brimming eyes. "Marla, I have not lost the music, I have only lost the source of my sinful pride and arrogance. As long as I have you, I have the music. Now, dry your eyes, and tell me where we will find this . . . What did Dr. Nichols call it? Oh, yes, this rubber ball. And why would a child have one?"

She smiled at him, wiping her eyes, and hand in hand they walked on down the sidewalk as she explained the nature of a child's toy from up-time and why it would help him regain partial use of his hand. It being Friday evening, they turned at the corner by unspoken consent and walked toward the Gardens.

"Is anyone playing tonight?" Franz asked as they drew near.

"Not that I know of. Couple of the guys in Mountaintop are out of town, so they haven't been doing anything lately."

Franz sniffed. "That is not a bad thing."

"Oh, now, you listened to them just fine the last time they played. You even clapped a couple of times."

"Do not mistake tolerance and politeness for acceptance," he said with a deadpan expression.

"You!" She poked him in the ribs. He poked back, and they scuffled together for a few moments until they separated laughing. She grabbed his left arm with both hands and leaned against him as they walked on. After a few quiet moments, she said, "You know, Franz, I'm awfully glad you came to Grantville."

"As am I."

"No, I'm talking about more than just our friendship." They walked a few more steps before she continued. "You know, I had my life all planned out before the Ring of Fire hit. I was set to graduate in a few weeks. I knew that I wouldn't be the valedictorian or salutatorian, but I knew that I would be like

number three or four in our class. I was going to college in the
fall. I already had scholarship offers from University of Virginia
and Belmont, and there were hints from University of North
Texas that they were going to offer me a good package, too. I
was going to double major in voice and piano, and with a little
luck I could be the band drum major as well. I even had hopes
for Eastman School of Music, although the odds were longer
there. Then I was going to do the master's degree, and then the
doctor's degree. I was going to be Doctor Kristen Marlena Linder
by the time I was thirty, show my family and everyone in this
one-horse town that I had what it took to be something other
than the little girl that sang in church and at the county fair, and
everyone said, 'Doesn't she sound good?' and patted me on the
head or someplace else."

Their pace had picked up a little. Franz waited a few more
steps, then said, "Marla?"

"Huh?"

"You are . . . steaming, I think Ingram called it."

She slowed down abruptly, sighed, and said, "You're right. I
can't help it. Every time I think about what happened, I just get
furious . . . with the universe, with God, with Grantville. My life got
screwed up royally. Everyone's did, I know that, but *my life . . .*"

She stopped, rubbed her hands across her face and brushed
her long hair back. "Sorry." She took his arm again, and they
started walking slowly.

"I was so angry. Aunt Susan can tell you that when we found
out what happened and that Mom and Dad and Paul were left
up-time, after I got over the shock I wasn't fit to be around. She
said I was like an old sow bear just woke up from hibernation
with a bad case of PMS. It was literally months before I could
talk to anyone without snarling at them, and probably over a year
before I actually smiled again."

Franz placed his hand over hers. "I find that hard to believe."

"No, seriously, I can't describe what I was like without getting
pretty vulgar." He snorted and she slapped his arm. "I mean it!
I was awful!"

"If you say so."

"I was! And I was a long time getting over it. Aunt Susan
finally talked me into going into the teacher training program.
Since I have no mechanical aptitude, I get sick at the sight of

blood and I can't hit the broad side of a barn with a shotgun, that was about the only thing that I could do to pay my own way in our brave new world." Her voice dripped sarcasm.

"It is a new world, at least for me."

Marla flushed, looked up at him quickly and then down again. "I'm sorry," she muttered. "That was rude."

A few more quiet steps, and she said, "Anyway, what I was trying to say is that I feel different since you came. I can talk music with you, and daydream about somehow starting a music school. I feel . . . happy."

She stopped and twirled once on the sidewalk, holding out her arms. "You are good for me, Franz Sylwester."

"You just say that because you love me," he joked.

She stopped and looked at him in all seriousness. "I do love you, Franz."

He stared back in amazement. "Are you . . . I mean . . . you mean . . ."

His head was spinning. Yes, they had kissed, and cuddled, but she had not allowed any more than that. They had joked about having a future together, he had dreamed it, but now in cold honesty he saw that he had never truly thought he had a chance at a lifetime with her, crippled and destitute as he was. Jokes and fantasies had all of a sudden become a reality, and he was totally speechless.

With a smile, she reached out and took both of his hands—whole and crippled—in hers, and said, "I love you, Franz Sylwester, I believe you love me, too, and I'm tired of waiting for you to say something about it."

He continued to stare at her, and she laughed. "Close your mouth, silly."

He did. "Well, say something."

He just looked at her, saying nothing. After a few moments, her smile faded away. "Franz?" in a small voice.

He pulled his hands from hers, and turned away, pushing his hands in his coat pockets and ducking his head. "I can't," he choked.

"Why not?"

He started to walk away.

"Franz Sylwester, you stop right there!" A sternness in her voice that he had never heard before stopped him without thought.

Her steps sounded as she walked around in front of him, and he looked away.

"Franz, look at me." He did, seeing the tears trickling down her face again, and looked away again quickly. "No, look at me." He did, swallowing.

"You look me in the eyes, and tell me that you don't love me, and I'll walk away. But until you do that, we're going to stand right here."

Despite her command, he looked down at his feet. "I . . . love you," he whispered.

"Then why—?" she started exasperatedly.

He snatched his left hand from his pocket and thrust it in her face. She stepped back, startled, as he snarled, "Because of this! Because I am crippled! I cannot hope for you or anyone to marry me. Your family would not allow it. I cannot support you. I cannot provide for a family, when all I can do is translate for one person here today, another person there on Thursday, or write two letters for someone next Monday. I cannot give you what you deserve, a husband sound in mind *and body*. I cannot protect you from the ridicule that people will heap on you for marrying a cripple! I love you more than my life, Marla, and because of that I cannot do this!"

She smiled, and said, "Oh, is that all?"

Franz was taken aback. "Is that *all*? Is that not enough?"

"No," she laughed. "I was afraid there was something seriously wrong."

She took his crippled hand in both of hers, and said, "Franz, you're still wrestling with the trauma—"

He looked at her quizzically.

"Okay, you don't know that word. You're still wrestling with the damaging mental effects from when your hand was shattered. You're dealing with anger, and grief, and bitterness, and finding out that bargaining with God doesn't work, and you're not able to see some things realistically because of that. Believe me, we in Grantville know all about this, me in particular. Trust me, no one whose opinion matters considers you less than a man, less than a whole person, because of what happened to you. In fact, a lot of people, me included, admire your courage."

*Courageous, him?*

"And besides, Doc Nichols called me a she-lion, Aunt Susan

called me a bear. What do you think I'm going to do to anyone who bad-mouths you?" She looked at him expectantly, and grinned in response as the corners of his mouth turned up.

"Franz," she continued more soberly, "we can find a way to make it work. If Grantville and Mike Stearns can remake Europe, then surely you and I can make a life together." She took his hands in hers again. "I ask you again, do you love me?"

"With all my heart," he said, his voice shaking.

"And you won't give me any more foolishness about your hand?"

"No," he told her, his voice stronger.

"Good." She hugged him and kissed his nose. "Now, it's dark and cold out, and after making me cry twice tonight you owe me a cup of coffee. Let's get to the Gardens."

They walked together hand in hand, his left in her right, contentedly. As they turned up the final walk, he said, "Marla?"

"Hmm?"

"If your name is Kristen Marlena, why do you say your name is Marla?"

She laughed. "I haven't gone by Kristen since the third grade. There was another girl in the same grade but a different class who was Kristin. Her name was spelled slightly differently, but sounded the same. She was a bully, and first she picked on me all the time saying I was stupid because I didn't spell my name like hers. Then she started calling me Kristin Junior, and trying to make me follow her orders during recess. So, I got sick of that name pretty quickly, but I didn't like Marlena either. According to Mom, Dad liked this German actress from old movies, so when they couldn't decide on a middle name for me, he suggested that one and it stuck. I told her, 'Gee, thanks.' Anyway, you remember the comics I showed you that my brother Paul used to have?"

He nodded.

"Well, at the time there was this one superhero comic book that had a strong female character in it named Marla. He started calling me that, and after he showed me the comic, I thought it was cool, so I started calling me that, too. Mom and Dad caved in pretty quickly. It took a couple of years for it to stick at school, though. I don't know how many times I got sent to the office for telling teachers, 'Call me Marla!' It wasn't until junior high that Mom was finally able to convince the teachers and principals that she wanted them to call me Marla even though that wasn't what was on my birth certificate. Mom was cool like that. And ironically enough, the cause of it all moved away from Grantville after fourth grade. I could have gone back to Kristen, but I liked Marla better. Marla it stayed."

"So, a name chosen and not bestowed. Appropriate for you, I would say."

She stared over at him suspiciously, making sure that he wasn't being sarcastic. He smiled back blandly as they walked through the door of the Gardens.

No sooner had they entered than a voice yelled, "Franz!"

Recognizing a voice from his past, he spun, looking for a familiar face. "Friedrich!"

A young man jumped up from a nearby table so quickly that his chair fell over backwards. Franz hurried to meet him, and they embraced in the aisle between tables, exclaiming loudly, pushing back for a moment to hold each other at arm's length, then embracing again in a ferocious hug. Franz literally picked his shorter friend up, then dropped him back on the floor and turned to the rest of the people at the table.

"Anna, it is good to see you!" She held her hands out, and as he took them she pulled him forward.

"Lean down, you oaf." He did so, and she stood on her tip-toes to kiss his cheek.

Next, the older man at the table received Franz's attention as he stood up straight and held out his hand. "Master Riebeck, I do not understand why you are here, but I am very happy that you are."

The gray-haired man shook his hand heartily, peering up at him and said, "These young ones said they would go. Old heads were needed, I said, so I come also."

"Even so, sir, thank you for coming."

Finally Franz turned to another young man of about his own age, one even taller than he was, thin but not gawky, and embraced him also. "Thomas, I knew you would come, even if the others did not. I knew the scent of new music would draw you like a starving hound."

"And draw me it did," Thomas rumbled in a full basso, face split by a large grin. "I hold you to your promise to show me all of the music from the future."

"Franz?" he heard from behind him. He turned and held out his hand to Marla. "Marla, here are most of my best friends from my old life, from the days before I left Mainz." He drew her up level with him, and said, "First, here are Friedrich and Anna Braun. You've heard me speak of them, my dearest friends. They are why I am alive today."

They smiled and nodded together. Friedrich was shorter than Franz, shorter than Marla as well, and Anna was just this side of tiny.

"Next, here is Master Hans Riebeck, Anna's father and Friedrich's craft master, maker of fine musical instruments." A distinguished looking older man, longish silver hair swept back, a short square-cut beard and faded blue eyes looking out from under bushy eyebrows nodded in turn.

"And finally, this human pikestaff is Thomas Schwarzberg, another good friend who stood by me in dark days." Thomas grinned and bobbed his head at her. Although unusual for a down-timer, he was taller than Marla, with an unruly shock of dark brown hair.

"Everyone, this is Kristen Marlena Linder—off!" Her elbow took him under the ribs. They took in the sight of a tallish, well-made young woman with long black hair, high cheekbones and piercing blue eyes that at the moment seemed to be dancing.

"Call me Marla, please."

"Please, come sit with us," Friedrich said. They busied themselves with taking coats off, pulling other chairs over to their table and waving at the server, who came over to take their orders. In moments, Marla had a cup of steaming coffee and Franz a mug of beer in front of them, and everyone settled in. There was a moment or two of awkward silence, which Master Riebeck broke.

He had been peering very closely at Marla ever since the introductions had begun. Now he sat back with a satisfied smile on his face and said something in German.

"Your pardon," Franz said quickly, "but as a courtesy to Marla, I ask that we all speak English tonight. She is learning German, but it is not easy for her yet."

"Of course," Master Riebeck said, and the others muttered agreement. He continued, "I said, now I understand."

"Understand what, Papa?" Anna asked.

"Ever since the letter from Franz you read to me, I wondered. The letter, it was Franz und it was not Franz. No anger, no bitter, no hurt was in it. We come here, und I see Franz, Franz mit joy in face, Franz with shadow gone from eyes. I wondered. Now I understand. You, young woman," he said, pointing at Marla, "you ist the reason. Compassion I see in your face. By God's grace, you bring healing to our Franz."

Marla blushed, looking down. Franz took her hand, and she smiled up at him, then turned to Master Hans and said, "Actually, sir, we bring healing to each other."

Anna was seated on her other side, and reached over and took her other hand. "Thank you, Mistress Marla."

"Just Marla, please. You make me sound like I'm an old maiden aunt!"

They all laughed, and Anna continued, "Marla, then, to please you. Again, thank you. Franz is very dear to us, and we worried so about him when he left. We were so surprised to receive the letter he sent. It was the first word we had had since he left over a year ago."

"Yes," said Friedrich, leaning over, sandy-colored hair falling into his eyes, "this crazy man took out on his own, leaving us behind to worry. And worry we did! Not a word for months and months, and then like a bolt from heaven comes his letter, sounding almost like a story of one taken under hill to the Erl-king's domain. First he tells of the wonders of Grantville, then he tells of music not known to mortal men, then he hints of a lovely lady." They all laughed again as Marla's blush renewed.

"Indeed," Thomas rumbled with that deep voice that was so surprising from his slender frame, "nothing would do for Anna but that we come immediately and make sure that Franz was safe and hale, that he was not lying in a delirium someplace, or under some kind of enchantment." Now it was Anna's turn to blush as the rest laughed.

"But I did not expect you," said Franz, as the laughter died. "I thought you would write to me a letter of your own. I have been looking for one these past few days, but instead, you are here yourselves. I do not complain, I am glad to see you, but why?"

"Because we care about you," said Master Hans. "We must see for ourselves your wellbeing, see for ourselves the wonders of Grantville, see for ourselves the *fraulein* who has lifted you up."

He raised his mug to Marla, then continued, "Und see for ourselves the music and the instruments you wrote about. Anna would see you, so nothing would do but that Friedrich and Thomas would come und see the other wonders you named. Me," he chuckled, "much have I heard about the new ways and devices of Grantville, of changes good und bad, of people growing rich who grasp change. If new music und new instruments come, then Riebeck will be at the front. Must see them all, especially *piano* that shames the noble clavier."

"So," Thomas said, leaning forward, eyes shining brightly "when can we see these marvels?"

"Thomas!" Anna hissed.

"What? What did I say?"

"Enough," the diminutive woman said sternly, looking around the table. "There is time enough to talk about that tomorrow. Tonight, let us just enjoy old and new friends together." And they proceeded to do so.

The next morning was bright and crisp and clear, the sun was shining brightly, and Franz's head was thudding like the tympani in the opening fanfare of Strauss' *Also Sprach Zarathustra*. As he turned onto the sidewalk leading to Marla's aunt's house, a particularly bright beam of sunlight made its way through the naked limbs of the trees and lanced into his eyes. He threw his good hand up to shade his eyes and stopped, swaying a little. Flinching when the front door slammed, he looked up and peered under his hand to see Marla walking toward him, smiling.

"I told you not to drink that wine last night, not after drinking all that beer." Marla's voice held a note of gleeful satisfaction, and pierced Franz's ears much as the light had assaulted his vision. He moaned a little. She took his arm and turned him, walking back out to the street. "Had anything to eat?"

"Please, not so loud. Some bread, some aspirin, a little water."

"You'll start to feel somewhat better soon, then. Next time, listen to me, all right?"

"Yes."

Aunt Susan's house was only a couple of blocks from the Methodist church, which was where their friends from Mainz were supposed to meet them this morning. As they turned the corner, they saw Friedrich helping Anna down from their wagon and Thomas tying the horse to a convenient tree in the parking lot. Master Riebeck was looking around, and he smiled and waved when he saw them. Within moments, they were all together. Franz was somewhat gratified to note that Friedrich and Thomas looked about as bad as he felt. Master Riebeck was apparently none the worse for the evening's experience. Marla began herding them through the main doors of the church.

"You wanted to see a piano, so I thought we'd start here." They could hear ringing tones unlike anything the visitors had ever heard before, which became clearer as Marla opened the doors into the sanctuary. They entered through the rear of the room, and stopped for a moment in awe. The room was not as large as a cathedral, but there was a certain majesty to it nonetheless, with its high ceiling, dark wooden beams and pews, and large stained glass windows. Marla led them down the aisle toward the platform at the front.

There was a large instrument on the platform which was the source of the tones they had heard. By deduction it must be the piano. A gray-haired man seated at it was banging on a key to produce the sounds. He looked up as they approached.

"G'mornin', Marla."

"Hi, Ingram. You going to be long?"

"Nope. Just about done. Reverend Jones called me a couple of days ago and asked me to check the tuning. Near's I can tell, it's right on."

"Great. Ingram, these are some friends of Franz's, from Mainz. This is Master Hans Riebeck, an instrument maker, Anna and Friedrich Braun, his daughter and son-in-law, and Thomas Schwarzberg, their friend. Everyone, this is Ingram Bledsoe, my friend and a good instrument maker in his own right."

There was much shaking of hands and exchanging of pleasantries, then Marla continued. "They came all the way down to see Franz, and to learn as much as they can about the music and instruments he wrote to them about. I brought them in to see the piano. I'm glad you're here, because I was going to call you about bringing them around to see some of your instruments and kits."

"No problem. It's Saturday, so I was going to putter around in the shop anyway. I'll just wait here and we can go on over there when you're done."

He got up from the bench and she sat down, while he raised the lid on the grand piano to its greatest opening. Marla rippled a chord up and down the keyboard, then looked up at the visitors. "How do you want to do this?"

Everyone looked at Master Riebeck, who simply said, "Play music, zings you know."

She looked down at her hands, and began with a short piece in the contrapuntal style. "Two-Part Invention Number 1, by Bach." Then came a slow legato piece with a repetitious arpeggio in the bass. She stopped after a minute or so. "Part of the first movement of the 'Moonlight Sonata,' by Beethoven." A martial theme. "'Onward, Christian Soldiers.'"

Master Riebeck raised his hand, and she stopped. "Good. The sound, we know it." He muttered in German to Franz, who said, "He wishes you to demonstrate the power of the piano, what it can do that the clavier cannot."

"I am not very accomplished," Marla began.

Ingram snorted, and said, "Girl, you're the best pianist in town, and one of the best I've heard, period. Just play that thing you were working on before the Ring fell."

She closed her eyes, took a deep breath, and sat motionless for several moments. Then she opened her eyes, raised her hands, and literally attacked the keyboard. Franz was astounded. He had never seen anyone's hands move so fast, and the volume of sound coming from the piano was amazing. The arpeggios of this piece made the Beethoven sound like a child's exercise, and the percussive hammering of chords was incredible.

All too soon it was over. Marla lifted her hands from the keys and sat back, breathing heavily. No one else moved. Friedrich and Anna were both staring wide-eyed at her, Master Riebeck was gazing at the piano through narrowed eyelids, and Thomas stood like a statue with his eyes closed.

She caught her breath, and said, "That was the "Revolutionary Etude," by Fredric Chopin, a Polish composer and pianist who would have lived about two hundred years from now. Or at least, it was supposed to be. I made so many mistakes it was ridiculous. Got to practice more. Anyway, he'll probably never be born, and the only place his music exists is here in Grantville. And Ingram, the A-flat three is a little flat."

Thomas broke out of his stillness, threw himself to his knees by the bench and took her hand in both of his. "Teach me."

Startled, she tried to pull away.

"I beg of you, teach me! I will pay anything to learn this!"

The happy-go-lucky young man of the night before was staring at her with burning eyes, and his clutch on her hand was fervent and strong to the point of pain. "Please, I must have this music! This power, this passion, this . . . this . . ."

"Thomas," Anna said, touching his shoulder, "let go, you're frightening her."

He dropped her hand as if it burned him, and shrank back, saying, "Sorry," over and over. "Please . . ."

"I'm . . . I'm not a teacher," Marla said unevenly. "I can't teach you. I don't know enough to teach."

"Marla," Ingram said. She looked at him. "You know plenty. What you don't know, you can find out or teach yourself. You can teach. You were going to eventually, before. Looks like you just get your chance earlier than you thought, is all."

She looked into his weathered face for long moments, and seemed to draw strength from his confidence in her. Squaring her shoulders, she turned to Thomas.

"What I know, I will show you. And maybe together we can learn what I don't know." Then she turned to Franz and held out her hand. "And you, too, dear heart. We will find a way for you to do music again."

The young people gathered around the piano, talking back and forth, chattering, even. Marla began playing something light and bouncy. Master Riebeck drifted over to stand next to Ingram Bledsoe. "She is good?"

"Oh, yes. For her age and the amount of study she had before the Ring of Fire, she's very good. And she has the potential, the talent, to be as good as they come. She's right, there's a lot she doesn't know, but even so I'd bet she knows more than anyone except Marcus Wendell, the school band director. Experience, he's ahead of her, but knowledge . . . she's probably not far behind him even now. She'd absorbed everything the piano and voice teachers here in Grantville could teach her a few years before the Ring, and was studying with teachers in Morgantown." He smiled in satisfaction. "Yes, she's good. She even has perfect pitch."

"She is . . ." he stopped, muttered in German, then called out, "Friedrich!" When his son-in-law stepped over, he spoke rapidly in German. Friedrich nodded, and said, "Strong-willed." Master Hans turned back to Ingram and raised his eyebrows.

Ingram laughed, but didn't say anything.

"A good match for our Franz, then." Riebeck nodded. "So."

With the air of a man who's settled his mind about something, the craftmaster marched over to the piano and declared, "Enough of this noodling. Time to talk about important things. Herr Bledsoe, this piano, it is *ein grosse* dulcimer, yes? Hammers strike the strings, yes?"

The others stepped back as Master Hans, Ingram and Friedrich took over the piano and spent the next little while examining its construction and mechanisms. Exclamations such as "*Himmel!*" and "Aha!" punctuated the conversation.

While this was going on, Anna visibly steeled herself, turned to Marla and said, "Franz says that you sing. Do you sing as well as you play?"

"Well . . ."

"Yes," Franz said. "If anything, she is better." Marla flushed again.

"Er," Anna hemmed, "um, if-you-teach-Thomas-will-you-teach-me-please?" It all came out in a rush, and she in turn blushed, but still continued to hold her head up and look the taller woman in the eye.

Marla reached out and took her hand, saying, "Of course. I would love to."

"You know," said Thomas, "that some people will disapprove."

Two heads turned as one toward him, two sets of female eyes focused on him, and if pointed glances had been daggers and stilettos he would have been well and truly nailed to the nearest wall. He quickly held up his hands in surrender. "Not me! I would never object. I just meant that others would."

"Smart man," Franz muttered under his breath.

He thought. The heads turned toward him now, the eyes boring, and Marla gently said, "Did you say something?"

"No, nothing, not a word."

"I didn't think so."

"I will deal with Papa and Friedrich and my brother Karl," Anna said. "No one else matters." The two women talked together about singing, while Franz and Thomas silently congratulated each other on narrowly escaping with their skins intact.

Finally, Master Hans pushed away from the piano, and said, "Enough. I must think. Herr Bledsoe, now go to your workshop? I would see more of the wonders of Grantville, *bitte*."

After Marla closed the piano top and put the quilted cover over it, nothing would do but for them all to bundle up against the cold and traipse back out into the bright day, all load into the visitors' wagon and drive the few blocks to the Bledsoe residence.

Ingram's workshop turned out to be in an old detached garage building behind his house. He ushered them into it and turned on the lights. They all looked around at the neatly racked tools, the power saws and lathe. Both Master Hans and Friedrich were immediately drawn to the workbench where a work was in progress.

"This is?" Master Hans looked to Ingram.

"A guitar, the kind that's called a classical guitar."

"Is this . . . what strange word was it, Franz?"

"Kit."

"Thank you. Is this *eine* kit?"

Ingram chuckled, and said, "Yep. I got this one and a steel-string guitar kit in right before the Ring fell. Didn't start it until recently, but it's coming along well. I had it in mind to build these, learn from them and try producing my own."

"So, this is apprentice work?"

Ingram blinked. "Well, you might say so."

"If you please, show me this kit."

"Sure." Ingram hauled out the box, laid out all the parts and showed them the instructions. Master Hans and Friedrich looked them over, examined everything, tried to read the instructions and understand enough to follow the pictures.

"Hmm. These writings—good. Friedrich, think about these, how we might use them." To Ingram, "How good will this guitar be?"

Turning to a nearby cabinet, Ingram brought out something wrapped in a scrap of old blanket, which he unwrapped to reveal a lap harp. "This was made from a kit from the same company. I assume the guitar will be similar in quality—not great, but good enough for a beginning student to play." He held it out to the two down-time craftsmen.

As they scrutinized the harp, Marla whispered to Anna, "Why is your father quizzing Ingram this way?"

"Quizzing?" with a perplexed expression.

"Why is he questioning him, and poking into everything?"

Anna shook her head, "I do not know. Papa always wants to know how good other craftsmen are, but I have never seen him this direct before."

"Good, Herr Bledsoe." Master Hans handed the harp back.

"Call me Ingram."

"Herr Ingram, have you zomezing of your own that I can see, zomezing not a . . . kit?" Master Hans seemed to be getting excited. His accent was getting thicker.

Wrapping the harp up and putting it back in the cabinet, Ingram said nothing. Marla could tell he was beginning to get irritated with the down-timers because a muscle in his jaw was jumping. She went over and helped him clear the guitar kit from the workbench. Still not saying a word, he went back to the cabinet and removed a much larger blanket-wrapped parcel which he carefully set down on the workbench and equally carefully unwrapped. Stepping back, he waved a hand at what was revealed—a dulcimer of beauty and quality. There was a faint "Oooh" sound from the others in the room, and they stepped closer.

Marla clapped her hands. "Ingram, you finished it! You didn't tell me!"

"Yep. Finished it last week. Figured I'd tell you the next time I saw you, which turned out to be today."

Master Hans and Friedrich peered at the dulcimer closely, muttering to each other. The craftmaster looked to Ingram for permission. At his nod, they picked it up carefully, turning it this way and that, examining the wood grain and joins, plucking at the strings, nodding approval at the sound.

"Pardon," Friedrich said, "I must be sure. This is not a kit?"

"Nope," said Ingram tightly. "I haven't made a hammer dulcimer from a kit in, oh, twenty years or more."

"A fine work, this," Master Hans declared. "Worthy of rank." Ingram looked pleased.

"Old Bessie MacLaren from Clarksburg commissioned that, before the Ring. She's . . . or I should say, she was . . . one of the best players in the country, and I was right pleased that she called on me. I finished it up after the Ring fell, even though she's not around to get it. Couldn't stand to leave it undone, and I figured that sooner or later I'd have a chance to sell it. Anyway, I have to admit that's probably the best piece I've done."

"*Ist gut,*" Master Hans repeated. "Master Ingram"—who now looked very pleased at the compliment—"from this I see that *du bist* craftsman." He waved at the dulcimer, which Friedrich was carefully placing back on the workbench. "You know wood, you have skills, yes? Now, let us talk of pianos. To make pianos, here, now, what do we need?"

The newly dubbed master pulled at his chin with his thick-fingered hand. "I'm not an expert," he said slowly. "I moonlighted for a music store in Clarksville, Tennessee, when I was working for a contractor at Fort Campbell a lot of years ago. That's where I learned what I know, including how to tune pianos. But I suspect you-all have a handle on the woodworking part of it. The soundboard is large, but shouldn't be a problem, and a cabinet is a cabinet."

Master Hans nodded impatiently, and motioned for him to continue.

"No, the two things that you will need to make one right are the cast-iron harp and the steel wire. You need the wire to stand up to the tension and the hammering and not stretch or break, and you need the harp to brace the soundboard so it will stand up to the tension that has to be placed on the wire to tune it. Otherwise, sooner or later the soundboard will warp and all your work will be wasted."

"As I thought," said the German craftmaster. "For the piano, for the music, it must be this cold heavy metal." Marla choked. He looked at her quizzically, but she waved him to go on. "Good copper and bronze and brass too warm, too soft would be, not hard as iron."

As the craftsmen discussed the metals and their availability, Franz leaned over to Marla and asked, "What was so funny?"

"Heavy metal . . . music. I'll explain later."

"Iron we can get," Riebeck concluded. "From Muehlhausen or even Nuernberg. Wire from steel, difficult."

"Especially that much of it," Friedrich said, "and in those lengths. Steel wire is not common, and is ruinously expensive."

There was silence in the shop, while they all ruminated on that thought.

"There might be a way around that problem," Marla said, "at least until they start making the stuff in Magdeburg that they keep talking about."

Both older men turned and looked at her, identical expressions with raised eyebrows on their faces. She smiled, and said, "You know, Aunt Susan's got that old upright piano in her parlor, Ingram? The one you said had a cracked soundboard? I bet you could buy it from her for not much, strip out the harp and wire and other fittings, and use them to build a new piano."

Simultaneous expressions of joy appeared on the three craftsmen's faces. "Of course!" Ingram enthused. "I don't know what it would take to adapt the works of an upright to a baby grand, but it's worth a try. If that can't be done, then we'll make uprights until someone starts making wire. In fact, I can name fifteen or more houses with old pianos in them that I can probably convince their owners to sell. Not to mention the fact that the Methodist and Baptist churches have at least half a dozen apiece in Sunday School rooms that nobody's played in the last twenty years. Give me two weeks, and I can probably buy enough old pianos to keep you in business for a year, maybe more!"

Master Hans nodded definitively. "Friedrich, Anna, we move to Grantville. Karl will take the shop in Mainz. We must be here to grasp the new, to grasp pianos."

They gaped at him. "I am not mad. It will be as I say." He seemed almost agitated as he turned. "Master Ingram," he began, then muttered to Franz once more in German. "Proposal," said Franz. "Master Ingram, I haff proposal for you. I will bring tools, wood, apprentices, money, even fumble-fingered journeyman." He slapped Friedrich on the shoulder. "You buy pianos, find bigger workspace. We will make pianos, sell to Hochadels, to burghers with more silver than sense. We will be first, we will be rich. Piano from Bledsoe and Riebeck everyone will want. And guitars," he added, almost as an afterthought. Ingram stared at him. It took a moment for him to realize that the German was very serious. A slow smile bloomed on his face, and the two men shook hands.

Pivoting, Riebeck pointed to Franz, Marla and Thomas. "Pianos need the new music, the new music needs pianos. You, you must learn the music. You must teach the music. You must make the people hungry for the music. I will help. Silver I will give, but your hearts must build road, must cornerstone be, must bring light for new music to all who can hear and see."

They stared at each other, light dawning in their own eyes, anthems sounding in their spirits. Marla reached out to the two young men. Hand in hand, they faced the others. "We will," they said, solemnly, soberly.

# FACT

# Drillers in Doublets

～

## Iver P. Cooper

I don't want to be critical of coal mining, especially not where Mike Stearns can hear me. But the fact remains that coal has some serious disadvantages, both as a fossil fuel and as a source of organic chemicals.

Extracting coal is labor-intensive; you have to dig shafts and tunnels, keep the works from flooding, and provide ventilation. It is also dangerous: the roof can collapse; methane gas in the mine can explode; and breathing of coal dust leads to "black lung." Once the coal is on the surface, it must be transported by trains or vessels.

If the coal has a high sulfur content, then the sulfur must be removed. Otherwise, burning the coal will result in the emission of sulfur oxides, and the formation of acid rain.

To obtain chemicals from coal, the coal is cooked and fractionated. This is a batch process; the coal is loaded into iron vessels with small vents. Hydrocarbon gases escape from the openings; the solid material which remains is coke. When the gases are cooled, some of the hydrocarbon will precipitate as coal tar. The remainder is subjected to fractional distillation and other processes, yielding ammonia, light oils, and "coal gas." You get only eight to ten *gallons* of coal tar from one *ton* of coal.

Because of the difficulties in handling solid coal, chemical engineers have developed techniques for converting it into a gas or liquid. Of course, these increase production costs.

213

Hence, this essay will examine the extent to which the United States of Europe (USE) might be able to exploit natural gas and petroleum.

Natural gas is mostly methane, with small amounts of ethane, propane, butane, isobutane and pentanes. These are all small linear hydrocarbons, and they are useful in the chemical industry. Still, I expect that the principal use of natural gas (especially the propane fraction) in the USE will be to keep gas-guzzling twentieth-century vehicles running.

We will want to obtain our aromatic hydrocarbons, such as benzene, from either coal or petroleum. Benzene is a trace ingredient (only about 0.06–0.29%) of coal tar, itself a minor product (in a quantitative sense) of coke production. Until World War II, benzene was nonetheless obtained from coal tar; afterward, to feed the growing plastics industry, it was produced from petroleum. Petroleum typically is around 3% benzene. Plainly, petroleum is the richer source.

What are the other advantages of petroleum? When you drill for it, there is no need to send anyone underground. Once the drill reaches the oil reservoir, the oil is driven to the surface by the action of an overlying "gas cap," gases dissolved in the oil, underlying water, or, on rare occasions, gravity. Indeed, in some cases, the escape is overly vigorous; the oil gushes out and the well must be brought under control so that it is not wasted.

Transportation costs are much less than they would be with coal, at least once oil pipelines can be constructed and protected. Finally, since oil is a fluid, it is easier to refine into its component hydrocarbons. For example, the refining can be conducted as a continuous process. (Natural gas has similar advantages over coal, at least if you can carry it in pipelines.)

## Local Resources

Fictional Grantville is based on historical Mannington, West Virginia, with one very important exception: it does not have Mannington's oil wells, or any of its drilling rigs. (It is unclear whether the oil wells just ran dry or never existed. If they merely ran dry, then there might be pumping equipment, casing and pipeline available for salvage.)

Fortunately, Mannington's natural gas wells have been bequeathed to Grantville, and we know that they are still productive. In *1633*, Chapter 34, Mike says, "we're getting a fair amount of oil now from the gas wells right here in Grantville, too, since we upgraded them." And in Loren Jones' "Anna's Story," from Grantville Gazette Number One, we are told, "like many of his neighbors, George ran his stove, water heater, dryer and furnace on gas from under his own land. The wellhead and compressor were out in the barn."

The Grantville (Mannington) public library owns a number of possibly useful accounts of the oil industry (see Appendix). There should also be some local knowledge independent of the library's resources. West Virginia has produced oil since 1859; it produced 16 million barrels in 1900. It was the leading natural gas producing state from 1906 to 1917. It is not unreasonable to suppose that pre-ROF Grantville high school students made field trips to the Oil and Gas Museum in Parkersburg, West Virginia. And perhaps they had to write research essays afterward . . . which are still in a box at the school somewhere.

Some displaced up-timers may have worked in the oil or natural gas business. We know from *1632*, Chapter 8, that some residents have at least participated in the West Virginia Oil and Gas Festival; that is how they know how to build steam engines. Perhaps one of them has a copy of a vintage Oil Well Supply Company catalog; these have impressively detailed drawings of drilling equipment, parts lists, and so forth.

In *1633*, Chapter 3, we are told, "downtown Grantville had some large and multi-story buildings left over from its salad days as a center of the gas and coal industry." So there might be some interesting artifacts in cellars or attics, or perhaps some resident has a little collection of souvenirs, collected when his grandpappy worked on a derrick.

Another point to keep in mind is that many of the techniques and much of the equipment used in oil and gas drilling are also used in drilling for water (or brine). According to the West Virginia Department of Natural Resources, a Mannington resident, Luther Dell Michael of Luke's Drilling, is certified to drill water wells within the state. Perhaps he has a Grantville counterpart; if not, there should be some residents with water well drilling experience and perhaps even a light drilling rig.

Also, drilling is performed in the *coal* mining industry: to find an underground coal seam, to start a shaft, or to vent methane out of the works. Chances are that there are UMWA members who know something about drilling, and there may even be drilling equipment.

## Down-timer Knowledge of Petroleum

In the ancient world, both bitumen (tar, asphalt) deposits and liquid oil seeps were observed. The tar was used as a binder (e.g., to mortar bricks together) and as a waterproofing agent (especially as caulking for ships). The liquid oil served as a medicine. Both were used as a fuel (e.g., in Persian fire worship) and as incendiary agents in warfare (notably the "Greek Fire" of Byzantium). While these ancient exploits were probably forgotten by the seventeenth-century Europeans, these are uses which I would expect to be rediscovered, time and again, whenever a curious passerby happened upon a lump of asphalt. Thus, there would be some local knowledge of petroleum wherever there were oil seeps.

Moreover, I would think that the peculiarities of petroleum, in particular the fact that it was a liquid that could catch fire, would cause it to be remarked upon to strangers, resulting in the dissemination of information about it.

According to Dr. E.N. Tiratsoo, "samples of petroleum oils were brought back to Europe by travelers from Baku, Burma and China" (Tiratsoo, 2).

Marco Polo visited the ancient Baku oil fields in 1250. He reported that "a hundred shiploads might be taken from it at one time" (James and Thorpe, 405). It was apparently used at that time both as a fuel, and as a veterinary ointment (for camels with mange).

There is also ample evidence of pre-Ring of Fire (ROF) knowledge of European oil seeps. The best known were those at Wietze (Hannover, Germany), Pechelbron (Alsace), Beziers (southern France), Agrigentum (Sicily), Modena (Po valley, Italy), and Tegernsee (southern Bavaria), and at various locations in Galicia and Romania. (HBS 2). The oil of Tegernsee was sold for medicinal purposes as "Saint Quirinus Oil" as early as 1436. The Alsatian oil was discovered in 1498, and the Galician "earth balsam" in 1506. The petroleum of Agrigentum was first mentioned by ancient Roman writers. Salsomaggiore in northern Italy had gas springs, which is why, in 1226, it adopted a salamander surrounded in flames (i.e., a fire elemental) as its municipal emblem.

There was a small scale local trade in European oil before the Ring of Fire. Moreover, if there were a sudden increase in the demand for oil, the down-time Europeans would look further afield, and they, or their trade contacts in the Ottoman Empire, would probably be aware of the Near Eastern seepages in Baku, Ecbatana (Kirkuk), Ardericca (near Babylon), Zacynthus (Zante), and Tuttul (Hit). Spanish and English mariners visited the Trinidad pitch lake in the sixteenth century, and Joseph de la Roche d'Allion commented on the oil springs of New York in *Sagards Histoire du Canada* (1632). The Spanish were probably aware, by 1632, of at least some of the oil seepages of Cuba, Mexico, Bolivia and Peru. (1911EB).

## *The German Oil Fields*

We first heard of the Wietze oil field, near the town of Celle, in 1633, at Jesse Wood's press conference. The extraction and refining operation is being supervised by Quentin Underwood, the secretary of the interior and would-be oil tycoon. Most of the financing is coming from unidentified Germans. It appears that the refined oil will be transported by river, specifically, by barges towed by the steam-powered tugs *Meteor* and *Metacomet*. The field lies within the province ruled by George, the duke of Calenburg, and he is already enjoying economic fringe benefits; the Abrabanels are opening a bank branch in the provincial capital, Hannover.

The 1911 *Encyclopedia Britannica* notes that Hannover has oil production from Pliocene, Cretaceous, Jurassic, Triassic and Devonian rocks. The Wietze field is famous in geological circles because half the total production comes from mining rather than drilling. This implies that some of the oil is quite close to the surface. Still, that doesn't guarantee that all drilling will be successful. In 1857–1863, Professor Hanaus of Hannover bored ten wells in its vicinity, but only three showed even traces of oil (HBS 4).

This field is one of a cluster of a score of small oil fields, which mostly lie on or southwest of a line running from Bremen to Magdeburg. The largest of the lot is Nienhagen, which produced 2,200,000 barrels of oil in 1940.

However, the most prolific oil field in all of Germany is the Reitbrook field, near Hamburg, which yielded over 2,500,000 barrels the same year. There are 1,000 acres of producing field, and they lie atop a salt dome (see below). If you drill in the right place, you will find a gas sand about 300 feet down, and below it, at 700–800 feet, the oil horizon, made of fissured Upper Cretaceous chalk. (If you hit salt, you know you are out of luck.) It will probably be discovered only once geologists thoroughly map 163x Germany; in our time line, the field was discovered in 1937. (Near Reitbrook we may find two more fields, Sottorf and Meckelfeld.)

North of the mouth of the Elbe, near Meldorf, are a few more small fields. They, too, are salt dome-associated. Oil from Reitbrook or Meldorf could be transported by barge on the rivers Elbe and Saale.

Borings in a potash mine resulted in the chance discovery of oil in Thuringia, specifically, at Volkenroda near (and northeast of) Mulhausen. That is less than 60 miles from Grantville.

Also worthy of note are the Bavarian oil seepages (near Tegernsee, home of the relics of St. Quirinus), and the small oil fields near Bruchsall and Heidelberg, opposite Pechelbronn in France. (See generally Tiratsoo,126–31.) Bruchsall and Heidelberg are south of Mannheim and east of the Rhine.

Only the Wietze and Tegernsee fields, and possibly the Mannheim fields, are likely to be known to down-timers (by "known," I mean, they know of the associated seepages). The other German fields must be located by prospecting. In some instances the field of search can be narrowed down by reference to up-timer geographic texts, such as the *Hammond Citation World Atlas*. This shows that modern Germany has seven oil sites and five natural gas sources. Comparing this map to Tiratsoo's 1949 map of German oil fields, it appears that the atlas will guide the USE to the fields at Meldorf, Reitbrook, and Nienhagen. It also shows three fields that Tiratsoo either ignored or didn't know about. These are southwest of Bremen, west-northwest of Osnabruck, and south of Frankfurt.

## *Other European Oil (and Natural Gas) Fields*

Discounting the North Sea, Europe is not a major producer of oil. The most productive portion is in the foothills of the Carpathian Mountains, especially in Galicia and Romania.

In the seventeenth century, Galicia (now the western "spur" of Ukraine) was part of Poland. There is some question as to how welcome USE entrepreneurs will be in Galicia, as Sweden and Poland were at war as recently as 1629 (Sigismund thought he was the rightful king of Sweden.)

The main Galician oil field is Boryslaw (over the period 1855–1949, it produced 180 million barrels), followed by nearby Schodnica-Urycz (with oil reserves about one-seventh those of Boryslaw).

Perhaps sixty miles west-northwest of Boryslaw, inside modern Poland, there is the small Gorlice-Sanok area. This includes Bobrka, which has an oil history museum. According to their website, the first Polish mention of oil was by Jan Dlugosz (1415–1480). In the seventeen century, they add, rock oil was found near Drohobycz and Krosno (west-northwest of Sanok).

Getting this Galician oil to Grantville or Stockholm would be rather arduous. Initially, the Krosno and Sanok oil would probably be transported down the San and Vistula to the Baltic Sea. The petroleum of Boryslav might need to ride the Dniester to the Black Sea, and then come around the long way through the Mediterranean Sea and the Atlantic Ocean.

The Romanian oil, in a geographic sense, is more accessible; oil from the many fields within a forty kilometer radius of Ploiesti can be hauled to the Danube and then shipped upstream (to Vienna) or downstream to the Black Sea. Unfortunately, this is Ottoman territory, and therefore hostile to uptimers.

Cardinal Richelieu is likely to make a grab for the small Alsatian oil field at Pechelbronn, discovered in 1498. (Historically, Alsace was not absorbed by France until 1639.) The oil is found in sand lenses. Of the oil here, about 43% can be removed by mining, and another 17% by drilling (the rest is considered unrecoverable). From 1745 to 1849, twelve wells were drilled or dug, to depths of thirty-one to seventy-two meters. Average production in the late Forties was about 500,000 barrels, and total production over the last 150 years has been about 3,000,000 metric tons.

The Italian oil fields are small, and thus it is likely that the only ones which will be exploited in the near future are the ones which are known to down-timers as a result of seepages, or through pirated copies of the *Hammond Atlas*. The latter only shows two oil sources, one near Ragusa in Sicily and the other in the Po river valley, to the northwest of the gas seeps of Salsomaggiore. The development of these sources are best considered as possible joint venture projects with our colleagues in the Most Serene Republic.

A very large natural gas field lies close at hand, in the northwestern province (Groningen) of the United Provinces of the Netherlands, and is still under Dutch control. This territory might well be subject to protective occupation by USE military forces, if that were considered desirable. Would-be natural gas tycoons would be well advised to read the "Fuels" essay in the Grantville Public Library copy of *Encyclopedia Brittanica* before they set out. This reveals that the Groningen field is large (24 kilometers wide by 40 kilometers deep), but the productive formation, a Permian sandstone, is deep (pay depth is 3,440 to 3,050 meters). That means it is not a good target for neophyte drillers.

## Oil Fields Outside Europe

One advantage that the transplanted West Virginians have over main timeline wildcatters is that they know in advance which parts of the world to start looking in.

Standard encyclopedias will tell them about the world's major oil fields. Unfortunately, they are all outside USE territory. Some might be developed as joint ventures with the Venetians or the Dutch.

As long as the Ottoman Empire remains hostile to Grantville, it will be difficult to directly exploit any of the oil fields in the Persian Gulf states (modern Iran, Iraq, Saudi Arabia, Kuwait, Bahrain, Qatar), in the Baku region on the west coast of the Caspian Sea, or in Libya. While some of the fields are controlled by the Persians, rather than by the Ottomans, the most direct shipping routes would still pass through the Sultan's domains.

But what we can't drill for ourselves, we can still buy. Muslims began commercial production of oil at a very early date. Baku oil was being sold as early as 885 AD, and crude oil was also produced commercially, pre-ROF, from seepages on the eastern bank of the Tigris, from the Sinai in Egypt, and from Kuzistan in Persia. (The wells were dug, not drilled.) Islamic alchemists were also able to fractionate naphtha by distillation. Hence, the USE could at least import petroleum, crude or partially refined, from the Ottoman Empire.

There are several noteworthy oil fields in Latin America, notably on Trinidad, and in Venezuela and Mexico. My initial concern was that this was within the Spanish sphere of influence. However, the island was only sparsely populated, and the natives were hostile to the Spanish. So a strong enough party of adventurers could certainly take over. In 1595, Raleigh made a surprise attack, with 100 to 200 men, and slaughtered the Spanish settlement. However, Raleigh was not interested in colonizing Trinidad himself, just in using it as a springboard for an expedition into Guyana (the fabled location of El Dorado).

Europeans first learned of Trinidad's oil in 1510, when Columbus shipped samples back to Spain. Prior to European settlement, Indians used Trinidad's asphalt to caulk dugout canoes, so Sir Walter Raleigh, who used it to repair his ships on his 1595 visit, was just copying native practice.

The Pitch Lake, now a tourist attraction, is large (95 acres), and 300 feet deep at the center. The asphalt can be broken out by picks; there is no need to drill.

Of course, there are other, less immediately accessible, sources of oil on the island. Even there, it should not be necessary to drill to great depths to obtain petroleum. In 1857, the Merrimac Company drilled a well to a depth of 280 feet, and struck oil. In 1867, Mr. Walter Darwent found oil on the Aripero estate at a depth of 160 feet. And the next year, the Trinidad Lake Petroleum Company was gratified by the discovery of oil at La Brea at a depth of 250 feet.

In 1902, a well was drilled to 1,015 feet in three months using the "Canadian Pole method of percussion drilling." It produced a small gusher (100 barrels a day).

The first big find was in 1911–12; one well yielded 10,000 barrels per day from a depth of 1,400 feet.

The Trinidadian reservoirs, when intact, have a high gas pressure. That is both good news (initial production can be high) and bad news (the well may blow wild, wasting oil and blasting casing, tools and rocks into the air). It became customary to keep an emergency crew on hand, armed with pumps, shovels and picks.

Venezuela also has a great deal of oil; in 1996 it ranked sixth worldwide in proven oil reserves. Its oil is already known to down-timers; "the first oil exported from Venezuela (in 1539) was intended as a gout treatment for the Holy Roman Emperor Charles." At Guanoco you can find the Bermudez Asphalt Lake, covering 1,100 acres with an average depth of six feet.

In what would have become the United States, were it not for the Ring of Fire, oil and natural gas can be found in the Appalachian mountains (Pennsylvania and West Virginia), in the midcontinent region (Louisiana, Arkansas, Mississippi, Oklahoma, Kansas and Texas), in the Rocky mountains (Colorado and Wyoming), in California, and in Alaska. (There is also oil in Alberta, Canada.)

In our own timeline, beginning in 1638, the New Sweden Company established colonies in modern Delaware, New Jersey, Pennsylvania and Maryland. It is possible that a similar venture in the 163x timeline could exploit the petroleum of Pennsylvania and West Virginia, but it is doubtful that it would be economical for them to ship it back to USE. Still, an advantage of an American expedition is that the Grantville Public Library is likely to have specific information (e.g., where and how deep to drill) only about American (especially West Virginia, Pennsylvania and Ohio) oil fields.

Nigeria is also a major oil country (in 1995 it ranked twelfth in proven reserves). In 1632, it was not dominated by any European power, and it is convenient from a transportation standpoint; oil could be shipped by sea all the way from Nigeria to Germany. This isn't as cheap on a per mile basis as pumping it through a pipeline, but it is certainly superior to transporting it by rail from Baku or Ploiesti.

However, an expedition to Nigeria is not for the faint-hearted. The *Encyclopedia Americana* will tell Grantville residents (and spies) to look for oil in the Niger river delta (first discovered there in the Fifties). What they won't know, until they get there, is that the oil fields are in swampland, and that they will probably need to drill from barges.

## Where Is Oil Found?

Oil is a liquid rock. In fact, another name for oil—petroleum—means "rock oil." Oil is formed primarily from marine sediments rich in organic matter (bacterial, plant, and animal remains). These deposits are usually found along the rims of ancient ocean basins, where sea life was most abundant. In these basins, as more and more sediment was deposited, the layers below were compacted, becoming rock. The compaction also resulted in physical and chemical changes in the organic matter, eventually resulting in the formation of oil in the pores of this source rock. Further compaction drove the oil out.

The first criterion for the formation of a useable oil pool is that the oil find its way into a suitable reservoir rock. This must be porous (so it can hold the oil) and permeable (the pores are interconnected, so oil can flow into and out of it). Think of the rock as being like a can filled with marbles. The usual reservoir rocks are sandstones and limestones.

Since oil is lighter than water, it constantly tries to migrate upward and outward. If it not somehow trapped, it will pass out of the reservoir rock, eventually reaching the surface, evaporating, and becoming lost to the atmosphere. Thus, to have a viable oil reservoir, it is therefore not enough to have a good reservoir rock; one must have an oil "trap."

The trap is formed of a rock which is relatively impermeable to oil. This is sometimes called the cap rock. Shales make excellent cap rocks. Of course, to form a trap, the cap rocks must be positioned to prevent the upward and horizontal movement of the oil in the reservoir rock. This kind of positioning can occur as a result of the folding or faulting of the earth's crust.

The same structures which trap oil can also trap gas, and the same field can produce both fossil fuels.

## Prospecting for Oil

Even if you know that there is oil in, say, Saudi Arabia, you still have to find it. In searching for oil you must strike a balance between trying to cover a large area and not overlooking any indications that oil might be present.

The simplest approach is that you walk over the land, looking for surface signs of oil or gas. A more sophisticated prospector will make an effort to deduce the subsurface structures by finding places where the underlying rock layers are exposed, such as outcrops, roadcuts, ditches, wells, and mines. By comparing the rock beds at different sites, you build up a picture of how the underlying rock layers are contorted. With enough information, you can identify a potential oil trap. Finally, you can also use geophysical methods to find out what is below the surface. These prospecting methods are discussed in greater detail below.

## Oil Signs

Early prospectors combed the land for signs of oil, such as oil and gas seeps, mud volcanoes, solid petroleum deposits, burnt clays, and "showings" of oil in water and salt wells. They then drilled nearby.

An oil seep or "spring" is a place where oil seeps to the surface. The La Brea Tar Pits in Los Angeles are a good example. The oil may reach the surface in a number of ways. The trap may be eroded to the point at which the reservoir surface "outcrops," that is, is exposed to the surface. Or the oil in a trap may be tapped by a joint (a crack) or a fault in the overlying rock. Either way, the oil reaches the surface and slowly evaporates. Typically, the seepages are tarry (asphaltlike), but a young seepage, or one warmed up by the sun, may become more liquid and flow. In 1864, the chemist Benjamin Silliman, Jr., remarked that in the Rancho Ojai area of California, "the oil is struggling to the surface at every available point and is running down the rivers for miles and miles."

Modern geologists regard oil seeps as proof that an oil-bearing rock is in the region. However, they do not necessarily mark a good place to drill for oil. An oil seep, after all, is a place where the oil is escaping to the surface. It escapes because the trap rock above the oil reservoir has been breached by erosion or faulting. The more prolific the seeping, and the longer it has been going on, the less oil is left to be drilled.

Oil seeps are often associated with water springs, possibly

because water springs are also formed as a result of outcropping and faulting. The oil forms an iridescent film on the spring water. If the water is stagnant, the oil may accumulate as a semisolid mass that remains after the oil evaporates.

Gas can also seep to the surface. Gas seepages are easiest to detect when they occur underwater, forming visible bubbles. Thus, gas seepages are most often spotted in swamps, streams, lakes, and coastal waters. Bear in mind that gas often travels greater distances than does oil.

Escaping oil and gas can catch fire, baking nearby rocks such as clays to give them a burnt appearance.

A mud volcano can cover an area of several square miles and be more than a thousand feet tall. It is a cone of mud through which gas escapes, perhaps through cracks in a layer of clay. As the gas rises, it mixes with the clay and ground water to form a mud, which erupts under the pressure of the escaping gas. Mud volcanoes have been found in the Baku region beside the Caspian sea, on the Arakan coast of Burma, on the island of Trinidad, and in Rumania.

Gas or oil may be found, not only in a well drilled for the purpose of finding oil, but also in a water or salt well. In major oil producing regions, minor oil showings may be found in nearly every exploratory well. Even if a showing itself is too minor for the well in question to be commercially viable, the driller may hope that the showing indicates that the well is on the edge of a pool.

## Anticlines and Geological Mapping

Beginning in 1861, geologists speculated that anticlines—rooflike arches (folds) of rock—could, if a layer of impermeable rock (the "trap" layer) overlaid a porous, oil-soaked layer (the "reservoir" layer), prevent the oil from escaping. In 1913, Charles Gould pointed out that all of Oklahoma's big pools lay under anticlines, and the rush to find anticlines began. The Mannington, West Virginia, oil field was one of the first discoveries made as a result of applying this geological knowledge.

The ability of an anticline to trap oil into a commercially

exploitable pool is dependent on many factors. Oil is usually not associated with large anticlines, i.e., mountain ranges. If the anticline is small, the amount of oil trapped may be insignificant. If the anticline's slopes are shallow, oil may escape, especially if assisted by a regional dip or by groundwater movement. If the anticline's slopes are steep, there may be little room to drill. If the anticline has been eroded or fractured, oil once trapped there may have escaped. If an anticline was formed too many millennia after oil entered the reservoir layer, the oil may have moved on before the trap was formed.

If an anticline traps gas as well as oil, the gas will be at the top. That means that the center of an anticline may produce gas, while wells on the flanks yield up petroleum.

A young anticline will form a hill-like surface structure. However, the geologist cannot safely assume that hills are anticlines and that valleys or plains are not. As a result of erosion, an anticline may be leveled, or even become a valley. For that matter, a syncline (the opposite of an anticline) can become a hill.

Therefore, to be sure whether an anticline is present, one must map the subsurface layers of rock. Mapping the subsurface geology is easiest in hill country (especially the western badlands), where there are numerous outcrops and cliff faces. Mineshafts and road cuts can also be revealing. In farmland, information can be gleaned by descending into irrigation ditches and water wells, as well as by studying occasional outcrops. Pits can be dug, or shallow holes (called "strat" holes) drilled, to gain more information. In forests, swamps, and jungles, of course, the rock formations are well hidden, and digging is also difficult.

If an anticline is fully exposed, you can "walk the bed," that is, trace one of its layers as it rises upward, levels off, and then dips back down. However, it is more likely that only bits and pieces of the structure are exposed. The geologist needs to be able to recognize that a rock layer at outcrop A is part of the same bed as a particular rock layer at outcrop B. Hence, specimens will be collected and carefully compared.

Care must be taken not to confuse two rocks that are similar in appearance but laid down in different geological periods. Fossils can be very useful in dating a rock layer. If the beds are correlated correctly, the geologist can compare the height of a bed, relative to sea level, at different points, and thereby discern whether an anticline is present. Unless distorted by later folding or faulting, the bed will be at its shallowest at the point corresponding to the crest of the anticline, and deeper elsewhere.

The ages of outcrop rocks can be an important clue as to the presence of an anticline. If an anticline is present, and has been eroded down to a plain, older rocks will be exposed at the center of the anticline, and younger rocks on its flanks.

## Faulting

A fault is a break in the continuity of a stratified rock. If you broke a plank of wood, and then stuck something underneath one half so the plank pieces no longer lined up, that would resemble a fault.

Faults can be bad news or good news for the petroleum geologist. The bad news is that a fault can break open an anticline, giving the oil a chance to escape along the gap between the fault blocks. The good news is that the faulting can result in an impermeable rock layer being moved alongside a reservoir rock layer, preventing oil from escaping on that side. They can thus help to form a trap and even, in some cases, form traps all by themselves.

Faults can also break up what would otherwise be a single reservoir into several noncommunicating sections. If so, then each section will have to be drilled by at least one well for the entire reservoir to be drained.

## Stratigraphic Traps

The term "stratigraphic traps" refers to various kinds of traps that are not formed by folding or faulting.

Paleogeomorphic Traps are aptly named, "buried landscapes," and they are derived from ancient coral reefs and sand bars. Corals are invertebrate sea creatures that form limestone skeletons. When the corals die, their skeletons accumulate to form hill-like coral reefs. In the meantime, their soft parts decay to form oil, which permeates the porous limestone. If the reef is buried by fine silt, which is compacted to form a fine-grained (impermeable) sedimentary rock, the oil will be trapped in the reef.

Sand bars are often found offshore. These sand bars can act as oil reservoirs if they, too, are covered over by silt. Ancient sand bars are the origin of Kansas' shoestring sands.

When one layer after another are laid in parallel, i.e., running in the same direction, they are said to "conform" to each other. If strata are eroded, resubmerged, and then covered with the new sediment, chances are that the new layers will have a different orientation. If the old strata were tilted, and the new strata are horizontal, oil can be sealed off where the old and new layers meet. This is called an "unconformity trap".

The grain size of sediment can change within a rock layer, leading ultimately to a change in permeability. This can prevent the oil from spreading out within the layer. If the oil-bearing layer is capped by an impermeable layer, the "facies-change" trap is complete.

A rock layer will not necessarily have the same thickness throughout. Often, sandstones will have a lenslike cross-section, pinching out at the edges. If the overlying rock is impermeable, it will seal off both the top and the flanks of the sandstone, resulting in a viable "pinch-out" oil trap.

It is relatively common for the basic kinds of traps to be combined within a single oil field. An anticline and a fault, or a fault and an unconformity, may work together to trap oil.

## Salt Domes

Sometimes, a deep-lying bed of salt will be pushed up, perhaps as much as 10,000 feet, to form a great dome. As this salt dome rises, it pushes through the overlying rocks. The rocks to either side will be tilted upward toward the dome, like the wake left by a passing ship. Since the salt is impervious to oil, oil rising along one of these tilted layers will stop, and be trapped, when it reaches the dome. Above, the dome, the layers of rock will be folded, forming an upside-down U much like an anticline. Here, too, oil can be trapped.

The first and perhaps the most famous of the salt dome fields was Spindletop, but there are many salt dome fields along the Gulf Coast in Texas and Louisiana. They are also found in the Zechstein basin of Germany.

## Geophysical Prospecting

In the mid-1920s, gravimeters, magnetometers and seismometers became important tools of the trade. The seismometer is the most effective of these devices, as it can detect a hidden anticline, i.e, one that does not outcrop. To use a seismometer, you must set off an explosion (in effect, an artificial earthquake). When the sound wave strikes the boundary between two rock layers, the sound wave is reflected (and refracted), and you can detect this.

Unfortunately, I don't think seismological prospecting will be practical in the 163x universe within a reasonable time frame. While I have no doubt that a pendulum-type seismograph can be constructed, I doubt that the necessary sensitivity and precision can be achieved.

Even if that barrier is surmounted, we will need to learn how to interpret the seismograms; this is very unlikely to be explained in a public library book. In effect, we will need to rediscover geophysics. It will happen, but not anytime soon.

## Percussive Drilling

If the oil has seeped to the surface, you may not need to drill a well at all. Depending on whether it is in a liquid or solid state, it can be scooped out or dug out.

In percussive drilling, the rock is fractured by repeated "hammer-blows" from heavy cutting tools. Such drilling was first performed in North America in 1808, using a device called a spring pole. This was a sapling bent to hang over the hole. (While the spring pole was initially used to drill for brine, the technique was readily carried over to petroleum extraction.) A rope would be tied to the sapling, hanging over the hole, and the drill would be tied to the free end. A second rope would also be tied to the sapling, but its free end would be tied into a loop. The operator would put his foot in the loop, and kick down, driving the drill into the hole. The natural springiness of the sapling would pull the drill back up, and the operation would be repeated. From time to time, you would replace the drilling tool with a bailer, so you could clear out the accumulated debris. To facilitate this, a large wooden tripod, with a hanging pulley at the top, was placed over the well hole. This tripod was the precursor of the derrick.

Drilling with a spring pole rig was slow work (one to three feet a day), and spring poles were suitable only for drilling shallow wells, usually less than 300 feet deep. On the other hand, the investment in materials was minimal, and the well could be drilled by one person. This is the drilling strategy that a farmer might use on his or her own land.

Could a spring pole rig be used successfully at Wietze? I can't say for sure, but I think it significant that in 1991, the Petroleum Museum in Wietze issued a commemorative medal that depicts the tripod of a spring pole rig on one side.

The spring pole rig was the precursor of the "cable tool" rig, in the sense that both break rock by percussion. The cable tool rig was so called because the drill (the "tool") was at the end of a cable. The cable ran up to a pulley mounted on the cross arm of a mast, and then down to the "tool string" hovering over the well hole. With the cable tool rig, the rock was worn away by the hammering effect of dropping the tool on it.

The tool string of the cable rig was raised by animal or steam power. For example, a walking horse or ox could pull a sweep (described by Agricola in 1556) or walk a treadmill. Or a steam engine could turn a capstan. The cable was initially a manila rope, and later steel wire.

In 1880, the total weight of the downhole tools was around 2,100 pounds. The drill bit was around four feet long and 140 pounds, and had a chisellike cutting edge. The heaviest tool, the auger stem (over 1,000 pounds), screwed into the bit, and increased the rigidity (and weight) of the drill. Above it were the "jars," which have a lower link that strikes against the auger stem on the upstroke, helping to dislodge (jar") the bit if it is stuck in the rock. The sinker bar, above the jars, has a similar purpose. The topmost downhole tool was the rope socket, which secured the tool string to the cable. The tool string is described in Grantville's copy of the 1911 *Encyclopedia Britannica*, which also comments on how the different components work together.

Percussive drilling techniques were known down-time. In the Artois region of France, a water well was drilled in 1126 by hammering down a rod with a chisel edge at the other end. (Gies, 112). A similar technique had previously been developed by the Chinese to drill both brine and natural gas wells, and it is a matter of scholarly debate whether the French were innovators or copycats.

I have not found a record of pre-ROF spring pole drilling in Europe. However, spring pole lathes were used in the Renaissance so, once a down-time engineer had the incentive to drill, this would not be a tremendous intellectual leap. However, the spring pole rigs would probably be used only by farmers on their own property, or on long distance expeditions on which you don't want to transport a full drilling rig yet expect that the oil will be found at a shallow depth.

Can the USE build cable tool rigs right away? I assume that cable is available, but if it isn't, you can still use a sturdy rope. Grantville residents know how to construct steam engines, which could provide the motive force. But animal power is an alternative. Then you need a connecting mechanism, such as a walking beam, to translate the steam engine's action into a pull-and-relax on the cable. This is well within down-time engineering skills (there are mills in pre-ROF Europe). Finally, you need the parts of the tool string. I believe that if you can cast cannon, you can cast the cable tools.

There are two basic problems with cable tool drilling. First, one has to stop every few feet to replace the tool string with a bailer, to haul out the debris. Second, the tool string could come loose inside the well hole. One then has to fish it out, which is easier said than done. As a result of these factors, the average pre-1940 cable tool drilling rate was about three feet per day, and the maximum rate, about ten feet a day. (Williamson I, 97; *Oil Century*, p. 93) A modern cable rig can pierce sixty feet a day (Anderson, 129).

It is often stated that cable tool rigs can be used to drill only to 2,000–4,000 feet. However, in 1953, a cable tool rig plumbed a depth of 11,145 feet.

## *Rotary Drilling*

In the 1890s, oil drillers began experimenting with a "rotary rig." In this rig, the rock was worn away by the cutting action of a spinning bit. The bit is attached to a hollow drilling rod, and, as the drilling progresses, you attach additional rod sections so you can reach ever further down.

Early in the development of rotary drilling, water was used to remove cuttings and lubricate the bit. It was discovered that the water mixed with the unconsolidated material to form a mud, and that this mud had advantageous effects, such as preventing fluids from flowing into the well and causing a blow out. Consequently, drillers began to deliberately formulate "drilling muds" for use in areas where the local materials were inadequate.

In soft and loose rocks, the rotary rig was much faster than the cable tool rig. For example, in Roaring Twenties East Texas, it averaged about 150 feet a day. Its maximum rate is perhaps 2000 feet a day. However, the cable tool rig remained the only practical equipment for use when exploring hard rock formations, until Howard Hughes, Sr., developed a special hard rock bit for rotary drilling.

Until the USE reinvents the Hughes technology, it could deploy a combination rig, i.e., one that could switch between cable tool and rotary drilling depending on what formations you encountered. In our history, combination rigs became available at the turn of the century. However, to operate a combination rig, you usually need a pair of drillers, one with expertise in cable tool operation, and the other knowledgeable in rotary drilling.

Can we teach down-timers how to do rotary drilling? We might not need to. Mark Kurlansky says that Europeans began using rotary drilling in the salt industry in the sixteenth century. In 1640, he adds, the Dutch drilled 216 feet under Amsterdam, using a rotating bit attached to extension rods, to obtain fresh water (p. 310).

## *Contemporary Chinese Drilling Techniques*

In the medieval Chinese version of cable tool drilling, a cast iron drill bit was suspended by a bamboo cable from a derrick. The cable was attached to a rocker (typically twelve feet long); it was lifted when the operator jumped on to the rocker, and dropped back when he jumped off. (Essentially, a human-operated walking beam). The Chinese were sufficiently sophisticated to use both "jars" and fishing tools.

Chinese borings were on a massive scale; in 1089, there were 160 brine wells just in the province of Cheng Tu. There is no doubt that, pre-Ring of Fire, the Chinese drilled wells of respectable depth, although there is some dispute as to just which depth milestone was reached when. A tenth-century source is quoted as saying that Lin-chiung has a "fire" (natural gas) well which is over 600 feet deep. James and Thorpe say that even during the Tang Dynasty (AD 618–906), the wells drilled in this manner were as deep as 850 feet (pp. 405–6). In 1944, a drilling engineer, M.T. Archer, was told that at the Tzu-Liu-Ching field in southwest China, wells over 2,000 deep were drilled "at least 200 years before Drake spudded in," i.e., before 1659. Typical progress was one to three feet a day.

According to the sinologist Joseph Needham, the traditional Chinese drilling technique, which was still used in the nineteenth century, could reach a depth of 4,800 feet. The adaptations that the Chinese made to deep drilling included tall derricks, double stranded bamboo cable, and giant rockers. The latter provided synchronized aerobic exercise for six laborers at a time. (Temple, 51–54).

It is presently unclear just how much early seventeenth-century Europeans knew about the Chinese drilling methods as a result of reports from merchants, missionaries and diplomats. If the Chinese knowledge is even hinted at in any of the books that would logically be consulted by someone starting an oil company, it would be wise to question these travelers closely and perhaps even ask them to send agents to China to study the local practices, which might help fill in any gaps in up-time knowledge of drilling.

## Drilling Operations

Beginning in the late 1800s, oil well supply companies provided plans for rigs, as well as all the necessary parts. They shipped the parts to you, and you assembled them at the site. If a piece broke, you ordered a replacement by number.

Alternatively, you could buy a portable drilling rig. The early ones were hauled, while some of the later ones were self-propelled.

My guess is that a USE oil company will begin by drilling for natural gas locally. Once they have mastered the techniques, they can disassemble the successful rig, and ship all the parts, or at least the essential ones that can't be made locally, to the new site. Before long, the parts of these rigs will be standardized, and the USE will have its own oil well supply companies.

There will usually be several crews, working either three eight-hour shifts or two twelve-hour shifts. A typical drilling crew, for working a single shift, comprises four workers: the "driller" (the shift supervisor), the "derrickman" (posted at the top of the derrick), and two "roughnecks" (on the derrick floor). The roughnecks do the grunt work and can be hired locally; the driller and the derrickman need training or experience. Sometimes a rotary rig will have additional crew members, such as a "mudman" to monitor and adjust the drilling mud, and a "motorman" to maintain and operate the power drive. Thus, a rotary drilling crew is often larger than a cable tool one. Indeed, a cable tool rig can be operated with as few as two people (the driller and a "tool dresser"), if need be.

Drillers were expected to keep track of the formations they were drilling through. Even if the well were dry, the information gained from a well log—especially when compared to other well logs and to other geological information—could help locate an oil pool. Well logs were supplemented by occasionally taking "cores": actual samples of the rocks being drilled through. Logging is easier if the well is drilled using cable tools, because the rotary drill bit pulverizes the rock.

Some of the German and Dutch fossil fuel fields are on tidal flats, and so we may have to experiment with near offshore drilling techniques. Piers were used as drilling platforms as early as the 1890s. At Huntington Beach, California, in 1929, directional (slant) drilling was used to reach offshore oil from derricks situated on the beach. Also in the Twenties, dredges were used off the Gulf Coast to create artificial islands for use as drilling platforms, and certain lakes were drilled from barges.

When the drillers are done, they must "complete" the well, that is, the well hole must be "cased" so that it is not infiltrated by water from the formations above the "pay" layer. (In soft formations, you case as you go along rather than wait until you're done. If you fail to strike oil, you then pull up the casing rather than let it go to waste in a dry hole.)

If the oil is gushing out, a manifold called a "Christmas tree" is attached to the wellhead, so that the flow of oil can be regulated. If the reservoir lacks sufficient driving force (gas or water) to push the oil up to the surface, the wellhead will be connected to a pump, which then provides the lifting force. It is not unusual for a single pump to be connected to multiple wells.

Gathering lines collect the fluid from several wells to a tank battery, in which gas, oil and water are separated. Clean oil is then stored in a stock tank. If you are drilling additional wells nearby (see below), you can use some of the oil as fuel for a suitably equipped drilling rig.

The first well drilled in a "virgin" oil field is called the "discovery" well. Once oil is found, "step out" wells are drilled to determine the limits of the productive territory, and then "development wells" are drilled to assure efficient exploitation of the discovery.

The ideal spacing is such that there is one oil well for every forty acres, or one gas well for every 640 acres. Otherwise, there is "well interference"; one well pirating oil or gas from another. In addition, it is not a good idea to run the wells "wide open"; the total production is reduced.

## Storage

Once you have productive oil wells, you have to deal with the problems of oil storage, transportation, and refining.

Oil was initially stored in artificial lakes. Since the oil was rapidly lost by evaporation, and was also very vulnerable to destruction by fire, better storage means were adopted. By 1866, wooden tanks holding 10,000 barrels of oil were in use. The wooden tanks, in turn, were replaced by iron tanks, which were more fireproof than the wooden ones.

## Overland Transportation

Shipping costs can be very significant. In the 1860s, Odessa bought Romanian oil, rather than the petroleum of Baku, because the "transport difficulties" were such that the cost of Baku oil rose one hundredfold en route. (HBS 5) (I am not sure why this was the case, since Baku oil could be shipped up the Volga, and then down the Don to the Black Sea. The Romanian oil came down the Danube and then across the Black Sea.)

During the American Civil War, Pennsylvania crude was placed in barrels, and the barrels were delivered to their destination by teamsters. Usually, the destination was just an exchange point where the barrels were loaded onto barges (see below) or rail cars.

Initially, the railroad carried oil by placing the barrels on flatbed cars. The first oil tank cars appeared in 1865.

The first pipeline laid for the purpose of carrying oil was constructed in 1862. Pipelines can carry oil or gas more cheaply than can railroads, as the railroads learned to their dismay in the 1870s and 1880s. (The railroads of course still had plenty of business carrying supplies and workers *to* the oil fields.)

So, can the USE build pipelines? In 1633, Mike Stearns expressed the concern that Quentin Underwood wasn't sufficiently worried about transportation issues: "He's probably assuming a pipeline will materialize out of nowhere. Made out of what, I wonder, and by who? A cast-iron industry that's just got up to cranking out potbellied stoves a few months ago?"

In 1632, the down-time engineers would have been familiar with the use of clay, wood or metal pipes to carry water. The Romans, of course, had made extensive use of lead pipe, and this had not been forgotten. In 1455, Dillenberg castle in Germany was supplied with water using a cast iron pipe.

By 1685, cast iron pipe sections, each one meter in length, were joined to form an 8,000 meter conduit carrying water from Picardy to Versailles. While this occurred after the Ring of Fire changed the course of history, I believe that this pipeline system was merely applying the earlier cast iron technology on a larger scale.

It is clear that if the iron can be spared and Sweden and Germany have plenty of iron ore, the USE can build pipelines in northern Europe. (Once it becomes available, steel pipe is preferred.)

It has been known since the 1860s that the joints of the pipe sections should be threaded and screwed together so that they don't leak as a result of the line pressure. (Welded joints ultimately replaced the screwed type.) I assume that we can either thread the pipes manually or build a machine to do this. If threading is not economical, then the alternative is some sort of flange.

If the cast iron cannot be spared, wood pipes are worth considering. Sir Hugh Middleton constructed 400 miles of wooden water mains for London in 1609–13; these used hollow logs (Wilson, 17–18). Their disadvantage was that they had to be dug up and replaced every twenty years. By 1666 (the time of the Great Fire), some of the wood conduits had been replaced with lead pipe. However, London did not completely switch over to metal pipe until the next century.

Hollowed wooden logs (or bolted planks) were used even in the United States (in part because timber was readily available). The first water mains of Boston used bored logs. New Englanders cut the logs with mating "V" ends, and forced one section into the next with a mallet.

Ceramic pipeline is also a possibility. It was used by the ancient Babylonians around 4,000 BC, so we are not talking about advanced technology here.

Oil can sometimes be moved by gravity feed, but it is more likely that it will need to be pumped. The early pumps were steam-powered, but later ones were driven by gas or oil-burning engines. Neither wood nor clay will withstand high pumping pressures, so the throughput of wood and clay conduits is limited relative to those made of copper, lead or iron.

Initially, the lines can be laid on the surface. However, the metal will expand in the summer and contract in the winter, causing buckling. It therefore is desirable to bury the pipe under several feet of earth, but digging the necessary trenches naturally increases the cost of construction.

In 1875, the 125 mile Big Benson line, crossing the Alleghenies, was built in nine months. The ten- and twenty-foot lengths of pipe were hauled 20 to 30 miles over primitive roads, screwed together, and buried. This makes me hopeful that USE will soon be able to build a pipeline to the refinery in Hannover, a distance of about 130 miles.

## *Water Transportation*

In the 1630s, it was cheaper to ship goods down rivers by barge than by road on wagons. Barrel-carrying barges were used in the early days of the Pennsylvania oil rush. However, they were effectively superseded by pipeline and rail transport.

But what if the oil needed to be shipped overseas? The simplest approach would be to stow oil barrels in the holds of merchant ships. Later, ships can be equipped with oil tanks; the first such vessel, the *Charles*, began operating in 1869. The first bulk tanker (oil stored in the hull) was built in 1886.

## *Oil Economics*

Private parties will prospect for oil only if there is a reasonable chance of making a profit. That is a function of the costs (of prospecting, leasing, drilling, completion and shipment) of oil production, the probability of success, and the price that the petroleum will command on the open market. The history of the oil industry in our own time line provides only limited guidance, but it is still our logical starting point. Since the industry is in a nascent state, I believe that it is appropriate to use pre-1940 cost data.

## *Oil Prospectors*

Geologists did not play a major role in oil prospecting until the early twentieth century. Down-timers can certainly search (and ask villagers about) oil signs. Thus, the cost of this crude form of prospecting is low; it is the cost of transportation, provisions, and salary for a small party of down-timers who are sent to a locale of interest. They will no doubt need an expense account for gratuities to pay to landowners or tenants in the area so that they aren't run off (or worse) for trespassing.

If a USE business venture wants to find anticlines, then it will need to hire (or train) up-timers or down-timers in the basic techniques of geology: identifying the common types of rocks; measuring the dip and strike of rock strata; making topographic and geological maps, etc. This is the sort of thing you learn to do in an introductory college geology course. The preferred equipment (geologists' hammer, chisels, a Brunton compass, a magnifying glass, etc.) are well within USE manufacturing capabilities. (A Brunton compass could be replaced, if need be, with an ordinary compass and an inclinometer with an inclination gauge and a bubble level. Da Vinci designed a scaleless inclinometer for airplane use in 1483–6.)

Individuals trained in geology and surveying will doubtless command higher salaries, but the costs of assembling a geologically oriented prospecting party should not be exorbitant.

## Leasing Costs

Assuming that a likely site is identified, you want to obtain drilling rights over a large block of land. Otherwise, if you are successful, others may drill wells nearby, competing with you for the oil in the local reservoir.

In the United States of our own timeline, oil on private land is owned by the owner of that land, not by the government. While it is possible to buy the land, ordinarily the oil company just leases drilling rights.

In "rank wildcat" territory (no producing wells nearby), it might pay a signage fee one dollar an acre. That is because the oil company is assuming the initial risk and expense of drilling. However, the company has to drill for oil on the lessor's land within one year of signing the lease. If not, it must either give up the lease, or pay a "delay payment." These delays can't continue indefinitely; the lease usually expires in five years unless oil or gas is being produced.

If oil or gas is found, the lease automatically continues for as long as oil is produced, and the landowner is entitled to the one-eighth of all of the oil or gas produced on the land (most just take the cash equivalent). This is called the "royalty interest."

You want your leases to cover a large acreage, without any gaps where a competitor could drill later (and siphon off your oil). Don't be shy about this; if an oil field is, say, three miles long and two miles wide, that's six square miles or almost 4,000 acres. By the same token, that's almost $4,000 in signage fees, and perhaps $4,000 a year in delay payments. So once you lease the block, don't dawdle.

Outside the USA, oil rights are usually publicly owned, and it is necessary to negotiate a concession from the government. Since the Ring of Fire has transported Grantville back to the age of monarchy, it is likely that if you are exploring in "civilized" areas, you will need to acquire rights from the local lord, and perhaps from the ultimate ruler. In the wilderness, you may still need to negotiate with native tribes so they don't harass you. In either case, there is the risk that if your operations are highly profitable, they will be taken away from you by force.

## Drilling Costs

Drilling costs depend on the depth that you are drilling to, the rock formations that need to be penetrated, the type of drilling rig employed, and whether you are buying the equipment yourself or engaging the services of a drilling contractor.

In the early days of the 1632 oil industry, you are probably on your own. However, costs are likely to then be comparable to those of the late nineteenth century.

In 1860, a spring pole well could be sunk to 200 feet at a cost of about $1,000. (Clark, *Oil Century*). In Appalachia, in 1886–88, a 2,000 foot well could be drilled and completed for a cost of about $3,000 using cable tools ($1.50 a foot)(Williamson vol. 1, 768). In Pennsylvania 95% of the wells of that period were shallower than 3000 feet.

As the industry matures, a petroleum entrepreneur will be able to engage the services of a drilling contractor (at least in northern Europe). The cost will then be heavily dependent on supply and demand. In the Burkburnett field (made famous by the Gable-Tracy movie *Boomtown)*, a 2,000 barrel a day gusher was brought in on July 29, 1918, and three months later there were 200 completed wells on Burkburnett townsite. The cost of rotary drilling down to 1600–1900 feet went from $10,000–12,000 in 1918 to $30,000 in 1920, as drilling contractors and supplies became scarce. Nonetheless, the average *non-boom* cost in the early twentieth century was $3/foot drilled. (Olien 36).

Drilling costs do increase with depth (you need heavier pipe, heavier and taller rigs, etc.). Nonetheless, prior to 1940, it was safe to assume drilling costs averaging $10/foot down to 7000 feet. In fact, some drilling contractors just quoted this as a flat rate.

In proven or semi-proven areas, drilling costs can be reduced by taking advantage of the logs from the successful wells. As early as the 1860s, geologists identified the formations which "paid out" oil. In Pennsylvania, the most important formation was the "third sandstone," at 300–800 ft., and if this did not produce oil (you hit a "tight" spot), the well was abandoned.

## Chance of Success

Please note that if you are drilling in "rank wildcat territory" on the basis of detection of oil signs, your chance of striking oil is probably on the order of one in thirty. Even with knowledge of favorable geology (you are probing an anticline), your chance of a strike is only about 10%. (Anderson, 95–6).

It can be argued that if you are exploring a region on the basis of twentieth-century knowledge, that the chance of success is higher. And I would agree, if your twentieth-century sources specify the location of the "known" oil field with an accuracy of about one mile.

That isn't likely to be the case, so you need to budget with the expectation that some of your wells will be dry. If you are drilling in a known oil field, the chance of success is closer to 75% (you could still hit a region where the reservoir rock is impermeable).

## Completion and Production Costs

Completing a productive well (putting in casing, constructing gathering lines and temporary storage, dismantling the derrick and rig, setting up the pump, etc.) might add 50% to the cost of drilling it.

Once production begins, costs are minimal if you sell the oil "at the wellhead" (i.e., the customer pays for transportation). If the well has to be pumped, there will be lifting costs; figure five to twenty cents a barrel.

Your ability to recover your exploration and drilling costs is going to depend, in part, on the productivity of the well. The average well produces perhaps ten barrels a day. (Ball, 137).

Storage tanks give you the ability to wait out a temporary drop in crude oil prices.

## The Price of Oil

The impetus for the drilling of the 1859 Drake Oil Well in Titusville, Pennsylvania was a report by Professor Benjamin Silliman, Jr., that "rock oil" could be refined, in place of whale oil, into kerosene for use as a lamp fuel. The Drake petroleum sold for about twenty dollars a barrel. A barrel, by the way, was later standardized as 42 gallons.

Thousands of miles away, Galician villagers hand-mined oil seepages, and sold their oil on the local market for a price of $140 a ton (likewise about twenty dollars a barrel) (HBS 3–4). Seepage oil was sold in Europe at least as early as 1480 (HBS 2), and I suspect that both supply and demand were constant until oil from drilled wells became readily available.

In America, as both demand and supply increased, the price stabilized to some degree. Overall, from 1880 to 1970, the average crude oil price was usually close to one dollar a barrel. (The "real" crude oil price, in 1991 dollars, was five to fifteen dollars a barrel during the same period.)

It is difficult to predict what oil prices will be like in the 1632 universe. Unlike America in 1869, the USE has plenty of uses for petroleum. However, it is also able to exploit nearby natural gas and coal reserves, and petroleum will have to be priced competitively with these alternative fuel and organic chemical sources.

## The Pipeline Business

The first successfully completed oil pipeline, two inches in diameter, built in 1865, carried 1,900 barrels a day a distance of six miles, and charged customers one dollar a barrel. I estimate that the cost of the pipeline was about $15,000–25,000 (based on Giddens, 142 et seq.). A turn of the century Gulf Coast six inch pipeline, delivering 7,000 barrels a day to the refinery, cost $5,400 to 6,500 per mile. (Williamson II, 87–8).

## The Refinery Business

If the oil field is far away from the USE, you will probably want to build a refinery nearby. You then export the refined products rather than the crude oil; this is more cost-effective. The cost of building a refinery depends very much on its processing capacity and sophistication. At the low end, in 1860, a simple still, with a five barrel a day capacity, cost $200. This was probably good only for producing kerosene. If you want multiple fractions, then you are going to be spending more money for the same refining capacity.

Whether it is desirable to refine the crude yourself depends on the profit margin. In early 1863, for example, crude oil was selling for two dollars a barrel (less then five cents a gallon), while refined oil brought in forty cents per gallon. Five gallons of crude oil made three gallons of refined product, and the refining cost five cents a gallon. On the other hand, in 1869, the price of crude was seven dollars a barrel (sixteen cents a gallon), the price of refined was 34 cents a gallon, while the refining cost was three cents a gallon. (Abels 50).

## USE Oil and Gas Law

Oil is subject to the rule of capture, that is, it belongs to whoever extracts it from the ground, not to the owner of the land where it lay originally. If a field had mixed ownership, that encouraged rival oil companies to drill wells close together and pump the oil out as fast as they could.

In the 1930s and thereafter, legislation in the "old" United States curbed waste in oil (and gas) production, and, not incidentally, put a floor under oil prices. The conservation methods included requiring minimum spacings between wells, limiting the amount of oil that an operator could produce each day from his well ("proration"), and in some fields providing that the field would be operated as a single unit with all owners sharing in the income ("unitization"). The USE might want to consider similar legislation.

## Natural Gas

Until 1960, natural gas was considered a waste product, and it was disposed of in the easiest manner possible, usually by "flaring it" (that is, burning it without even attempting to derive any benefit from it). It is now considered an important fuel.

Natural gas is lower in density than oil, and hence more expensive to ship. It usually is moved by pipeline, rather than by tankers. In the 1960s, natural gas was liquified for more convenient handling. Unfortunately, the necessary cryogenic facilities and cold-resistant alloys put this strategy beyond the pale for USE, at least in the near future. Hence, USE will probably exploit only the natural gas fields that it can access by protectible pipelines.

## Conclusion

Even before the Ring of Fire, the Europeans were collecting and selling oil on a small scale. Even if Grantville residents knew no more about the intricacies of oil prospecting and extraction than they did, the down-timers could supply us with petroleum. Given the financial incentive to do so, they could go beyond mining asphalts or oil sands, and actually drill for oil; they had already developed rudimentary percussion and rotary drilling techniques for obtaining both water and salt. What Europeans lacked, before the Ring of Fire, were parties willing to invest in land and drilling equipment (HBS 3–4), and these were absent, in part, because there wasn't enough assurance of profitability. The history of the spice industry gives us ample evidence of the length to which seventeenth-century merchants were willing to go if the rewards for success were great enough.

As the known sources of oil become exhausted, up-timer-trained geologists (and up-time atlases) will become more important in finding new fields, and up-time drilling techniques will allow the deeper sections of old fields to be exploited. But this doesn't need to happen all at once.

Likewise, we cannot ignore the problem of transporting the oil. But neither do we need to make an immediate jump to steel pipelines and supertankers. It is likely that the during the early years of the oil industry in the 163x universe, petroleum (and its refinery products) will be shipped by a combination of wagon trains, barges, barrel- or tank-carrying ships, and wood or iron pipelines.

I close with the words of Everette L. De Golyer: "In the finding of oil, it's good to be good, but it's better to be lucky."

# *Appendix*

## Works Listed as Owned by the Mannington (Grantville) Public Library:

Cranfield and Buckman. *Oil*

Whiteshot, The Oil-well Driller : a History of the World's Greatest Enterprise, the Oil Industry (Published in Mannington!)

Sampson, The Seven Sisters : the Great Oil Companies and the World They Shaped

Yergin, The Prize : the Epic Quest for Oil, Money, and Power

Mallison, The Great Wildcatter

Canadian Association of Oilwell Drilling Contractors, *Introduction to Oilwell Drilling and Servicing*

Thomas, The Quest for Fuel

Alth, *Constructing & Maintaining Your Well & Septic System* [water well books often discuss cable tool and rotary drilling]

Kurlansky, Salt : A World History.

*Encyclopedia Americana* (note articles on "Petroleum", "Gas, Fuel," "Geophysical Exploration," "Wells and Well Sinking," "Artesian Well," "Pumps," "Tanker," "Oil Sand," "Oil Shale," "Paleontology," "Rocks-Petrology," "Coal Liquefaction," "Salt Dome," "Salt," "Pipeline," "Tanker," "Asphalt")

I have been informed that Grantville has both the 1911 Encyclopedia Britannica and a more recent edition.

While it is not in the Mannington Public Library, I would be very surprised if none of the local Oil and Gas Festival buffs owned a copy of McKain's *Where it all began: the story of the people and places where the oil & gas industry began: West Virginia and Southeastern Ohio* (1994).

## Works Consulted by the Author
(starred references are of particular interest)

**PETROLEUM GEOLOGY AND PROSPECTING**

Lalicker, Principles of Petroleum Geology (1949)

North, Petroleum Geology (1985)

Crump, Our Oil Hunters (1948)

Gould, Covered Wagon Geologist (1959)

*Pearson, Surface Marks of Oil Deposits (1920)

*Hager, Practical Oil Geology (1951)

Ver Wiebe, Oil Fields in the United States (1930)

Dobrin, Introduction to Geophysical Prospecting (1976)

Nettleton, Geophysical Prospecting for Oil (1940)

King, Stratigraphic Oil and Gas Fields: Classification, Exploration Methods, and Case Histories (1972)

Moody, Petroleum Exploration Handbook; a Practical Manual Summarizing the Application of Earth Sciences to Petroleum Exploration (1961)

Cunningham-Craig, *Oil Finding* (1921)

*Ver Wiebe, *How Oil is Found* (1951)

Egloff, *Earth Oil* (1933)

Levorsen, Geology of Petroleum (1967)

Lalicker, Principles of Petroleum Geology (1949)

*Tiratsoo, *Petroleum Geology* (1951).

Hobson and Tiratsoo, Introduction to Petroleum Geology (1975)

Blakey, Oil on Their Shoes: Petroleum Geology to 1918 (1985)

**PETROLEUM ENGINEERING (DRILLING AND PRODUCTION)**

Thomas, Principles of Hydrocarbon Reservoir Simulation

Muskat, Physical Principles of Oil Production (1949)

Crichlow, Modern Reservoir Engineering: a simulation approach (1977)

Pirson, Oil Reservoir Engineering (1958)

Clark, Elements of Petroleum Reservoirs (1960)

*Brantly, History of Oil Well Drilling (1971)

*American Petroleum Institute, *History of Petroleum Engineering* (1961)(HPE)

Institute of Petroleum, "Oil, A Natural Resource" http://www. energyinst.org.uk/education/natural/3.htm

## OIL ECONOMICS

Grayson, Decisions under Uncertainty : Drilling Decisions by Oil and Gas Operators (1979)

Harbaugh, Probability Methods in Oil Exploration (1977)

Thompson, Oil Property Evaluation (1984)

Campbell, Oil Property Evaluation (1959)

## AMERICAN OIL HISTORY

*Williamson and Dunn, The American Petroleum Industry (1963) (2 vols.; v. 1. The Age of Illumination, 1859–1899. v. 2. The Age of Energy, 1899–1959.)

*Olien and Olien, *Easy Money* (1990)

*Fanning, Rise of American Oil (1948)

Donahue, Wildcatter: The Story of Michael T. Halbouty and the Search for Oil (1983)

Mallison, The Great Wildcatter (1953)

Ezell, Innovations in Energy: the Story of Kerr-McGee

Franks, Early Oklahoma Oil—A Photographic History 1859–1936 (1981)

*Giddens, *Early Days of Oil* (1948)

Giddens, Pennsylvania Petroleum, 1750–1872 (1947)

Rister, Oil! Titan of the Southwest (1949)

Roberts, Salt Creek, Wyoming; the story of a great oil field (1956)

Rundell, Jr., Oil in West Texas and New Mexico: A Pictorial History of the Permian Basin (1982)

Tennent, The Oil Scouts: Reminiscences of the Night Riders of the Hemlocks 1915 (1986)

Hughes, Oil in the Deep South (1993)

Latta, Black Gold in the Joaquin (1949)

Welty and Taylor, *Black Bonanza* (1958)

Clark, *The Last Boom* (1972)

O'Connor, The Oil Barons: Men of Greed and Grandeur (1971)

White, Formative Years in the Far West: a history of Standard Oil Company of California and predecessors through 1919 (1976)

Franks and Lambert, Early Louisiana and Arkansas oil : a photographic history, 1901–1946 (1982)

*Clark, *The Oil Century* (1955)

Clark and Halbouty, *Spindletop* (1952)

Marcossan, Isaac F., The Black Golconda: The Romance of Petroleum (1923–4)

Presley, Saga of Wealth: The Rise of the Texas Oilmen (1934)

Getty, My Life and Fortunes

Abels, The Rockefeller Billions (1965)

Knowles, First Pictorial History of the American oil and Gas Industry, 1859–1983 (1983)

West Virginia Geological and Economic Survey, "History of WV Mineral Industries—Oil and Gas" http://www.wvgs.wvnet.edu/www/geology/geoldvog.htm

### STORAGE AND TRANSPORTATION

*Wilson, Oil Across the World (1946).

Labouret, "A World Athirst for Oil; from Square-Rigger to Supertanker," UNESCO Courier, June, 1984 http://www.findarticles.com/p/articles/mi_m1310/is_1984_June/ai_3289708

### EUROPEAN OIL FIELDS

Scholle, "Petroleum-Related Medals and Tokens" http://geoinfo.nmt.edu/staff/scholle/graphics/medals/wietzel.jpg

Bobrka Oil Museum, http://www.geo.uw.edu.pl/BOBRKA/index.htm

*Harvard Business School, Oil's First Century (1959) (HBS)

Tiratsoo, *Petroleum Geology* 121–139 (1951)

Implications for Oil Potential in the Rhine Graben" http://www.crpg.cnrs-nancy.fr/MODEL3D/SOULTZ/TRANSFERS_SOULTZ/oil.html

### NIGERIA

Nigerian Oil Fields, http://www.eia.doe.gov/emeu/cabs/ngia_fields.png

photo of inland drilling barge in Nigeria, http://www.rigzone.
com/images/rigs/opt/Parke_PRig_ID637_175x225.jpg
www.nigerianoil-gas.com/industryprofile/index.htm and www.
nigerianoil-gas.com/industryprofile/niger-detla-fields.htm

**TRINIDAD AND VENEZUELA**

Barbour, "Privateers and Pirates of the West Indies," *American Historical Review*, vol 16, No. 3 (Apr., 1911), 529–566.

Porter and Prince, Frommer's Caribbean 2004 (p. 661)

Lonely Planet, http://www.lonelyplanet.com/destinations/caribbean/
trinidad_and_tobago/history.htm

Chaitan, "A Gravity Investigation of the Pitch Lake of Trinidad and Tobago," http://www.gstt.org/Geology/pitch%20lake.htm

"History of Trinidad's Oil" http://www.gstt.org/history/history%20
of%20oil.htm

Tiratsoo, *Petroleum Geology* pp. 250–69 (1951).

Seaman, "Trinidad's Pitch Lake" http://www.richard-seaman.com/
Travel/TrinidadAndTobago/Trinidad/PitchLake/

"How Ancient People and People Before the Time of Oil Wells Used Petroleum," http://www.leeric.lsu.edu/bgbb/2/ancient_use.
html

Trevelyan, *Sir Walter Raleigh* (2002)

Lacey, Sir Walter Raleigh (1973)

**OTHER REGIONS**

Al-Hassan and Hill, Islamic Technology: An Illustrated History (1986)

Tiratsoo, *Petroleum Geology* (1951)

Yergin, The Prize: The Epic Quest for Oil, Money, and Power (1992)

Temple, The Genius of China: 3,000 Years of Science, Discovery and Invention (1986)

**GENERAL OIL AND GAS INDUSTRY**

Boatright, Folklore of the Oil Industry (1963)

*Anderson, Fundamentals of the Petroleum Industry (1984)

*Ball, The Fascinating Oil Business (1965)

Deaton, U.S. Patent No. 2,299,803

American Oil & Gas Historical Society (museum links), http://
www.aoghs.org/MuseumLinks.asp

Malkamaki, Blake, "Oil History: An Index to Early Petroleum Historical Sites" http://www.petroleumhistory.com/

Oil and Gas Museum, Parkersburg, WV, http://www.aoghs.org/MuseumLinks.asp

*Pees, Oil History http://www.oilhistory.com

*"Petroleum," 1911 Encyclopedia Britannica, http://73.1911 encyclopedia.org/P/PE/PETROLEUM.htm

## GENERAL GEOLOGY

Levin, The Earth Through Time (1991)

Cooper, A Trip Through Time: Principles of Historical Geology (1986)

Gilluly, Principles of Geology (1968)

Chesterman, Audubon Society Field Guide to North American Rocks and Minerals (1979)

## GENERAL HISTORY, HISTORY OF TECHNOLOGY

James and Thorpe, Ancient Inventions: Wonders of the Past (1994).

Teresi, Lost Discoveries (2002)

"A Brief History of New Sweden in America" http://www.colonial swedes.org/History/History.html

"Cast Iron Pipe through the Ages," http://www.acipco.com/international/ductileiron/history.cfm

Gies, Cathedral, Forge and Waterwheel: Technology and Invention in the Middle Ages (1994).

Clarkson, "History of Alsace and Lorraine" http://feefhs.org/frl/fr/sc-alhis.html

*Kurlansky, Salt: A World History (2002)

"Animal Treadmills on the Farm" http://www.americanartifacts.com/smma/power/tread.htm

Vogel, "A Short History of Animal-Powered Machines: What Goes Around Comes Around, and Does Useful Work" *Natural History* (March 2002)

## MISCELLANEOUS

Chemlink, *Benzene* http://www.chemlink.com.au/benzene.htm

*West Virginia Library Catalog gateway (includes Mannington Public Library), http://clarkbrg.clark.lib.wv.us/vtls03/english/

History of Mining in Cape Breton, http://collections.ic.gc.ca/coal/impact/coaluse.html

Coal Tar MSDS, http://www.intlsteel.com/PDFs/coaltar.pdf.
USE Map, http://www.biel.ca/gville/smeurope1632.jpg
*Encyclopedia Americana
*1911 Encyclopedia Britannica
*current Encyclopedia Britannica

# How to Keep Your Old John Deere Plowing: Diesel Fuel Alternatives for Grantville 1631–1639

~~~

## Allen W. McDonnell

The Ring of Fire has left many of the farms around Grantville scrambling to train enough horses for the fall harvest. About half of the tractors that came through the Ring Of Fire were designed to burn gasoline and with the help of the agriculture department they will be converted to use pressurized natural gas in its place in 1631. Grantville has an abundance of natural gas; therefore, this conversion will put half of the modern equipment back into service for the first year. The tractors that are the topic of this article are farm size tractors, not the smaller lawn tractors people with large yards like to use for mowing their grass. The small lawn tractors are mostly gasoline powered but with conversion to run on natural gas they will come in handy for a lot of other jobs outside the farming industry. Examples of those alternate uses include the drawing of wagons and carriages designed for horses or serving as stationary PTO sources to operate machinery where electricity is not easily available.

With the exception of the old steam tractor, which was being rebuilt for the county fair, the rest of the tractors that came through the Ring of Fire are diesel engined machines. These diesel machines are sturdy beasts of burden; some of them are 30 years old and still running well. Several of the farms have their own diesel fuel storage tanks and can keep their equipment in the field with a little extra effort. In addition to petroleum diesel in these farm grade tanks, some isolated farms and homes outside of town use heating oil #2 in oil furnaces. Heating oil #2 is almost identical to farm grade diesel fuel #2 and burns quite well in diesel engines.

The question of how to keep these diesel tractors and the modern diesel trucks and cars also in the area fueled is the central focus of this article. Four different fuel alternatives and one fuel additive are explored. First is the petroleum diesel that came through the Ring of Fire and additives to it, including propane. Direct use of biologically derived oil is a second method, and the easiest short-term solution. Third, for the long run beginning in late 1634 the most likely method will be to burn crude diesel refined from petroleum sources. This crude diesel is easy to make once petroleum is available. Until that time, however, it would be a waste to let the diesel engines in Grantville sit idle. Finally, there is bio-diesel, which is a form of diesel fuel made from biologically derived oil.

Two methods are available to extend the petroleum derived diesel in up-time tanks. The first method is mixing. Any diesel engine, modern or archaic, will function quite well on a mix of 75% petroleum refined diesel and 25% light vegetable oil. Of course, this presumes the availability of cheap vegetable oil, which may be problematic in seventeenth-century Germany. The second alternative, if a competent mechanic is available, is to add propane injection to the diesel engine. Propane injection, also known as fumigation, will give an increase in diesel combustion efficiency. The propane acts as a combustion catalyst during the power stroke of the cylinder. If you are not a good mechanic let an expert do the conversion, otherwise you may get the propane amount too high and cause severe engine damage. When a turbo-charged diesel engine is properly fumigated with propane it will get a boost in torque and fuel economy resulting from the more complete combustion of the liquid fuel. Typical tractor engines are not turbo-charged and will only receive a small boost in efficiency from propane fumigation; many diesel farm trucks and pick-up trucks on the other hand are turbo-charged and would greatly benefit. No information is available on propane fumigation for engines that burn unrefined plant or animal oils; however with diesel or bio-diesel the engine boost amounts to a 10% increase in fuel economy. Combined with a 25% light vegetable oil mix in the fuel, this will total up as a 38% increase in fuel economy per unit of petroleum derived diesel used. The propane tanks used for this fumigation are generally the same ones found on backyard barbecue grills. With proper treatment some propane can be recovered from raw natural gas and used to refill these tanks if the knowledge and ability to install them on the diesels is available.

One of the most surprising things to come to light in researching this article was how easy it is to produce propane and butane from raw natural gas. Both propane and butane may be adapted to power gasoline engines where they provide 80% of the range of an equal volume of gasoline. This is an increase in range of 240 to 1 over low-pressure natural gas. To refine butane and propane out of raw natural gas you can follow any of several methods. The easiest one to explain is condensation.

Butane vaporizes at just below the freezing point of water, and propane vaporizes at about 45 degrees F below that. Using a metal coil run through a freezer you can condense butane out of the raw natural gas at about 10 degrees below freezing. The liquefied butane is separated out through a drip tube and stored in a regular propane cylinder like those used on portable backyard barbecues. When removed from the freezer, the butane will naturally warm to ambient temperature but will remain a liquid in the tank due to vapor pressure. If sufficient (probably cascaded) freezing is available, the partially refined natural gas can then be fed through a second condensing coil in a much colder freezer at about −30 C where the propane condenses. The propane may also be stored as a liquid under pressure in another tank. Natural gas in the eastern USA averages about 10% butane-propane-ethane and 90% methane. Using the freezing condenser method above refines about 2% butane and 4% propane by volume from the raw natural gas.

The second method to conserve up-time diesel works best with older diesel engines, but with a relatively simple heating set it will work for modern diesel engines as well. The newer machines in the diesel group can run on straight vegetable oil (SVO), or the animal equivalent, with a simple tank and fuel system heater added. These modifications involve installing a simple resistance heating element in the fuel tank, very similar to the ones used in engine blocks for winter weather. This can even be an electric heating pad fastened onto the bottom of the fuel tank. When the engine is not running, the heating element can be connected to an electrical outlet, to maintain a hot liquid oil temperature in the fuel tank and fuel system. While the engine is running, the waste heat from the liquid cooling system takes over. A copper tube is wrapped around the exterior of the fuel tank and attached to the tractor cooling system between the engine block and the radiator. This copper tube forces the hot engine coolant to circle the fuel tank several times before going to the radiator and maintains the oil as a hot liquid.

Hot and thin waste cooking oil or fresh vegetable oil burns just fine in older diesel engines; those that predate late twentieth-century pollution controls can be expected to have zero problems. Lighter oils such as corn or soybean oil work best. If the oil is kept sufficiently hot and thin; tallow, butter or lard can also be used as fuel. If bio-diesel or stockpiles of fossil fuel derived diesel are available, it is recommended that a small diesel tank be added to the newer equipment. This will allow the more refined fuel to be utilized when starting the engine and bringing it up to full power. Once at full power, one can switch to the biologically derived unmodified fuel oil. About five minutes prior to shutting down the engine, it should be switched back to the refined fuel. While these modifications are not mandatory, they do ensure that the equipment will have very little problem with clogged fuel injectors. The refined fuel serves as a fuel system cleaner during startup and shutdown, purging the lines and filter. Using refined fuel in this supplemental tank requires less than one percent of the total fuel supply for the newer vehicle and keeps the fuel pump and filter full of refined fuel when the equipment is shut off. This in turn helps prevent any pitting or premature wear that in some rare cases may be caused by free fatty acids that are present in all unrefined biologically derived fuel oils. Of course, again, this technique is dependent on the availability of animal or vegetable fats.

The third supply of fuel for the up-time diesel engines that came through the Ring of Fire will be crudely refined from down-time petroleum, most likely the Wentz oil fields. These oil fields are well known. Drilling for petroleum in this location has begun in

1633. Modern style multiple fractional distilling however, is several years in the future and only the much cruder pot distilling method will be available for several years. Pot distilled diesel fuel is very crude compared to that which came through the Ring of Fire with Grantville. The older diesel equipment, both the farm tractors and older farm trucks, can burn this crude diesel with minimal problems. The more modern heavy equipment, cars, and turbo-charged trucks on the other hand will suffer if they must use it. Crudely refined diesel tends to be high sulfur and it also has a broader range of chemicals in its mix. The turbo-charged engines of the late twentieth century are specifically designed to produce low exhaust emissions burning highly refined fuel with very low sulfur content and do not run well on crude diesel. To a small extent removing pollution controls on these engines will help, however the fuel filter and pump systems will be very hard to duplicate or modify until Grantville has built up an extensive manufacturing capability. Added to these difficulties is the expense of hauling either the crude petroleum or crudely refined diesel from the Wentz area to Grantville. This adds even more cost and complexity to the task of keeping the modern diesel engines of Grantville operational. The available hauling methods amount to wagons loaded with heavy oil barrels hauled over dirt pathways, with the option of using a barge for portions of the trip. All of the loading, hauling, unloading and reloading involved, when combined with wages and supplies for the teamsters and fodder for the livestock, make this process slow, complicated and expensive.

The medium-term solution to the general diesel fuel supply problem and the medium- to long-term solution for the modern diesel equipment is to create an alternative to the crude pot distilled diesel that will be coming from the Wentz petroleum fields down-time in 1634 and later. Bio-diesel can fill the gap during the period between 1634 when the crude refinery will be available and the projected fractional distillery five to ten years in the future.

What is bio-diesel? Regular cooking oil, no matter if it is vegetable oil or pork drippings, consists of triglyceride molecules. A triglyceride molecule consists of three fatty acid molecules that are bound to one glycerol molecule. The longer the fatty acid molecules, the more viscous the oil is. To make bio-diesel the triglyceride molecules have to be broken down to separate out the glycerol, which is a useful byproduct of the whole process but not a good thing to burn in a modern computer-controlled diesel engine. The easiest method of separating the glycerol from the triglyceride molecule is to break it down with a catalyst and substitute another alcohol molecule for the glycerol molecule. Most recent tractors and modern diesel farm trucks can have problems burning raw cooking oil; these engines work much better when operating on bio-diesel fuel.

Feedstocks to be used to manufacture bio-diesel will not be cheap to acquire. There is very little waste oil and fat to make fuel from. Most fats are eaten. Transportation costs in the 1630's were extremely high, effectively doubling the cost of any raw materials transported a long distance due to taxes, tolls and labor expenses.

One possible plant oil source in 1631–1633 will be the traditional seed crops grown by the local farmers as livestock feed. This leads to resource competition for any food crop such as oats or rice and it is believed that they will be only minor sources for biological oils. In 1631 linseed oil averaged 40 guilders per aum in Amsterdam, with one aum roughly equal to 30 gallons. With a monetary exchange rate of 50 to 1, a gallon of linseed oil in Amsterdam would cost $60.00, or about $120.00 per gallon by the time it is transported to Grantville.

The most economic animal derived oils in 1631–1633 will be cod liver oil, which sold for 60 guilders per tun, with one tun roughly equal to 252 gallons, or just over 4 gallons per guilder. This gives a price of about $11.91 in Amsterdam or $25.00 per gallon delivered in Grantville. As a final example tallow, made from the fat of cattle and sheep, sold for 16 guilders per 100 pounds. One gallon weighs six pounds so each gallon costs just over 1 guilder in Amsterdam and would be about twice that in Grantville, $100.00 per gallon.

While many people like the idea of corn oil because corn is available in Grantville, at the 2004 minicon the West Virginia extension agent explained that the Mannington area was a grass-based agriculture and that corn was not grown in Marion county. Corn crops will have to be built up from small amounts of seed, which will take years. Additionally, other oil crops have a much higher yield. Corn has an average yield of 18 gallons of oil per acre while pumpkin seeds yield 57 gallons per acre. Sunflowers seeds yield 102 gallons and pecans 191!

While the corn and sunflowers used in this example are modern hybrids with very good yield per acre, that would likely decline over the course of years. Pumpkins on the other hand are bred for size and weight, not seed content, and should remain fairly constant.

Another biological oil source is cow's milk. This can be made into butter at a ratio of about 21 pounds of milk to 1 pound of butter. Cow's milk weighs about 8 pounds per gallon and this means that for every 3.5 gallons of fresh milk you get 1 pound of butter. Six pounds of butter yields about a gallon of bio-diesel. A good down-time milking cow will yield about 1 gallon a day of milk when in season. Therefore, every cow in the pasture has the potential to produce about 8 ounces of bio-diesel per day while in season. Because down-time milk is a seasonal product the local people are not conditioned to getting butter with every meal as the up-timers do. To entice them to sell the butter instead of eating it will be expensive, but not impossible. A package deal could be made to purchase the cooking oil, the pork drippings, and the lard given off by cooked beef or mutton along with the butter. To make it attractive for the down-time farmers up-timers would need to offer a moderate income, otherwise they will eat the butter and grease. The added benefit to down-time farmers of having up-time farmers help with planting and harvest will also encourage them to provide oil and some butter.

Animal fats tend to have longer fatty acid molecules and hence are thicker than most plant oils. Some common examples of this are tallow, lard, pork drippings and butter. On the contrary side, some plant oils like coconut oil are very thick in their own right, but few of these are present in Europe in the seventeenth century. Much more common will be linseed oil, which is made by pressing the seeds from the flax plant that is grown throughout northern Europe to provide flax for linen cloth. Any viable sunflower or safflower seeds that made it through the Ring of Fire will need to be conserved and planted; they yield considerable oil and the pressed seeds make good livestock feed after the oil has been extracted. Corn, soybeans and cottonseeds are also good sources of vegetable oil but do not yield as much per acre as sunflower seeds.

Making bio-diesel from any of these biological oil supplies will require a moderate knowledge of chemistry. The high school chemistry teacher, his lab assistants and Frank Stone all would be able to follow the simple recipes given in this article and produce a product that would burn correctly in modern diesel engines.

Most people who "home brew" bio-diesel use methyl alcohol, also known as methanol, because it is cheap and is the easiest alcohol to use. Methanol is made industrially by combining natural gas, heat and steam through a series of catalytic chambers. The end result is a very pure form of methanol which can be burned in modified Otto-cycle engines, used as an industrial solvent, or used as the starting point in manufacturing products like bio-diesel fuel. Methanol is being produced down-time, and is a major component of the fuel for the down-time air force.

Larger bio-diesel processing plants usually use ethanol, also known as moonshine, because it is easy to produce on an industrial scale. Ethanol is much less toxic than methanol if it is accidentally spilled or the vapors are inhaled. Methanol is a nerve poison. It can cause blindness followed by death if it is swallowed, absorbed through the skin, or the vapor is inhaled. Ethanol used in the bio-diesel process must be 199 proof or higher. You cannot just distill it; you have to dry it completely afterwards. Fortunately, you can dry ethanol to 199 proof by straining it through a tank filled with diatomaceous earth. The diatomaceous earth can be reused indefinitely. After a batch of moonshine is fully dried out the earth is gently heated and the water is driven off as low energy steam. When the heated diatomaceous earth stops steaming the heat is removed immediately and it is allowed to cool before more distilled ethanol is poured through it for drying. Methanol is not as sensitive to water contamination and if all you have is 190 proof moonshine you might be able to force the process to work by substituting 40% methanol in the process, but there are no guarantees.

Diatomaceous earth is also known as *kieselguhr* and has been mined in Thuringia since at least the 1860's. It consists of the fossil remains of millions of nearly microscopic water plants that form beds of tiny seashells. It is almost pure silicon dioxide; the same stuff sand is made from, but with hollow centers. This makes diatomaceous earth very absorbent, and an excellent filter. It was be the preferred material used by Alfred Nobel in the late nineteenth century in the manufacture of dynamite up-time.

Two different catalysts can be used for the bio-diesel conversion process and both are commonly called lye. Cleaning lye (NaOH), also known as sodium hydroxide, is very slowly and carefully added to the methanol to form a compound called methoxide. Alternatively potash (KOH), also known as potassium hydroxide, can be used and is available by dripping boiling hot water through wood ashes and through a filter, then evaporating off the water to leave crystalline potassium hydroxide.

Bio-diesel is made by substituting the glycerol in biologically derived oil with light alcohol molecules such as methanol or ethanol. Because it is a substitution process you get the same volume of materials out as you put in. Biological oil and alcohol go in, bio-diesel, glycerol and a little soap come out.

## *Small Batch Process*

Beware! The methoxide reaction is exothermic. It releases large quantities of heat and if done too quickly will release deadly methanol vapor or explode in your mixing chamber. For unused oil the average ratio of lye to methanol is 3.5 g sodium hydroxide lye or 4.9 g potassium hydroxide to 200 ml of methanol per liter of oil. Potassium hydroxide is less reactive than sodium hydroxide so you need 1.4025 times as much. 1.4 works fine for the small batches you would be making at home. When the methoxide solution is slowly added to the heated oil and stirred, the lye acts as a catalyst. It strips the fatty acids from the triglyceride molecules in sequence by reacting with the fatty acids directly. The process creates first one free fatty acid and a duoglyceride molecule, then a second free fatty acid and a monoglyceride molecule, and then ultimately a third free fatty acid and a free glycerol molecule. As each of the free fatty acids separates, it is in a reactive state and quickly binds with one of the methanol molecules in the mix, forming a methyl ester molecule.

If too much lye is added to the mix it will attack the methyl ester molecules once all of the glycerides have been broken down into glycerol and free fatty acids. In a normal reaction with fresh oil most of the lye will mix with the glycerol, which is denser than the methyl ester solution and naturally separates into layers after the stirring is stopped. The methoxide and oil mixture is stirred for an hour while being kept at a moderate temperature of 130 degrees Fahrenheit, which is the temperature of hot water straight out of your average hot water heater. Much hotter than this and the methanol will boil out of the mix. This results in poisoning and also means it will not be available to react with the free fatty acids in the mix to form methyl ester. Any of the above mentioned biologically derived fats are appropriate for this use.

If you are using oil that has been kept at high temperatures for an extended period of time, such as waste fryer oil, it will have a lower pH level. In this case you would need to increase the lye portion in the methoxide solution to compensate for the increased acidity of the used oil. To do this most accurately you would need a pH meter or simple litmus paper, which should be available before the end of 1632. As a general rule you will need a 20% increase in lye for used cooking oil and the end product will contain more soap than you would get with fresh oil. For recycled used cooking oil you need to not only increase the lye concentration 20%, it is also helpful to dry out the used cooking oils as much as possible. This is done by heating the used oil to about 190 degrees Fahrenheit and maintaining that temperature for 15 minutes to drive off all suspended water in the oil. Make sure you allow the oil to cool to 130 degrees Fahrenheit before adding the methoxide or the methanol will vaporize back out and poison you. Having too much methanol in the mix results in more methanol in the crude glycerin, but does not cause any problems as a result. Having too much lye does cause problems. When in doubt err on the low side for the lye component and increase the agitation or stirring time from 60 minutes to 90 minutes.

After an hour of mixing allow the mixture to cool to room temperature and stand for 12 hours. If you did everything correctly you will have light straw-colored liquid on the top of the settling tank and darker, thicker liquid in the bottom of the tank. If you have a proper settling tank with a spigot drain on the bottom, drain the glycerol mix into another container. If the tank does not have a drain, use a siphon pump to draw the liquid off the top of the tank into suitable containers, making sure to stop above the glycerin layer. This is the raw bio-diesel. More cautious people will wash the bio-diesel before utilizing it to remove the small percentage of free fatty acids, lye and soap that are suspended in it. If you wish to wash the bio-diesel, simply add a small quantity of water, about a quart per gallon, and bubble air through from the bottom of the container. The water will mix thoroughly with the raw bio-diesel causing bubbles to form on the top and the water to change to a milky color from absorbed impurities. To thoroughly wash the raw fuel you should wash it for several hours, let it settle, and drain the milky water from the bottom of the tank. Replace the dirty water with fresh water and bubble the tank for several more hours. Repeat as needed until the water returns to a clear color after the liquid separates. The top of the tank is bio-diesel solution and it is ready to use in your modern equipment exactly as is.

Once the raw bio-diesel is removed from the mixing tank, the mixture of lye, methanol, soap and glycerol, remaining at the bottom, is crude glycerin. Using a sealed still, gently heat the crude glycerin and capture the vapors distilled off in a cooling chamber. This will be about 20% of the total volume of methanol used in the methoxide mix. Through more difficult processing the lye can also be separated from the glycerol as a soap compound leaving nearly pure glycerol. Glycerol is a very valuable byproduct. It is nontoxic, tastes sweet, and can be used in a wide range of products from soap to diabetic friendly sweetener. It is also the foundation for nitroglycerin types of explosives. Glycerol can even be burned in modified kerosene lanterns giving off light and heat without the bad smells or indoor air pollution. It can also be added to crude jell soap as a conditioner.

For the near-term future most of the bio-diesel available in 1632 will be made by the small batch process given above. Once capital is raised for construction, a large batch industrial scale plant could be built to keep Grantville supplied with nontoxic bio-diesel made with the ethanol process. The ethanol process for making bio-diesel is somewhat more difficult as it requires more precise temperature and mixing processes to work correctly. This will only happen if petroleum derived diesel remains unavailable, as the most economic sources of biological oils will remain waste cooking oils and butter purchased from local farms for about $2.00 per gallon. The farmers will gain spending cash while giving up a seasonal resource that they could not transport to market for a profit.

## The industrial process

The first step in creating bio-diesel with ethanol is to prevent soap formation during the process. Soap is one of the by-products of the small batch process for brewing up bio-diesel. Soap is a chemical compound formed when the metal component of the lye, sodium or potassium, binds with a free fatty acid and loosely attaches itself to a methyl or ethyl ester in the bio-diesel. These molecules in turn bind with water during the washing stage and draw the attached bio-diesel out of the solution. A similar process occurs when you use soap to wash your hands and body. The metal ions bind the water to the natural oils secreted by your skin as well as the dirt that is sticking to these oils. Raw soap does this so well that it will make your skin dry and chapped in short order. One of the first remedies for this problem with raw soap was to mix 20% pure glycerol into the formula, which acts as a conditioner and has the added benefit of being a disinfectant.

The first stage of the industrial process prevents the soap formation by eliminating the free fatty acid component, which is bound to the metal ions at the start of the soap chain of reactions. This is done by adding 98% pure sulfuric acid to the incoming oil. Any solution of less than 95% pure sulfuric acid will not work well for this process. Sulfuric acid in a lead acid vehicle battery is only concentrated to 50% but in the industrial processing plant they will make their own acid. At all costs avoid using other acids for the first stage. If you were to use nitric acid for instance, it would bind with the glycerol to form nitroglycerin and likely destroy not only the processing plant but a good piece of territory around it. Because you are using very dry sulfuric acid you must make sure the oil is as dry as possible by simply heating it and driving the water out before you add the sulfuric acid. If the oil has more than .5% water in solution it will derail the reaction, so the solution must be very dry. Once the oil is fully dry allow it to cool to 95 degrees Fahrenheit. Make sure that all of the solids in the oil such as lard or butter are completely melted. Add 12% pure ethanol by volume to the oil and mix for 5 minutes. Maintain the temperature and continue stirring while slowly adding 1 ml concentrated sulfuric acid per liter of oil. Stir at temperature for 60 minutes, remove the heat source and continue stirring for an additional 60 minutes as the solution slowly cools. Move the solution to the settling tank and let it settle for 12 hours.

Prepare sodium ethoxide by mixing pure 199 proof ethanol with potassium hydroxide. This is impractical for home use because the sodium hydroxide does not dissolve easily in ethanol, but for the industrial plant, sustained temperature and agitation of the mix will result in the compound needed. The potassium ethoxide mix is made at a ratio of 3.5 grams pf lye to 350 ml of ethanol per liter of oil undergoing processing. After 12 hours of settling, warm the oil mixture to dissolve the solid fats and mix at a low speed. Once the solids are dissolved, add 175 ml of potassium ethoxide solution per liter of oil, but do it slowly. The potassium ethoxide will neutralize the sulfuric acid creating potassium sulfide in the process.

The processing plant then raises the temperature of the neutralized oil mixture to 140 degrees Fahrenheit and maintains this temperature throughout the remainder of the process. An additional 175 ml per liter of potassium ethoxide is added to the oil mixture while stirring continuously for 30 minutes while maintaining heat. Allow the mixture to settle for 10 minutes. At the end of the settling period, the plant drains the settled glycerol from the bottom of the mixing chamber and removes the glycerin to the soap processing portion of the bio-diesel plant. Resume mixing for an additional 15 minutes. Then the processing vat repeats the settling and draining procedure. As the glycerin is settled out of the reaction chamber and drained off, the mixture will become lighter in color until it achieves a straw yellow color. At this point the mixing and heating are stopped and the product is allowed to settle for 60 minutes. After this long settling period the residual glycerin is drained off and the raw bio-diesel is transferred to the washing chamber. A very weak phosphoric acid water solution is used to wash the raw bio-diesel through three stages. The water is stirred with the raw bio-diesel for 60 minutes and then allowed to settle out for another 10 minutes between draining and water changes. After the third wash the refined bio-diesel is filtered through diatomaceous earth filters and placed in storage containers for sale.

## Conclusion

Feedstock for all of these processes will be expensive, and even using the oil collected for a fee does not change that fact. After 1634 petroleum derived diesel will be more economical to produce than bio-diesel. In 1631 and 1632 the citizens of Grantville will have feedstocks of up-time fuel to consume, and these can be stretched with the addition of local waste oil at a ratio of 75% petroleum diesel to 25% waste cooking oil. By 1633 these up-time supplies will be exhausted, even with careful conservation and boosting through addition of local waste oils. This is the crucial year when bio-diesel would be most valuable to Grantville since it can be manufactured with relatively simple technology. Key materials for the process such as methanol, ethanol, and potassium hydroxide (lye) will already be in production for use as a gasoline fuel substitute and for soap manufacture. Diatomaceous earth will most likely have been found and quarried because it is located inside Thuringia. It is easy for an amateur geologist to identify and is useful for many industrial processes as an absorbent or as a filter. If a supply of diatomaceous earth does not get discovered before 1633, the safer ethanol process can be set aside in favor of the methanol process. Of fresh biologically derived supplies only cod liver oil, a by-product of the intensive north Atlantic cod fishing by the maritime nations, will remain cheap for the near- and medium-term future of 1631–1634. Buying butter from down-time farmers will supplement this source with a moderate economic cost, but is only available in quantity about 5 months of the year. With adequate supplies of the feedstock materials one competent up-timer using a 55 gallon oil drum, a low fire, thermometer, and stir stick should be able to make 100 gallons of bio-diesel per week, along with 20 gallons of glycerol and a gallon of soap. An amateur up-timer using the recipe given in this article would be able to make at least 45 gallons if they take extra time and caution at each step of the process.

In conclusion, without shorting any other critical resource, a small batch bio-diesel facility would give Grantville the crucial supply of fuel it will need in late 1632 through early 1634 to keep its diesel farm equipment and heavy mine trucks available for use. Due to the costs of transporting any of the materials for long distances, bio-diesel will only be economically feasible in localized areas such as in Grantville and in Magdeburg where the up-time diesel engines are positioned. Bio-diesel cannot compete with petroleum diesel except for this narrow window of time when highly refined fossil fuel is not available, but may be a vital fuel supply during that period of time. Additionally, liquid butane and liquid propane production is within the reach of Grantville from their natural gas supplies and can be used to power up time gasoline engines, and extend the fuel life of uptime diesel engines.

# How to Build a Machine Gun in 1634 with Available Technology: Two Alternate Views

*Editor's note: The firearms round table that produces these articles on firearms doesn't always reach agreement on a specific issue. They didn't on this one, and asked me how to proceed. Since I don't see any reason the fictitious universe of the 1632 series should be any less contentious than the real one, I told them to produce both views and we'd run them simultaneously in the magazine.*

*So. The question now raised is: which of these alternatives will be chosen in the series?*

*And the answer is . . .*

*Probably both. Not only is the Europe of the 1632 series full of disputing nations, but none of those nations— certainly not the USE—has a command economy to begin with. Most likely, someone will produce one variant, and someone else will produce the other. And then, it wouldn't surprise me to see someone produce something else entirely.*

*That's how it happened in our history, after all. Why should an alternate history be any tidier?*

## *First alternative*
### by Leonard Hollar, Tom Van Natta and John Zeek

One question that is always coming up on Baen's Bar is why are there no new machine guns being built in the 1632 universe. The one M-60 is wearing out and spare parts are three hundred years away. What is going to replace it on the battlefields of 1634? One thing to note is the replacement will not be a home built copy of the M-60 or even a mechanical gun like a Gatling. A real machine gun is beyond the gun makers of the USE for a while, possibly until 1639 or 1640.

A real machine gun would require inside-primed brass cases and smokeless powder. Both of those are coming to the 1632 universe, eventually, but not right away. The ability to make guncotton (nitrocellulose) and nitroglycerin exists by 1634 with the first advent of nitric acid, but not the ability to completely stabilize it so the acids used to make it do not cause it to deteriorate into an unstable state—nothing worse than having a soldier's cartridge go "boom" when dropped, or go "click" when fired. This took some 20–30 years to figure out in Our Time Line (OTL).

Brass was made from Roman times on in Europe, though zinc was not known as a separate element. By mixing zinc ore with copper ore and heating it together, brass was produced; some brass church plaques made this way were the correct 70% copper, 30% zinc ratio for rifle brass, but this was a happy accident. Reliably getting a 70/30 ratio to make good rifle brass is another problem; delivery of metallic zinc from Japan may help solve this.

So we are not going to have a new machine gun—but as of 1634, the armies of the USE don't need the best, just something better than any enemy can come up with. And they need it on the battlefield *now*, not in the design room or even being made in a factory somewhere.

First of all, let us look at what a machine gun is. No, that doesn't mean a physical description, or a description of how it works, but more what its presence on the battlefield accomplishes.

First and foremost, a gun like this is a force multiplier. That means that the crew of a machine gun, usually two to four, can take the place of many more riflemen. As an illustration let's look at two weapons from our world that fire the same caliber round, the M-60 machine gun (as found inside the ROF) and the

M-14A1 rifle. Both use the same .308 cartridge, the same round Julie Mackay uses in her sniper rifle.

But first a definition is required from the *Combat Leader's Field Guide*, 9th edition (1980): Maximum Effective Rate (MER) of Fire (Rounds per Minute) . . . The rate at which a trained gunner can fire and obtain a reasonable number of hits (50%).

Now, one man firing an M-14 rifle in semi-automatic mode has a MER of 20 to 40 rounds per minute (RPM). Compare this to the 200 RPM of the M-60. Simple math shows that the (normally) two-man crew of the M-60 can produce the rate of fire that it would take as few as five and as many as ten men with M-14's to produce. If one now compares the rate of fire of the semi-automatic (and the fully automatic mode has been purposely ignored here) M-14 with the muzzle loaders found on the battlefield in the sixteen hundreds it is easy to see why the M-60 has been such a big boost in battle. The "Battle of the Crapper" scene in 1632 shows this very vividly.

Second, a machine gun is an area denial weapon, meaning it prevents an enemy from using an area. This area may be a bridge, a path or a line of attack. Basically the machine gun crew has the job of making an advance by an enemy force through the covered area too expensive in manpower. To put it in even simpler terms, those Spartans of old could have held that pass with thirty troops and four machine guns, and the other two hundred seventy could have been watching for that flanking movement.

After much discussion, we have concluded that the best bet to have a weapon that does these two jobs, and to have it quickly, is to construct a ribauldequin, or "organ gun." This is a multi-barreled gun in a rifle caliber on a two-wheeled carriage. Search Google for ["ribauldequin"], and you will find a number of pages about these so called "Organ Guns," including this one with an illustration way down towards the bottom (http://xenophongroup. com/montjoie/gp_wpns.htm).

Historically, these guns often have about 6 barrels, each one to two inches in bore diameter. We are proposing a larger number of rifle diameter barrels, in rifle calibers of .50 to .75 calibers (one-half to three-fourths of an inch). For ease of production the .58 caliber of the SRG may be best.

Sometime in 1634, USE Steel will go online and one of their first products will be rifle barrels for the SRG and other uses.

These are simply tubes of steel that are then rifled by cutting spiral grooves inside to make the bullet fired from it spin-stabilize. We expect that this will be the easy part of a rifle to mass-produce and that their ability to make these will exceed the number of skilled craftsmen making the rest of the rifle. Ever heard the expression "lock, stock and barrel"? —this refers to the gun maker's craft. The lock and the stock take as much or more work than making a barrel by hand-forging it—and we won't be hand-forging. Barrels not used in making rifles can be made into organ guns.

So, why didn't this get used before? Well, it did. By 1632 multibarrel guns, including organ guns that looked like this design, had already been made and used. But, they were still muzzleloaders—loaded from the same end the bullet goes out. Thus loading was such a slow process that once they made their initial shot, they might as well be removed from the field. Organ guns that loaded from the muzzle were probably best relegated to defending a fortress wall against siege, since several could be positioned with interlocking fire zones for mutual protection during reloading. Such a fixed emplacement weapon is seen here: http://www.museumonline.at/1999/schools/classic/wiener_neustadt_2/objekte/etadt153.html

Both cluster barrel and "duck foot" guns (a pistol with three or more barrels splayed out like a duck's foot) already exist and have been used by 1632. Since they are muzzle loaders and very slow to reload, they were not found useful other than as a means for an individual to intimidate a group. The classic use for a "duck foot" pistol is for a naval officer trying to suppress a mutiny. There are some excellent images at this site: http://website.lineone.net/~da.cushman/ducksfoot.html

As was pointed out in the SRG report, the SRG as it exists *can* be modified from flintlock, to percussion, to a Snyder, or some such self-contained cartridge breechloader. But the reality is that as soon as cartridges become available, the USE is likely to have better things to do with them than stick them in Snyder or Springfield trapdoors. To all intents and purposes the SRG is a dead end... but it was a weapon that could be done fairly quickly at the time.

The organ gun is the same; it can be done using the technology of the time, with only a little up-time help in the design. The USE armies might be able to wait on a true machine gun if they were the absolute strongest power on the continent, not just militarily, but in all categories. They are not. They need a force multiplier now, not three or four years down the road.

Although all elements for this gun were available in 1632, and the need for such a gun was clear (take a look at Gustav Adolf's own desperate search for antipersonnel artillery), 200 years would pass before someone put them all together. Then they were obsolete within 6 years when cartridge-firing Gatlings and other magazine-fed mechanical machine guns were introduced, which were then made obsolete themselves in another dozen years.

In this light, there have been a number of proposals for defeating the problem of loading time. All, of course, involve various schemes for loading from the breech. Whether the resulting weapon will have preloaded blocks that attach to the back of the barrels, or individual breech mechanisms using paper cartridges remains to be seen, but rest assured, someone is going to introduce multi-barreled guns to the battlefield in the near future.

Indeed, someone will develop these guns, and who's to say it's our friends in Grantville?

It could go like this . . .

As head of the gun makers' guild in St. Etienne, Andre Gueydan had been called to Paris where he had been handed a number of pages of information on firearms he had never dreamed of. Today, a Sunday, he had been sitting quietly watching the organist in the cathedral and contemplating the problem of making a device that would produce the same volume of fire as the American's "machine gun." It was then that the epiphany struck.

Tubes! He could make tubes to preload with powder and shot and then load them into the back end of barrels. Barrels which would be clustered just as were the pipes of the organ. Even the holes in the bottom of the organ's pipes were part of the vision he had been presented with; powder could be trailed into those holes and used to fire the "cartridges" sequentially. *It must be God's will,* he thought, *why else would I have had such a vision in such a place, at such a time?*

"God's will," or a good guess on the part of Andre, or someone of whatever nationality, finally figures out how to build an organ gun, or to use the correct term, a volley gun.

1634-era USE organ guns would have the following features: 18 open-ended rifle barrels (or more, or less—depends on weight and width desired) affixed to a wheeled frame, capable of being pulled by a single horse (or perhaps a pair of horses). They would be fastened to the frame near the back end with a bolt that would allow the barrel to pivot in a limited range (without moving the gun carriage), and the front would be adjustable with a lever that directed the barrels into "straight" or "spray" configuration. The organ guns will be able to bring all their barrels to parallel, for longer shots or massed targets, or splayed a bit to provide greater area of coverage.

Usually the organ gun cartridge will be the same one used by the infantry (a hollow base minié bullet out front, and a tapered nitrated-paper tube full of powder behind, tied with thread to the bullet). However, a buckshot load (5 or 6 .35 caliber lead balls) may be useful for organ guns. Rifled barrels will spray multi-shot loads into a donut-shaped pattern—not very accurate, and a definite hole in the middle of the pattern, but a good spread. Occasionally, a good spread of bullets at short range is exactly what is desired in an organ gun.

The back end of the barrels would have a smoothbore chamber about two inches long, to hold a bullet and powder. Behind the back of the barrels is a hinged plate (breech block) that seals the barrels for firing, and a groove for the priming powder trail.

In the United States (in Our Time Line), volley guns were patented just a bare month before the Gatling gun, which proved to be a superior weapon. Despite this, Billinghurst-Requa volley guns, to use their true name, were used in at least one major Union attack and in defense of Washington City (Now commonly known as Washington, D.C.) A brief history of the weapon, along with digitally enhanced photographs, may be found at this site: http://www.virginialighthorse.freeservers.com/catalog.html

Please note in the second from last photo the design of the cartridge used. As you can see, while similar to a standard rifle cartridge, instead of being flat on the end there is a slight dome. In this cartridge there was a hole in the center of the dome which was covered from the inside by a piece of nitrated paper. The powder train lay against this dome and the paper burned through to allow the bullet to be fired.

The powder "tubes" for our organ gun would work in the same manner, except they would use a preloaded paper-wrapped packet containing the bullet and powder, or perhaps an unprimed metallic cartridge. For the paper cartridge, the powder could be preloaded and the back covered with nitrated paper, or the powder could be loaded into the cartridges by a gun crew member just before firing; this method would allow for reloading during combat and eliminate the need for specialized machines to form rimmed cartridges such as the one shown on the Virginia Light Horse site. Probably a mixture of these methods would be used.

Once the cartridge tubes are loaded, they will be laid in grooves at the rear of the barrels. A hefty hinged block (called the breech block), running the width of the weapon, lays open below the barrels. Behind the cartridges, a priming trail of loose powder would be poured into the priming groove in the breech block—better too much than too little, the excess priming powder will be forced into the chamber.

Then the breech block will be closed, which pushes the cartridges into their chambers; the breech block is then put under tension sufficient to withstand the recoil of firing—and locked in place. A flintlock would be snapped (or some sort of fire applied, like a matchlock) and the priming trail would ignite, firing all the barrels in a very rapid sequence.

After firing, the breech would need to be swabbed with a mop (putting out any smoldering powder residue and cleaning up a bit) and dried a little—just so it's not dripping wet, and the firing process repeated. In wet weather, a simple tarp to keep the rain off the back of the gun and the powder would be all that is needed.

Grantville needs the best gun that can be fielded next spring, not the best gun that can be made in five years or one that has limitations placed on it by someone planning to use parts of it or its production machinery five years (or even next year) down the road. They need to get through the coming year to even worry about what might come. There just isn't time for "nice to haves." In five years these organ guns will be scrap. They are very much a dead end. They are also where we need to be now. (The guns are not useless after they are obsolete on major battlefields. Rest assured that after the USE develops superior follow-on weapons, these guns will be valuable trade items with everyone from those with "private ventures" in the outer world, to other empires.)

Once the volley guns have been developed might we see this scenario?

The chasseurs had worked for nearly ten hours clearing a path to get the three pipe organs into position on the hill, and another two clearing lanes of fire that wouldn't be obvious from the road below. At last the supply column hove into view and began to bunch on the approaches to the narrow bridge, just as had been expected. The captain raised his sword and with a swift slicing motion gave the signal to fire . . .

The massed fire was as unexpected as it was devastating. The screams of the horses was as from the blackest of nightmares and was matched by the agonizing cries of the teamsters and their escort. Cries from the enemy officers to rally fell apart when the guns fired a second time, and then a third, all within one minute. The carnage was dreadful, and the screams of the wounded men and horses assailed their ears.

To a man, the organ gun crew preferred their ears to be assailed than the enemy to attack after crossing the bridge. Far more than their ears would be hurt if the bridge was crossed. And the new guns could hold here until help arrived.

Now the only question is; who's going to get this weapon first? Exit right with evil laugh.

P.S. Thanks to Rick Boatright for nagg—I mean encouraging us.

## Second alternative
### by Bob Hollingsworth

Grantville and its allies need a machine gun!

Fortunately, there is an excellent example of late-middle twentieth century general purpose machine gun available in the former U.S. Army M-60. Unfortunately there will be no way to truly duplicate that gun in the near future. Many of the same arguments that applied to the adoption of the SRG flintlock minié rifle apply here.

Grantville has only one M-60 machine gun; they have no others and only a limited amount of ammunition for it. What is it going to take to keep that gun functioning until it is no longer needed?

Let's take a look at the M-60 machine gun.

The M-60 machine gun is a 7.62 mm NATO caliber fully automatic, gas operated, air cooled, belt feed weapon, firing from an open bolt, that uses disintegrating ammunition feed links and may be fired from the hands, off a bi-pod, or from a tripod or vehicle mount.

It weighs 23.06 pounds when properly lubricated and is 43.75 inches long overall and features a 25.6 inch barrel.

It can fire at a cyclic rate of 600 rounds per minute, though to do so necessitates a barrel change to continue firing at a high rate. It is normally fired in bursts of from 6 to 9 rounds and at a rate of about 200 rounds per minute.

It may be fired against area targets to a range of 900 meters from the bi-pods or 1100 meters from a fixed mount such as the M122 tripod.

(Thank you, Drill Sergeant.)

The gun is made mostly of steel, with a few minor aluminum parts, with plastic to be found on the front hand guard, trigger group "pistol grip," and the buttstock. To assist in controlling the weapon when it is fired from the shoulder and bi-pod, there is a small folding rest in the buttstock that rests on top of the firer's shoulder in use.

The most common problems with the gun are user malfunctions. That's right, operator error.

It is possible to assemble the gun with two important parts backwards. The gas piston can be installed backwards, making the gun effectively a manually operated repeater. The other and more common error is that the firing pin may be installed backwards and the gun will then not fire at all.

Another common assembly error is to reverse the flat spring that places tension on the trigger group retaining pin, which may then become loose and fall from the gun, resulting in the loss of the trigger group, the pin and the spring. The gun may be fired without those parts, but it is more difficult to control and accuracy suffers.

Finally there is the common problem of losing the pin that locks the rear of the bolt and so retains the firing pin spring and its guide in position. This can result in the firing pin, and its associated parts, coming out of the bolt while firing and causing a serious stoppage.

The likelihood of all of those problems occurring can be reduced by having a written checklist and always having two people involved in assembling the weapon and using the checklist.

The gun is not invulnerable to knocks and bumps or even wear. Common problems demonstrated in service were things ranging from something as simple as the cocking handle being rammed into a tree or stone and bent or broken, to the receiver tube that holds the barrel and gas system in place cracking from the strain of bi-pod use. Feed trays become worn and allow misfeeds and feed tray covers become bent and restrict the movement of parts. Barrels and gas systems become overheated and can erode or warp from exposure to high heat and pressure. The feed system can be damaged by an inexperienced user attempting to force-fully close the feed tray cover while the bolt is forward. There is no support depot repair facility for the Grantville M-60 and for that matter, no mail order parts houses or internet web sites to provide replacement parts directly to the users.

Army technical manuals call for special lubricants, but in real-ity anything oily beats nothing and guns have been operated on used motor oil or sewing machine oil or WD-40 (TM) more than once. For extended firing, the synthetics do seem to work best as they do not evaporate as easily.

The gun depends on steel links to feed ammunition. Each link is stamped from steel, hardened, and given a protective finish. A link firmly holds one cartridge in position for feeding by friction around the body of the cartridge and what is essentially a flat spring that snaps into the extractor groove of the cartridge. The link also has a piece that snaps over the next cartridge in between the front and rear of its link. Once links become damaged by being flattened or bent or lose their metal temper or are heavily corroded, they are of no use. Fortunately links that are recovered undamaged can be reused many times. Links are normally deposited just below the link ejection port to the right of the gun, as they are not forcefully ejected. When the gun is tilted to the left, links may be struck by the forcefully ejected fired cartridge cases and scattered. For the purposes of Grantville, it may be best to make some sort of bag to catch both the used links and ejected cartridge cases so they may be more easily recovered for re-use.

Ammunition is the most important factor for keeping Grantville's M-60 working and the gun's biggest weak link.

The best ammunition for the M-60 is 7.62 NATO ammunition having the "NATO cross" on the case head. How much of this is in Grantville? The ammunition for the gun should drive a 147 to 152 grain bullet at 2800 +/- 40 feet per second from its barrel. As the weapon is gas operated, it is critical that the correct amount of gas pressure be available at the gas port in the barrel to cycle the action for the next round. Any factory loaded military round of 7.62 NATO ball or tracer ammunition that bears the cross in a circle stamp should function the M-60 or any NATO standard weapon in that caliber.

Obviously it is possible to reload some ammunition. U.S. military 7.62 NATO ammunition can be reloaded by sport shooters who reload .308 Winchester. This has led some to call for the seizure of all .308 ammunition and components to feed the M-60. Besides the political problems this may cause, there is a technical problem. Commercial .308 Winchester or hunting ammunition typically do not have cartridge cases constructed to the same hardness as NATO standard. Firing some hunter's .308 ammunition in the M-60 can cause stoppages and likely ruin the cartridge case for further reloading. The commercial brass tends to be far softer than the NATO standard, resulting in bent and creased cartridges on loading and more importantly, bent, torn, or broken rims upon extraction. Should the bend, tear, or break be large enough, the cartridge will fail to extract and require a cleaning rod be run down the barrel to extract the case.

Owners of military style semiautomatic rifles will also often note this problem. Some, like the FN FAL type rifles that have a gas regulator, can be adjusted to slow their action speed and not damage brass as much. But they are best served with ammunition intended for such rifles.

A problem for reloading the 7.62 NATO military ammunition that may be in private hands is that much of it may be of foreign manufacture and have a Berdan primer rather than the U.S. standard Boxer large rifle primer. Berdan primers are much harder to remove than Boxer designs and few Americans reload them or have tools to do so. There are a number of ways to remove the Berdan primers, each much more time and material consuming than the removal of Boxer primers.

Another problem facing reloading for the M-60 is the availability of usable primers. It may be several years before new primers of any type can be reproduced. For the immediate future only the primers in the hands of reloaders or already loaded in cartridges are available. A factor that comes into play when loading for military weapons is the hardness of various primers. The firing pin strike of the M-60 is substantial and because the round is being fired from a hot, and possibly as a result, tight chamber, pressures can be higher than normal. These factors can result in ruptured primers that allow hot gas and molten metal from the primer to be sprayed into the bolt and feed areas of the gun. Military primers are harder than most commercial primers. Many who reload for such weapons will not use some of the major and most common brands of primers for this reason.

Next there is the issue of bullets. The NATO standard is for a full metal jacket bullet with a pointed nose. There may well be feed problems if bullets of a different shape are used. Also bullets must be loaded to the same overall length as the 7.62 NATO standard. This means considerable load development may be necessary to use longer and heavier bullets that might be available from hunters and target shooters who reload. Also part of the M-60 feed system pushes down on the front of the bullet, possibly damaging sporting bullets such as soft points with their exposed lead and hollow points with their unsupported cavities. Reloaders tend to purchase and have on hand sporting type bullets suitable for hunting and target shooting. Most states do not allow the use of full metal jacket ammunition for taking game and the full metal jacket bullets tend to not be as accurate as most available hunting or target bullets. Their only advantage for sport shooters is a slight savings in purchase cost. There is actually likely more loaded surplus 7.62 NATO ammunition with such bullets in Grantville than there are unloaded bullets suitable for reloading them.

Finally there is the issue of available powder. Grantville will not be able to produce smokeless powders of any sort for quite some time. All the smokeless powders that exist are in the hands of sport reloaders who recognize its value for their own use. Further, not all smokeless powders are suitable for reloading the 7.62 NATO cartridge. Even among the powders that are suitable, different powders may need a good bit of load development work done to get a load that functions the M-60 and shoots reliably and accurately from it. Given the small amount of powders available, all this testing may be seen as a waste of what could be valuably used in a hunting rifle. Any load development also uses up primers and bullets that cannot be currently replaced. While there are many loads that will function fine in a manually operated rifle like a bolt action, getting a series of loads for different powders that produces that critical gas-port pressure for the M-60 will be an expensive chore.

One possible alternative for arming the M-60 may be to convert any military loadings of the older US M-2 Ball loadings of the .30-06 caliber. These cases will be of or near the same hardness as the NATO brass. The bullet falls within the proper weight range and the powders will be suitable for loading to 7.62 NATO pressures and velocities. The bullets would be pulled and saved for use, the powder saved, the cartridge cases run through a .308 sizing die and the excess removed and the necks turned to the correct size. Loads may then be developed using the original powder. Each lot of ammunition must be processed separately for this type of conversion. This might work well if 1000 rounds of a specific lot of .30-06 ammunition were available, but it would not be suitable for a few mixed rounds. One certainly would not wish to mix powders of two different types or even lots when doing these conversions.

It may be possible to obtain usable primers and brass by converting other old military ammunition. If large lots of 7.92 mm, 7.65 mm or 7 mm Mauser cartridges can be found, they can be converted to 7.62 NATO cartridge cases and their original primer used. Again the original powder might be used to develop loads if proper bullets are available. The bullets for these rifles cannot generally be used in .308 caliber guns, though it might be worthwhile if a large quantity of 7.65 Mauser ammo were found to attempt to swage the bullets down a few thousandths of an inch to proper diameter. Finding enough of that round with a spitzer shaped bullet to make it worth while is unlikely, though.

At best the Grantville M-60 machine gun is a stopgap weapon of limited use. It may be a guide for future machine gun development, if not for a copy of itself, in ten or fifteen years as a starting point or for taking ideas from. It may actually be little more than a good luck talisman having a short useful life on the battlefield from lack of suitable ammunition and repair parts.

Something that performs the same functions as the M-60, that can be produced and operated with 1633 materials and technology with as little help from Grantville as possible, needs to be developed as soon as possible.

Even disregarding all of the above arguments, copying the M-60 requires machine time and tools that are not available. Also the quality of the steels needed for the barrel, gas system and the all important springs that will be necessary for an "automatic" machine gun, whose action is cycled by the firing of its ammunition, are not available.

Many have suggested that a "manual" machine gun driven by an external power supply, such as a gunner turning a crank, would solve the spring problem. It does not, however, deal with the problem of primers and cartridges.

The best known of the manual machine guns is the Gatling gun. It is interesting to note that it was perfectly legal to own an untaxed or federally registered manually operated machine gun in the USA and West Virginia in the year 2000 when the Ring of Fire occurred. There are likely to be not only illustrations in books available in Grantville, but it is not impossible for there to be a set of detailed blueprints for building a late model, cartridge-type Gatling gun somewhere in town in private hands. Unfortunately, such designs call for modern ammunition exactly like the automatic machine guns demand.

The original Gatling guns (as were in use during the first half of the 1860s) used a special firing chamber rather than a fixed cartridge. Each of these was a steel tube with one end open to accept powder and bullet and the other end closed by a plug having a nipple for a percussion cap to be affixed. These chamber pieces were treated like and performed like cartridges, though they were simply pushed up against the end of each barrel rather than sliding into the barrel as cartridges do in later designs. Still, there is the need for percussion caps and a great deal of machine time and tools just to produce the guns and enough firing chambers to make production worthwhile.

In perhaps five or six years, Grantville can have cartridges loaded with black powder equal to anything available in the 1870s. When that happens, Gatling guns will certainly be doable and perhaps, if steel production and manufacturing techniques are advanced enough, the Gatlings may be skipped in favor of a Maxim or Browning 1895-type automatic machine gun.

But does Grantville have five years to wait for a machine gun?

A machine gun is what military planners refer to as a "force multiplier"; that is, if you only have a few men, something that gives them greater ability on the battlefield than their raw number suggests. To be worthwhile, a machine gun in 1632 would have to be able to deliver more effective shots on an enemy force than the same number of men armed with the SRG, a muzzle loading Flintlock that fires minié ball ammunition. For five men with SRGs, we might expect that to be between 15 and 20 shots per minute, with the ability to actually hit a predicted area at ranges up to 300 yards.

Was there a weapon that could do that, which did not need modern cartridges, heavy and expensive chamber pieces, percussion primers, and perfect springs? A design likely to be known or recorded in Grantville?

Yes.

During the American Civil War (ACW) the most-purchased and used "machine gun" fits this description. Most schoolboys can tell you about the Gatling guns bought by General Butler of the Union Army and even a few are aware of the single barreled "Auger Coffee Mill" that outnumbered the Gatling in the field. Very few, however, seem to recall the less glamorous Requa battery gun or "the covered bridge gun" as it was frequently called. Almost as heavy as a light field howitzer and drawn much the same way by a team of only two horses on a carriage, the Requa bears little physical resemblance to the one M-60 machine gun in town.

But it is capabilities, not looks, that count.

The original Requa battery (or volley) guns fired up to 175 rounds of rifle-power shots per minute when served by a crew of three. It could fire these bullets with some accuracy and power to a range of over 900 meters. The guns fired their shots either at a concentrated spot or spread out horizontally and equally spaced over a wider area. While not as effective as an M-60 GPMG, the Requa could outshoot 40 SRG armed men with a crew of only four, three to work the gun and one to hold the horses.

So what is the Requa battery gun, as it was originally built and as it might be produced for the use of Grantville's allies?

The original Requa battery guns in U.S. service during the American Civil War (ACW) had 25 barrels laid out horizontally on a light artillery carriage. The barrels were often described as .50 caliber, but surviving bullets seem to be .52 caliber. The caliber of the original guns is not a concern for Grantville, and it may be that a larger or smaller bore size would work as well or better. Certainly there is no reason not to use the same .58 caliber barrels that are being produced for the SRG, a specially designed bullet that would take advantage of the breech loading ability of the battery gun, and the barrels rifled with an appropriate twist. A longer, heavier, solid bullet of boat-tail construction would provide far better performance than the regular .58 caliber minié ball in use with the rifles. The bullet would be made so that its diameter equals the bore size of the barrels, as measured to the bottom of the rifling lands. Such bullets would retain velocity much better than minié balls and, owing to the fact that they can be made as hard as linotype if the materials are available, would have far greater ability to pierce body armor than the soft lead minié ball.

The barrels must be mounted in a frame that will hold the rear of the barrels in a fixed position, yet allow the muzzle end of individual barrels to be adjusted to fire at a common point or spread to make a fan-shaped swath of fire. This can be accomplished by a set of steel wedges between the mounts of each barrel that, when pulled to the rear, would splay the muzzles apart a known amount. Two potential methods of controlling this movement are available: a simple lever having locks at three or four range settings, or infinitely adjustable via a large screw and adjustment wheel having gradations for various ranges. It would work well to have marked adjustments for parallel firing ( all barrels pointed at the same place), and then perfect separation (bullets strike a foot apart horizontally at a given range) for the ranges of 150, 300, 600, and 900 meters.

The metal frame holding the barrels and their adjustment system needs to be adjustable so both sides can be raised or lowered to take into account "cant"—that is to say, level the barrels for best effect. It also needs to have an elevation adjustment like a common artillery piece. These can all be done with large threaded screws, as was done in the original.

The feed strips for the ammunition are strips of steel or iron with holes for the individual cartridges. These consist of two strips joined in a piano-hinge fashion to make a single loading strip. The cartridges are shoved through one set of holes and the other portion of the strip is then swung up to prevent cartridges from falling back out.

The cartridges may be made of copper rather than cartridge

brass, or turned from iron or steel. They need not have a complex primer pocket or hollow rim and will thus be easier to make with fewer culls. Unlike the firing chambers for the Gatling or Ager Coffee Mill guns, these are true cartridges that are fired inside the gun rather than simply butted against the back of the barrel, though they have no primer. Like the Maynard carbine cartridges used in the ACW, the Requa cartridge simply had a small hole in its base to allow the flame of the external priming system to flash through. Since this is a preloaded cartridge, it may have as many features to improve its accuracy as desired, such as waxed felt discs and paper cards between the bullet and powder or a paper-wrapped bullet. For extreme close range work, shot-cartridges may even be issued.

The rear of the gun consists of a breech that is little more than a hinged piece whose front end bears a curved lower edge that will force the cartridges and feed strips forward as it closes. This is attached through a simple lever to a series of "fingers" that will extract the clip a short distance when fully opened. Imagine a piano hinge running the length of the rear of the barrels mounted horizontally and this breech attached to the hinge. When the piano-hinged breech is fully forward and down, the cartridges are loaded into the chambers of each barrel and await firing. Along the top edge of the breech piece is a groove and in the bottom of that groove are 25 holes that align with the hole in the bottom of each loaded cartridge. This groove is simply filled with loose gunpowder from a powder measure or horn and is ignited to fire. The original gun used a percussion cap for this ignition, but a flintlock or even a bit of glowing slow match from an artillerist's linstock would work as well. Ignition is from the center-most barrel outward and all barrels typically fire in a ripple in about one second.

Since the battery gun is an artillery piece with its own mount, lock time—the time between initiating firing and the bullet leaving the barrel—is not as critical as it would be on a shoulder-fired weapon. While such a system may not be practical for producing a cartridge-firing flintlock rifle, it works fine in this usage.

The sighting system for the guns may take two forms. One is a single sight and a spirit leveling bubble to ensure that the barrels are level. The other would be a set of two or more sights that could each be set for range and then checked to ensure the gun was aimed to cover the area intended. A sight on each of the outer two barrels might do this and would allow the gun to be intentionally canted to shoot over ground sloping to one side.

Horizontal adjustments may be made either by moving the gun carriage trail, or the gun mount may be made more complex to allow it to function as a turn table. Such a system as the latter was familiar to Swedish King Gustav's gunners, who had such on some of his light guns, but it adds complexity to the design.

During the ACW, the battery gun was made at a cost of about $500 U.S. of that time. By comparison, some iron 2.12 inch rifled cannon were made for about $275 U.S. that same year. Grantville must determine which use of its resources would give it the greatest return, building 20 battery guns or building 36 little cannon. Certainly one battery gun can out-perform 50 average riflemen in the field at volley firing. A cannon might get off three shots of canister in a minute, the typical load for a two pounder being only 46 round musket balls or 138 total for 3 shots. A battery gun gets off seven volleys totaling 175 shots of a better-shaped, more easily aimed bullet and can control dispersion over range. With a fan-shaped beaten zone, rather than the cone of fire of an artillery piece, half those shots are not wasted going high or low, as would be the artillery's cloud of shot.

Forty loaded strips would provide a gun with 1000 rounds of ammunition and would be easily carried on the gun carriage in ammunition boxes. And the gunner and his number one could each carry sufficient powder to prime that many strips. Additional loaded cartridges and a few spare strips could be carried on pack animals or in a battery wagon. A battery of two guns firing in sequence could fire 14 volleys in one minute, or a volley of 25 shots about every four and half seconds.

While Grantville and her allies begin to adopt the open-order skirmish formations that disperse riflemen and make volley fire less effective, a few battery guns in a battle can keep the benefit of volley fire at a low expense of man and horse power. This technology can be ignored only at great risk, for surely the French and Austrians have obtained history books that mention such a gun and are hard at work on their own versions. Grantville has the choice of experiencing this primitive machine gun from the point of view of the shooter or the target.

Which would you choose?

# A Looming Challenge

~~~~~

## Pam Poggiani

Grantville needs people to work in the munitions factories. And the steel mill. And the brick factories. Where will they come from? Why, all those poor women who have to spin and weave all the time can be emancipated right away—just build a spinning jenny and power up those looms!

Grantville needs more cloth, to make uniforms and to provide everyone with a change of clothing. What can be done? Why, build a spinning jenny and power up those looms!

Now, wait just a doggone minute—it is not that easy!

Among the up-timers there are no textile mill workers, no hobby spinners, no hobby weavers. Some up-timers will be sure that great-grandmother's spinning wheel and loom in the attic must be better than anything down-time and want to show them off—those wheels and looms that have not, over the years, been fed to the stove (*Foxfire 10*, 362). But the down-timers may be hard put to keep straight faces. The spinning wheels used in American homes were great wheels, a design that down-time spinsters on the Continent abandoned over a hundred years before the Ring of Fire. American home looms were simple two- or four-harness looms; seventeenth-century weavers use multiple-harness or draw looms.

The spinning jenny pictured in encyclopedias is not the original of 1764, nor even the patented jenny of 1770, but an improved

287

version from 1815. Except in the Encyclopedia Americana, the parts are not labeled. Even there, the description of how it works is incomplete, and the drawing does not show how the drive wheel at the side turns the spindles. Constructing a spinning jenny from the up-time knowledge known to be in Grantville will be a long, frustrating engineering exercise involving much experimentation.

The seventeenth-century loom is not suited to power. Several inventions and adjustments must be made before weaving, just of wool, can be mechanized.


## *First Steps*

### Spinning Wheel.

The simplest improvement that up-timers can suggest is that the down-timers convert their spinning wheels from hand power to foot power: crank the hub of the drive wheel of a low spinning wheel, set a **treadle** below, and put a connecting rod (known in OTL as the *footman*) between.

Later historians assumed that the low wheel, with the flyer/bobbin spinning mechanism and the treadle to power it, appeared complete in 1530, replacing the thirteenth-century great wheel. Perhaps, in the absence of written evidence—women's work was seldom documented—these writers assumed that spinsters enjoyed walking a prescribed course while spinning, manipulating the supply of fiber, the thread being spun, and the drive wheel, and that only the treadle could have convinced them to sit. The crank-and-connecting-rod system has been known since about 1500 (HOTb 653–4), for turning wood lathes. But would a wood-turner watch his wife spinning and thereby realize how useful a treadle would be? Not to mention that these later writers attribute the invention of the treadle and/or flyer/bobbin to a mason of Brunswick, one Johann Jürgen. A drawing of the low wheel with flyer/bobbin appears in a household journal of about 1480 (HOTa 204); there is no treadle.

Spinning wheels were hand-powered until late in the seventeenth century (Feldman-Wood). "A Woman Spinning," painted in 1655 by

Nicolaes Maes, of Amsterdam, shows the earlier, treadle-less design, as do several earlier paintings, while "Interior with a Woman at a Spinning Wheel," by Esaias Boursse, also of Amsterdam, from 1661, shows a primitive treadle. "The Spinner," painted a generation later by Willem van Mieris, of Leiden, shows a wheel with a fully developed treadle. This indicates that the treadle was first applied about 1660, and modified later.

A few minor tweaks may be necessary: The crank and the far end of the treadle must be in line, and making the table three-legged instead of four-legged is advisable. The treadle must be able to drive the wheel in either direction, according to need, so footman and treadle are tied together with a bit of leather lacing through a hole bored in each. The bearings, probably of leather, between crank and footman and between treadle bar (replacing a stretcher) and the table legs, should be firm enough to hold the wheel in position when the spinster stops it, so that she can stop it exactly when she wants to, and restart it going in the same direction easily.

Photographs of a treadled spinning wheel in operation can be found in the newer encyclopedias (not in the 1911 Britannica), and in *Foxfire 10* (356; not in the article on spinning and weaving found in *Foxfire 2*). Grantville's museum contains a low wheel with treadle, but no up-timer knows anything about spinning wheels and may not even notice the differences between it and the wheels used by down-timers.

## Loom.

The first improvement to the loom is the **flying shuttle**, which will provide some ease for the weaver. The two looms in Grantville's museum do not have flying shuttles; although of late twentieth-century manufacture, they are simple versions of the looms used in the home by women of the seventeenth century. However, the text and drawings available in several encyclopedias should be sufficient once the desire for the invention occurs.

A loom holds the *warp*, the lengthwise threads of a textile, taut, and provides a mechanism to lift certain of these threads—in the simplest case, every other—while pulling the rest down, creating a *shed* for the passage of the *shuttle*. The shuttle carries the *weft*, the crosswise thread, over and under the warp threads. The usual shuttle of the seventeenth century is a shape known and used at least since the thirteenth century—a *boat shuttle*. This is a rectangular block with pointed ends; in the top is a trough wherein a bobbin full of yarn can spin, letting the weft pay out through a small hole in the side of the shuttle as it travels across the warp. The weaver opens the shed by pressing treadles with his feet. While holding the treadles down, he stretches forward and to one side to throw the shuttle through the shed with a snap of his wrist, then quickly reaches to the other side of the loom to catch it. A man of average height, or less, can weave on a warp two ells in width, an ell on most of the Continent being 26 or 27 inches. Before opening the *countershed* and throwing the shuttle back, the weaver swings the *beater* (or *batten*) to snug the *shot* (British: *pick*) of weft against the growing edge, the *fell*, of the cloth. The beater is made of two heavy lengths of wood hung vertically from above, holding the *reed* between the lower ends. The reed, extending across the loom, is strips of reed, set vertically and edge-forward, between two laths. The warp threads pass through the *dents* between the individual reeds. As well as beating up the weft, the beater and reed help keep the warp threads from clinging to each other.

The flying shuttle, invented by John Kay in 1738, will permit one weaver (instead of two or more) to produce wider cloth, and will improve the ergonomics of weaving. But it will increase the speed of weaving very little. Although Aspin uses the term "doubled" for the increase in speed (p. 14), the actual numbers recorded at the time, and reported by Aspin, show that after the invention, a weaver needed yarn from five or six spinsters instead of only four.

Invention of the flying shuttle begins with modification of the beater. The bottom lath is widened so that it extends forward of the reed to make a *shuttle race* on which the shuttle can slide. At each end of the beater, beyond the edges of the warp, a box big enough to hold the shuttle is added, with the end toward the beater open for the shuttle to leave by and enter through. The shuttle is thrown from one box to the other across the warp by the impact of a *pick block*, a small wooden block deep in the box that is jerked or knocked so that it hits the end of the shuttle and then encounters a stopper. There are several ways to move the pick block: the original invention had the ends of a loose cord fastened to the pick blocks through a slot in the front of the box, and the weaver jerked a handle fastened to the center of the cord to left or right.

The shuttle used in the twentieth century with the flying shuttle mechanism is the *boat shuttle*, but having metal caps on each end with a spring inside instead of being a solid block of wood. These caps came fairly early in the development, as did tiny wheels set in the bottom of the shuttle.

The weaver will still need to check the length of weft left behind by the shuttle before beating it into place. It must be enough to keep the weft from pulling the edges in, but not so much that there are loops of it beyond the edges of the cloth. A neat selvage is the mark of a good weaver.

The treadle and the flying shuttle are minor improvements—they are evolutionary, not revolutionary—but they could incline down-timers to look favorably on more up-time innovations.

## Changes: Down-time to Up-time

The modern, up-time, textile industry depends not only on machines—a multitude of them!—but also on improved crop yield, good transport, and, yes, cheap labor even yet.

The down-time European fiber crops are wool, linen, hemp, and silk. The first three are grown almost everywhere; silk is produced in Italy, and in France in an area around Lyons. Cotton is grown elsewhere and imported. Ramie, jute, and other natural fibers are native to, and used in only, the Far East.

## Raw Material Supply.

**Wool** (undercoat of *Ovis aries*) is from sheep that have been bred for the purpose for millennia. A major part of the wool supply comes from Britain, which, in the 1630s, does not tax its export. For more wool, there must be more sheep. What will they eat? Australia or America could feed them, but not Europe. Breeding for quantity as well as quality of wool has been underway for something over 6,000 years; formal Mendelian theory may be of interest to down-timers.

**Flax** (*Linum usitatissimum*) and **hemp** (*Cannabis sativa*), bast fibers, can be grown anywhere in Europe; at this time, flax is a major crop in areas just south of Thuringia, and hemp is major in several areas of Germany. They will grow in almost any soil, as long as it is deep enough for the roots.

When grown for the fiber rather than the seed, flax is sown thickly, to keep the plants growing straight with little branching. Weeding is necessary only once, when flax has grown to about six inches. Modern fertilization might help, but if the soil contains too much nitrogen, each flax plant will yield less fiber (EB14f 430). When grown for the seed, flax is sown much less thickly, so that each plant branches and produces more seed.

Flax is subject to wilt, and several other fungi and viruses. For this reason, flax is not planted in the same field year after year; a field should have at least five years between crops of flax. Resistant strains of flax were developed early in the twentieth century, becoming available around 1920 (EB14f 431). No flax was grown in the area transferred in the Ring of Fire, however, and redeveloping resistant strains, starting with only the conviction that it can be done, will take some time.

**Cotton** (*Gossypium* spp.) is a tropical plant. It is imported from the Levant (Syria to Egypt); most of it is grown in India, and nearly all of it, no matter where it is grown, is *G. herbaceum*, Indian cotton. Some is *G. arboreum*, tree cotton, also a native of India. Up-time Egyptian cotton is not a native of Egypt; *G. barbadense* is a native of South America and, down-time, is grown only as Sea Island cotton, not having been introduced to Egypt yet. The English colony of Virginia began cultivating *G. hirsutum*, Upland cotton, which is native to tropical North America, in 1621 (Hartsuch 164); there was still very little cotton in England as late as 1640. The German states, being closer to the Levant, may have more cotton at this time.

Cotton is subject to many insect pests; the boll weevil is simply the most famous. Cotton must be hoed to reduce weed growth, *chopped*, constantly, as the plants are grown too far apart to shade out weeds.

Grantville can do little to affect the cultivation of cotton, as most of it is grown far away.

**Silk** (cocoon of *Bombyx mori*) needs a warm climate. James I of England tried to find one in his own territories, but was unsuccessful.

Silkworms cannot be cared for by machines; in fact, up-time silkworms get more human attention than down-time worms did. In the nineteenth century, the silk industry experienced a great die-off. Pasteur was consulted and determined that the worms must not be crowded, that the eggs must be microscopically inspected for disease, that only the best cocoons should be allowed to produce breeding stock (Barker 297–8).

An important part of sericulture is the cultivation of mulberry; an ounce of silkworm eggs plus a ton of leaves yields 12 pounds of reeled silk (EB14h 522).

Up-timer biological and agricultural knowledge will be useful. While specifics known to Grantvillers may not be applicable, the general principles can be applied in the search for improvement.

## Harvesting and Processing.

Much of the initial processing of the fibers is done where the product was raised, primarily because of the cost or difficulty of transport and the lack of any use for the by-products. Wool grease and the accompanying dirt are washed out of the fleece a week or more before the sheep are sheared. Cotton seeds weigh about three times as much as the lint, and are discarded in place.

**Wool.** The shearing of sheep is much faster up-time than down-time. With the old-style hand clippers, a man could shear 30 plus or minus 10 sheep in one day; with modern powered clippers, he can do about 100 plus or minus 20 (Van Nostron). This does not mean that the same shearing will be accomplished by a third as many people; individual sheep will have to be captured and dragged to the shearer at the greater rate, and their fleeces folded and packed. Up-time, a shearer works four two-hour sessions in a day.

Down-time, all sheep are sheared with scissor-style clippers: shearing blades set on a flat spring. Up-time, most sheep are sheared with an electric handpiece, invented about 1900, much like the ones used to shear recruits in boot camp. But the desired outcome of shearing sheep is not a bald sheep; it is a good fleece. While the up-time handpiece can shear closer than the old clippers can, it also requires more care in avoiding skin tags and bits of sheep that protrude. Nicking the sheep's skin is a very bad thing—it exposes the animal to infection and infestation, and besides, blood is so hard to get out of wool.

In the twenty-first century, the modern shears are powered by distributed electricity or individual batteries. Before the power grid spread everywhere, they were powered by small motors set on the rafters of the shearing shed, or by someone turning a crank.

When a sheep is sheared, the locks of wool cling to each other, forming a fleece. Shearing usually begins down the middle of the underside of the sheep, so that the edges of the fleece are belly wool. This permits *skirting* of the fleece, the removal of the matted belly wool, which can be sent to the lanolin boilers. Then the fleece is folded, tips in and cut ends out, rolled up, and tied. The fleeces are packed into *woolsacks*—the English woolsack held 364 pounds of wool (Hartley 135)—ready for shipment by the wool merchants. Up-time, compressing the pack is done with a mechanical press, instead of by people walking on the fleeces in the sack.

**Flax** and **Hemp**. The harvesting of flax is done by hand—even up-time. These plants must be uprooted, pulled up by hand; if the plants are cut from the roots, or the roots removed later, the fibers will be degraded in the process that separates pith and outer coating from the fibers of the phloem (EA 576). A field of flax is harvested all at once, by a line of all available people crossing the field, although the shorter plants and the longer are separated. Harvesting of flax for fiber is best done before the seeds are ripe; harvesting later yields less flax of poorer quality. A field of hemp is harvested in two passes, the male plants first and the female plants ten days or two weeks later.

Different regions handle harvested flax somewhat differently, but in nearly all, the seeds are *rippled* free immediately; the tops of the plants are pulled through a comb with the seeds falling onto a sheet below. After that there is a drying period; the flax is *stooked* in the field to dry for a few days in the sun. In parts of Flanders, the flax is then stored in a shed for a full year, but in most places, it is retted immediately.

*Retting* is the way that the *boon*, the pith and the outer coating, is partially rotted to free the fibers. Down-time, retting is often done in a pool dug near a stream. The length of time depends on the weather; it takes at least ten days, and can take up to three weeks. The water left after retting cannot be discarded into the stream, as it will have a detrimental effect on the fish, but can be spread over the fields as a fertilizer (Moore 50). Up-time, retting is done in huge, temperature-controlled, indoor tanks; with the temperature at a constant 80°F, retting takes about a week (EB14f 430).

When retting has progressed as far as it should, the flax is dried again, and the boon is broken, by means of a hand-operated *breaking box*. *Scutching*, done with a board and a paddle, removes the *boon* completely. Then the flax must be *hackled*, combed, to separate the *line flax*, 20 to 30 inches long, from the shorter *tow*. (Line flax becomes strong linen thread; tow is used unspun for stuffing, or can be spun into a softer, weaker thread.)

Up-time, all of these procedures, rippling through hackling, even drying, are performed by machine, instead of by hand with simple tools. In both systems, the plants and the resulting fibers are kept as parallel as possible.

After breaking, scutching, and hackling, the flax goes to the women of the area for spinning. Most of the hemp will go to the men of the *rope walk*; a nineteenth-century man-of-war used 80 long tons of hemp, the yearly product of 320 acres (Hartley 157). The longer fibers of hemp are not easily handled by distaff and spinning wheel (Davenport, *Spinning* 98); only the shorter hemp fibers go for clothing.

**Cotton.** Harvesting cotton continues through much of the growing season, as each plant has flowers, developing bolls, and ripe cotton all at once. The first harvester was developed in the 1850s; it stripped the plants, leaving only the stalks. This was extremely wasteful, and required more hand labor to separate the mature cotton from everything else. Immature ("dead") cotton cannot be spun and woven. It was not until the 1940s that the modern *spinner* harvester was fully developed; it pulls the mature cotton, which is expanding out of the bolls, free (EB14c 90H). The spinner designed for Upland cotton, which bursts upward, cannot be used for Indian cotton, which spills downward.

Up-time, cotton is shipped with the seeds still present. Down-time, seeds are removed by hand right after the cotton is picked.

When the gin was first invented, it was used on the farm, because of the costs of transportation—cotton seed is two-thirds or more of the weight (Peake 19)—and because there was little use for cotton seed. Without modern oil-pressing machinery, cottonseed oil is somewhat toxic (EB14a 615).

Three different cotton gins have been invented. The wire teeth gin invented by Eli Whitney, and the saw gin improvement of it by Hodgen Holmes, damage the *lint*, especially lint of longer fibers, more than roller gins do (EB11a 259–260). Some seeds are broken in ginning, and the bits often stay in the cotton, needing to be removed later—which is, with the full machine processing and handling of up-time, after it is woven. Up-time, the Whitney-Holmes gin is still used for Indian cotton, which produces very short lint.

Cotton *linters*, the very short fibers that coat the seeds of Indian and Upland cotton but not those of Sea Island or Egyptian, will not be available. These were ignored until the second decade of the twentieth century (Peake 18), when they were found to be useful in several industries (paper, rayon, and "Boom!").

**Silk.** Up-time, cocoons that have set (about a week after being spun) are subjected to high heat, or poisonous fumes, to kill the chrysalids before they can break out of the cocoons; they are stored until the factory rep collects them. Down-time, reeling is done on the farm from "live" cocoons—they are put into very hot, but not boiling, water to soften the sericin enough to allow unwinding. Live cocoons produce silk that is more lustrous; dead ones yield a more even yarn, better for power weaving (Hooper 33).

One silk fiber (a *bave* of two *brins* of fibroin embedded in sericin) is only 1/3000 inch thick (Hooper 4). Several cocoons are reeled off together (three to eight—Patterson II 197, or six to twelve—Hooper 34). Of the 4,000 yards a silkworm spins to make one cocoon, only about half a mile (give or take a couple hundred yards) can be reeled for use (Hartsuch 286–287). Down-time, the rest is discarded; not until 1671 was silk waste carded and spun (Hooper 112).

As each cocoon is exhausted of reelable silk, another cocoon is added to the pot, until the required length to make a *hank* has been reeled. The ends are tied together and secured so that they can be found later. Twine is tied around the silk threads at several points in the circle to keep them from tangling, and the hank is removed from the reel.

Some of the methods used in reeling are fairly late: Up-time, cocoons are unwound from two pots next to each other, each group onto its own reel, but between the pots and the reels, the two threads are twisted around each other about six times. This *croisseur* (*croissure, croisure*), this "essential part" (Hooper 36) that presses the filaments together so that they consolidate, dates from 1828 (Barker 301). The use of glass rods and rings to guide the fibers between pot and reel is probably established in down-time Italy already; smooth glass does not snag and impede the silk fibers the way bronze or iron can.

## Spinning.

Spinning is the process whereby fibers, either animal or vegetable, are turned into yarn. There are three phases: the fibers are drafted, pulled partway past each other; the resulting length is twisted, so that the fibers curl around each other and do not pull apart; and the spun yarn is wound onto a stick so that it can be stored without unspinning itself or tangling up.

A spinning wheel is a machine that, in combination with a human, performs these tasks, originally a mechanization of the *drop spindle*. The drop spindle dates back thousands of years; it is a stick with a weight: gyroscope and flywheel. The spinster hitches the spun yarn to one end and starts the spindle spinning; as it spins the fibers, its weight pulls more out of the spinster's upraised hands. When the spindle reaches the ground, the spinster stops it, unhitches the yarn and winds it around the stick, rehitches the yarn, and starts the spinning and drafting anew.

The most obvious part of a spinning wheel is the *drive wheel*, turned by the spinster. The rotation of this wheel is transferred to a small wheel, a *whorl*, part of the spinning mechanism, by way of a *drive band*, a length of linen or hempen twine. This length is spliced, preferably, but can be tied, into a loop; Amos recommends a knot he calls the "Fisherman's Bend," but the accompanying illustration shows the Fisherman's Knot (Ashley #1414). The spinster controls the drafting of the fiber and the amount of twist.

There are two mechanisms by which a spinning wheel imparts twist, the *spindle* and the *flyer/bobbin*.

A spinning wheel's spindle is a straight stick, pointed at the front end and with a whorl at the other; with drafted fibers held at a 45° angle to the spindle, the fibers wrap around it and then drop off the end with each rotation, producing one twist in the fibers. The spindle is also the stick for the yarn to be wound upon. This winding is accomplished by first turning the drive wheel the other direction just enough to free the yarn from the point. Then the spinster moves closer to the drive wheel, moving the hand holding the end of the spun length so that the yarn is at a 90° angle to the spindle. When the wheel is rotated again, in the same direction as for spinning (not, as many technology historians report, the opposite direction), the yarn winds onto the far end of the spindle and she moves toward the spindle as it does so.

The flyer/bobbin is a multipart mechanism. The flyer is wishbone-shaped, with the addition of a central shaft ending in a whorl at the far end—overall, it looks like the Greek letter psi. The fiber goes through the *orifice*: into a hole in the base of the flyer and out through a hole in the side of the base. From there, the fiber goes along one of the arms and is turned around one of the bent metal wires on the arm, a *heck*, to the bobbin. The bobbin is a hollow cylinder with a flange, a *cop*, at each end; it fits loosely on the central shaft of the flyer. The bobbin usually has a whorl attached outside the far cop (or the far cop is a whorl), so that it can be turned by the drive wheel too; the drive band describes a folded figure eight, twice around the drive wheel and once around each whorl. The whorls of flyer and bobbin are of different diameters so that their speeds differ. As the flyer rotates, the drafted fibers are twisted, and then wound onto the bobbin. Of course, as the bobbin fills up, the relative speeds need to change; either flyer or bobbin can slip against the drive band. The bobbin is filled in sections; when the diameter of the wound yarn gets too great, the spinster stops the wheel and moves the yarn to the next heck to fill the next section. Leonardo da Vinci drew an oscillating mechanism to wind yarn onto the bobbin from one end to the other and back, obviating the necessity for the spinster to move the yarn (Ponting 30–31), but it was never adopted—perhaps not even known to others at the time. When the bobbin is full, the mechanism must be dismantled so that the bobbin can be removed; the drive band is taken off the whorls, the flyer whorl is removed, and the bobbin is slipped off the shaft. A new bobbin is installed, the whorls are replaced, and the drive band is set in place again.

The drive wheel was originally powered by hand. Often, when the drive wheel was supported on only one *upright*, a peg was attached to one of the spokes for the spinster's use; her right hand on this peg constantly described a circle, turning the drive wheel. The original spinning wheel, with a drive wheel about 5 feet in diameter, required that the spinster stand. This version is now known as the *great wheel*.

As far as can be determined at this date, this great wheel always had a spindle. To change the angle of the fibers, the spinster had to walk from one point to another. Her task was complex, especially when she was spinning line flax: She had to turn the wheel, carry the distaff that held the fibers, and use both hands on the fiber itself.

The *low wheel*, with a drive wheel as small as 18 inches, could be turned by a woman seated in front of it, still using her hand on a peg, with the distaff set conveniently on the spinning wheel's table. If she was spinning a fiber that needed both hands, she could give the wheel intermittent power pulses. Small drive wheels often have heavier rims, indicating some pre-Newton understanding of angular momentum. The earliest drawing of the low wheel shows the flyer/bobbin, fully developed; of course, the low wheel could also operate with a spindle.

The low wheel replaced the great wheel on the Continent well before the seventeenth century. About the middle of the seventeenth century, some wheels were made with the drive wheel between two uprights, which makes for more stability, but of course the peg could no longer be used. Instead, a hand-crank might be applied to the front of the wheel. While the low wheel could be fitted with a spindle, nearly every drawing and painting of a low wheel shows the flyer/bobbin, which is excellent for flax. England and her colonies lagged behind the Continent in this area. As a result, the only low wheel in Grantville is the one in the museum, which may be of twentieth-century commercial manufacture. This wheel has a treadle, and the mid-seventeenth-century improvement of a *tensioner*, too.

The only visible part of the tensioner is the *tension handle*, a peg sticking out of the left-hand end of the table, which may be mistaken for a decorative element, or a handle to assist in lifting or moving the spinning wheel. But the tensioner is a useful addition to the flyer/bobbin. Turning this peg moves the *mother-of-all*, the assembly holding the spinning mechanism, toward and away from the drive wheel, allowing ease in putting the drive band on or removing it. A smaller movement, changing the tension of the drive band just a little, permits the whorls to slip more or less so that the relative speeds of flyer and bobbin change.

The flyer/bobbin mechanism puts strain on the yarn; it works very well for line flax, but not with weak fibers. On the Continent, spinsters used a low wheel fitted with a spindle for cotton and for weaker wool fibers, while in England and her colonies, the great wheel continued to be used for these (even after the low wheel was known there), earning the alternate name of "wool wheel."

Wool, flax, and cotton are very different fibers, requiring different preparation for spinning and different spinning techniques. Silk is in a category of its own, being *thrown* instead of spun, but the process will be included in this section.

**Wool.** While each breed of sheep produces wool of an expected type, different flocks of sheep, and different parts of one animal, undergo different stresses (weather and friction from botanic and manufactured items). A fleece comprises many locks of wool; within that fleece, these locks vary in color, length, fineness (diameter), handle (the "feel"), and amount of crimp. Before it can go to a spinner, each fleece must be *sorted* by an expert; each fleece will have six or more grades of wool in it. The sorter will also pull the *kemp*, the outer coat, which cannot be spun with the wool. Domestic sheep have very little kemp; certain breeds have more than others, and within breeds, the weather affects how much kemp a sheep grows each year.

As a general rule, longer wool fibers are coarser and have less crimp than shorter ones; these coarser fibers, as long as 18 inches, are *worsted*, and the finer, crimpier ones, as short as 1.5 inches, are *woolen*. Worsteds produce a harder yarn, suitable for (up-time) suits and dresses; woolens produce a softer yarn, more easily felted, suitable for (up-time) coats and blankets. Although both trap a lot of air in the yarn because the crimp guarantees that the fibers cannot be completely against each other (worsted is at least 60% air, by volume [Davenport Spinning 20], and woolen more), they feel quite different, and are prepared and spun differently. Each fleece will be all, or primarily, worsted or woolen—or even, perhaps, entirely of very coarse wool suited for carpets.

For worsteds, the longer, coarser wool is *combed*: A lock is drawn through tall, fixed combs, working bit by bit from tip to middle and then from cut end to middle, to remove all tangles. The shortest fibers are removed in the process; these *noils* can be mixed with woolen fibers. The combed lock of *tops* is called a *sliver*.

For woolens, the short, fine wool is *carded*: a lock of wool is spread across a hand card (of wood, studded with bent wires); an identical card, held in the other hand, is drawn across the first. The wool tangles are straightened out as the wool is transferred from one card to the other and back several times. When the fibers are neatly parallel (not tangled and going in every direction as stated by many technology historians), the wool is rolled up, cut ends toward tips, so that the fibers form a cylinder; this is called a *rolag*.

Up-timers may have heard of the hand-tool called the *drum carder*, intended to replace the hand cards. The drum carder has two cylinders of different sizes, both studded with bent wires. The wool is spread out carefully and one of the cylinders is turned with a handcrank; the other cylinder turns too and, ideally, the wool fibers are parallelized in one rotation of the larger cylinder. The *lap* is then carefully removed by hand and rolled up. With only the name of the tool, and no drawings or descriptions available, an up-timer may produce a better version of this tool.

Wool needs to be at least a little greasy during combing and carding. If the wool has already been *scoured* so that all the natural grease, the *yolk*, has been removed, olive oil is added, deemed the best grease for the task as it can be washed out easily later. (Even up-time, the preferred grease is oleic oil.) Either oil is added to each lock of wool in the hand as it is prepared for combing or carding (Davenport *Spinning* 39), or the comb is greased (with either olive oil or butter) and, if necessary, kept near a source of heat to keep the grease soft (Hunter 44). However, unless the wool was dyed *in the fleece*, requiring scouring beforehand, it should not need to be oiled; wool is best stored and shipped *in the grease*. (If it was stored too long, the yolk may have solidified, requiring olive oil anyway.)

The worsted slivers and the woolen rolags can now be spun. The spinster will hold a sliver or a rolag in her left hand; while she turns the drive wheel with her right hand, she moves her left hand back away from the spinning mechanism, permitting the fibers to be pulled between her thumb and fingers and to be twisted by the action of the wheel. Both sliver and rolag are fed end-first, the sliver from the end of the fibers, and the rolag from the end of the cylinder. As the spinster nears the end of sliver or rolag, she picks up another and its beginning meshes with the end of the first as she drafts.

Some spinsters prefer to join the worsted slivers end to end before actually spinning them, twisting (by hand) just enough to encourage them to hold together; the result can be rolled into a ball. Sliver, ball, or rolag can be kept ready near the wheel: in a bag or basket, or on a shelf.

**Flax.** Flax-spinning is a delicate process. The spinster dresses the distaff with an ounce or so of fiber. On the Continent, it is common for the *strick*, a bundle of parallel fibers, to be tied at one end and dropped onto a *lantern distaff* (cone-shaped) so that the fibers hang all around, then secured by a ribbon wound around. Less common on the Continent, but standard in England, is for the fibers to be layered accordion-fashion on a flat surface, forming a fan-shape; this arrangement is then positioned around a lantern distaff and secured with a ribbon (Davenport *Spinning* 83–88). The Dutch paintings of the time appear to show distaffs dressed by both methods.

When spinning flax, a spinster must apply both hands to the fiber, with the right hand supplying power to the wheel intermittently, as mentioned above. One hand controls supply of fibers near the distaff; the other hand drafts the fibers and then smooths them down, running up ahead of the twist. The smoothing fingers must be wet—water will do, but saliva is better (Davenport *Spinning* 82; Barber 49n); saliva predigests the flax enough that the individual fibers stick together better than they do with water. Moving the thumb between flax and lip produces a condition known as "flax mouth," with a bad taste for the spinster and foul breath for everyone she meets.

Tow, the shorter lengths separated out by hackling, may be spun, worsted fashion, or used unspun as stuffing in bedding, pillows, and other items.

The more humid the air, the finer the flax can be spun. Damp basements are a good location if extreme fineness of the yarn is a goal.

**Cotton** is tightly packed in bales; an up-time Indian bale is 400 pounds, and it is likely that this size dates back a very long time. The cotton lint must be loosened from the pack. A section is removed, placed on a flat surface, and either *whipped* (beaten with a springy stick that ends in several branchlets) or *bowed* (vibrated by a string snapped above the mass). The spinster will pull a *slub* free from the mass and spin it much the way worsted is spun, except that cotton is smoother than wool, with the cotton fibers slipping farther past each other more easily.

Cotton is a very short, weak fiber, and Indian cotton is shortest, coarsest, and weakest of all, being only 3/8 to 5/8 inch long (Peake 40), having a diameter of 25 micrometers (EB14d 226), and having a breaking strain of perhaps 46 grains (Peake 47). A drop spindle cannot be used to spin cotton, as the spindle weighs too much to be supported by the growing yarn. Even the flyer/bobbin may put too much strain on cotton yarn; on the Continent, cotton may be spun on a low wheel with a spindle. In England, as noted above, the great wheel continued in use much longer, used for cotton as well as for wool.

## Differences in Commonalties.

In spinning, details matter. Spinsters learn what is appropriate for each fiber, and may well specialize in spinning yarn of only one.

Yarns must not be underspun, or they will part. Neither may they be overspun, or they will tangle unmercifully. Each individual fiber must go around 4 or 5 times (Elliott); cotton requires more twists per inch than worsted or line flax does. With the flyer/bobbin mechanism, the yarn must often be retarded from winding onto the bobbin for the drafted length to acquire sufficient spin. When the spinster arrests the feed, the bobbin's whorl will slip against the drive band, permitting the bobbin and the flyer to spin as one while the flyer imparts twist. Many up-time technology historians state that the flyer/bobbin sped up spinning because it winds yarn at the same time yarn is spun; this is not strictly accurate.

Different fibers are spun in different directions. Down-time, there were many names for the two directions, and neighboring spinsters often used the same word for opposite directions. Not until 1934 did an unknown American suggest the terms "S-spun," with the far end turned counterclockwise, and "Z-spun," with the far end turned clockwise (EB14b 622); these names are from the match of the visible slant of the helix with the slant of the middle stroke of the letter. Individual plant fibers have twists themselves; for tighter, more durable yarns, these fibers are spun in accordance with their innate twist. Flax is S-spun; hemp and cotton are Z-spun (Barber 66). Down-timers will not know of the innate twists of the individual fibers, good microscopes being necessary, but women learned, 3,- or 4,000 years ago, that spinning *this* fiber *this* way gave more durable yarn with more luster, and passed the knowledge to their daughters. Animal fibers have no predilection, but, except for special effects in the eventual cloth, wool has always been Z-spun. No one knows why, but this tradition began long, long ago. With the spinning wheels described above, turning the drive wheel clockwise will produce Z-spun yarn, and turning it counterclockwise will produce S-spun yarn.

To measure the lengths of the new yarn, and to be able to see the length and inspect the quality of the yarn, the spinster winds the yarn off the bobbin into a hank. The *niddy-noddy* is the standard tool: a wooden rod a foot or so long with a shorter wooden cross-piece at each end; these cross-pieces are at right angles to each other—an artifical forearm. The yarn is hand-wound up, down, and around, to make a hank of known circumference, with the spinster counting as she goes. The hank is secured so that there is no strain on the yarn, and removed from the niddy-noddy.

Yarns must not be too thick, but each fiber is spun within its own range of fineness. Down-time, there may not have been specific measuring guides; while Master Weaver Ziegler wants the yarns he uses to be fine, he specifies no further (Hilts). *Gauge systems* may have come into use only with spinning machinery, size having been judged by the spinster's hand before that. Stating the diameter does not work; too many things affect that: the spinster, the stage in bleaching and dyeing, the loft of the yarn, even the color of the dye. Instead, the gauge is defined by the length of a certain weight, and expressed as the number of hanks of specified length in a specified weight. Woolen, worsted, linen, and cotton each have their own hank-lengths—in fact, woolen has several scattered around England and Scotland, and two more in the United States. The one most commonly used for woolen yarn is the Yorkshire *count*, the number of 256-yard hanks that weigh 1 pound. Other systems for woolens are usually called *cut*; these vary in both hank-length (200 or 300 yards) and weight (1 pound or 24 ounces). Unique to the U.S. is the *run*, which is expressed as the multiple of 1,600 yards needed to make 1 pound. The worsted *count* states the number of 560-yard hanks in 1 pound. Linen is measured by 300-yard *leas* in 1 pound, cotton 840-yard hanks in 1 pound—in England. On the Continent, cotton is gauged by the number of 1,000-meter hanks in a kilogram; this system is obviously no earlier than the late eighteenth century. With these systems, as with wire, the smaller the number, the thicker the yarn. In 1956, ASTM established the metric *tex* system, intended for all these fibers, which gives the weight of a specific length of yarn; 1 tex is 1 g/km.

Yarns straight from the spinning are called *singles*; except for some spun from line flax, they are not strong enough to be stretched over the loom as warp. Singles are *plied* (British: *folded*; industry: *doubled*): two or more singles are spun together, in the opposite direction from the original spin. That is, Z-spun woolen, worsted, and hemp are S-plied, like the yarn and strands of plain-laid rope; S-spun linen is Z-plied, like the yarn and strands of reverse-laid rope. (Spun yarns ply naturally in the direction opposite to the spin.) To ply singles, the spinster transfers the hanks of singles back to bobbins, sets the bobbins in a frame that permits them to spin easily, and uses her spinning wheel to spin the singles together, turning the wheel the opposite direction from that used for spinning those singles. Plying more than four together is difficult; each single is most easily controlled by being passed individually between two of her fingers.

Once plied, the gauge of the yarn changes. For plied woolen and worsted yarn, the gauge is now figured on the plied weight, with the number of plies indicated also. That is, four singles of 32s plied together become 4/8s. Plied cotton retains the gauge of the singles, with the number of plies indicated: either 4/32s or 32/4.

Plied yarns are wound into hanks, for measuring, quality inspection, and their transfer to bleachers and dyers.

**Silk.** Reeled silk is already a long string; unlike the shorter fibers, it does not need spinning to become one. However, reeled silk is not round in cross-section. Twisting the strand will round it, but the strand is many yards long (up-time, 10,000 yards). This twisting is called not spinning, but *throwing*.

After the hank of silk has been graded and lightly washed, it is placed on a swift, a rotating device that will hold the hank spread out, from which it is wound onto a bobbin. Up-time, it is wound from that bobbin onto another, being *cleaned* by its passage through a double knife—cleaning removes bumpy imperfections. Finally, it is thrown by being transferred from that last bobbin to another, with the two bobbins set at right angles to each other, and the silk going through a flyer set atop the source bobbin. The amount of twist, which varies according to the intended use of the silk, is set by the speeds of the bobbins. In Italy, throwing machines are water-powered, and the receiving bobbins oscillate so that the silk is wound evenly on them.

Down-time, the Italian silk workers are jealous of their methods, which have been little changed for about two centuries (Ponting 3). Italian machine-throwing methods were unknown elsewhere until 1717, when John Lombe, working in an Italian filature, made drawings of the machines and smuggled them to his family in Derby, England (Hooper 46). However, silk throwing without these Italian machines is known in seventeenth-century England; the Livery Company of Silk Throwsters was founded in 1629 and the Company of Silkmen in 1631 (Hooper 112). While *books* of silk, packages of hanks, are being exported to England, they may well be still unknown in Thuringia.

The thrown silk is then plied, onto another bobbin, which must be stopped immediately if one of the threads breaks or otherwise fails. This plied silk then goes through the throwing process, being twisted in the opposite direction to that in which the individual threads of reeled silk were. Finally, it is wound from the take-up bobbin into a hank.

The gauge of thrown silk varied from place to place. In nineteenth-century Italy and France, it was the weight in grams of a certain length of silk—450 to 500 meters, but a different length in every city—divided by an inconstant constant—different in every city. In nineteenth-century England, the gauge was expressed as the weight of 1,000 yards, the weight being given in drams (1/16 ounce avoirdupois) or deniers (1/12 of a sou; French for *pennyweight*). Eventually, the *international denier system* was agreed upon: the weight in grams of 9,000 meters. However, the tex, grams/kilometer, may also be used for silk. (After its introduction, spun silk was gauged the same way as cotton.)

**Bleaching, Dyeing, and Mercerizing.** Before it can be dyed, or woven, yarn of any fiber must be washed to remove oil, wax, and dirt. Wool is *scoured*; this term does not imply the application of elbow grease, but the removal of all grease and oil, both natural yolk and added olive oil. Linen and cotton are washed; flax contains so much stiffening wax that the weight of a lea of linen yarn may be reduced as much as a quarter. Cotton must be freed of the simple dirt acquired in its processing. Silk, too, gets a gentle wash.

If the yarn is to be dyed a pale color, or is to show as white when woven in combination with yarn of another color, it must be bleached, as its natural color is either yellow or gray. Up-time knowledge of bleaching chemistry, even the small amount acquired in an introductory chemistry course, will be helpful to down-timer bleachers. Up-timers can provide different ways to apply sulfur to wool—not the "black" wool, which can be brown, gray, or black, and is not bleached—to turn it from creamy white to white, and knowledge of hypochlorites for linen and cotton—of which the active element is oxygen, not chlorine (Hartsuch). Bleaching of silk is accomplished by *boiling off*—the color is in the sericin, and boiling the hanks removes much of the sericin. Linen intended as white goods may be bleached after it is woven, in the piece instead of in the yarn.

Most yarn is dyed before it is woven into cloth; much fabric design depends on the use of different colors of yarn. One thing to consider: "Aniline dyes . . . are not worthy to be used on silk"—silk should be dyed with alizarine dyes, which are closer to the natural dyes (Hooper 49).

About 1850, John Mercer discovered that exposing cotton yarn to alkali made the fibers shorter and thicker, increasing their strength and their tendency to accept dye. However, *mercerizing* was not accepted by the cloth trades until the 1890s, when Horace Lowe discovered that holding the yarn under tension during treatment made it lustrous too (Hartsuch 189–190). The increase in strength is not great; in the 1960s, mercerized sewing thread was easily broken between the fists, and cotton fabrics for home-made summer dresses were not cut from the bolt, but torn. However, longer-fiber cottons are easier to mercerize than short-fiber ones, and the cotton available down-time is the shortest-fiber species.

**Tools and machines.** Up-timers could invent several small tools that would benefit spinsters and dyers. If the up-timers notice all the hand-winding from bobbin to niddy-noddy and onto bobbins again, the mechanically inclined could make bobbin winders and ball winders very easily—just a little cam and gear work. To replace the niddy-noddy, the *swift* is needed: a rotating frame, with a vertical axis, clamped to a table or standing on the floor, of known circumference, that yarn can be wound on to or off of. Primitive swifts were in use at least by 1657 (Velázquez, *Las Hilanderas*), but an up-timer might invent the *umbrella swift*, which can be adjusted to different circumferences, and collapsed to make removing the hank easy, ahead of its time.

In OTL, all the machines designed for spinning many yarns at once were designed with cotton in mind—American Upland cotton, *G. hirsutum*, with lint averaging about an inch instead of Indian cotton's five-eighths inch (EB14d 226). These machines were later modified to accommodate the lengths of wool and, much later, flax.

The **spinning jenny** produced very poor yarn, weak and slubby, which broke often during the spinning, and is suitable only for weft. The jenny replaced the spinster's fingers with the *clamp*, a piece of wood split lengthways, through which the cotton was drawn from the *slubbing bobbins*. The drive wheel was turned by hand so that the spindles rotated, twisting the drafted fibers. The *deflection wire* was moved by foot to change the angle of the yarn and the clamp was moved by hand toward the spindles so that the yarn was wound onto the spindles. The operator balanced on one foot to work this machine.

For strong, smooth cotton threads suitable for warp, hand-spinning continued for some years. As late as the second decade of the nineteenth century, while the low wheel had been introduced to England, the version used for cotton still had no treadle. Spinsters sat, but still had to spin the drive wheel manually, faster than required for the great wheel (Aspin 45).

Another item to note is that the spinning jenny cannot be operated with a supply of individual slubs. A number of slubs must be joined, end to end, and twisted slightly so that they will stay together; this *roving* is then wound onto one of the slubbing bobbins.

However, poor as the spinning jenny was, adapted versions of it, some powered, were used for wool well into the twentieth century.

Other machines, invented during the next sixty years (the **water frame**, the **mule**, the **billy**, and more), worked differently, some using *rollers* and others retaining the clamp. The up-time mechanisms that replaced the spindle, *flyers*, *cap spindles*, *throstles*, and *ring frames*, are nineteenth-century inventions (EB14j 35; Barker 12). Different mechanisms are suitable for different fibers and twist those fibers more or less tightly. Good machining is a necessity; up-time machines work well only at high RPMs (Barker 16).

Up-time spinning mills are filled with machines, a sequence of about a dozen taking the farm-fresh fibers through every operation to finished plied yarn. While there are some sketches of principles in the encyclopedias, there are no detailed drawings, and no examples in Grantville. The reinvention of mechanized spinning will be a substantial engineering exercise.


## Weaving.

Textiles are made by interlacing yarns at right angles; at its simplest, many yarns several yards in length are laid side by side (the *warp*), and another length of yarn (the *weft*) crosses the warp, following a path over and under alternate yarns, and then back again, reversing the under and over. A loom is a machine designed to facilitate this process, by holding the warp yarns in place, in order, and straight, and then separating the warp yarns into two banks; between the banks is the *shed* through which a shuttle may carry the weft—effectively, under and over the warp threads. The two banks then exchange places, creating the *countershed*.

**The physical loom.** In seventeenth-century Europe, the *horizontal frame* loom is standard. Horizontal means that the warp is parallel to the ground, not hanging vertically; frame means that the warp is surrounded by beams and rails, not pegged out on the ground. Warp threads are stretched between the *back beam* and the *breast beam*, both solid, fixed lengths of wood. Both the *warp beam*, below the back beam, and the *cloth beam*, below and set back from the breast beam (knee room), turn to *let off* the warp and *take up* the cloth. The warp and cloth beams can be braked at many points in their rotations in order to maintain the proper tension of the warp threads between them. Between the back and breast beams is the *castle*, two uprights capped with a lintel, from which depends the mechanism for opening the sheds; this mechanism will be described below. Between the castle and the breast beam is the *beater*, two heavy lengths of wood hung vertically from above, holding the *reed* between the lower ends. The reed, extending across the loom, is strips of reed, set vertically and edge-forward, between two laths. The beater, also called the *batten*, is swung by the weaver after every shot of weft to press that weft thread against the growing end, the *fell*, of the cloth.

The basic shedding mechanism permits warp threads to be lowered or raised in groups. Each warp thread is controlled by a *heddle* (British: *heald*), a length of string that has at its middle an *eye*, tied in the string itself, or a *mail*, a bronze ring held by the string, which the warp threads pass through. Many heddles are held by each *harness* (British: *shaft*), a wooden rectangular frame wider than a warp can be, with the heddles fastened to the top and bottom rails. Two pulleys hang from the top of the castle, one near each side, and a pair of harnesses depends from these pulleys. In the simplest threading pattern, the *draft*, the warp threads alternate between harnesses, each thread passing alone through one heddle—except that, at the outside edges of the warp, two or three threads will be doubled, each of the first two or three heddles will hold a pair of threads, for the *selvage*, which forms a stronger edge on the cloth. Each harness is tied to a treadle, through intermediate *lamms*, paired laths each half the width of the loom, to even the pull across the width. The warp and the harnesses must be balanced to keep the loom operating easily and efficiently. Down-time, this standard seventeenth-century shedding mechanism has been in use for about a millennium. Up-time, it is known as *counterbalance* (a retro weaving term made necessary by the nineteenth- and twentieth-century inventions of the *jack* and the *countermarche*); when one treadle is depressed by the weaver, that harness is pulled down and the harness hanging from the same pair of pulleys goes up.

**Warping.** Hanks of yarn delivered to a weaver become the

warp. The yarn will be wound onto hollow bobbins, so that it can be controlled easily, and the bobbins will be placed on pegs upon which they can turn easily, in a *bobbin frame*.

Measuring out the length of each warp thread while keeping the threads from tangling, *warping*, is an easy task. If the warp is no more than seven or eight yards, a *warping frame* is used; for longer warps, the tool is a *warping mill* (Davenport *Weaving* 78). The warping frame is two columns of pegs about a yard apart; the yarn is wound back and forth, down the frame over as many pegs as needed to reach the intended length plus *loom waste*, and then back to the beginning. The warping mill, known down-time, is a large, rotating, vertical cylinder with columns of pegs at intervals; the yarn is spiraled down to the right, between the pegs, while the cylinder is turned, and back up while the cylinder is turned the other direction. At the beginning of either frame or mill are two subsidiary pegs between which the yarn going down follows one path and the yarn going up follows the opposite path, creating an "X" that keeps the warp threads in order while they are transferred to the loom. While a hobby weaver using heavy yarn may warp one thread at a time, professional weavers working with fine yarns may feed from as many as 12 bobbins at once. The X is preserved by a tie as soon as the entire warp has been measured out. Now the warp is ready for *dressing the loom*.

**Dressing the loom.** The warp is removed from the frame or mill starting with the bottom loop: the warp is tied loosely in a chain sinnet (Ashley #2868) or crochet chain as it is removed from the pegs, and then carried to the loom. The tie around the X is replaced by two *leashes*, wooden slats that fit between the rails but are a little longer than the warp beam; these leashes are tied together at their ends so that the warp may be spread without the threads escaping. The beginning end of the warp is then secured to the warp beam; a metal rod is put through the loop and tied to the rod that is held at the end of the *apron* (a length of cloth attached to the beam). With the warp threads passing over the back beam and held under tension, and the two leashes being pulled forward to move the X toward the other end, the warp beam is turned to wrap the warp onto it. More leashes are positioned every few inches around the warp beam so that the warp threads do not bury themselves in earlier layers (modern hobby weavers often use brown paper, wound along with the warp, instead). The warp is wound until only enough length is left free to finish the dressing.

The free, forward end of the warp is cut and each thread is passed through the shedding mechanism in the castle—between the heddles in the harnesses behind and before the harness holding the heddle for that thread—then the reed is *sleyed*—the warp threads are passed through the *dents*, the spaces between the reeds. These operations are best performed by a two-person team, one behind the castle presenting the warp threads in order, and one in front pulling the threads through with a hook.

Last, the warp is fastened to the cloth beam, tied to a rod that is secured to that cloth beam. The tension of the warp threads is checked, by patting with a hand, and corrected by retying wherever needed.

The two looms in the Grantville museum are of this type, except that they are of twentieth-century manufacture: the reed is of steel and the heddles in one are of aluminum instead of string. These two looms also have *rollers*, long wooden poles, taking the place of the pulleys, and the beaters are *standing*, pivoted at the bottom where they are permanently fastened to the base of the loom, instead of *pendant*. The shuttles on display with these two looms are *rag shuttles*, designed to hold torn strips of cloth to be woven over a coarse cotton or linen warp in making rag rugs.

**Types of weave and bigger looms.** Two harnesses are sufficient for the simplest "over one, under one" weave, which is called *tabby*, and for the tabby variation called *basket weave*, with the shots of weft in pairs. More complex weave patterns require more harnesses. For example, for the weft to go over two and under two, with each shot offset one warp thread from the last (basic *twill*), four harnesses are needed. The second pair of harnesses will hang from their own pulleys, and the four primary pulleys (or *horses*, strips of wood hung by their centers with the harnesses tied to their ends) will hang from the secondary pulleys, so that any three of the four harnesses can be pulled down at once. (As long as the number of harnesses is a power of two, all but one harness can be treadled down at the same time.) For the simplest twill, the arrangement of the warp threads through the harnesses, the *draft*, is: first harness, second harness, third, fourth, repeat, and the treadling is first and second, second and third, third and fourth, fourth and first, repeat. Variations of twill are produced by changing either the threading order or the treadling or the number of harnesses used. *Denim* is over one, under two—from the right side of the fabric, which faces the floor as it is being woven on a counterbalance loom, so that the weaver sees under one and over two. The draft for denim is first harness, second harness, third, repeat, and the treadling will be all but first, all but second, all but third, repeat. Careful choice of drafts and treadling patterns produces more variations of twill, like the *herringbone* and the *pointed* (*diamond*, etc.) weaves. Every fiber can be woven in tabby or twill.

In s*atin* weave—or rather, its reverse, *sateen*—the weft floats over more warp threads, requiring yet more harnesses. A total of eight, two groups of four depending from a third level of pulleys, is sufficient. For *five-shaft* (or *harness*) satin, the weaver treadles for over four, under one, offset two; for *eight-shaft satin*, over seven, under one, offset three. Turned right-side up, satin shows longer expanses of exposed, floating warp threads. It is a more fragile fabric, more subject to pulls, and this weave is not used for any fabric subject to hard use or provided to the poor.

*Damask*, fabric with designs—geometric figures, animals, plants—produced by floating warp threads within the design element over weft threads, requires looms with shedding mechanisms that can produce many more sheds.

**Draw loom.** The draw loom has harnesses only for the *binder* (or *ground*) weave, which was usually satin; it secured each warp thread more often than the pattern called for. Each warp thread passes through one mail in the pattern and one in the binder. As the pattern shed opened behind the binder harnesses, and the shuttle was thrown in front of them, the heddles in these harnesses had *long mails*, elliptical instead of round, so that the shed extended through them.

For the pattern shed, each heddle hangs free, with a weight, a coil of lead wire called a *lingoe*, hanging from it to pull it down. The cord above the mail is called the *first leash*, which rises through the *comber board*. The comber board is as long as the warp is wide, and consists of *slips*, thin pieces of wood, as many as there are repeats of the pattern across the cloth, each slip having a rectangular arrangement of holes equal in number to the number of warp threads in the pattern. The first leash for the pattern goes through the first hole in the appropriate slip (and its terminology changes to *necking cord*), the second through the second, and so on. The comber board forms the bottom of the *necking box*, in which all the cords through the first hole of all the slips are tied to a *pulley cord*. Each pulley cord goes through the appropriate hole in the *top board*, a single slip, and leaves the necking box by way of a pulley, becoming a *tailcord* as it goes horizontally to the side. The end of each tailcord is fastened to the far end of a beam extending from the top of the loom. Another cord is tied around the standing part of each tailcord; these *simple cords* are fastened to the floor directly below, with no slack in them. If, for example, there are four pattern repeats across 1,000 warp threads, there are only 250 simple cords. Following the pattern draft, the weaver ties *lashes* around the standing part of the simple cords, a set for each row of the pattern; if several adjacent warp threads are to be raised at the same time, one lash can serve the adjacent simple cords.

In weaving, the weaver's feet control the sheds for the binder weave. The pattern sheds are provided by a *drawboy* seated on the ground who pulls the lashes according to the pattern.

Some damasks are woven with one weft yarn for the pattern and a finer one for the binder, so that the occasional specks of weft appearing inside a pattern element are even less noticeable. The flying shuttle will be of limited use in this case. For that, the invention of John Kay's son Robert, the *drop-box*, which fed several shuttles in sequence, is required. The drop-box was patented in 1760 (Peake 6)

Originally, the drawboy perched above the loom, drawing the necking cords. Tailcords and simples, invented in Lyons in 1606 (HOTd 189), may not have spread across Europe yet. French inventors worked on simplifying the operations further. J.M. Jacquard, building on the work of three inventors of the first half of the eighteenth century, completed the task in 1803, before power was applied to weaving at all. The mechanism of the Jacquard loom replaces the draw-loom mechanism, necking box through draw-boy.

**Multiharness loom.** Smaller, simple damask patterns can be produced on multiharness looms—as many as 32 harnesses, one harness for each row of the pattern. These looms will, however, often have two groups of harnesses: 8 at the front for the binding weave, and 16 or 32 at the back for the pattern weave. (In British weaving terminology, each group of shafts is a harness: the binder harness and the pattern harness.) Depressing all those treadles would, it seems, require considerable mass on the part of the weaver. By early in the eighteenth century, there was the *small draw-loom*, which had treadles only for the binder group, the pattern harnesses being raised by a drawboy.

**Treatment of fibers.** Yarns used as warp require treatment if they are not to break often. How the yarns are treated depends on the identity of the fiber:

*Woolen* can be used as warp if it is not too soft, but it is more often used as weft on a worsted or a linen warp. Woolens can be heavy, like up-time blankets and coats, or thin; wadmal is a very thin woolen fabric.

*Worsted* makes a good warp, and a good weft.

*Linen* is a strong fiber, especially when it is wet. Even single, unplied linen yarn from line flax can be used as warp. If the weaving shop is not humid, wet towels can be laid on the warp between the back beam and the shedding mechanism. If the linen is not damp enough (or even if it is), it will break, as the flax fiber has no elasticity. Up-time, it is coated with a paste of Irish moss (*Chondrus crispus*).

*Cotton* used as warp must be *sized* to keep the warp yarn from breaking too often. Boiled rabbit skins are sometimes used by up-time hobby weavers; a flour paste with tallow, and sometimes paraffin, is used commercially. Cotton can be used as weft on warps of worsted or linen.

Broken warp threads are dealt with immediately. The hand weaver will darn a new thread into the cloth and tie the other end to the broken warp thread, then weave to the knot. He will then remove the knot and darn the ends in. The Weaver's Knot that Davenport (*Weaving* 61) recommends is the true Carrick Bend (Ashley #1439).

**The act of weaving.** Once a loom has been dressed, the weaver is advised to weave an inch or two, to check that the draft has been executed correctly. He then falls into a rhythm. He opens the shed by depressing the appropriate treadles. He leans forward and to one side, positions the shuttle at the end of the shed, and, with a snap of his wrist, throws the shuttle through the shed, the full width of the warp. He quickly leans to the other side, and catches the shuttle with his other hand, and stops the rotation of the spindle with a fingertip to keep more weft thread than needed from being left in the shed. With his free hand, he yanks the beater forward to position the weft thread properly against the fell.

Each of these actions must be properly timed, in sequence.

When the weaver has woven a few inches, the warp must be advanced: a few inches of warp must be let off the warp beam and a few inches of cloth taken up on the cloth beam, with the tension of the warp being maintained. Every few inches, but not at the same time as let-off and take-up, the *temple* must be advanced. The *temple*, or stretcher, keeps the warp as wide as it should be instead of getting narrower as it is woven. It is two laths, each about half as long as the cloth is wide, hinged together so they are end to end. A flat side of the outside ends holds pins, which are inserted into the new cloth near its edges; the temple is then flattened. Without a temple, the piece of cloth may be not a rectangle, but a trapezoid. It is required on woolens, and advisable on all others.

## Power looms.

In 1785, Dr. Edmund Cartwright patented the very first power loom; he designed it without having ever seen a loom, and, surprisingly, his design did not work (Barker 9). He patented his second design in 1787. Other designs were patented over the next fifteen years, and finally, very early in the nineteenth century, power looms overcame—or outlived—the weavers who wanted nothing to do with them. However, only wool and worsted could be woven on them. Power weaving of cotton was delayed by the need for sizing, as the sizing could be applied only to warp that had been let off the warp beam. It was not until 1836 that sizing the warp before it was wound on the warp beam was worked out (Peake 7). As linen has no elasticity, it broke too often without the feedback that only a human can supply, until the effects of a vibrating roller were found to alleviate this problem, about 1840 (Moore 71, 78).

These early power looms still had to be stopped for warp advancement and temple movement. The first automatic temple was invented in the United States, in 1816 (Chase 4). The standing beater was a necessary part of the invention.

When a warp thread breaks, the loom must stop. When the shuttle runs out of weft, or the weft breaks, the loom must stop. If the shuttle does not exit the shed as it should, the loom must stop immediately—beating the shuttle into the cloth is total catastrophe. Automatic stop-actions that do not vibrate or shake the entire mechanism are needed for each of these certainties, if each loom is not to be attended by its own personal fast-reacting weaver.

Broken warp threads are dealt with immediately by up-time industrial weavers, but, it seems, differently from the way the hand-weaver does. The knots that Clifford Ashley, who was consulted by the twentieth-century weaving industry, reports as having been used in weaving as far back as anyone knows are all permanent knots (78–81, 259), not the strong but transitory knots that a hand-weaver prefers. Ashley implies that commercial cloth keeps those knots forever.

Another difficult item to automate is the *beater*, which beats the latest shot of weft up against the *fell* of the cloth. This beating must not be too hard or too light; the correct amount varies according to the type of cloth being woven. A weft-face textile requires a harder beat than an even weave does. Down-time, beaters are pendant; up-time, hand-looms can have either a pendant or a standing beater. Up-time powered looms have standing beaters.

## Finishing.

Down-time, all textiles are inspected for mistakes in the weave, of either warp or weft; the *menders* correct these as best they can with needle and thread. The pieces are then *burled*: knots, knops, neps, foreign matter, anything affecting the appearance and the acceptance of dye, are searched for and removed. This must be done before the piece can be approved by guild and city council quality inspection teams. They will need to be washed, bleached if the yarn was not bleached and dyed before it was woven, and pressed or calendered.

**Woolen** textiles, including those of woolen weft over linen or worsted warp, are *fulled*, matted and shrunk (when this is done to unwoven wool, it is called *felted*). Fulling mills exist down-time, with wooden drop-hammers operated by waterwheels (Hartley 136). Fulling makes the fabric less likely to tear, and shrinks it about 50% (CHWTa 205). Next, it is *tentered*: the selvages are hooked on pins fastened to heavy lengths of lumber to stretch the fabric out evenly; this does not counter the shrinking. Then it is *teased* and *shorn*: the piece is laid over a board, thistle heads set in a frame are used to raise loose fibers and ends, and shears are used to cut these off. The gig mill, for raising the fibers, was invented no later than the sixteenth century (HOTc 172); the textile is carried on a leather belt past teasels—and its use was not widespread. The saving in man- and boy-power is significant, personnel requirements dropping from 18 men and 6 boys to 2 men and 1 boy (CHWTa 205), although shearing still had to be done by hand. Various methods of mechanical shearing were invented late in the eighteenth century, leading to a spinning cylinder bearing a spiraling blade at the end of that century (HOTe 304–5)—which was still marveled at early in the twentieth (Hunter 62).

**Worsted** textiles are subjected to a process called *crabbing*, which evens the tension so that the threads do not pull up unevenly over time.

Both woolen and worsted fabrics are pressed by being folded accordion-style into presses.

**Linen** is polished, laid flat on a board so that the flat side of a stone, or perhaps of a lump of glass, can be rubbed over it.

**Cotton** has loose fiber ends; the cure is singeing, done by passing the fabric over a source of heat, originally a hot copper plate, later a gas flame—followed immediately by quenching.

Linen and cotton fabrics are *calendered*: pressed between rollers.

## Acceptability of Innovations.

Some of the new procedures will be welcome; others will not be. Jobs, wages, and product quality will be questioned. Even if farmers and prospective mill owners have capital to expend now for increased profit later, spinsters and weavers will fear for their jobs—as they have done in centuries past. New textile machines (spinning wheel, gig mill) were prohibited by law, in the German states, in France, and in England, as early as the thirteenth century, partly over quality concerns, but also for job protection.

## Spinning.

Spinsters are self-employed, and may not want to work in a mill at someone else's orders. A cottage spinster chooses her own hours for spinning. Hand-spinning can be stopped at any moment if a toddler or infant screams; spinsters who work in mills will have to find others to care for their children.

Up-timers know that modern sewing thread is very strong, but it is polyester. Few will remember the mercerized cotton thread that could be snapped between fists. Even fewer will remember the days when clerks in fabric departments would tear cotton fabrics from the bolt, instead of using shears to cut it. Up-timers will also know how fine and smooth up-time thread, both sewing and woven, is, and may think that handspun always means thicker, slubbier, and weaker—which it does not. Human fingers are marvellous tools, but up-time hobby weavers have learned that if their yarn is slub-free, people accuse them of passing off machine-spun yarn as their own work. Down-timers may well have opposite suspicions of machines, especially if they are not properly tested before being revealed.

In OTL, the machines were first developed to handle cotton, and modified to deal with linen and wool, but there is still a maximum length allowed. Up-time, many sheep are sheared twice a year, instead of the old standard of once. Line flax of 20 to 30 inches will be no more; up-time flax must be cut short, perhaps as short as 3 to 5 inches (Crockett 175). Effectively, all flax up-time is tow, and more twists per inch are required. Perhaps the up-time inventors, lacking knowledge of modern machinery and the OTL abundance of cotton, will develop machines intended for linen and wool as they are, not as they have been modified to suit.

In OTL, machinery could not produce linen yarn as fine as hand-spinning could, until wet-spinning machinery was developed in the 1820s (CHWTc 478).

## Weaving.

Weavers pride themselves on the quality of their finished goods. The German cities with major cloth-production have quality inspection teams, from weaving guild and city council, who stamp each piece that meets minimum standards. When rogue weavers, usually farmers in the surrounding territory, counterfeit-stamp their own pieces of cloth, the cities adopt new stamps.

The weaving guild of each city has two levels: masters and journeymen. A master weaver has worked his way up through the ranks until he could produce a masterwork (demonstrating his ability to design and create) and amass the funds necessary to purchase his own home and looms and to employ journeymen. The master weavers define the names applied to textiles, determining the fiber content, the thread count, and the weave necessary for a particular textile. They set minimum and maximum prices, to avoid both undercutting each other and overcharging the customer.

In the German-speaking states, a journeyman weaver is at least eighteen years old, and has put in three years as an apprentice, to learn the basics of the craft. He becomes a journeyman when three journeymen decide he has learned all an apprentice must and sponsor him. And then he must journey—to another town, where he reports to the Gasthaus frequented by the journeymen of that town. The head journeyman checks his bona fides—where he apprenticed and who sponsored him—and leads him to a weaver with a job opening. He is expected to join the guild of the town. The journeymen of the town meet at the Gasthaus about once a week, paying their dues, electing a new head journeyman when called for, and then draining their steins between songs.

Guild dues are a source of relief to members too sick to work, to bereaved dependents, and so forth. Much social life is organized through the guild. A master weaver can hire only through the head journeyman.

## Luddites and featherbedders.

Over the centuries, workers have objected to their jobs being made redundant by machines. Inventors have often moved from one city to another, after the first production run of their machines: James Hargreaves set up a building full of spinning jennys, which were destroyed by his townsmen. Barthelemy Thimmonier in France had 80 sewing machines in use; his fellow tailors destroyed them.

Up-time, destruction is not as common, but the twentieth century has seen objections from auto workers, steelworkers, longshoremen, railroadmen, those in the printing trades, and many more—all of whom wanted job security rather than an easy way for the few to do the work of many. Even musicians have objected to the theater practice of hiring only the number of musicians needed for a play's music, rather than as many as can fit into the space provided by the theater's architect. "Solutions" have included delays in adopting innovation, keeping unnecessary positions filled, and encouraging early retirement: American automobile factories fell behind those elsewhere; the railroads had to maintain firemen, ready to shovel coal into diesel engines; dockyard workers were supported by a make-up and pension fund set up by union and management together.

Even if there are jobs available in other fields, how many workers will be willing to learn a new skillset?

Those who keep their jobs worry about their pay. Will it be piecework, or time? There are many arguments on this issue, both directions. Pay by the piece must be set high enough that a worker can earn enough to live on. Those who work quickly can earn more; quality inspection is required to separate the deft from the hasty. In the view of the business owner, hourly wages will encourage slackness.

Finally, there is capital expenditure: who can invest in invention and development? Do the fiber merchants, master weavers, and drapers have the capital necessary to purchase these new machines? Improvements will provide savings over time, but the initial expense can be great.

## Conclusion

Technological advances in the textile industry have many aspects, requirements, and effects. Machines must be invented and tested. The site of the factory or mill must be chosen carefully, preferably near water power, without taking land out of cultivation. Transportation of the raw material and the finished goods must be facilitated. The resistance to new ways of those already in the field must be overcome.

As in OTL, it will take time.

## Further Reading and Partial Bibliography

CHWT = Cambridge History of Western Technology; EA = Encyclopedia Americana; EB = Encyclopaedia Britannica, with the number immediately following "EB" indicating the edition; HOT = A History of Technology.

Those works of particular use to authors are marked with an asterisk.

Amos, Alden. *Spinning Wheel Primer*. Loveland CO: Interweave Press, 1990.

Ashley, Clifford W. *The Ashley Book of Knots*. Garden City NY: Doubleday & Company, Inc., 1944.

* Aspin, C. and S.D. Chapman. *James Hargreaves and the Spinning Jenny*. Helmshore Local History Society. Preston UK: The Guardian Press, 1964.

Barber, E.J.W. Textiles: The Development of Cloth in the Neolithic and Bronze Ages. Princeton NJ: Princeton University Press, 1991.

* Barker, A.F., M.Sc. *Textiles*. Rev. Ed. London: Constable & Company Limited, 1922.

*Cambridge History of Western Textiles*. 2 volumes. Ed. David Jenkins. Cambridge University Press, 2003.
  a "Medieval Woollens: Textiles, Technology and Organisation 800–1500." John H. Munro
  b "The Western European Woollen Industries 1500–1700." Herman van der Wee.
  c "The Linen Industry in Early Modern Europe." Leslie Clarkson.

Chase, William. H. *Five Generations of Loom Builders*. Hopedale MA: Draper Corporation, 1950.

Crockett, Candace. *The Complete Spinning Book*. New York: Watson-Guptill Publications, 1977.

Davenport, Elsie G. *Your Handspinning*. Tarzana CA: Select Books, 1964.

————. *Your Handweaving*. Tarzana CA: Select Books, 1951.

Dulles, Foster Rhea. *Labor in America*. Binghamton NY: Vail-Ballou Press, 1966.

Elliott, Connie. Member, Contemporary Handweavers of Houston. Personal Communication, May 2004.

*Encyclopaedia Britannica*, 11th Edition. New York: The Encyclopaedia Britannica Company, 1911.
a "Cotton." A.N. Monkhouse. Vol. 7.
b "Cotton Manufacture." Sydney John Chapman, M.A. Vol. 7.
c "Cotton Spinning Machinery." Thomas William Fox, M.Sc. Tech. Vol. 7.
d "Flax." Thomas Woodhouse. Vol. 10.
e "Linen and Linen Manufactures." Thomas Woodhouse. Vol. 16.
f "Silk." Frank Warner, et al. Vol. 25.
g "Spinning." Thomas William Fox, M.Sc.Tech. Vol. 25.
h "Spinning Machinery." Thomas William Fox, M.Sc.Tech. Vol. 25.
i "Weaving." Alan Summerly Cole, C.B. Vol. 28.
j "Wool, Worsted & Woollen Manufacturing." Aldred Farrer Barker, M.Sc. Vol. 28.

*Encyclopaedia Britannica*, 14th Edition. Chicago: William Benton, Publisher, 1972.
a "Cotton." John Melvin Green. Vol. 6.
b "Cotton Manufacture." Alan Ewart Nuttall. Vol. 6.
c "Farm Machinery." Walter M. Carlton and Eugene C. McKibbon. Vol. 9.
d "Fibre" (Plant Fibres). Mills Herbert Byrom and Ernest Ralph Kaswell. Vol. 9.
e "Fibre" (Animal & Mineral Fibre). Ernest Ralph Kaswell. Vol. 9.
f "Flax." John H.Martin. Vol. 9.
g "Silk," Part I: History. Unsigned. Vol. 20.
h "Silk," Part III: Sericulture. Unsigned. Vol. 20.
i "Silk," Part V: Silk Manufacture. Milton H. Rubin. Vol. 20.
j "Spinning." Virginia P. Partridge and Frank Charnley. Vol. 21.
k "Technology, History of." Unsigned. Vol. 21.
l "Textiles." N.K.A. Rothstein. Vol. 21.

*Encyclopedia Americana*. "Textiles," Part 3: Fabric Construction. Evelyn E. Stout. Vol. 26. Danbury CT: Grolier, Inc., 1999.

Feldman-Wood, Florence. *The Spinning Wheel Sleuth*: http://www. spwhsl.com/. FAQ page: accessed January 2004. Personal e-mails: January 25 and March 17, 2004.

*Foxfire 2*; *Foxfire 10*. New York: Anchor Books, 1973; 1993.

Geijer, Agnes. *A History of Textile Art*. Pasold Research Fund Ltd. in association with Sotheby Parke Bernet Publications. London: Philip Wilson Publishers Ltd., 1979.

\* Hanton, William A., M.Sc.Tech. *Mechanics of Textile Machinery*. London: Longmans, Green and Co., 1924.

Harris, Jennifer. "I: A Survey of Textile Techniques." *Textiles: 5,000 Years* (edited by J. Harris). The Trustees of the British Museum. New York: Harry N. Abrams, Incorporated, 1993.

Hartley, Dorothy. *Lost Country Life*. New York: Pantheon Books, 1979.

\* Hartsuch, Bruce E. *Introduction to Textile Chemistry*. New York: John Wiley & Sons, Inc., 1950.

\* Hilts, Patricia, ed. *The Weavers Art Revealed*. Vols. 13 and 14 of *Ars Textrina*. (Facsimile, translation, and commentary, Marx Ziegler's *Weber Kunst und Bild Buch*, 1677, and Nathanael Lumscher's *Neu eingerichtetes Weber Kunst und Bild Buch*, 1708). Winnipeg, Manitoba: Charles Babbage Research Centre, December 1990.

A History of Technology. 5 volumes. Vol. II, The Mediterranean Civilizations and the Middle Ages; Vol. III, From the Renaissance to the Industrial Revolution c. 1500–c. 1750; and Vol IV, The Industrial Revolution c. 1750–c. 1850). Ed. Charles Singer, et al. London: Oxford University Press, 1957.
a   Vol. II: "Spinning." R. Patterson.
b   Vol. II: "Machines." Bertrand Gille.
c   Vol. III: "Spinning and Weaving." R. Patterson.
d   Vol. III: "Figured Fabrics." J.F. Flanagan.
e   Vol. IV: "The Textile Industry." Julia de L. Mann.

\* Hooper, Luther. *Silk: Its Production & Manufacture*. (Pitman's Common Commodities of Commerce.) London: Sir Isaac Pitman & Sons, Ltd., N.D. (1911).

\* Hunter, J.A. *Wool: From the Raw Material to the Finished Product*. (Pitman's Common Commodities of Commerce.) London: Sir Isaac Pitman & Sons, Ltd., N.D. (1912).

\* Moore, Alfred S. *Linen: From the Raw Material to the Finished Product*. (Pitman's Common Commodities of Commerce.) London: Sir Isaac Pitman & Sons, Ltd., N.D. (1914).

Morton, W.E. and J.W.S. Hearle. *Physical Properties of Textile Fibers*. Butterworth & Co. (Publishers) Ltd. and the Textile Institute, 1962.

\* Peake, R.J. *Cotton: From the Raw Material to the Finished Product*. (Pitman's Common Commodities and Industries.) Revised Edition. London: Sir Isaac Pitman & Sons, Ltd., 1925. (Reprint, Wachtung NJ: Albert Saifer Publisher, 1997.)

\* Polleyn, Friedrich. *Dressings and Finishings for Textile Fabrics and Their Application*. Translated from the third German edition by Charles Salter. London: Scott, Greenwood & Son, 1911.

Ponting, Kenneth G. *Leonardo da Vinci: Drawings of textile machines*. Bradford-on-Avon, Wilts: Moonraker Press, 1979.

Pratt, Fletcher. *All About Famous Inventors and Their Inventions*. Chapter 3: "The Cotton Gin and the Reaper." Chapter 5: "Inventions for the Home." New York: Random House, 1955.

\* Radcliffe, Wiliam. *Origin of the New System of Manufacture Commonly Called Power-Loom Weaving*. Clifton NJ: Augustus M. Kelley Publishers, 1974 (reprint of 1828 edition).

Shanks, Clarice. Owner, Upstairs Studio (Weaving & Spinning). LaPorte TX. Personal communications.

Van Nostran, Don. Mid-States Woolgrowers Cooperative Association. Personal correspondence (email), April 20, 2004.

Wild, J.P. *Textile Manufacture in the Northern Roman Provinces*. Cambridge: at the University Press, 1970.

\* Woodhouse, Thomas. *Jacquards and Harnesses: Card-Cutting, Lacing and Repeating Mechanism*. London: Macmillan and Co., Limited, N.D., 1923.

# Images

**Note from Editor:**

There are various images, mostly portraits from the time, which illustrate different aspects of the 1632 universe. In the first issue of the *Grantville Gazette,* I included those with the volume itself. Since that created downloading problems for some people, however, I've separated all the images and they will be maintained and expanded on their own schedule.

If you're interested, you can look at the images and my accompanying commentary at no extra cost. They are set up in the Baen Free Library. You can find them as follows:

1) Go to www.baen.com
2) Select "Free Library" from the blue menu at the top.
3) Once in the Library, select "The Authors" from the yellow menu on the left.
4) Once in "The Authors," select "Eric Flint."
5) Then select "Images from the Grantville Gazette."

# Submissions to the Magazine

If anyone is interested in submitting stories or articles for future issues of the *Grantville Gazette,* you are welcome to do so. But you must follow a certain procedure:

1) All stories and articles must first be posted in a conference in Baen's Bar set aside for the purpose, called "1632 Slush." Do *not* send them to me directly, because I won't read them. It's good idea to submit a sketch of your story to the conference first, since people there will likely spot any major problems that you overlooked. That can wind up saving you a lot of wasted work.

You can get to that conference by going to Baen Books' web site www.baen.com. Then select "Baen's Bar." If it's your first visit, you will need to register. (That's quick and easy.) Once you're in the Bar, the three conferences devoted to the 1632 universe are "1632 Slush," "1632 Slush Comments," and "1632 Tech Manual." You should post your sketch, outline or story in "1632 Slush." Any discussion of it should take place in "1632 Slush Comments." The "1632 Tech Manual" is for any general discussion not specifically related to a specific story.

2) Your story/article will then be subjected to discussion and commentary by participants in the 1632 discussion. In essence, it will get chewed on by what amounts to a very large, virtual writers' group.

You do *not* need to wait until you've finished the story to start posting it in "1632 Slush." In fact, it's a good idea not to wait, because you will often find that problems can be spotted early in the game, before you've put all the work into completing the piece.

3) While this is happening, the assistant editor of the *Grantville Gazette,* Paula Goodlett, will be keeping an eye on the discussion. She will alert me whenever a story or article seems to be gaining general approval from the participants in the discussion. There's also an editorial board to which Paula and I belong, which does much the same thing. The other members of the board are Karen Bergstralh, Rick Boatright, and Laura Runkle. In addition, authors who publish regularly in the 1632 setting participate on the board as *ex officio* members. My point is that plenty of people will be looking over the various stories being submitted, so you needn't worry that your story will just get lost in the shuffle.

4) At that point—and *only* at that point—do I take a look at a story or article.

I insist that people follow this procedure, for two reasons:

First, as I said, I'm very busy and I just don't have time to read everything submitted until I have some reason to think it's gotten past a certain preliminary screening.

Second, and even more important, the setting and "established canon" in this series is quite extensive by now. If anyone tries to write a story without first taking the time to become familiar with the setting, they will almost invariably write something which—even if it's otherwise well written—I simply can't accept.

In short, the procedure outlined above will save *you* a lot of wasted time and effort also.

One point in particular: I have gotten extrxemely hardnosed about the way in which people use American characters in their stories (so-called "up-timers"). That's because I began discovering that my small and realistically portrayed coal mining town of 3500 people was being willy-nilly transformed into a "town" with a population of something like 20,000 people—half of whom were Navy SEALs who just happened to be in town at the Ring of Fire, half of whom were rocket scientists (ibid), half of whom were brain surgeons (ibid), half of whom had a personal library the size of the Library of Congress, half of whom . . .

Not to mention the F-16s which "just happened" to be flying through the area, the Army convoys (ibid), the trains full of vital industrial supplies (ibid), the FBI agents in hot pursuit of master criminals (ibid), the . . .

NOT A CHANCE. If you want to use an up-time character,

you *must* use one of the "authorized" characters. Those are the characters created by Virginia DeMarce using genealogical software and embodied in what is called "the grid."

You can obtain a copy of the grid from the web site which collects and presents the by-now voluminous material concerning the series, www.1632.org. Look on the right for the link to "Virginia's Uptimer Grid." While you're at it, you should also look further down at the links under the title "Authors' Manual."

You will be paid for any story or factual article which is published. The rates that we pay are six cents a word for any story or article up to fifteen thousand words. The rate for anything beyond fifteen thousand words drops to five cents a word. The drop is not retroactive—i.e., regardless of the length of the piece, the first fifteen thousand words will always be paid six cents a word. These pay rates are professional rates, as established by the Science Fictions & Fantasy Writers of America, Inc. In the event a story or article is later selected for inclusion in a paper edition, you will get no further advance but will be entitled to a pro rata share of any royalties earned by the authors from that volume.

# Grantville Gazette

*An electronic-only magazine of stories and fact articles
based on Eric Flint's 1632 "Ring of Fire" universe*

The *Grantville Gazette* can be purchased through Baen Books'
Webscriptions service at www.baens.com (then select Webscriptions)
or you can subscribe through www.grantvillegazette.com, which
is an electronic magazine that publishes six issues per year.

Each electronic volume of the *Gazette* can be purchased individually for $6.00 from either site, or you can purchase them in
packages from Webscriptions as follows:

- Volume 1. This volume is free and can be obtained
  from the Baen Free Library. (Once you're in the Baen
  web site at www.baen.com, select "Free Library" on the
  left hand side of the menu at the top. Then, select "The
  Books" and you'll find *Grantville Gazette Volume 1*.)
- Volumes 2–4, $15.
- Volumes 5–8, $15.
- Volumes 8–10, $15.
- Volumes 1–10, $40. This special offer allows all of
  our fans to read all of the stories published so far
  at a bargain rate.
- Volumes 11–13, $15.
- Volumes 14–16, $15.
- Volumes 17–19, $15. Volume 17 is already available
  with Volumes 18 and 19 in production.